ACES

A MAFIA REVERSE HAREM

CASSANDRA DOON
J.N. KING

Aces Copyright 2024 by Cassandra Doon and J.N. King

All Rights Reserved. No part of this book may be used or reproduced in any manner whatsoever without written permission except in the case of brief quotations embodied or critical articles or reviews.

This book is a work of fiction. Names, Characters, Businesses, Organisations, Places, Events and incidents either are the product of the author's imagination or are used fictitiously. Any resemblance to actual persons, living or dead, events or locales is entirely coincidental.

First Edition 2024

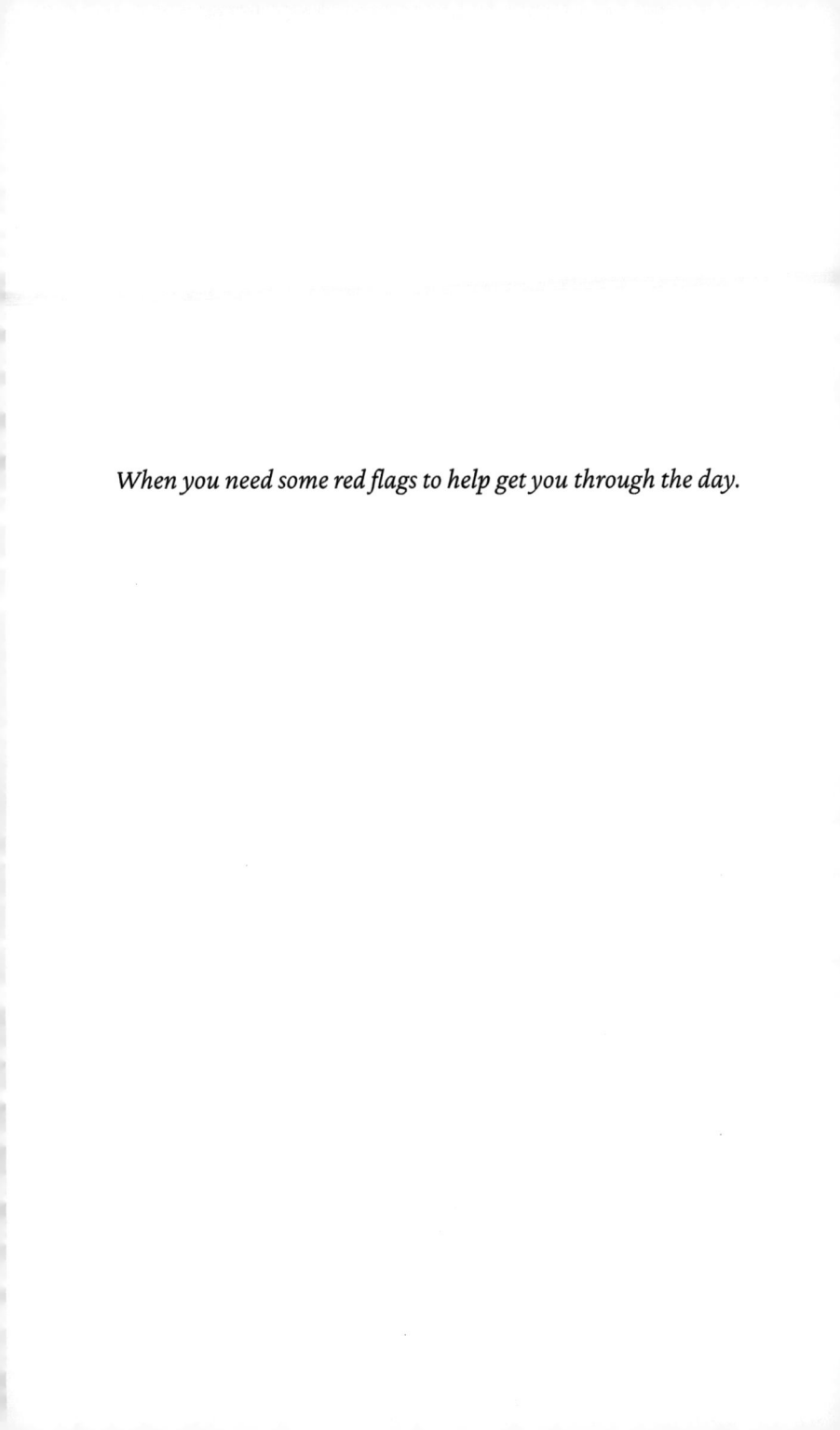

When you need some red flags to help get you through the day.

1

EMBER DANG

As I finalized my second complex sale, a wave of accomplishment rippled through me, followed closely by a quiet sense of relief. To celebrate, I slipped into a flowing dress and draped a long coat over my shoulders before entering the night. For me, celebrating didn't mean loud music or crowded dance floors—it meant unveiling something more profound. Tonight, it was the grand opening of a new art gallery in the City, where I could lose myself in the quiet brilliance of human expression.

Unlike the masses, my age, nightclubs, and parties only stirred a discomfort I could never shake—too much noise, too many faces, all merging into a cacophony that set my nerves on edge. Art galleries offered something else—a serenity, an intimacy that called to me like a secret.

Tonight's event showcased two emerging local artists. Their work was displayed with such elegance that each piece felt like a whispered confession waiting to be heard. Their rise in the community had been swift, but their talent made it inevitable. I wandered the gallery, captivated by the rawness of their creations—so full of life and unrestrained passion that it left me both in awe and silently hungry for more.

Success, these days, has its strange arbiters. Social media can transform the mundane into the extraordinary with the right complaint or controversy. The so-called 'Karens' of society had worked their peculiar magic on these two artists, catapulting their work into the limelight.

One artist's paintings were rife with erotic tension—couples entangled with unconventional objects, their forms bold and unapologetic. The surrealism of it tugged at something in me, a quiet fascination mixed with unease. The provocativeness was undeniable, though, and I found myself lingering on the details, drawn to the audacity.

The other artist delved into distorted humanoid forms, sculpted and painted like gods from some ancient myth, though with exaggerated, almost grotesque features. Their work had an Omegaverse fantasy quality, and as a fan of the genre, I felt a shiver of recognition ripple through me. It was strange and sensual all at once, leaving me to admire their ability to make something primal.

Isolation has been my constant companion since I was seventeen. My mother succumbed to cancer in my final year of adolescence. At the same time, my father had been ripped from me even earlier—gunned down in a shootout when I was just twelve. Alone, I learned how to adapt and exist in the quiet spaces most people ran from. Solitude became a choice, a preference, rather than a condition to be pitied.

Two years ago, I made a decision that some might call

Chapter 1

reckless, but for me, it was necessary. I left everything behind and moved to England. With the inheritance from my mother, I bought a small unit in London, immersing myself in the city's pulse by day and revelling in the dark mystery it became at night. I felt alive in the nocturnal hours, when the streets emptied and the air thickened with a kind of dangerous promise.

But London was more than a refuge. It became a canvas for my love of Gothic architecture, a passion I could no longer ignore. I used part of my inheritance to buy and renovate three properties, each a tribute to the macabre elegance that had always drawn me in.

My first venture was a two-unit townhouse just outside the city. Sandwiched between restored, historic homes, it stood out with its newly painted black exterior. It was crowned with intricate gargoyles and fronted by a fountain that seemed to belong in some forgotten Gothic novel. I had finally brought to life a piece of the dark, romantic world that had always existed in the corners of my imagination.

Word spread quickly about my eccentric style and obsessive attention to detail despite my lack of prior experience in property sales. Even Karen, my ever-inquisitive neighbor, couldn't resist sticking her nose where it didn't belong. She sent formal complaints to the council and contacted local news reporters, all desperate to unearth more about my so-called "Dracula" residence. It amused me, honestly. The more she poked and pried, the more I reveled in the attention. It proved that my dark and unapologetic vision had unsettled the right people.

In pursuing architectural perfection, I found William

Henry—the only man capable of bringing my wildest dreams to life. He wasn't cheap, but art rarely is. Every penny was worth his meticulous care in translating my ideas into something tangible. My crude sketches paled in comparison to his. It was like watching chaos transform into elegance on paper, all with a flick of his pen.

William was among the few who embraced my nocturnal tendencies without a second thought. We often met over dinner or late afternoon tea, making plans and decisions under dim lighting. Being a night owl, I preferred my work hours to start when the world began to quiet, usually in the early hours when most people were asleep. My visits to the properties were brief—once to acquire them and then weekly to ensure steady progress. Always in the afternoon, when I felt most alive.

I wasn't the stereotypical goth cloaked in black velvet, slumbering through the daylight. But the night—it was mine. My mother had called me her little night owl, and I wore that nickname as a badge of honor. The darkness had always felt like home.

One of the best parts about city life was that it never truly ended when the sun went down. Unlike the oppressive small towns, London hummed nicely past sunset. Shops stayed open, lights twinkled from all corners, and the streets held a stronger pulse with the hours. It was a world where I fit perfectly and didn't have to shrink to accommodate anyone else's expectations.

Tonight was different, however. I felt the rare urge to sell my second townhouse, netting me over half a million. That's how I found myself at an art gallery opening—some-

Chapter 1

thing I usually avoided, but tonight felt like a fitting celebration.

I hadn't anticipated the crowds of people that packed the gallery, shoulder to shoulder, barely room to breathe. The heat of all those bodies pressing together was suffocating, the air thick and stifling. Sweat began to bead at the back of my neck, reminding me why I preferred solitude. I needed to escape, to feel the cool night air of London against my skin. I wound my way through the crowd, avoiding brushes with strangers, seeking the sanctuary of the exit.

Once outside, I found my place along the edge of the bustling street, a glass of champagne in hand as I watched the city unfold before me. The night was alive, a tangled mess of light and shadow. My gaze drifted, catching on a man across the road. He was dressed in a sharp, tailored suit, but his movements were anything but composed. He stumbled and swayed, glancing nervously over his shoulder as though something—or someone—was hunting him. His steps were unsteady and erratic, and he struggled to hold them together.

Something off about him caught my attention, even in the night's chaos. I watched him, curiosity pulling me into the scene as the city buzzed around me.

As the man staggered to a halt directly across from me, I saw him nearly collapse, his legs buckling under him. Instinct took over, and before I could second-guess myself, I was rushing toward him, offering support as he crumpled to his knees. That's when I noticed the blood—a deep crimson spreading across his pristine white button-up shirt. The sight of it made me gasp, my mind racing.

"Mate, need an ambulance?" The words tumbled out, urgent and instinctual.

"Fuck no, please don't," he slurred, his eyes wild and hollow as if the light had long since left them. Something about his gaze sent a shiver down my spine, stirring an unease I hadn't felt in years.

"What do you need then?" I asked, calculating how quickly I could escape this unpredictable stranger. This was precisely the chaos I had fled from back in Australia. The last thing I wanted was to get entangled in it again.

"I just need to make it to the end of the road... my car's waiting." He lurched as he spoke, his body swaying with the effort.

I hesitated, my instincts at war with my conscience, but something compelled me to stay. "All right, I'll help you," I muttered, slipping an arm under his and hoisting him to his feet. We staggered down the street, his weight heavy against me. As we moved, curious eyes tracked us, suspicion lingering in every glance.

Quickly thinking, I pressed him against a nearby wall and pulled off my coat, draping it over his shoulders to obscure the bloodstains. We continued down the road, my arm still propping him up, until we reached the end, where a sleek black Rolls Royce with tinted windows awaited. The man who stepped out from the driver's seat looked almost identical to the stranger I was supporting—same sharp features, same cold eyes.

"What the hell happened?" His voice was sharp and concerned, but there was something else, too, something darker.

Chapter 1

"I have no idea," I replied, keeping my voice flat. "Found him slumped back there." I jerked a thumb toward the alley behind us.

His eyes narrowed, suspicion evident. "And you just... helped a random guy down the street?"

I shrugged casually, forcing indifference into my tone. "Yep. And now I'm done." Without waiting for a response, I turned on my heel and walked away, picking up my pace as I returned to my unit.

The night air felt cooler against my skin as I neared my building, and by the time I reached the entrance, my heartbeat had slowed to a steady rhythm. Tim, the doorman, greeted me with his usual smile—handsome, as always. I had thrown more than a few flirtatious glances his way since moving in, but he never took the bait. The wedding ring on his finger seemed to mean something to him. Good for him. The commitment wasn't something I had ever craved.

The very thought—domesticity and monotony—made my stomach twist. I preferred variety and freedom. It was easier that way and less complicated. My collection of toys had always been a more reliable outlet for my desires, each chosen carefully and catering to a different need. The idea of being tethered to one person for a lifetime was suffocating. Thankfully, modern technology has made it far easier to find like-minded individuals without messy attachments. Apps, websites—endless possibilities.

I couldn't imagine how women like me had survived the years before. Men always seemed to want more—more than a casual encounter than I was willing to give. They got attached too quickly, their expectations escalating. And that wasn't the life I wanted. Not now. Not ever.

2

EMBER DANG

As I stumbled into my apartment at 2 a.m., the weight of chaos and adrenaline still clinging to me, I cursed under my breath. I had left my phone in the pocket of the jacket I'd thrown over the bloodied man.

"Shit," I muttered into the space, frustration twisting inside me. It meant one thing: I'd either have to brave the streets tomorrow to retrieve it or order a new one and endure the days-long wait for delivery. The idea of using my iPad to track it flashed through my mind, but I quickly dismissed it. The last thing I wanted was to deal with prying eyes while trying to recover my phone. Not worth the risk.

With a resigned sigh, I accepted my fate, pulling up the nearest site to order a new one. It wasn't a disaster—William and the builders were the only contacts I needed to keep in touch with, and the club only reached out when necessary. But what truly gnawed at me was the thought of that stranger now holding my phone, scrolling through personal photos and videos documenting my private encounters. My taste in partners was specific, and I had always enjoyed reliving those moments in the safety of my own company.

Frantically, I logged into iCloud and downloaded everything I could, hoping to salvage whatever I might need. As I did, my heart sank. My phone had disappeared from the "Find My" list—as if it had never existed. I stared in disbelief. Could someone have turned it off already? Panic surged. It had only been an hour since I lost it. My fingers flew across the screen, checking the list of devices, searching for any sign of it. Nothing.

How had they done it so quickly? Who the hell were these people? A sickening thought crept into my mind—was I somehow tangled with the CIA? Did London have the CIA, or was that only in America? I shook my head, forcing the paranoia down, but the fear remained, humming beneath my skin.

Feeling defeated, I clicked "express shipping" on a new phone order, praying that "express" meant tomorrow. The lingering tension in my muscles led me to the bathroom, where I saw the small bloodstain on my dress. I cursed again, pulling the fabric close.

I peeled off the dress, tossing it into the laundry room sink, filling it with hot water, and emptying an entire bottle of bleach over it. My time around my dad's motorcycle club back in Australia taught me one thing—random blood on your clothes was never good. Evidence. That word alone made my stomach turn. I wasn't about to get dragged into anyone else's shady business. Not again.

The dress was ruined, of course, but better ruined than

Chapter 2

bloodstained. I made a mental note: no more dangerous situations. My dad hadn't raised a fool.

I shuffled toward the bathroom, the weight of the day pressing on my shoulders, pulling me down. Each step felt heavy as it echoed against the tiles. I stepped into the shower, determined to scrub away the memory of that man—his eyes, blood, and presence. I turned the water as hot as I could bear, washing myself from head to toe three times, desperate to erase him from my skin.

But no matter how hard I tried, his eyes—those sharp, electric blue eyes—clung to my mind. Something about them, wild and untamed, repelled and attracted me all at once. The kind of dangerous pull I should know better than to get close to.

I chastised myself for not being more competent, for not seeing the signs and steering clear. But something inexplicable had drawn me in, even though I knew better—always knew better.

After the shower, I changed into pajamas and began blow-drying my hair. My long black hair was my pride and joy, but it was a labor of love, requiring constant maintenance to keep it sleek and straight. As I stood in front of the mirror, drying section by section, I envied women with their effortless "mum buns." My routine was far from effortless. Three times a week, I endured this ritual, and it never seemed to get easier.

Feeling refreshed, I headed to the kitchen and grabbed a pre-made chicken and green beans meal from the local restaurant down the street. They delivered a week's worth of dinners every Monday—a lifesaver for someone like me.

Cooking had never appealed to me. It was one of the many life skills I lacked; frankly, I had no interest in acquiring it.

As I ate silently, I wondered what kind of person willingly raised a child, cooked for them, and devoted their life to such tasks. I was content with my solitude, my freedom, for now.

The truth was, I wouldn't say I liked cooking. My parents hadn't bothered teaching me much about life skills growing up. Instead, my father had focused on training me in boxing and MMA, ensuring I could defend myself as the president's daughter. On the compound, I never had to lift a finger—there was always someone to do it for me. Cooking and cleaning—it was always taken care of by the club girls, and I had never seen the need to learn. Now, at twenty, those same gaps in my knowledge didn't bother me.

I have an appointment to check out a new townhouse outside the city tomorrow. It had renovation potential, and the profits from my latest projects had been staggering. Thanks to Karen's meddling, my properties had attracted quite the attention, and buyers were now lining up, sight unseen. I no longer needed to advertise—my realtor had clients ready to purchase at the mere suggestion.

As much as I might complain, the truth was that this was my dream. Beautiful spaces, massive profits—who could have predicted this life for me just two years ago?

I sank into bed, pulling the doona to my chin as I reached over to switch on the air conditioning. A cool breeze washed over me, soothing my tired muscles. The city might have been sweltering during the day, but at night, it was mine. The hum of life outside was my lullaby.

Chapter 2

But sleep didn't last long. My eyes flew open, panic flooding my veins as a large hand clamped over my mouth. A crushing weight pinned me to the bed. My heart pounded against my chest as I realized it was him—the stranger from earlier. He straddled me, his hand firm but not brutal around my neck, another covering my mouth.

I managed to mumble through his grip, "If you're going to sit on me and cut off my oxygen supply, you at least need to buy me a drink first."

3

JAX STEVENSON

In my 22 years, I'd never felt the sharp, burning agony of a knife slicing into my stomach without my consent. The pain ignited a rage deep within me, but what fueled that fury even more was the person responsible—Shelby, the backstabbing bitch. We had a tumultuous thing for over a year, but when I refused to give in to her constant demands, she snapped. Today, she'd delivered an ultimatum: commit to her, or she'd expose all my secrets to the police. In that split second, I knew I had to silence her for good. But in the midst of it, she managed to land a blow, driving a small switchblade into my gut. It wasn't fatal, but blood poured from me like a broken dam.

As I sprinted towards the car, desperation gnawed at me. Each step weakened me, the blood loss taking its toll. Panic surged when I spotted a police officer on patrol, forcing me to veer away from Shelby's lifeless body. My only hope was Declan. I needed him, fast.

Blurring through the street, I noticed a crowd gathered

outside a shop. Among them, a woman in a striking blue dress and black trench coat caught my eye, leaning against the wall. Just as my legs gave way and I collapsed, she rushed over, her concerned face looming over me.

"Mate, need an ambulance?" she asked, her thick Australian accent oddly comforting.

"Fuck no, please don't," I slurred, my voice barely holding together.

"What do you need then?" she pressed, her gaze locking with mine—stunning eyes that flickered with curiosity.

"I just need to make it to the end of the road... my car's waiting," I muttered, nodding towards the waiting car.

"All right, I'll help you," she offered without hesitation, slipping an arm around me and hoisting me to my feet. For someone so small, she was surprisingly strong. As blood seeped into my shirt, she swiftly took off her coat and draped it over me, covering the mess.

Who was this woman? Most people would recoil at the sight of blood, yet she covered it up as though it were nothing. I was intrigued.

With urgent steps, she guided me towards the car, where Declan waited, his expression grim as he entered the scene.

"What the fuck happened?" Declan growled at her.

"No idea," she replied, pointing behind her. "Found him slumped against the wall."

Declan's eyes narrowed. "And you just helped some random guy down the road?"

She shrugged nonchalantly. "Yep. Now I'm off." Without waiting for a response, she spun around and took off into the night.

Chapter 3

As I watched her disappear, curiosity gnawed at me. There was something about her, something I couldn't shake. But my focus was abruptly snapped back when Declan shoved me into the car, inspecting my wound with a grimace.

"You're a reckless cunt," he muttered, shaking his head.

I smirked, leaning back. "Shelby's dead," I said matter-of-factly. "Gave me an ultimatum—either date her, or she'd go to the cops."

A low growl rumbled in Declan's throat. "Good riddance. I would've handled her if you hadn't."

He glanced back at my wound. "How'd you let her get the drop on you?"

"Lucky shot," I shrugged. "It's not deep—just needs a stitch."

"Knox will deal with it," Declan sighed, driving us back to the apartment.

He parked outside the lift in the underground carpark, helping me out and slinging an arm around me as we made our way upstairs to the penthouse. It had been Tommy's home for the last three years, ever since the old compound was attacked and his wife killed. He couldn't stand to live there anymore. I never understood his grief—she was a nightmare, constantly stirring up trouble. Her death brought a strange satisfaction.

Moving in with Tommy had been the best thing for us. Deck and I had been living in one of the off-site units, and commuting to and from the compound was getting old fast.

The penthouse was a marvel—sleek, modern, towering over the city with two levels, six spacious bedrooms, a state-of-the-art gym, and an office for Tommy. Deck and I had rooms, but we had a door between them for easy access. Even at 22, being separated from him felt wrong. Despite our differences, there was a connection—when one of us was off, the other balanced things out. Yin and yang. Deck, with his rough exterior, was a sweetheart at heart. Women would fall over themselves for a loyal, kind guy. But after his heartbreak at 18, he swore off dating and buried himself in work.

As we stepped into the apartment, Deck called out for Knox.

"Knox!"

"Knox!"

"All right, I'm not deaf," Knox grumbled, appearing around the corner. Seeing me draped over Deck, he chuckled. "What did you do this time?"

"Shelby stabbed him," Deck replied, barely holding back his laughter.

Knox gestured to the medical room, smirking. "Get him in here before I'm late for my meeting."

The familiar scent of disinfectant hit me when I entered the medical room. Knox, our twisted doctor, got to work quickly, stitching up my wound with deft hands. He hooked me up to a blood bag, grumbling about how lucky we were. Tommy had just restocked.

Knox's mind always drifted to experimentation, and he joked about using me as a guinea pig for expired blood. I shuddered at the thought, knowing that Knox's brand of fun was much darker than mine. But we all had our quirks. His bedroom antics were legendary—women left his room

Chapter 3

dazed, never to return. Whether out of fear or Knox's preference for variety, I wasn't sure.

As I shrugged off my jacket, I casually mentioned it wasn't mine and gave a brief explanation of the woman who helped me. "Belongs to the girl who helped me earlier," I said, searching the pockets. My fingers brushed against something—her phone. Holding it up, I grinned at Knox.

"Looks like she left me a little gift."

Knox raised an eyebrow and slid his laptop over. We weren't above a bit of entertainment, even in moments like this.

With a wicked grin, I plugged in the phone, quickly disabling the "Find My" feature and erasing her device from all her systems. Time to dig.

As I scrolled through her contacts, surprise flickered. No endless stream of messages, no constant pings from friends or lovers. Just a few names—"bricky," "plumbers," "builder"—people connected to some project she was working on. One stood out—William Henry. The full name is distinct from the others. Curious. The rest were restaurants around Essex Street. She must live close by.

Frustrated, I jumped into her messages. They were more mundane texts about renovations and projects. Dinner plans with William and meetings for tea all seemed too innocent. Was he a builder, too? Or something more?

I shook my head, pushing away the speculation. Opening her photo reel, my jaw dropped. Knox leaned in, laughing beside me.

"Holy shit!" he grinned.

Holy shit, indeed. We needed her. Now.

4

EMBER DANG

The rush of blood in my ears drowned out everything as I locked onto his piercing blue eyes. I was trapped beneath his weight, his hand pressing firmly over my lips and chin, stifling my breath but igniting something darker inside me. This was wrong—so fucking wrong—but I couldn't help it.

"Your pupils are blown out, Ember," he taunted, a wicked grin curling at the edges of his mouth. He knew exactly what he was doing to me.

"Fuck you," I spat, though the words were muffled against his palm. My tongue slipped out involuntarily, grazing his skin, tasting the salt of it. His eyes flickered, widening slightly at my boldness, but I could see the lust flicker brighter beneath the surface.

I hated the way my body responded, heat pooling between my thighs, my panties already dampening. This wasn't the time for arousal—this man had broken into my apartment and pinned me down, and yet my body didn't seem to care. It wanted him, fiercely and urgently, ignoring the chaos of the situation.

His eyes darkened like a storm brewing, his voice low and dangerous. "If you keep that up," he growled, his breath hot against my skin, "I won't be responsible for what comes next."

"Don't threaten me with a good time," I mumbled through his hand, my voice betraying both fear and the undeniable thrill coursing me. But we both knew it wasn't just a threat.

"Consider it a warning," he hissed, loosening his grip on my throat just enough. It was all the space I needed.

Adrenaline surged, and I flipped our positions in one fluid motion, straddling him and grinding against his now rock-hard cock. "How's this for an arrangement?" I teased, satisfaction washing over me as his green eyes widened with surprise and hunger.

"Fuck," he muttered, his control slipping, but I wasn't done. I wanted this—the danger and reckless thrill of it. My issues? I'd embraced them long ago, and right now, I didn't give a damn.

The air between us thickened with the scent of sweat and adrenaline, mixing with the heady haze of my desire. I leaned in close, my breath skimming his ear as I whispered, "How'd you get into my apartment?"

My tongue trailed up his neck, feeling the rapid pulse beneath his skin, alive and electric.

"You're like the sweetest poison," he breathed, his voice sending a shiver down my spine. His hands gripped my hips, guiding me to grind harder against him. "You are mine."

Chapter 4

"Am I?" I teased, a wicked grin curving my lips as I continued my assault, the feel of him only feeding the fire inside me.

"Shit," he groaned, his voice thick with need. "Oh, Poison, I think I'm in love." He began thrusting up, dry humping me, his eyes locked onto mine. Everything about this was wrong, but the wires in my brain had been crossed long ago. Why the hell not?

My fingers traced the fabric of his shirt, feeling the rise and fall of his chest as he panted beneath me. The raw hunger in his gaze only spurred me on.

"Like what you see?" I taunted, dragging my hands down his chest and lifting his shirt just enough to reveal the bandage covering the wound. My fingers poked at it playfully, earning a hiss from him. My grin widened.

"Fuck," he groaned, his voice a low rasp. "Do you like that, Poison?"

"Maybe," I replied, sliding lower and undoing his slacks. As I pulled his cock free, I couldn't help but marvel at it—thick, with a head that made my mouth water.

"Jesus Christ," he muttered, clearly struggling for control. In a desperate attempt to regain some semblance of power, he lifted me slightly off him, providing better access to sink into me. I grabbed his belt, pulling it free from the loops with an almost predatory grin as pressed his thick cock against my slick entrance, the sensation sending a shudder through me. As I slowly sank onto him, my body welcomed his girth with ease, the wetness of my pussy easing his entrance.

"Fuck," He groaned beneath me, his blue eyes burning

into mine as he struggled to maintain control. "You're so damn tight."

I reached for the belt I'd removed from his pants, looping it back on itself to create a makeshift set of handcuffs. With a wicked grin, I secured his hands to the headboard, leaving him at my mercy.

"What the fuck are you doing?" he growled, tugging at his restraints in a futile attempt to break free. His eyes flicked between the belt and my face, searching for some hint of my intentions.

"Relax," I purred, resuming my rhythmic movements atop him. "You're the one who came to play."

His breathing hitched as I continued to grind down on him, matching each of his desperate thrusts with my own. "You're fucking insane," he muttered with a grin.

"Shh," I whispered, pressing my fingers against his lips.

My hands moved to his chest, nails clawing at the skin as I ground my hips harder against him. Each deliberate movement drew out my pleasure, making me feel alive. It was like dancing on a knife's edge – dangerous, reckless, but undeniably seductive.

"Fuck," He muttered through gritted teeth, his body tense beneath me. "I'm going to cum"

"Don't you dare" My voice was sharp, cutting through the air like a whip. "You don't get to cum until I tell you to."

"Jesus Christ," he gasped, his hips twitching in a futile attempt to find relief. "Poison, please..."

I couldn't help but laugh; how quickly he broke under my touch was almost pathetic. I liked it when they begged.

Chapter 4

"Tell me how much you want it," I demanded, my inner thighs slick with arousal as I continued to ride him. "Say it."

"Fuck, I need it so bad," he moaned, his desperation sending a thrill racing through me. "Please, just... let me cum."

"Is that the best you've got?" I taunted, feeling the familiar tingle in my feet and the tightening sensation deep within me. My orgasm was close, and I knew he could feel it, too.

"God, Please, I'm begging you," He panted, his voice raw and broken. "I can't hold on any longer."

The sound of our mingled breaths filled the room, a symphony of lust and desperation. I tightened around him, my muscles clenching as I neared the precipice. "Cum for me," I breathed, crashing over the edge as my orgasm exploded like fireworks in the night sky.

His eyes widened, a single tear escaping to trace a path down his cheek as he released inside me, hot and pulsating. It coated my walls; my heart raced with the exhilaration of it all.

"Fuck..." he gasped, chest heaving beneath me. Unable to resist, I leaned down and licked the tear from his face, savouring the salty tang that lingered on my tongue.

"Delicious," I murmured before laying down on top of him, our bodies slick with sweat.

"Can you please undo my hands?" he asked, his voice strained but still commanding.

"Nope," I replied, smirking at his predicament. Rising from the bed, I reached down to his pants halfway down his legs and rummaged through the pockets until I found his phone. Turning it towards him, I watched as the screen unlocked with his face ID.

"Smile for the camera," I teased, snapping a photo of him in all his chaotic glory – wet, soft dick and hands bound by his belt to my headboard. My fingers danced across the screen as I sent the image to his last contact, Deck.

"Hey, come pick up your lost puppy," I typed, hitting send without a second thought.

5
DECLAN STEVENSON

Jax had bolted from the apartment like his ass was on fire. The second Knox had stitched him up, he was gone, determined to bring that girl back with him—something he'd never done before. I couldn't blame him; my brief encounter with her had left me wanting more too.

She was possibly the most stunning woman I'd ever seen; her features were a perfect blend of Asian heritage that I couldn't quite place. Her long, glossy black hair cascaded down her back, and the delicate tattoos peeking out from under her clothes only added to her allure. She was ultimately my type, yet there was something more—something pulling me toward her like an invisible thread, irresistible and dangerous.

As I made my way toward Tommy's office, I bumped into Knox, dressed sharply in a three-piece suit that looked like it was strangling him. He tugged at the collar, clearly irritated.

"I don't know how you wear this shit every day," he

muttered, shifting uncomfortably. "It's like having an anaconda around my neck."

I chuckled, brushing past him. "That's because your neck's too thick. You need tailored shirts." Knox, never one to pass up on sarcasm, asked if Jax had found his 'Little Witch.'

"He's not back yet," I replied, glancing at my watch. "Been gone a while though."

Knox smirked. "I'm sure he's tied up somewhere. I'll check in later," he called over his shoulder as he strode off.

I headed upstairs, my mind already swirling with thoughts about Shelby and ensuring nothing would blow back on us. As I approached Tommy's office, muffled groans seeped through the closed door. Without hesitating, I twisted the knob and stepped inside.

There was Tommy, bent over his desk, hammering into a blonde hooker who moaned loudly beneath him. I took a seat at the front of the desk, watching as his grip tightened on her hips, his knuckles turning white. He forced her face into the wood as he worked her over.

He glanced up at me, smirking, but didn't slow his pace. Tommy took what he wanted, without a second thought for anyone else. Since his wife's death, he'd been a cold, selfish lover. He didn't chase women—he bought them. To him, it was just a transaction, a way to scratch an itch. I couldn't judge, however. It had been four years since I'd touched a woman, and even now, watching his animalistic movements, I felt nothing stir in me.

Finally, Tommy pulled out, panting heavily as he slumped back into his chair, lighting a cigarette.

"Get on your knees and suck me off," he ordered, his

Chapter 5

voice rough. The girl obediently dropped between his legs, eager to please. He must pay them well for their submission.

"What can I do for you, Deck?" he asked, exhaling a cloud of smoke, his eyes gleaming as the woman worked him over.

"I can wait," I said, nodding towards her as she bobbed on his cock.

"Candy, wait outside until I tell you to come back in," Tommy commanded, his voice cold. She obeyed without question and left the room.

"All right, out with it. I was close to blowing my load," Tommy said, leaning back, his cigarette hanging between his fingers, his cock still standing at attention.

Shaking my head, I got to the point. "Jax killed Shelby tonight, got stabbed, and a stranger helped him out. After Knox patched him up, he went after her."

Tommy's expression shifted, the usual smirk fading. "Was Shelby dealt with?" he asked in a low voice.

"Yeah, I sent a crew to clean up after I picked him up."

Tommy nodded, satisfied. "And the woman?"

"No idea what to make of her," I shrugged. "She's... interesting."

"In what way?" he pressed, taking another drag.

"Well, for starters, she found Jax bleeding out in the street, covered him with her coat, walked him to the car, and then saluted me before heading home." The confusion in my voice mirrored the look on Tommy's face.

"So she wasn't fazed at all?" Tommy asked, his brows furrowed. "And she helped Jax escape?"

"Yeah," I nodded.

Tommy's grin returned, wide and wicked. "And now Jax is out there... what? Kidnapping her?"

I chuckled, unable to resist. "That was the plan, but he hasn't returned yet."

"Well, now my interest's piqued," Tommy said, tucking himself away and adjusting his pants.

Just then, my phone pinged loudly. I pulled it out, scanning the screen. The caption read: "Hey, come pick up your lost puppy." Beneath it was a photo of Jax, his black hair a mess, blue eyes wide with that familiar mischief. He was tied to a bed, pants halfway down his legs, cock out for all to see.

"Jesus Christ," I muttered, a grin tugging at my lips. Jax, always unpredictable, was diagnosed as a psychopath at five. He might've been my twin, but we were opposites in every way. I tried to keep us out of trouble; he dove headfirst into it.

"What's going on?" Tommy asked, arching an eyebrow as he leaned in to look at my phone.

"Take a wild guess," I replied, holding the screen.

"Fuck me," Tommy laughed, his green eyes gleaming as he took in the image of Jax tied up.

"So much for kidnapping the girl," I sighed, shaking my head but unable to stop laughing.

"Guess we better go rescue him, huh?" Tommy adjusted his tie, his cufflinks gleaming as he straightened up.

"Looks like it," I agreed, typing a response and asking for the address.

Tommy's eyes twinkled with amusement. "Your brother's always getting himself into shit, isn't he?"

"Trouble sticks to him like glue," I muttered, rubbing my

Chapter 5

forehead. This wouldn't be the last time Jax found himself in a mess, and it certainly wasn't the first.

"I'm very interested in meeting this woman," Tommy mused, his eyes narrowing slightly.

My phone buzzed again, and another message came—an address and apartment number. I took a deep breath, preparing for whatever insanity awaited us.

"Well, we know where he is," I said, showing Tommy the information. "Let's go."

As we reached the door, Tommy turned to Candy, the girl who had been on her knees moments before. "Get dressed; you're not needed now," he ordered, his voice sharp. She nodded, hurrying out of sight.

6

EMBER DANG

I shoot off my address to someone named Deck, then flop back onto the bed beside the stranger. His scent fills my senses—sweat, sex, and something primal that lingers in the air between us. My heart still races as I glance at him, the memory of his hands around my neck vivid, almost electric. He's an enigma, and I crave answers.

"All right," I say, staring up at the ceiling with a wicked grin. "I've got some fuckin' questions for you."

He laughs, a low, rich sound that sends a shiver down my spine. "You wanna play twenty questions or something?"

"Why not?" I shrug, trying to act nonchalant. "We've got time while we wait for your ride. Might as well get to know each other."

"Fair enough," he smirks, amusement flickering in those intense blue eyes.

"Name?" I ask, raising an eyebrow.

"Jax," he replies, the smirk still firmly in place. He watches me like he's in on a joke I haven't figured out yet.

"All right, Jax," I say, rolling my eyes at the smugness in his expression. "My name's Ember." I lift my hand as if to shake his, only to remember it's still tied to the headboard with his belt. I laugh at myself, shaking my head at the absurdity of it all.

"Hi, Ember," he says, his grin widening, clearly enjoying my predicament.

I bite back a smile as I take in his face, tracing the sharp lines of his jaw and the way his lips curve in that maddeningly confident smirk. He's got that dark, brooding thing going on—exactly the kind of man who gets under my skin and stays there.

"Okay," I continue, trying to keep the conversation casual, though my pulse betrays me. "How old are you, Jax?"

"Twenty-two," he answers, his blue eyes locking onto mine with an intensity that makes my stomach flip. How he looks at me is unsettling, like he sees through every layer I've built around myself.

"I'm twenty," I say, shifting slightly under his gaze. "Guess we're not too far apart."

"It seems like it," Jax agrees, his eyes never leaving mine. In the dim light of the room, his gaze is almost hypnotic, and those blue orbs glow with a raw energy that makes me uneasy and intrigued all at once.

"Are you Australian?" he asks suddenly, throwing me off with his question.

"Fuckin' hell, what gave it away?" I reply with exaggerated sarcasm, rolling my eyes. "The accent, maybe?"

"Could be that," he says with a teasing smirk. "But you

Chapter 6

never know. People can sound all kinds of ways, accents and shit."

"True enough," I admit. "Yeah, I'm Aussie. Born and raised. What about you? I take it you're English, with that lovely accent?"

Jax smiles again, a mischievous glint in his eyes. "I'm English, but Irish blood is in the mix. Though, it's never been confirmed."

"Ah, so Black Irish then?" I ask, raising an eyebrow with mock intrigue. His dark hair and blue eyes scream Irish ancestry, but how he plays it down makes me smirk.

He leans in a bit closer, a teasing gleam in his eyes. "Let me guess—my black hair and blue eyes gave it away?"

I laugh, enjoying the playful back-and-forth more than I should. There's something about the ease of this conversation, the way it feels natural like we've known each other far longer than a few chaotic hours. I know I shouldn't feel this comfortable with him, but I do.

"You've got me there," I say, my tone light but my gaze fixed on his. Those eyes, deep blue and full of intensity, seem to pull me in more profound, and I can't help but get lost in them for a moment. "Your eyes are... something else," I murmur, the words slipping out before I can stop them.

He smirks, leaning in closer, his breath brushing against my skin. "What are you? A siren? I've never felt this drawn to anyone before."

I laugh, the sound sharp and unexpected in the small room. "Oh, don't flatter me now. We've already fucked, remember?"

His grin widens, the amusement never leaving his face.

"I'm not flattering you. I'm stating a fact. You've got me hooked, and I don't let go."

I lean in without thinking, pressing a soft kiss to his lips. Something about Jax pulls me in, like gravity, and it's impossible to resist. "Well, it's a good thing I do let go," I whisper against his mouth, my lips lingering for a second longer than they should.

A loud knock echoes through the apartment, snapping us both out of the moment. The sound is jarring like a bucket of cold water dumped over my head, and I pull back, glancing toward the door.

Jax raises an eyebrow, amusement still dancing in his eyes. "Guess that's my ride."

7

TOMMY PERCIVAL

The hallway lights were too bright, almost obnoxiously so, as I raised my fist and knocked hard on the apartment door. I didn't have patience for this kind of nonsense. Two minutes—two bloody minutes, that's all it took for the door to open, and when it did, my heart nearly skipped a beat.

Standing before me was a tall woman, Asian descent, with glossy black hair that flowed like silk over her shoulders, as if she'd stepped out of some high-end fashion magazine. Her eyes were the color of warm, rich chocolate, which only highlighted the bleakness of the world around her. It all made sense now—why Jax had gone tearing off to kidnap this woman. I could feel it too, the pull, the allure. She was wearing nothing but a black silk nightdress that barely skimmed the tops of her thighs, and I found myself momentarily entranced by her ethereal beauty.

"Can I help you?" she asked, her voice like honey with just enough venom to make it dangerous. Her amusement was clear in the glint of her eyes, as if she already knew exactly who we were.

I had to clear my throat, annoyed that she'd caught me off guard. "Yeah," I stammered, pulling myself together. "We're here for Jax."

The chandelier in the entryway cast a dim, eerie glow across the room, stretching shadows in unnatural directions. It felt like we'd walked into some kind of lair, where she was the predator and we were the prey. A chill crawled down my spine, but I wasn't about to show weakness—not in front of her.

"You're here for the lost puppy?" she asked, a wicked smile playing on her lips as she gave me a once-over, eyes lingering just a bit too long. There was something bold, calculating about her—she was toying with us.

"Hardly a puppy," I shot back, forcing a laugh that sounded far more confident than I felt. "More like a rabid mutt. But yes, we're here for Jax. Maybe we should get him chipped so he doesn't wander off again."

Her laugh echoed through the air, soft and mocking, wrapping around me like a silk noose. I felt that same tug Jax had felt, an inexplicable pull. She closed the door with a soft click, locking us inside with her—an invitation into her world of mystery and danger.

"Follow me," she commanded, her voice leaving no room for argument. She turned on her heel, the black silk of her nightdress fluttering with each step, offering tantalizing glimpses of her perfect ass. I felt my fingers twitch, the desire to reach out and claim what I saw almost overpowering. But

Chapter 7

before I could lose myself entirely, Declan's elbow jabbed into my ribs, pulling me back to reality.

"Focus, Tommy," he hissed, clearly unimpressed. "We're here to rescue Jax, remember?"

"Right," I muttered, tearing my eyes away from the hypnotic sway of her hips. But it was difficult to concentrate with that woman leading the way, like some seductive siren tempting me to crash against the rocks.

We entered a dimly lit room, and my attention immediately shifted to Jax. There he was, wrists bound to the bedpost with a thick leather belt, a look of pure excitement on his face. Of course, the crazy bastard was enjoying every second of this.

Ever the responsible, Declan knelt next to the bed and began working to undo the restraints. "Let me get you out of this," he muttered, while Jax grinned like a lunatic.

Ember leaned against the wall, watching with that same amused smile. "Your lost puppy is quite charming," she remarked, her voice laced with playful mockery. "But maybe he could try knocking next time instead of breaking in?"

"Sorry about that," I said, leaning back and crossing my arms. "Jax has always been impulsive." I couldn't help but notice how my voice sounded too casual, like I wasn't completely distracted by her.

"No harm done," she replied, her melodic laughter filling the room. "He's behaved himself... mostly. But next time, he needs to knock." She cast Jax a glance that was both predatory and playful, her lips curving into a grin that showed she was in full control of the situation.

Jax's head snapped toward her, his eyes widening in disbelief. "Next time?"

"Of course," she said, her gaze never leaving his. The tension between them was palpable, thickening the air until it was almost suffocating.

With one last look at us, Ember turned and walked toward the door, her hips swaying with every step, the nightdress barely concealing what lay beneath. I couldn't take my eyes off her and knew Jax felt the same. She had us both on a string, and she damn well knew it.

"Goodbye, gentlemen," she said, opening the door for us with a flourish. Her voice had a dismissive tone, like she was already done with us, but the pull I felt hadn't lessened. I could see it in Jax's eyes too. She had him hooked, and I wasn't far behind.

"Can't say I expected that," Declan muttered as we stepped into the hallway, the dim light of the apartment still casting a shadow in my mind. As the click of the door closing behind us echoed through the hallway.

"Neither did I," I admitted, though I hated how much she'd gotten under my skin. No woman did that to me—not anymore.

"Oi, Tommy," Jax called out, snapping me from my thoughts. "You've got that look in your eyes. Don't tell me you've fallen for her too."

"Who the fuck was she?" I growled, frustration lacing my words. This wasn't like me. I didn't get rattled.

"Ember," Jax replied, his smirk still in place, eyes glazed with lust. "Australian, 20 years old."

"Really?" I raised an eyebrow, trying to understand why

Chapter 7

this woman was in London. "And how the hell do you know all that?"

Jax laughed, his wicked grin widening. "We played twenty questions. Right after she pinned me to the bed and used me like a fuck doll."

I clenched my jaw, fighting off a surge of jealousy. It wasn't like me to feel that—especially not for someone like Jax. But something about her... something about Ember got under my skin in a way I couldn't shake.

8

JAX STEVENSON

That girl. That beautiful, manipulative, and utterly mesmerising girl had just had her way with me. I wasn't even mad about it. If anything, I was fascinated. Every move she made was like a choreographed performance, perfectly calculated to pull me deeper into her orbit. I could feel her wrapping herself around my mind, and it only made me want more. I never let go of control easily, but with Ember, it was a different story. As we made our way home, Tommy and Deck kept shooting me knowing looks. They could sense it too. They were just as intrigued, especially Tommy, who usually couldn't care less about women unless they were high-end escorts. Even Declan, who had sworn off women entirely, seemed affected by her. And me? I was consumed. Consumed by the fire she had lit inside me. She was my next obsession, and I wasn't about to let her disappear.

Back home, the guys were eager to know what had gone down with Ember, their questions coming at me rapid-fire.

But I wasn't in the mood to share. I wanted to keep her—what had happened between us—just for me. So I brushed them off and retreated to my room. I needed something to calm my racing thoughts, and Jimi Hendrix's voice floating through my record player did the trick. His smooth melodies worked like a drug, easing my mind into quiet. As I lay sprawled on top of my plush four-poster bed, still wearing the scent of sex and sweat from Ember, the music lulled me into sleep.

I WOKE WITH A START AT 4 P.M., MY HEART POUNDING IN MY CHEST. I couldn't remember the dream, but I knew it had been about her. Ember. That woman had worried my mind so deeply that even my dreams weren't safe. I rolled out of bed and headed into the en-suite bathroom, flipping on the shower. I stank of her, and yet the thought of washing her off felt wrong.

As I stripped off my trousers, I glanced down, gripping my semi-hard dick. The memory of her hips rolling against me, the way she commanded my body with every touch, sent a shiver through me. Each caress felt like a live wire, igniting something primal and uncontrollable. And the way she made me beg—fuck. I couldn't remember when anyone had driven me to that point. I stared at my reflection in the glass, my fist moving up and down my rigid cock with clinical precision. The image of her haunted me, clinging to my every thought like a dark, enigmatic shadow. I couldn't shake it—her scent, taste, and essence invading my mind like an inescapable parasite.

Chapter 8

My hand worked itself faster, edging me closer to the precipice. My muscles tensed as the memory of her tight cunt clenching around my cock sent shivers down my spine. Her face, contorted in pleasure, played on repeat in my twisted mind, spurring me on.

"Fuck!" I grunted, my breath fogging up the glass. It wasn't enough—nothing was enough without her. My balls tightened in anticipation, the pressure building in me like a coiled snake ready to strike. My hand moved in sync with the imaginary ghost of her, my other hand resting against the cool glass as if it could somehow bring me closer to her.

Pictures of her invaded my mind, her lips curved in a mocking smile, her eyes boring into my soul. Ember was my kryptonite, my weakness.

With a final, desperate stroke, I came, my release painting the pristine glass before me. Cum splattered against the pane. My breathing ragged, I stepped back, a sneer twisting my lips.

I quickly soaped myself up then hurriedly rinsed it off my skin, my mind already spinning, thinking of how I could make her mine. Fully mine. A sly smile crept onto my face as a devious plan started to form.

I dressed in my most casual suit—grey dress pants, a charcoal button-up, and a waistcoat. I didn't need to dress like this all the time. Still, I wasn't about to risk running into anyone important looking like some common idiot. After slicking back my black hair and spraying some cologne, I grabbed my keys. If things didn't go according to plan, maybe I'd still get lucky. I'd learned from last time, though—I left the belt behind.

As the evening crept in, I entered the underground garage and slid into my Aston Martin. My heart raced as I started the engine. Ember's apartment was only twenty minutes away, but the universe had other plans. Traffic was a nightmare. Thick, humid air clung to everything as I sat in bumper-to-bumper congestion, cursing at the drivers around me. I honked, shouted, flipped people off—every second spent sitting in traffic felt like wasted time.

After what felt like an eternity, I finally arrived. The doorman at her building opened the door for me with a nod, and I made my way to the elevator. No one in London would dare stop me from entering any building unless it was owned by Adrian Romano—something Ember didn't need to know just yet. The elevator dinged as I reached her floor, pulling me from my thoughts. I strode out and reached her door, pulling out my lock-picking kit. A skill I'd perfected since I was ten. The tools gleamed in the dim hallway light as I worked the lock. The satisfying click of the door unlocking sent a thrill through me.

Stepping inside, I strained to hear any movement. The apartment was quiet—eerily so. Still, her scent lingered, wrapping around me like a drug. That intoxicating smell only intensified my desire. I crept down the hallway, my footsteps silent on the plush carpet. I heard a faint sound as I neared her bedroom door. A podcast? Maybe a TV show? Gently, I pushed the door open. The room was dimly lit, her laptop casting a soft glow as it played some podcast about serial killers.

And there she was. Ember lay sprawled in the center of the bed, her raven black hair fanning like dark waves against

Chapter 8

the sheets. One bare leg peeked out from beneath the duvet, her skin glowing in the low light. She looked peaceful, asleep amidst the faint glow of the room. Alluring, intoxicating—but I didn't want to wake her. Not yet. This wasn't a night for chaos. I had other plans.

With a soft click, I closed the door behind me and ventured back into her apartment, making my way toward the kitchen. It didn't take long to find—a bright, spacious room bathed in the warm evening light. I opened her fridge and frowned. Nearly empty. A few eggs, some milk, and a bunch of untouched takeout containers. The cabinets weren't much better—flour, sugar, and coffee. I shook my head. Does this woman not eat?

I rummaged through what little she had, deciding I'd have to order groceries for her. In the meantime, I set about making something simple. The pancakes sizzled in the pan, and despite my best efforts to stay quiet, I couldn't help but make some noise. By the time I flipped the last pancake, I felt the cold barrel of a gun press into the back of my head.

Fuck. This girl...

9

EMBER DANG

A soft, ruffling noise greeted me as I slowly surfaced from sleep, consciousness seeping back into my groggy mind. Squinting against the dim light filtering through the velvet curtains, I tried to focus on the sound. It was coming from the kitchen, and it was all too familiar.

"Damn it," I muttered under my breath, knowing exactly who was brazenly trespassing in my sanctuary. That infuriatingly attractive man dared to waltz in again despite me making it crystal clear he was supposed to knock first. My annoyance simmered just beneath the surface, threatening to boil over.

With a resigned sigh, I swung my legs over the edge of the bed and reached for the bedside drawer. My fingers curled around the cold metal of my 9mm Beretta, the same gun I bought shortly after moving to London. There was something about the weight of it in my hand that brought comfort, a strange sense of security that had its roots in the violence and loss of my childhood. PTSD clung to me like a shadow, always there, lurking just out of sight.

I moved silently, the carpet muffled my footsteps as I made my way down the hall, grip tightening on the gun. The smell of freshly cooked pancakes filled the air, a scent that would have been comforting if not for the fact that Jax was in my kitchen, uninvited.

Peeking around the corner, I saw him standing there like he belonged—rolled up sleeves of his charcoal button-up shirt, his grey waistcoat snug against his broad chest. He wasn't wearing a belt this time, which at least showed me he wasn't a complete idiot. My eyes traced the lines of his forearms, muscles rippling as he flipped a pancake. It was hard to deny how gorgeous he was—those broad shoulders, the memory of his sculpted abs, and the way his cock had felt pressed against me. But I had to stay cautious around him. He was dangerous in more ways than one.

I approached him as quietly as I could, the gun heavy in my hand, and pressed the barrel firmly against the back of his head.

"Good morning, Jax," I whispered.

He froze and slowly turned to face me, his infuriating grin spreading across his face. His blue eyes locked onto mine, daring me to pull the trigger. Without breaking eye contact, he leaned in closer, resting his forehead against the gun barrel.

"Poison," he breathed, the nickname sliding off his tongue with a mix of honey and venom. "If you don't want me to fuck you over this stove right now, I suggest you move the gun."

Chapter 9

I couldn't help but look down at the bulge in his pants, clearly visible even with the gun pointed at his head. The realisation sent a shiver down my spine, part fear, part something else I wasn't ready to admit.

"Is this how you get your kicks, Jax?" I asked, barely audible over the sizzling of the frying pan.

"Life's too short for anything less," he replied, his tone playful, as if daring me to go further.

My eyes flicked to the plate of pancakes, their aroma rich and inviting. With a sigh, I flicked the safety on the gun and lowered it, though part of me stayed on edge. "I usually take my pancakes with butter and maple syrup," I said.

"Your wish is my command, Poison," he said with a wink, stepping closer until he was inches from my face. He leaned down and kissed my cheek, a soft and unexpected gesture that sent an involuntary shiver through me. "Go get ready. I'll have everything set in ten minutes."

Nodding, I retreated to my room, still unsettled by how easily he got under my skin. I changed into sweats and an oversized t-shirt, throwing my hair into a messy bun before heading back out. Just as I re-entered the kitchen, the apartment's door phone rang and Jax answered it, barely hesitating, and granted access to whoever was there.

A few minutes later, a man arrived at the door with three bags of groceries. "Here you go, Mr. Stevenson. Anything else I can do today?" he asked humbly.

"Nope," Jax replied dismissively, waving the man off as he closed the door. My heart was pounding, a strange mix of curiosity and unease swirling in my chest. Who exactly was Jax, and why did he have people serving him like that?

"Looks like we've got everything we need," Jax said, unpacking the bags and setting out butter and maple syrup. He prepared the pancakes with a care that felt oddly out of place, given who he must be, and then gestured for me to sit.

"Who are you, Jax?" I asked quietly, frustration and desire battling within me. Every move he made sent tremors down my spine, my body betraying me.

Who the fuck was this man, and why did he make me feel like this? My thighs were slick with wetness, my mind screaming at me to get a grip. We didn't know him, yet every fiber of my being was drawn to him.

"Poison," Jax said softly yet commandingly, placing a plate of buttery, syrup-soaked pancakes before me. His gaze was penetrating, and despite my better judgment, I sat without protest.

"How do I know you didn't lace it with rat poison?" I challenged, narrowing my eyes. I needed to push him, to test the boundaries of this dangerous game.

His jaw tightened, eyes boring into mine as he spat his reply through clenched teeth. "If I wanted you dead, Ember, I would just shoot you between the eyes."

A shiver ran through me at the coldness in his voice, but it was quickly followed by a thrill that I couldn't ignore. This man was lethal yet intoxicating. I knew he wasn't about to kill me, but the tension between us remained thick and simmering. I lowered myself into the chair, setting my gun on the table beside me. I didn't trust him, but there was no denying the magnetism between us.

"Fine," I muttered, focusing on the plate of pancakes in front of me.

Chapter 9

"Good," Jax replied curtly, his icy facade softening slightly. He watched me intently as I picked up the fork, the sound of silverware scraping the plate cutting through the silence.

"Doesn't mean I trust you," I mumbled, stabbing a piece of pancake and bringing it to my lips. The syrup's sweetness and the pancake's buttery richness hit me like heaven on my tongue, momentarily distracting me from my spiralling thoughts.

"Trust is earned," Jax agreed, leaning back in his chair, his gaze never wavering. "And I intend to earn yours, Ember."

I glanced up, meeting his eyes as I chewed. "Can't believe you cooked this," I muttered between bites, still unsure what to make of him. A smug smile curled on his lips as if he'd just won some unspoken challenge.

"Nothing's impossible when you put your mind to it, Ember." He grabbed a plate and served himself, sitting across from me with an easy confidence that deepened the mystery surrounding him. Leaning in, elbows on the table, he locked his gaze onto mine. "So, tell me about yourself."

The question hung between us, pulling at a vulnerability I wasn't ready to expose. My past was a tangled web of pain and darkness, and I wasn't about to unravel it for someone like him. As I was about to speak, my iPad rang, the sharp sound slicing through the moment.

"Excuse me," I said, pushing away from the table. I grabbed the iPad, swiped it to answer the call and placed it on speaker so I could continue eating. "Hello, Kelly. What can I do for you?"

"Ember, I've got a new townhouse listing that I think you'll love," my real estate agent's voice came through, her excitement palpable even over the tinny speaker. "I can arrange a walk-through tonight at 8 p.m. if you're interested."

I glanced at the clock on the screen—6:37 p.m. Plenty of time.

"Sure," I said, excitement creeping into my voice despite my best efforts to stay composed. "How far is it?"

"About a thirty-minute drive," Kelly replied, typing faintly in the background. "I'll send you the address now."

"Great. See you there." I ended the call and turned back to Jax, who had been watching the entire exchange with amusement and curiosity. "Can I have my phone back now?" I asked, but its absence was an annoying reminder that the express shipping on my new one was a lie.

Jax reached into his pocket, pulling out my phone, its screen as dark as the mystery behind him. "I'm coming with you to see this place," he declared, his tone leaving no room for argument.

I raised an eyebrow, incredulous. "Why would I let a stranger tag along with me?"

"Stranger?" Jax smirked that dangerous glint returning to his blue eyes. "After everything we've been through, I think we're well past that stage, don't you? Besides," he added with a cocky grin, gesturing toward the pancakes, "I made you breakfast."

I eyed him warily, fully aware that beneath the charm and confidence lurked a predator. He was dangerous, no

Chapter 9

doubt about it. But there was something about him—something I couldn't shake.

"Fine," I relented, my voice edged with resignation. "You can drive me because I don't own a car."

Jax's grin widened, acting like he won the lottery, and I hated how much I liked the idea of him coming with me.

The cold leather of the Aston Martin's seat pressed against my bare thighs as I slid into the car, adjusting the hem of my short black suit dress to keep it from revealing too much. Jax, dressed in a tailored grey suit, moved with a grace I couldn't help but admire, and I didn't want to stand beside him.

"Here's the address," I murmured, handing him a slip of paper with the townhouse location. We were off when he typed it into the car's navigation system.

As Jax navigated the streets, I was captivated by his presence behind the wheel. The deep growl of the engine felt like a dark symphony, ideally in tune with his every shift of the gears. His hands flexed on the steering wheel easily and confidently, sending shivers through me. I hated how easily he made me feel this way. Sitting beside him, my body reacted like we were locked in another dangerous game. I knew it wasn't expected to be this wet around a man I barely knew.

The city lights blurred past us, and I wondered about the townhouse and the dark sanctuary I could create within its walls. I had been toying with the idea of incorporating gold accents into my next project, and this place could be the perfect canvas for that vision.

As we approached the townhouse, I was immediately struck by its presence. It was a gothic masterpiece draped in shadows, nestled among a row of similarly imposing structures. The light from the Victorian street lamps cast eerie patterns across the weathered stone and wrought iron banisters, heightening its dark allure. My heart leapt in my chest. This was the one.

"Here we are," Jax announced, effortlessly pulling the car into a parking space. He then moved around to open my door, his actions smooth, controlled, and practiced.

"Thank you," I murmured as I stepped out onto the cobblestone street, the chill in the air biting against my skin. I smoothed down my dress, tugging at the hem as the cool night air wrapped around me. London nights had a way of sinking into you, seeping into your bones, just like the darkness that permeated the city.

I walked toward the townhouse, my heels clicking against the pavement in a rhythmic pattern. The place called to me, its silent whispers promising sanctuary and secrecy within its walls. I could envision myself inside, reshaping its worn bones into something dark and beautiful.

"Quite the impressive building," Jax commented as he stepped beside me, his eyes glinting with curiosity. There was something about how he observed everything, like cataloging each detail for some hidden purpose.

As we approached the door, a gust of wind chilled the air further, and the sound seemed to carry whispers meant only for the night. The door creaked open, and Kelly stood wide-eyed as she took in Jax.

"Oh, Mr. Stevenson, I didn't know you would be

Chapter 9

attending as well," she stammered, trying to keep her composure but failing miserably.

I narrowed my eyes at Jax before turning to Kelly. "Mr. Stevenson is joining me today, but he's irrelevant. It's only me who will be buying the place."

Kelly's surprise was palpable as she glanced between us, clearly struggling to reconcile the dynamic she witnessed. But she nodded quickly, regaining her professional composure. I decided to dig deeper into Jax's background as soon as possible.

"All right then," Kelly said, her voice steady again. "Let's start the tour."

We stepped inside, and the townhouse's darkness immediately enveloped us. The moment Jax's hand brushed against the small of my back, a warmth surged through me, spreading like wildfire. I had to remind myself that I needed to stay in control. For all his allure, this man was dangerous, and the power he held over me after such a short time was alarming.

"Welcome to your potential new project," Kelly chirped. The outdated 1970s decor was an eyesore, a mix of dull browns and faded patterns that immediately offended my senses.

"Interesting choice of color," I said dryly, barely concealing my disdain.

Kelly smiled awkwardly, clearly picking up on my distaste. "It could be transformed into something spectacular with some work."

The rest of the tour passed in relative silence. Each room told a story, secrets hidden within the worn walls, and I could feel the townhouse's history hanging in the air. It was old and tired, but it had potential. I could already see the dark elegance I could craft from its bones.

As we returned to the front door, Kelly turned to me expectantly. "What do you think?"

"Tell me the asking price," I demanded, mentally redesigning every room.

"850,000," Kelly replied smoothly, clearly expecting negotiation.

"Put in an offer for 750,000," I instructed. "And get a building inspector in here. I suspect there's water damage on the second floor."

Kelly nodded quickly, jotting down my demands. "Anything else?" she asked, poised to finalize the details.

I smiled, its edge sharp and full of intent. "Yes. Let them know it's a cash offer, with a four-week handover."

Her eyes widened slightly, but she nodded and scribbled down the details. With the business concluded, we stepped outside, the cold air biting into my skin again. Jax offered his arm quickly, and though I hesitated momentarily, I allowed him to lead me back to the Aston Martin. His touch was warm, almost soothing, but I couldn't ignore the dark undercurrent of power that radiated from him.

Once inside the car, I settled into the leather seat, glancing at Jax from the corner of my eye. He was quiet, his brow furrowed in thought. His blue eyes seemed darker now, like something was brewing behind them, a storm waiting to be unleashed. The engine roared to life beneath us, breaking our heavy silence.

Chapter 9

"Ember... who the fuck are you?" Jax asked suddenly, his voice cutting through the tension like a blade.

The question hung in the air, and I turned to meet his gaze, my brown eyes locking with his. The intensity between us crackled like a live wire.

"Jax," I replied, my voice low and steady. "Who are you?"

10

TOMMY PERCIVAL

An eerie silence draped over the warehouse like a heavy shroud as I scanned my men's faces, unease settling into my bones. The room felt too tense, too thick with expectation. My chest tightened. Something was off. Jax was missing. That nagging absence pulled at me like a loose thread.

"Where's Jax?" My voice was sharper than I intended, but I couldn't mask the frustration and concern that churned inside me. I turned to Declan, standing beside me, expecting something—anything.

His nonchalant shrug made my jaw clench. "I have no idea. He left around 4 p.m. and hasn't been back."

The vagueness of his answer sent a ripple of annoyance through me. Jax wasn't just one of us but integral to our operations. His absence didn't just disrupt the plan; it fractured the entire structure. Jax had been running point on this job, and now we were running blind. It was infuriating.

I dismissed the men, who lingered in intense uncertainty.

Their hushed conversations did not interest me; I was preoccupied with the looming gun shipment and the mounting frustration of Jax's absence. His job was to gather us and lay out the final details. Now, that responsibility fell to me, unexpectedly and unwelcomely.

As I thought about Jax, I couldn't shake the image of him with Ember—the woman who had become his latest obsession. She had him wrapped up, twisted around her like a vine. It wasn't the first time Jax had been consumed by something or someone, but this felt different. Ember felt like more than just a passing fixation. And that unsettled me.

Ember was a complication I couldn't afford. Not with the way she stirred something deep within me. She represented a past I'd buried, and her presence was like a dark whisper, pulling me back into memories I fought to suppress. She had no idea of the danger she posed—to me, to us. And the worst part? I couldn't keep her out of my head.

I pushed her out of my thoughts, tried to at least, but her allure lingered, haunting the edges of my mind like a persistent shadow. She wasn't just dangerous because of what she represented but because she made me feel again. And that... that was a weakness I couldn't afford.

As I climbed into my car and left the dimly lit warehouse behind, I felt a pull I couldn't ignore. To confirm my suspicions, a drive past Ember's place seemed like the next logical move. Jax was reckless, but he wasn't careless. Still, the thought of him being at her place gnawed at me. Ember's address had been seared into my memory from the moment Declan showed me the message from her on his phone.

The drive was filled with my usual conflicting emotions.

Chapter 10

Every mile brought me closer to the questions I was too afraid to ask myself. Could Ember be the one to break through my carefully constructed walls? Or was she simply another reminder of why I needed to keep them up in the first place? Part of me feared that she would weaken me, while another part... hoped. Hoped she could free me from the labyrinth of lies and betrayals I'd woven over the years.

But that hope was dangerous. I didn't have room for it. Not now. Not ever.

As I pulled up to Ember's building, frustration simmered beneath the surface, my knuckles gripping the steering wheel tighter with each passing second. Then I saw it. Jax's Aston Martin was arrogantly parked out front, like some brazen flag marking his territory.

Rage boiled in my veins, hotter and more violent than I expected. It wasn't jealousy—I was better than that. But the sight of his car, sitting there as if he had the right to take what he wanted, set something off inside me. What made it worse was the realization that I had entertained the idea of longing for a woman like Ember, even for a fleeting moment. I'd allowed myself to feel something—a crack in the armour I wore so tightly. And that was unforgivable.

Fool, I thought bitterly. My heart and mind had let down its guard for a brief moment, and here I was, sitting like an idiot in the dark, grappling with emotions I'd spent years pushing away. It was pathetic. I was pathetic.

The air in the car felt heavy, charged with tension and bitter resentment. My fingers curled into fists as I slammed them against the steering wheel, the sound reverberating through the empty space. The sharp pain that shot through my hand only fueled the anger coursing through me. How had I allowed this to happen? How had I let my emotions get tangled up in something as dangerous as desire for a woman I barely knew?

But as the anger subsided, a cold clarity set in, chilling me to the core. I couldn't afford to entertain fantasies of connection or closeness. I couldn't afford to be weak. I wasn't built for it. I had chosen my path long ago—one of solitude, shadows, and survival. There was no room for love, no room for trust. Especially not with someone like Ember.

The truth hit me hard: I wasn't meant for anything other than this life. And in this life, women like Ember only led to ruin.

I shifted the car into gear, pulling away from the curb with a sense of finality. As the tires rolled over the cobblestone streets, I left Jax, Ember, and all the foolish hopes I'd entertained in a cloud of dust. I was nothing more than a lone wolf, destined to walk the shadows. The ghosts of my past clung to me like chains, and I knew I'd never be free.

Not with secrets like mine. Not with the path I had chosen. I was meant to be alone. And that was the way it had to stay.

I SAT AT THE HEAVY OAK DESK IN MY OFFICE, A SINGLE DIM BULB casting ominous shadows across the room. My fingers tapped restlessly against the polished surface while I mulled over the shipment details. With every second that ticked by, the room's quietude grew increasingly unbearable.

Suddenly, the door to my office creaked open, and Jax

Chapter 10

stumbled in, flopping down into the chair across from me. His disheveled hair, usually slicked back in perfect control, was now a chaotic mess atop his head. He looked like a wild-eyed animal, cornered yet ready to lash out at the first threat.

"Where the hell have you been?" I asked, trying to keep the frustration from creeping into my voice. "We had a meeting today about the shipment arriving tomorrow."

"Shite," Jax muttered, running a hand through his unruly hair. "I completely forgot. I was..." He hesitated, something I'd rarely seen him do before. "I was with Ember."

That name. Her name. It hit me like a brick, and I fought to suppress the unexpected pang of jealousy that twisted inside me.

"Ember?" I repeated, my tone sharper than I intended. I forced myself to stay composed, but the tension coiled tight in my gut. "What were you doing with her?"

For a moment, he paused, looking conflicted in a way that was entirely unlike him. Then, with a heavy sigh, he admitted, "I don't know, Tommy. There's just something about her... It's like she's taken over my mind. I can't think straight since I met her."

I clenched my fists, my knuckles turning white as I tried to shake off the discomfort settling like a heavy weight in the pit of my stomach. Jax's sudden vulnerability was unsettling. He wasn't supposed to be distracted, especially not by a woman. Not by her.

"Jax," I said, my voice low and serious. "You need to get your head back on straight. We have a job to do, and we can't afford any distractions right now."

"Tommy, you don't get it," Jax's voice cracked with

strain, a rare moment of emotional vulnerability leaking through. "It's not like my other obsessions. With Ember... I want to protect her, not kill her. And I don't know what to do with that."

"Protect her?" I raised an eyebrow, my surprise evident. Jax? Protecting someone? That was new. And that made Ember even more of a problem. His obsessions usually ended in bloodshed, but now he was talking about keeping her safe. I wasn't sure if that made things better or worse.

"Yeah," he muttered, almost as if he didn't believe it himself. "I know how I get with things, with people. But this? This is different."

"Alright," I said slowly, trying to make sense of the shift in him. "So, what were you doing with her today?"

Jax's brow furrowed, his confusion deepening. "She went to look at a townhouse outside the city. The place was a wreck—old, seventies decor, peeling wallpaper—but she seemed excited. I couldn't figure out why."

A spark of something dark flickered in my chest. Was Ember playing a game with him? Or was there more to her than any of us had realized?

"Jax," I said, leaning forward, my voice sharp and direct. "You're the tech guy around here. Have you not thought to simply Google her name?"

Jax's eyes widened, as though the idea had just hit him. Without another word, he pulled out his phone and began typing furiously, his fingers dancing over the screen like a pianist in a frenzy. I watched as his expression shifted from curiosity to something darker—confusion, awe, and maybe even fear.

Chapter 10

"Take a look at this," Jax whispered, holding up his phone for me to see. "Ember's big in the interior design and architecture world. She's not just some random woman. She's a name. A known entity."

I took the phone, scanning through the articles and images of Ember. There she was, standing beside some dark, Gothic-style homes, her eyes gleaming with pride as she showcased her creations. The articles praised her for her unique designs and ability to transform old spaces into modern marvels with a moody edge. There was a depth to her work, a sense of something... sinister. And it made sense, in a way. That darkness she carried wasn't just in her eyes; it was in everything she touched.

"So what?" I tossed the phone back to him, unimpressed. "She decorates houses. What does any of this have to do with us? Or the job?"

Jax's gaze remained on the phone, but his mind was elsewhere. "Tommy, I'm telling you, there's more to her. I can feel it. She's... under my skin. I've never felt this way about anyone."

I could feel the tension in the room growing thicker, suffocating. Jax was unraveling, and I couldn't allow that to happen. Not when we were so close to pulling off one of the biggest deals we'd ever had.

"Listen to me," I said, standing up and walking around the desk to stand before him. "I don't care how you feel about her. I don't care what you think she's done to you. We have a shipment coming in tomorrow and need you at your best. Whatever this is with Ember, you must put it aside until this deal is done. Understood?"

Jax clenched his jaw, and the internal struggle was clear in his eyes. He hated being told what to do, especially when it involved something—or someone—he was fixating on. But he knew I was right.

"Yeah," he muttered, his voice barely audible. "I get it."

"Good." I clapped a hand on his shoulder, trying to ground him. "We'll deal with Ember later. Right now, we focus on the job."

Jax stood, pocketing his phone with a weary sigh. "I'll handle it. But Tommy... she's not like the others."

I raised an eyebrow. "What do you mean?"

"I don't know yet," he admitted, his voice distant. "But I'm going to find out."

As he left the office, I sat back at my desk, my mind racing. Jax was right—something about Ember didn't add up. She wasn't just a woman who caught his eye. She was more dangerous than that. And if I weren't careful, she'd become a problem for all of us.

Because in this business, the most dangerous enemies were the ones you never saw coming.

11

KNOX HOLLAND

Steam billowed around me as I stepped out of the shower, water dripping from my body. The heat clung to my skin, but the cold air that hit me as I grabbed a towel sent a familiar jolt through me. I quickly dried off and threw on some sweat and a t-shirt, the fabric clinging to my damp skin. My mind wasn't on the chill—it was on the man I'd spent the day with. The little piggy had squealed within hours, breaking faster than I liked. Pathetic. I preferred it when they lasted longer when I could play with my toys.

It had been years since I'd come to terms with my... tastes. Twisted, dark. Most people couldn't handle it. My family sure as hell couldn't. Pity. They were missing out on so much.

I strode into Tommy's office, slamming the door shut behind me. The room was thick with cigarette smoke, and Tommy was hunched over his desk, buried in papers. Jax sat across from him, glued to his phone, tapping away like a man possessed. The tension in the room was suffocating, an almost tangible fog that seemed to press in on all of us.

"Finally," Tommy muttered without looking up. "Took you long enough."

"Got held up," I shrugged, not caring about his annoyance. I dropped onto the so-called "occasional" lounge in the corner of the room, the cushions digging into my back. Who the fuck calls it occasional when we sit on it every day?

"Whatever," Tommy grumbled, still rifling through his paperwork. "You get what we needed?"

"Of course," I said, a grin spreading across my face. "But I've gotta say, it was too easy. Barely any fun at all."

"Quit your bitching," Tommy snapped, finally looking up, eyes narrowing at me. "Did you find anything useful?"

"Didn't take long for the piggie to squeal," I replied, disappointed. "He spilled what he knew about the Russians."

"Which was?" Jax's voice cut in as he finally lifted his gaze from his phone.

"Something big's brewing," I said, flexing my hands, still imagining them covered in blood. "But they're keeping it close to the chest, even from their people."

"Shit." Tommy slammed his fist on the desk, sending papers flying like startled birds. "We don't need more trouble."

"Tell me about it," Jax muttered, already distracted again, eyes back on his phone. Whatever had him so fixated was starting to piss me off.

"Good work," Tommy grunted, his voice softer now, but still full of tension. "You need a girl today?" He smirked,

Chapter 11

knowing I usually got riled up after a good session. But not this time. Not when Jax's little witch was still dancing around in the back of my mind, her pictures from her camera roll burning into my memory.

"Pass," I said, trying to sound casual, but even I could hear the edge in my voice.

Jax perked up, like he was sitting on a secret he couldn't wait to spill. "Hey, Tommy, did you know she's well sought after?"

I shot him a glare, my curiosity spiking despite my efforts to stay composed. "Who?"

"Ember," Jax replied, a smirk tugging at his lips as he held up his phone. "She's an interior designer. She's built herself a name—selling properties for millions in cheap areas. People can't get enough of her designs."

"Show me," I demanded, unable to hide the hunger in my voice. The thought of Ember—this mysterious woman—sent a shiver of something dark and exciting through me.

Jax turned his phone around, showing me a picture of a black townhouse, sitting stark between two white ones. It looked like something out of a horror movie, and I couldn't help but smile. She had taste. I liked it.

"Where did she buy the townhouse?" Tommy's voice was low, dangerous. I could feel the jealousy radiating off him, though he tried to mask it under the guise of business.

"What townhouse?" I snapped, glaring at Jax.

"Jax went house shopping with Ember today," Tommy explained, his green eyes gleaming with something sinister as he watched my reaction. He was enjoying this, seeing us both circling around the same woman like wolves. "Why do you want to know, Tommy? You interested in her too?"

"Business purposes," he replied with a shrug, feigning indifference. "I want to know what she's buying and selling in our city."

There was more to it than that, and we both knew it, but Tommy wasn't about to let anyone in on what was going through his mind. He was too calculated for that.

Jax looked up from his phone, a wicked grin on his face. "Oh, she's under your skin too, huh?"

The tension in the room thickened, buzzing like static in the air. Tommy's gaze locked onto Jax, and for a moment, I thought he might snap. But instead, he leaned back, his voice calm and measured. "You need to work today. Go see the men handling the gun shipment from the Irish at 9 am. Take Declan with you."

I raised an eyebrow. Jax never missed a job. Was Ember really that much of a distraction? If so, she was heading for trouble. Everyone Jax got close to ended up dead.

"Alright," Jax agreed, still glued to his phone. A soft chime broke the silence, and he grinned as he tapped out a response.

Tommy's eyes narrowed, suspicion darkening his expression. "Who are you messaging?"

"Ember," Jax replied without looking up. "She's got all our numbers now. I put them in her phone before I gave it back."

Tommy frowned, and I could see the wheels turning in his head. "Why does she need all of them?"

Chapter 11

"Because she'll be one of us," Jax said, his tone final, almost daring Tommy to argue. "I'm not letting that bunny slip away. She's ours now. Did I mention she held a 9mm to my head while I was making her breakfast this morning? Clicked the safety off and everything."

My heart pounded. Ember was a wild card, dangerous in ways none of us could predict. The image of her holding a gun to Jax's head flashed through my mind, and I couldn't help the reaction it stirred in me. Jax noticed, his eyes locking onto mine as he smirked, grabbing at himself.

"Never been so damn hard for a woman," he said, his voice dripping with excitement. "Tommy, she's gonna be permanent around here. I'll make sure of it."

With that, Jax stood and strode out of the office, leaving me and Tommy in the thick silence that followed. Tommy's gaze lingered on the door, frustration and something darker flickering across his face.

"Jesus, Knox," he muttered, running a hand through his hair. "That girl's got everyone wound up."

"Seems like it," I replied, though my mind was already spinning with thoughts of Ember. What kind of chaos was she about to unleash on us?

"Jax better be careful," Tommy said, his voice low, dangerous. "We can't afford distractions. Not now."

"Agreed," I said, though deep down, I craved the chaos she'd bring. The thrill of violence, the satisfaction of tearing apart anyone who crossed us... it was only a matter of time.

"Keep an eye on things," Tommy ordered, his eyes cold and hard. "If she becomes a problem... deal with her."

"Understood."

As Tommy left the room, the darkness around me thickened, the air heavy with anticipation. Without a doubt, I knew that blood would be spilled before this was over. And I was ready for it. Ready to meet the little witch who had turned Jax upside down.

I stood, feeling the excitement buzzing through my veins. My phone buzzed in my pocket, and I pulled it out, smirking at the message from Jax.

"Go keep my little poison company," it read, followed by her address. I chuckled under my breath, anticipation building inside me.

"Guess we'll see what all the fuss is about," I muttered, heading for the door. The thrill of the unknown—and of meeting Ember—was already making my blood sing.

THE COLD METAL OF THE ELEVATOR BUTTON PRESSES AGAINST MY finger as I descend to the underground garage, a faint smile playing on my lips. Stepping out into the dimly lit parking area, the scent of gasoline and rubber fills my nostrils as I stride toward my Harley Davidson Breakout 117, its matte black paint gleaming under the soft glow of the overhead lights.

"Let's ride, baby," I murmur, grabbing my helmet from the rack and securing it onto my head. With one swift motion, I mount the bike, feeling the familiar power thrum beneath me. Tommy had bought this entire level for us—no prying eyes to disrupt our business here.

Cranking the engine to life, the Harley roars between my

Chapter 11

legs like an angry beast, eager to be unleashed upon the city streets. I shift down into first gear, slowly releasing the clutch as I guide the motorcycle out of its den. The darkness outside welcomes me, along with the cold bite of air.

I take off, speeding through the night, the wind tearing at my clothes, and the thrill of danger pounding in my veins. The cold air stings my exposed skin, a pleasurable pain that makes my pulse quicken, adrenaline coursing through me like a drug. The city's veins pulse with life, prey just waiting to be hunted. It's intoxicating—the power I feel on my Harley, weaving through traffic, dodging death at every turn. A grin spreads across my face as I ride, free from the constraints of the world.

"Twelve fucking minutes," I mutter under my breath, impressed by how fast I reach the address Jax sent me. Patience has never been my strong suit, but riding? That's where I find peace—if you could call it that. The thrill of speed is the closest thing to salvation I've ever known.

"Keep clear," the sign reads, but I pay it no heed as I park right in front of the building, relishing the blatant disregard for authority. My hand grips the key, wrenching it from the ignition, a shiver of excitement rippling through me.

The doorman's eyes pierce through me, his gaze cold and unreadable, like those of the steel doors he guards. He nods, granting me passage without a word. I smirk, pushing past him into the foyer.

I shoot a quick text to Jax. "Get some boys to watch the door. We'll get noticed if we keep walking in and out like this." Almost instantly, a reply flashes back. "Already done. Jimmy and Lemon are there."

Satisfied, I stride back outside into the frigid night air, raising two fingers in a peace sign. The familiar sound of bird whistles—Jimmy and Lemon's signature signal—slices through the darkness, confirming they're on guard duty.

"Good," I think, feeling the anticipation rise inside me. Time to meet Little Poison.

Making my way back inside, I walk toward the elevator and glimpse my distorted reflection in the polished metal. As I press the button for Ember's floor, the doors slide open without hesitation, like they were waiting for me. Stepping inside, I hum the tune of "Come Josephine in My Flying Machine" as the elevator ascends. My heart races, a mix of adrenaline and curiosity fueling my nerves. Jax is obsessed, and Tommy's intrigued—this woman must be something.

The elevator jerks to a stop, and the doors part, revealing a dimly lit hallway. Shadows cling to the walls, stretching like long, thin fingers. I follow the faint glow of light to her door and knock, the sound echoing through the quiet corridor. A moment passes, then another. Impatience simmers in my chest.

Finally, the door swings open, and there she is.

She's even more stunning than I imagined—her Asian heritage clear in her sharp, angular features. Shiny black hair falls around her face, her eyes dark and calculating. She's wearing a tight black business dress that hugs every curve. But the thing that demands my attention is the 9mm she's aiming right at my head.

"Who the fuck are you?" she snarls, eyes narrowing.

"Knox," I reply, my voice calm despite the gun inches

Chapter 11

from my face. "Jax sent me to keep you company while he works."

Her gaze follows me, lingering like a predator assessing its prey. The tension between us crackles like a live wire. "Can I come in?" I ask, my tone steady, though my pulse hammers beneath my skin.

She exhales sharply, the sound more of an irritated hiss. Slowly, she lowers the gun and flicks the safety back on with a practiced ease. Her lips twist into a sardonic smile. "Fine, Knox. You better not be a fucking serial killer."

I smirk, stepping past her into the dimly lit apartment. "Sweetness, I am," I say with a grin. "But don't worry, I'm not here to kill you."

Her scent hits me as I pass, something sweet and musky, like honey mixed with something darker. She gestures toward the hallway. "Please, have a seat, Knox the Serial Killer. I'm in the middle of working and eating, but you're welcome to join me."

I follow her into the kitchen, where the warm glow of the city lights streams in through the massive windows. The table is a chaotic mess of papers, drawings, and takeout containers, a collage of ideas that's both cluttered and strangely captivating. Chinese takeout. That's the scent. It mixes with the musky perfume, creating an unusual combination that clings to her.

She drops into a seat and picks up a chopstick, gesturing to the food. "So, Knox," she says, her voice playful but sharp, "Want to play a game of 20 questions too?" One eyebrow arches as she waits for my response, daring me to take the bait.

I smirk, settling into the seat opposite her, resting my arms on the back of the chair. "Sure, Sweetness. Let's see what I can learn about you."

She raises an eyebrow, a small smirk playing at her lips. This woman is dangerous—no doubt about that. But she's not just dangerous in the way most people are. She's a different breed. And I can't help but feel the pull too.

12

DECLAN STEVENSON

Tonight felt different. The air was charged with something I couldn't quite place, an awkward tension that hummed beneath the surface. Jax, usually oozing his unsettling aura, seemed strangely subdued. His atypical demeanor piqued my curiosity, making me wonder what twisted scheme he might be planning. Jax had always terrified me, despite being my flesh and blood. Our twin genes may have linked us, but we were stark contrasts in every other way. While I managed to control my impulses, Jax reveled in unleashing his inner psychopath without a second thought. The mere idea of killing someone that annoyed me sent shivers down my spine, but for Jax, it was just another day in his twisted existence.

We stood in the dimly lit warehouse, waiting for the Irish to complete our exchange of guns and money. My attention drifted from the business to my brother, who was unusually fixated on his phone. But the rare sight of him smiling caught my attention even more. Not his typical, unsettling grin that made people's skin crawl—this was different. It was genuine, softening his usually hardened features. Despite being undeniably handsome, when Jax smiled like that, it was as if the veil of his psychosis lifted, revealing a glimpse of humanity. The warm light from his phone illuminated his face, casting shadows over his sharp jawline. For a moment, I wondered what life would be like if he showed this side of himself more often.

I couldn't resist asking. "What's making you so happy, brother?" I glanced at him while carefully counting the bills in my hand. His answer caught me off guard.

"It's Ember," he admitted, running his hand through his usually perfectly styled black hair, now tousled in a rare display of openness.

"The girl?" I asked, intrigued but cautious. I knew who he was talking about—how could I not, with the way he had been acting since meeting her? But I needed to understand more. Could it be that my brother had finally encountered his equal? Someone who could control the chaos that raged inside him?

Jax nodded, his attention drifting back to his phone, a faraway look in his eyes. "Yeah. There's something about her, Dec. She's got me feeling things I never thought possible. It's like a whirlwind—like she's pulling me in and I can't escape."

I blinked, taken aback by his admission. Jax was never one to talk about feelings. He didn't feel things like normal people, or at least he never admitted to it. But now, sitting here in the darkened warehouse, he seemed almost vulnerable. It unsettled me.

Chapter 12

"So, sapart from helping you out when you got stabbed," I reiterated, trying to connect the dots. "What's with her then?"

He hesitated, the usual mask of indifference slipping as he spoke. "I don't know. She's unlike anyone I've ever met. Her eyes... they're like a witch's spell. And her body? Mesmerizing." He paused, frustration flickering across his face as he struggled to articulate what he felt. "But it's her attitude, Dec. It's more reckless than mine. She put a flipping gun to my head while I was making her breakfast, and you know what? It turned me on."

He chuckled, a warm and dangerous sound, but his eyes were serious, locked on mine. "I told Tommy she's one of us now. In all ways."

The weight of his words hit me hard. "In all ways," he repeated, his tone resolute.

I stared at him, heart pounding, trying to make sense of it. Jax wasn't just talking about claiming her like one of his usual obsessions. This was deeper, darker. He meant to pull her into our world—mind and body. But did she even know? Did Ember understand the peril she was in, the danger she was courting by being involved with my brother?

"Does she even know about your plans?" I asked, my voice tinged with concern. "Has she agreed to this, Jax? Willingly?"

He avoided my gaze, a sign that Ember was walking into this blind. My stomach twisted. She may have been reckless, but being reckless in Jax's world didn't end well. Holding a gun to his head in a country with strict gun laws meant she was involved in something far from innocent. But still, did she know what she was up against?

"Why does she even have a gun?" I pressed, trying to understand the depth of this. "Do you know anything about her background?"

Before Jax could answer, the sound of two cars pulling up interrupted us. Showtime.

We turned our focus back to the task at hand. The Irish were here, ready for the exchange. As much as I wanted to dive deeper into the enigma of Ember, I had to put it aside for now. The job always came first.

The exchange went off without a hitch, smooth as always. Our usual contact, Sean, didn't even bother with a thorough inspection of the money. After years of doing business together, he trusted us, though I wondered if that trust was misplaced given the storm brewing between my brother and this girl.

"Everything's in order, lads. Give my regards to Tommy and the unhinged one," Sean said with a grin, nodding toward Jax.

I chuckled, knowing he referred to Knox, but it struck me how little Sean understood Jax's volatility. Among us, it was hard to tell who was the most unhinged.

As Sean and his crew departed, I returned to Jax, the weight of our earlier conversation pressing down on me. I couldn't let this go. We were on the verge of something dangerous, and I wasn't sure if my brother could see the consequences.

"Jax," I began, but the words caught in my throat. I didn't want to sound doubting him, but I had to know. "You need to

Chapter 12

be sure about this. Ember... she's different, but that doesn't mean she should be pulled into our world without knowing what she's getting into."

Jax's expression hardened. "She's already in it, Dec. She just doesn't know it yet."

And with that, he walked away towards the car, leaving me standing alone in the warehouse, my heart heavy with uncertainty. Ember was a dangerous wild card, but my brother's obsession was the real danger. I wasn't sure if I could protect her from Jax or if I should even try.

One thing was clear—this wasn't going to end well.

THE SUN PLAYED PEEK-A-BOO WITH THE CLOUDS AS I SLID INTO THE passenger seat of Jax's Aston Martin. The air between us was thick with tension, heavy with words we hadn't yet spoken. I figured now was as good a time as any—trapped in this car, speeding through the city—there was nowhere for him to run, no distractions to turn to.

London blurred past, a cacophony of wet pavement and streaks of color reflecting the turmoil swirling inside us. I stared straight ahead, gathering my thoughts before cutting right to the heart of the matter.

"So, what are your intentions with Ember?" I asked, my tone more direct than usual. A part of me dreaded his answer, but I had to know.

Jax's grip on the steering wheel tightened, his knuckles turning white. His usual smirk faded into something colder, more calculating. "Didn't I already tell you?" he said, his voice edged with ice. "She's ours now, no matter what."

I felt a knot tighten in my stomach. Jax was many things—reckless, dangerous, unpredictable—but the certainty in his voice made this feel different. This wasn't one of his passing obsessions. This was something far darker.

"Jax," I sighed, trying to keep my voice steady and reasonable, "you can't just decide that for her. You need her consent; otherwise—"

"If I have to kidnap her and hold her hostage for life," he cut me off, the menace in his tone unmistakable, "then I will."

The chill in his words made my skin crawl. I turned to face him, taking in the familiar lines of his face, the same face as mine—yet we couldn't be more different. I'd always known he was dangerous, that he reveled in the chaos that came with being who he was, but this... this was about love. Or, at least, Jax's twisted version of it.

"Is that really what you want, Jax?" I asked softly, trying to break through the wall he'd built around himself. "If you force her, you'll destroy whatever chance you might have. You'll ruin it before it even begins."

He sneered at me, throwing that condescending smirk my way. "Since when did you become an expert on love, little brother?"

The nickname stung, as it always did. He liked to remind me of those three minutes he had over me, even though we both knew it didn't mean anything.

"Jax," I pleaded, "just talk to her. Be honest. Ask her. It's really that simple. Most people don't need to kidnap someone to get them to stay."

Something flickered in his eyes for a moment—doubt,

Chapter 12

hesitation, maybe even fear—but it was gone as quickly as it came. "Declan," he said, his voice soft but full of steel, "we both know I wasn't born like you."

I clenched my jaw. He wasn't wrong. Being diagnosed as a psychopath at the age of five had set him apart from the world and from me. It was why our mother had abandoned us—at least, that's what we suspected. She'd dropped us off at an adoption agency with our birth certificates and a folder of medical paperwork that warned us not to separate us unless they wanted Jax to turn into something worse. Something that even Knox, with all his sadistic joy in murder, couldn't compare to.

The car came to a smooth stop in front of our building. I glanced at the clock on the dash—8 AM. No wonder my head felt heavy. Jax turned to me, his expression unreadable, though something dark simmered just beneath the surface.

"Get the fuck out, little brother," he said, his voice hard. "I'm going to Ember's. I've done what Tommy asked. If he needs me, tell him to call."

I hesitated momentarily, staring at him, wondering if anything I'd said had reached him. But I knew better. Jax wasn't someone you could reason with—not in the way most people understood. He was a force of nature, and right now, Ember was standing in the path of that storm.

Reluctantly, I opened the door and stepped out, the cold morning air biting at my skin. I watched as Jax tore off down the road, the sound of the engine fading as his taillights disappeared into the distance. I stood there for a moment longer, staring after him, the weight of the conversation still pressing down on me.

With a sigh, I turned toward the building's entrance. We usually used the private lift from the underground garage, but today, I was going to walk through the lobby. We rarely used the front door, and I liked watching the staff scramble to open it, their faces a mix of fear and respect.

As I walked toward the elevator, I hit the button for our floor. My reflection stared back at me in the polished metal doors, and I couldn't help but wonder what would happen next. Would Jax heed my advice? Would he let his obsession consume him, pulling Ember into a world she couldn't understand?

With each floor that passed, my thoughts spiraled deeper. Jax had always been a time bomb, but now that bomb had a focus, a target. And I wasn't sure if either of us could stop it from going off.

13

EMBER DANG

The incessant knocking on my front door jolted me from the fog of sleep, leaving my heart pounding in my chest. My bleary eyes shifted to the digital clock on my nightstand—8:37 AM. Who the hell knocks at this hour? Groaning, I threw the duvet aside and dragged myself from the warmth of my bed, irritation bubbling beneath the surface. As an afterthought, I reached for my silk robe hanging on the door and grabbed the 9mm from the drawer of my nightstand. The cold weight of the gun in my hand grounded me as I clicked the safety off and crept toward the door.

With each step, my heartbeat grew louder in the apartment's quiet, and my breaths measured and shallow. When I peered through the peephole, my irritation shifted to confusion. Jax was standing there, looking... disheveled. The grey suit and charcoal button-up he wore yesterday were rumpled, and his usually neat hair was a chaotic mess. Dark shadows underscored his eyes, betraying his exhaustion.

"When did you start knocking?" I asked, cracking the door just enough to meet his gaze, gun still in hand.

Without a word, Jax stepped inside and, to my surprise, sank to his knees before me. I closed the door behind him, letting the soft click echo in the silence. He wrapped his arms around my legs, resting his head against my knees. The vulnerability in his gesture caught me off guard. Jax, the man who tried to kidnap me, now at my feet, felt... wrong. But there he was, holding on as if I was the only anchor in his turbulent sea.

A sigh escaped my lips as I placed the gun down on the nearby table, where my handbag and keys lay. Its presence felt unnecessary now. I ran my fingers through Jax's messy black hair, and in that small act, I felt a strange tenderness wash over me—something I hadn't expected to feel for him.

"Jax, are you all right?" I asked, my voice softer than intended as I spoke to a child needing comfort. I wasn't used to seeing him like this—so vulnerable, so raw.

He didn't answer right away, but I felt the warmth of his breath against my legs as he sighed. "Ember, I like you. Please tell me you'll be one of us."

"One of who?" I asked, my brow furrowing. His words carried weight, though the meaning wasn't immediately clear. I had an inkling, but I needed him to say it.

"The Aces," he murmured, almost reverently. "I need you to be one of us."

"Is that... like a gang?" I whispered, feeling a knot form in my stomach.

"Sort of," Jax replied. "We head up the Aces—Tommy,

Chapter 13

Knox, Declan, and me. But we have room for a queen. I want you to be that queen, Ember."

I swallowed hard, the gravity of his words sinking in. A queen in his world of chaos? My mind spun between the seduction of belonging to something and the dread of being pulled deeper into his dangerous orbit. "Jax, I can't join a gang. I just left the life of a club. I don't want to get sucked into another."

His head lifted, and his blue eyes met mine—pleading, desperate. "Poison, I don't think I'll be able to let you walk away. You have to join. I can't stand the idea of you not being with us."

I looked down at him, seeing something in his eyes I hadn't expected: fear. Not of me, but of losing control. "Jax, I don't like being owned. I'm not the type of woman to belong to just one man, and honestly, I'm not sure I want any man in my life at all."

A small smile played on his lips. "Who said you'd only belong to one? There are four of us."

I blinked, incredulous. "Are you offering me to your brothers without their consent?"

Jax shrugged, completely unbothered. "Why does consent matter so much? You and Declan keep going on about it."

I shook my head, amused and frustrated by his warped logic. "Consent is everything, Jax."

Silence stretched between us as I mulled over his offer, the weight of his words settling heavily on my shoulders. I knew men like Jax—men used to getting their way, used to controlling everything around them. But there was something different about him that intrigued me more than it should.

"Stay on your knees," I said suddenly, my voice taking on a commanding tone.

Jax blinked up at me, hesitating for only a second before he complied, shifting slightly so that he was fully on his knees before me.

"Now strip," I instructed, my voice firm as I tested our power dynamics. Slowly, Jax removed his shirt and waistcoat, his movements deliberate and measured. "And your pants," I commanded, watching him half squat so he could remove his pants and boxes, then return to his knees again. As each piece fell away, I stepped back, watching him.

Once he was bare, I walked toward the dresser and retrieved a red rope from the drawer, my heart racing with anticipation. "Stand and hold out your arms," I commanded.

He obeyed, and I began weaving the rope into an intricate shibari pattern around his wrists, binding them together. The air between us crackled with an unspoken tension.

"Pick a safe word," I whispered, tightening the knots.

"Yellow," he replied, his voice breathless.

I leaned in close, my lips brushing against his ear. "Remember it. You're mine to control now."

With slow, deliberate motions, I removed my silk robe and nightdress, feeling the cool air caress my exposed skin. Kneeling between Jax's legs, I gazed at his dick, now hard and leaking. My fingers trailed lightly up the length of him, making him jerk from the sensation.

"Under no circumstance are you allowed to cum," I

Chapter 13

warned, wrapping my hand around him and leaning in to lick the precum from the tip. The taste of him on my tongue sent a shiver down my spine, and I revelled in the power I held over him as he moaned loudly.

"Oh, Ember," he panted, desperation lacing his voice.

I could feel the heat of his cock as I took the head of him into my mouth, the thick girth hitting the back of my throat as I slid him down in one go. Jax panted and moaned beneath me, his body trembling with desire. I revelled in the intensity of his reaction to my touch, knowing that I held sway over this man who was so accustomed to wielding power over others.

"Ember," he gasped, his voice barely a whisper as I continued to suck him. His legs began to shake, signalling that he was nearing the edge of his control. With a devilish grin, I released him from my mouth with an audible pop, leaving him teetering on the precipice of an orgasm.

"Fuck...," he breathed, his eyes locked onto mine as I stood up. I ran my hands through my pussy juices, feeling the slick wetness between my fingers before placing them in his eager mouth. "Lick them clean," I commanded, and he obeyed without hesitation, moaning at the taste of me.

"Your taste is intoxicating," he murmured, his gaze never leaving mine. I turned him around and pushed him onto his back on the bed, then I climbed onto him, straddling his face, and lowered myself down to him. His tongue flicked out, finding my clit with unerring accuracy. The electric sensation of his touch sent shivers down my spine as if he had tapped into a hidden reservoir of pleasure that I never knew existed.

"Is this what you want, Jax?" I asked, my voice taunting

and sultry. "Do you like being under my control, tasting me like this?"

"Yes," he replied, his words muffled against my pussy lips. "Please, Ember... let me worship you."

"Jax, suck my clit," I commanded, the words coming out more breathless than intended. He complied without hesitation, his tongue working magic against me as he sucked and licked with a fervour that drove me crazy. I could feel my core growing tighter, getting ready to crest. I quickly slide off his face and straddle his hips, my hands eagerly grasp onto his hard dick. With a deep sigh, I slowly lower myself onto him, feeling him fill me up completely. As we both moan in pleasure, I begin to rock my hips, grinding my clit against his pelvis with each movement.

"Please, Ember," he moaned, his voice strained and desperate, "I need to come... Please let me."

The sound of his begging was music to my ears. "You beg so beautifully, Jax," I purred, denying him the release he craved. Instead, I focused on my pleasure, feeling it cresting within me like a tidal wave. As my core tightened, I ground down harder onto him, his pleas falling on deaf ears.

"Please, please, Ember... I can't hold on any longer," he whimpered beneath me, but I refused to relent. My climax crashed through me, shattering my resolve and setting me ablaze with unbridled passion. At that moment, I screamed for him to come, and he did, releasing his hot load deep inside me.

As I slowly come down from my high, I slide off him, and we lay side by side. I reached between my legs, running my fingers through our sticky wetness. With a wicked grin, I

Chapter 13

brought them to my lips, tasting the sinful combination of us both. Addiction coursed through my veins, this man's dangerous allure pulling me deeper into the abyss.

"Jax, taste us," I whispered, offering him my glistening fingers. His eyes locked onto mine as he opened his mouth, his tongue flicking out to lick them clean while moaning at our combined taste.

"Ember, you're... incredible," he murmured, the intensity of his gaze never faltering.

"Flattery will get you everywhere," I replied, smirking as I rose from the bed. With a glance back at him, I walked to the bathroom, leaving him tied up and vulnerable as I went to shower.

The hot water cascaded over my body, washing away the remnants of sweat and cum that clung to my skin, the heat soothing the muscles I didn't realize had tensed. As the steam billowed around me, I let the last traces of the night melt away, trying to regain some clarity. Once done, I stepped out of the steam-filled bathroom, padding softly across the floor, leaving a trail of water in my wake. Jax was still sprawled out on the bed, his eyes fixed on me, never wavering as I moved through the room.

"Stay," I commanded, my tone firm yet calm. A thrill surged through me at how effortlessly he obeyed, his submission sending a ripple of excitement through my core. With a cloth in hand, I gently wiped his face and cock clean, the intimacy of the gesture somehow more intense than anything we'd done before. Slowly, I loosened the knots binding his arms, releasing him from the restraints I had so carefully tied.

"Here," I said, handing him a dry towel. Dry me off." He took it, his fingers brushing mine for just a moment before he set to work. His touch was slow and deliberate as he dried every inch of my damp skin, his eyes following the path of the towel as if memorizing the curves of my body.

"Thank you, Jax," I whispered, stepping away from him. The night dress I pulled on felt weightless compared to the heaviness of the thoughts swirling in my mind. I reached out for him again, taking his hand and guiding him back to the entryway where his discarded clothes lay crumpled on the floor, a stark reminder of the chaos he'd brought into my life.

"Get dressed," I instructed, releasing his hand. Without a word, he complied, pulling on his charcoal button-up and sliding back into his grey suit, the ease with which he did it almost unsettling. Watching him, I felt a tug of something deeper, something dangerous. Could I become the queen of a gang like the Aces? Did I even want to? The darkness surrounding Jax called to me, familiar and comforting in a way that terrified me.

"Go," I finally said, pointing toward the door, trying to mask the uncertainty in my voice. He nodded but didn't leave right away. Instead, he stepped closer, pulling me into him, his mouth crashing into mine with a force that left me breathless. His kiss was desperate, all-consuming like he was trying to claim me, mark me as his in a way that words never could. His hands tangled in my hair, his body pressed against mine, and for a moment, I let myself get lost in the feeling of him—his taste, his touch, the fire he ignited in me.

"I love you, Ember," he whispered against my lips as he pulled away, his eyes locking onto mine with an intensity

Chapter 13

that made my pulse quicken. "You will be our queen." The weight of his words hung in the air between us, heavy with promise, with threat. And then he was gone, slipping out into the hallway, closing the door softly behind him.

For a long moment, I stood frozen, my heart pounding in my chest, my body still buzzing from his touch. I stared at the closed door, trying to make sense of everything, but the only thing I could focus on was the sinking realization that I was completely fucked. I liked Jax. No, I fucking *liked* Jax. And now, I was in deeper than I ever intended.

What the hell had I gotten myself into?

14

TOMMY PERCIVAL

I sat in my office, running a hand through my hair as the day's weight bore down on me. Declan had returned home far earlier than Jax, so I didn't need to ask where his brother had been. His obsession with Ember had become more than just an infatuation. I'd say he was falling in love if I didn't know any better. But Jax didn't do love—at least, I didn't think he did. And now he had this ludicrous idea of bringing her into the Aces. Was he completely out of his mind? We didn't need a woman in our crew, especially one Jax was ready to fight over. Sure, the idea of having someone steady to fuck wasn't exactly unwelcome, but it wasn't practical. I wasn't easily pleased, Knox was too dangerous for a real relationship, and Declan... well, he fell too hard and fast.

As for Jax, I didn't know what was happening to him anymore. It had only been a few days, but he had shifted; something inside him turned. And it scared me, as much as I hated to admit it.

When Jax finally returned, I wasted no time bringing up Ember. "You all right, brother?" I asked, stepping into his dimly lit bedroom. He sat on the edge of the bed, his head in his hands. When he finally looked up at me, devastation filled his blue eyes.

"No, Tom," he murmured. "I'm not all right. I'm a mess, and I don't know what to do about it. The only thing that makes sense is bringing her here, making her part of us." His voice was quiet yet filled with an intensity I hadn't seen in him before. I stood there, leaning against the wall, letting him vent whatever had been twisting his mind.

"You need to get a grip, Jax," I said, trying to keep the frustration from seeping into my voice. "You sound like a begging puppy." At the word "begging," Jax's eyes shot up, filled with something I couldn't quite place. But I didn't dwell on it. There was too much to address.

"What's going on with you?" I continued. "We can't just take in some girl and make her a part of this. It's too dangerous, and you know it."

"That's the thing, Tommy," he replied, his voice breaking. "If I don't bring her here, I'm going to lose it. She scares me, but I can't deny what I feel." His eyes, usually so cold and detached, were haunted. Desperate.

"She told me today she's never going to be with just one man," Jax went on. "She likes variety. She wants multiple men, more than one at a time. Isn't that perfect for us?"

I stared at him, letting the words sink in. "Multiple guys?" I repeated, disbelief thick in my tone. "She actually said that?"

Jax nodded. "She said it outright. But despite all that, I'm

Chapter 14

hooked. I can't get her out of my head, Tommy. I need her in my life, even if it's unconventional."

I pinched the bridge of my nose, trying to make sense of the situation. "Look, I get it. She's got you twisted up inside. But this? Bringing her into our circle? That's reckless."

Jax's jaw clenched, his eyes locking onto mine. "I trust her, Tommy," he said firmly. "More than I've trusted anyone in a long time."

I sighed, knowing I wouldn't be able to change his mind. "Fine," I relented, my voice heavy. "But if this goes bad, it's on you."

"It'll work," Jax said, nodding with grim determination. "I'll take responsibility for whatever happens."

As I left his room, a deep unease settled in my chest. Jax was playing with fire, and I wasn't sure any of us would come out unscathed. Ember was no ordinary woman, and she had already managed to embed herself in Jax's mind, body, and soul. But was she a blessing or a curse?

As I walked past Knox's room, I knocked on the door, but there was no answer. Typical. He must be in his playroom, probably caught up in one of his twisted hobbies, or maybe already dealing with that bastard I sent him after. I had asked Knox to get some information from a guy who had been feeding intel to Frank DeLuca, and I was hoping he'd drag the truth out of him before things got bloody.

Knowing Knox, though, that might be wishful thinking. The man lived for the bloodshed, and sometimes, the answers came too late.

With no response from his room, I sighed and headed to

my own. Tomorrow, I'd check in and find out if that rat squealed before Knox did what he did best.

Later, as I lay in my own bed, thoughts of Ember refused to leave me. Damn, girl had gotten under my skin too. I couldn't stop thinking about what Jax had said—that she liked multiple partners, that she was into the kind of dynamic we could offer. I felt a heat rising in me that I hadn't experienced in years. How could I tell Jax to get his head straight when I was spiraling myself?

I entered my en-suite, hoping a cold shower would clear my thoughts. I stripped off my clothes, tossing them aside as the cool water hit my skin. The freezing cascade did little to quell the fire Ember had sparked inside me. No matter how hard I tried to shake her from my mind, her image stayed. The curve of her body, the way her eyes could hold you in place… it was all too vivid.

Before I could stop myself, my hand slid down, and I gave in to the need that had been building all night. My mind raced with thoughts of her—those dark eyes, her sharp wit, the way she seemed to own every room she walked into. My hand moved up and down my length, giving it a small twist at the top, just the way I liked it. I could called Candy here to deal with it, but I wanted to get some sleep, and wasn't keen on waiting for her to arrive. I moved my hand faster, feeling the telltale signs of my balls starting to tingle as I finally cum, ropes of it now lying on the shower floor. But instead of feeling satisfaction, all I felt was frustration.

As the water continued to pour down around me, I cursed under my breath. We were in deeper trouble than I'd

Chapter 14

thought. Jax wasn't the only one caught in Ember's web. And I had no idea how we were going to get out.

15

KNOX HOLLAND

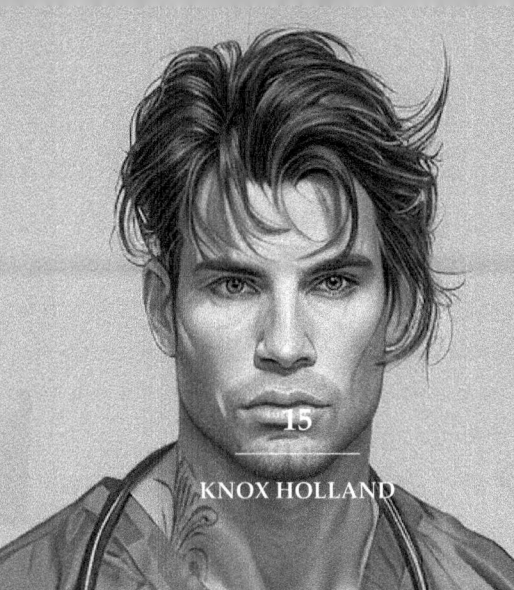

The sharp tang of iron fills my nostrils as I walk around the man strapped to the gurney, his body trembling uncontrollably. Blood oozes from several shallow cuts I'd made earlier, the crimson staining his skin as it drips onto the cold floor. "Don't struggle so much," I purr, a twisted grin pulling at my lips. "You'll pull the cannula out, and then this will get messy."

"Fuck you!" he spits back, wild-eyed, his voice breaking from fear. The defiance is weak, though. They always break faster than they think.

God, this is fun. I don't get to indulge like this often, not with Tommy watching over everything so closely. But today? Today, I've been given a special treat. The bastard writhing beneath me had crossed us—feeding intel to Frank DeLuca, of all people. Tommy wants answers, but he's given me free rein to get them however I see fit.

"Keep that attitude up," I taunt, flexing my massive

hands, the knuckles cracking. "And that'll take longer. You don't want that. Trust me."

His lip quivers, and then, like they all do, he breaks. "Please... just let me go," he begs, his eyes wide with desperation, tears streaming down his grimy face. Pathetic. Yet, it stirs a thrill in me—watching that moment when hope starts to slip from their grasp.

"Let you go?" I chuckle darkly. "Tommy wouldn't like that." I crouch down so my face is inches from his, the scent of sweat and fear intoxicating. "And I'm having way too much fun."

His breath hitches, and he stares at me with a mix of terror and disbelief. Most people think I'm just the muscle, but I've always had a deeper understanding of pain. I live for moments like this. It reminds me of when Tommy found me ten years ago after they took my medical license away. My "unorthodox" practices didn't fit the system, but they fit our world just fine. Tommy saw the potential in me then, and ever since we've been inseparable. Brothers, in a world where trust is worth more than gold.

"Look, I'll tell you what you want to know," the man pleads, his voice cracking. "I swear. Just please, don't hurt me anymore."

I smirk, rising to my full height as I pull the scalpel from my tool kit. It gleams under the dim lights, its edge sharp enough to slice through flesh like butter. I twirl it between my fingers, the anticipation bubbling in my chest. "Oh, you'll tell me," I say softly, "but we'll still have a little fun first. You see, I'm curious... how much pain can you take before you pass out?"

Chapter 15

His eyes widen in horror as I step closer, the scalpel gleaming. "The more you cooperate, the quicker that'll be over. Understand?"

He nods frantically, sweat beading on his forehead, soaking his collar. Good. Fear always makes the blood rush faster. Makes it taste sweeter.

"Let's start with something simple," I murmur, dragging the cold metal lightly across his thigh. His reaction is immediate—a gut-wrenching scream, raw and primal. The sound sends a delicious shiver down my spine. I press a little deeper, watching as the blood wells up from the cut, trickling down his leg. "Scream all you want," I say, licking my lips. "No one's coming for you."

"Please!" he shrieks, his voice breaking as his body convulses in pain.

"First question," I say calmly as if we're having a casual chat over coffee. "Why did you feed information to DeLuca?"

His head jerks, tears mixing with sweat as he tries to choke out a response. "Because... he paid me!"

"Is that so?" I hum, making another shallow cut, this time along his arm. The blade glides easily, splitting skin with the precision of a surgeon. "And did we not pay you enough?"

"Y-yes! I mean, no!" he stammers, his voice desperate. "I have a gambling problem... I needed the money... to pay off bookies."

"Ah," I say, mock understanding in my tone. "Gambling. That'll get you in trouble every time." I press the button on the IV, releasing a small dose of morphine into his bloodstream. "Here's a little reward for being honest."

He lets out a soft gasp of relief as the drug takes hold, but it's fleeting. It'll dull the edges of the pain, but not enough to make this easy. I watch with satisfaction as his muscles twitch, his body relaxing slightly under the effects of the morphine.

"Now," I continue, circling him slowly, dragging the scalpel lightly over his skin. "What did DeLuca want?"

"He... he wanted information," the man gasps, his breathing labored. "About who mans the doors, who handles the shipments. I didn't know most of it, I swear!"

I make another cut, this one deeper, and he lets out a wail, the sound echoing through the room. His agony fuels me, pushing me forward. The blood pools beneath him, staining the gurney, and I can almost taste the coppery tang in the air.

"Keep talking," I urge, my voice a low growl. "You're doing great."

"I... I gave him what little I knew!" he sobs, his body trembling violently. "I swear! That's all... I... I don't want to die!"

"Too bad," I whisper, leaning in close, my breath hot against his ear. "You crossed us, and now... well, now you'll bleed for it."

With a wicked grin, I make the next incision, watching as his screams fill the room once again. It's music to my ears, the symphony of suffering, and I revel in it. Today, I'm not just extracting information. Today, I'm indulging.

A glorious day, indeed.

16

EMBER DANG

A stream of light crept through my velvet curtains, rousing me from a fitful sleep, the clock said 3pm. My body ached, stiff from tossing and turning, the restless dreams swirling in my mind long after Jax left. The silence in my apartment felt suffocating, pressing down on me, amplifying the absence of the chaos he always brought with him. Every breath felt heavy as if I was waiting for something, anything, to break the oppressive quiet.

"Jax?" I whispered though I knew there would be no response. He hadn't returned. I wasn't sure how to feel about that until relief flooded through me—he was intense and consuming, and his unpredictability kept me on edge. But at the same time, disappointment settled like a weight in my chest. How had he gotten under my skin so quickly? It had only been a few days, but somehow, I had come to expect the whirlwind that was Jax Stevenson.

I sighed, dragging myself out of bed and across the cold floor toward the window. London's grey gloom greeted me, casting a dull light through the glass. My fingers traced patterns on the frosty windowpane, a chill running through me as memories of Jax's piercing blue eyes burned into my mind.

"Damn you, Jax," I muttered, the mix of longing and resentment twisting in my chest. I didn't want to miss him. Hell, I didn't even know him well enough to feel this way, but there was something about him—something dangerous and magnetic that pulled me in even when I knew I should keep my distance.

The cold floor beneath my feet snapped me out of my thoughts, and I moved with renewed determination. I needed to shake off this feeling and get on with my day. The shower was brutal, cold needles of water pelting my skin as I stood under the spray, letting it wash away the remnants of last night's dreams. Dreams where Jax's voice filled the darkness, his desperate pleas to cum still echoing in my ears.

Wrapping a towel around myself, I dried off quickly and set about taming my hair. The heat from the blow dryer was almost too much, but I needed the distraction. I yanked my hair into submission, the sharp tug at my scalp a welcome distraction from the chaos in my mind. A quick swipe of concealer hid the evidence of my sleepless rest, though nothing could erase the turmoil brewing just beneath the surface.

I stepped out of the bathroom, the scent of something floral catching my attention. It drew me toward the kitchen like a siren's call. There, on the counter, sat a vase filled with black roses. They were striking, their velvety petals a stark contrast to the grey world outside. My heart skipped a beat.

Chapter 16

"Jax," I breathed, the sight of the flowers sending a surge of heat through my body. He had been here, slipping in while I slept, leaving a trace of himself in my space. My body responded instantly, a familiar ache settling low in my belly.

"Calm down, hussy," I scolded myself, though my body ignored the command, my core tightening with need. I reached for one of the roses, twirling it between my fingers, the soft petals brushing against my skin like a lover's touch.

Nestled among the flowers was a card. I pulled it free, unfolding the paper, my eyes scanning Jax's messy handwriting.

"Please come to ours for dinner tonight?"

A smile tugged at the corners of my lips. Of course, he'd leave me a note like this, as if inviting me over for dinner was the most normal thing in the world. I wasn't lying when I told him I couldn't commit to one person. I never could. My attention always wandered, never content with just one. But Jax had offered me something different. He had offered himself and the rest of his group. The idea intrigued me.

Could I do it? Could I commit to a relationship if it meant I didn't have to choose just one? The idea of sharing myself with more than one man was both thrilling and terrifying. My thighs clenched as the thought of it sent a rush of heat straight to my core. Knox's image flashed in my mind, his dangerous energy pulling at me since the moment we met.

Knox... He had caught my eye immediately. The way his broad shoulders and thick neck filled out his clothes and the tattoos that peeked out from beneath his shirt hinted at a story I wanted to explore. His intensity was intoxicating, and

I couldn't help but wonder what it would feel like to be at the mercy of someone like him.

The sharp chime of my phone snapped me back to reality. I glanced down, my heart skipping a beat when I saw the name on the screen: "Compound." The familiar name sent a wave of longing through me, a reminder of the world I had left behind in Australia. My finger hovered over the screen for a moment before I pressed decline. The ache of homesickness gnawed at my insides.

"Damn it," I muttered, tracing the edge of the counter with one hand, memories flooding back. The people I had grown up with weren't blood, but they were my family. The motorcycle club had raised me, and though I had left that life behind, they were still a part of me. Loyalty, love, and violence ran in my veins because of them, and I missed it. I missed the camaraderie, the sense of belonging.

But I wasn't that girl anymore. That life was behind me. Now, there was a new game being played, and I was part of it, whether I liked it or not.

"Ember, don't get lost in the past," I muttered to myself, though the words felt hollow against the loneliness that always lingered at the edges of my soul. Of all the people I left behind, Killer haunted my thoughts the most. Now the Vice President of the club, he had always held a special place in my heart. We grew up side by side, our childhood filled with muddy adventures and mischief. He had been there for me through everything—until I was too broken to accept what he offered.

When I turned fourteen, Killer began to show an interest in

Chapter 16

me, but by then, I had already been shattered beyond repair. "Fuck," I sighed, the memories washing over me like a tide I couldn't hold back. I remembered the night my father was gunned down in cold blood, the night the compound was stormed by a rival MC. That night left me twisted inside, craving solace in the dark corners of the world. Killian had been my best friend through it all, yet I could never let him be more. The friend zone was where he stayed despite his unwavering loyalty. I didn't believe I was capable of love—not real love, not anymore.

I glanced at the clock—3.45 p.m. A single ray of sunlight broke through the kitchen window, casting a golden spotlight on the dust particles floating lazily through the air. The stillness of the apartment wrapped itself around me like a heavy blanket, reminding me that no matter what I did, the loneliness would always return. It clung to me, following like a shadow I couldn't shake. Not even the thought of Jax could completely banish it.

"Get a grip, Ember," I said more forcefully this time. I needed to get moving. I had an inspection of the townhouse later, and there was no use wallowing in memories. Grabbing my phone, I hesitated before typing out a message to Jax: "What time's dinner tonight?"

The reply came almost immediately, as if he had been waiting for me. "11 pm okay? I have some work to do, and everyone should be home and finished with work by 10."

"Perfect," I texted back, feeling an unexpected flutter in my chest.

A second message popped up with the address for dinner, along with an assortment of heart emojis that made me laugh. But it was the P.S. that really caught my attention: "Your breakfast is in the fridge."

I raised an eyebrow, intrigued, and made my way to the kitchen. Sure enough, there on the middle shelf sat a ham and cheese croissant on a plate, accompanied by an iced coffee. The ice had long since melted, but the gesture sent a wave of warmth through me.

As I sipped the watered-down coffee and nibbled on the croissant, I slipped into my shoes. My eyes drifted toward the gun still sitting on the table from the night before. I paused for a moment before slipping it into my pocket. In this city, it felt like a necessary precaution—one I couldn't afford to leave behind. I had to go check my mailbox and grab something to wear tonight before the shops closed.

Descending in the lift, I waved at Tim, the doorman, who offered nothing more than a curt nod in return. The city outside buzzed with its usual energy, a familiar symphony of honking cars, bustling crowds, and distant sirens. I hailed a cab, and within minutes, one pulled up to the curb like a faithful steed waiting to whisk me away. I slid into the backseat, telling the driver to take me to a clothing shop I fancied in Camden, and leaned back, letting the city blur by as we sped through the streets.

London's gothic architecture loomed overhead, dark and imposing, its ancient facades whispering stories of love, betrayal, and survival. The romanticism of the city called to me, pulling me deeper into its folds. It was a place for those who understood its shadows, for those who danced between the light and the dark.

Chapter 16

. . .

A FEW HOURS LATER, I SAT AT MY DINING TABLE, FLIPPING THROUGH emails and paperwork from the housing inspectors for the townhouse I had just purchased. The deal had gone better than expected—the owner, desperate to be rid of the place, had accepted my lowball offer of 750,000. There was some water damage on the second floor, but nothing that couldn't be fixed quickly. With the four-week turnaround agreed upon, I now had the pressing task of booking builders and sending my ideas to William to sketch out. The place had potential, and the excitement of transforming it pulsed through me as I sketched rough plans on my notepad.

I was interrupted by a sudden beep from my phone. Glancing at the clock, I realized I had only ten minutes to get ready for dinner at Jax's place. I stood up, smoothing out the black silk slip dress that clung to my body like a second skin. It was the perfect balance—not too revealing, but seductive enough to catch attention. The red heels I'd paired with it were a bold choice, designed to draw eyes. I hoped I'd struck the right balance between alluring and not too over-the-top.

The chilly London air nipped at my exposed skin as I stepped out of the apartment building. The sky was a deep shade of indigo, and my breath puffed out in little clouds as I cursed myself for not bringing a jacket. The city buzzed around me, alive with its usual evening energy—traffic humming, distant conversations drifting through the night.

Before I could even lift my hand to hail a cab, the deep growl of an engine drew my attention. Jax's Aston Martin slid up to the curb, its glossy black surface gleaming under the streetlights. The passenger window rolled down, revealing his intense blue eyes locked on me.

"Forgot you don't drive," he said smoothly, his signature smirk tugging at his lips. "And I don't want you in a taxi at this hour. Jump in, poison. I'll drive you."

"Thank you," I replied, doing my best to sound casual despite the fluttering in my stomach. As I slid into the passenger seat, the luxurious leather cooled against my skin, the scent of his cologne wrapped around me like a magnetic force. My pulse quickened as I took in the sight of him in his perfectly tailored black suit—dark, dangerous, and utterly tempting.

"Ready?" he asked, his voice low and charged with tension.

"Absolutely," I murmured, my voice barely a whisper. The engine roared to life, and the car glided smoothly into the stream of traffic.

Our conversation was sparse, each exchange heavy with unspoken meanings. Every glance Jax threw my way felt loaded, as though he was devouring me with his eyes. It wasn't just words—it was a battle of wills, each of us testing the other, the tension simmering beneath the surface.

"Almost there," Jax said as the cityscape blurred around us, his voice smooth and dark like velvet.

The drive took about twenty minutes, the streets growing quieter as we left the city's main arteries behind. We descended into a gated underground parking lot, the metal gate sliding open as Jax tapped his fob. Two floors down, the car purred to a stop in a private section of the garage—clearly theirs. They clearly owned the entire level if

Chapter 16

the second gate that opened with a different fob was an indication of that.

Jax jumped out of the car and walked around to my side, opening the door like a gentleman. I raised an eyebrow at him as he tossed the keys casually onto the roof of the car.

"We've got someone who parks the cars properly," he explained with a sly grin.

With a smirk, I took his hand and let him lead me to the lift. "Clearly not stressed about scratching the roof with those keys then," I muttered. Once inside, Jax swiped his fob and pressed the button for the penthouse. The hum of the lift rising echoed the anticipation building inside me. The small, enclosed space made his cologne feel even more intoxicating. I could feel his eyes on me, burning through the dim reflection in the mirrored walls.

"What's for dinner?" I asked, trying to ease the tension, though my voice came out softer than I intended.

His gaze locked on mine, and the corner of his mouth lifted in that irresistible smirk. "I would love to eat you for dinner," he said, his voice a low growl. "But maybe I'll save you for dessert."

Heat flushed through me, and I struggled to keep my cool. "Did you cook, or did you order in?"

"Knox cooked," Jax said, his grin widening. "I've been busy all day. Let's hope it's edible, though."

I raised an eyebrow in suspicion. "Why wouldn't it be?"

Jax let out a low, rich laugh. "One time, he tried to serve us all a boiled head. Thankfully, Tommy stopped him before it hit the table."

I blinked, unsure whether to laugh or feel horrified, but

the amusement in Jax's eyes was contagious. The doors slid open, revealing the luxurious penthouse that awaited us. The space was vast and dimly lit with modern design touches, but it exuded an aura of masculinity and control.

"Welcome to our home," Jax murmured, taking my hand and leading me inside, the scent of something delicious—hopefully not involving a boiled head—drifting from the kitchen.

The space stretched out before me, a monochrome canvas of shadows and light, stark black furniture contrasting against pristine white walls. It felt cold, minimalistic—void of comfort or warmth. It wasn't my style, but it wasn't enough to make me cringe, either.

"Ah, Ember, you've finally arrived!" Knox's voice boomed through the penthouse, his massive frame bounding toward me with an enthusiasm that was almost jarring in contrast to the dark atmosphere. Clad only in jeans and an apron that did little to hide his shirtless torso, he held a wooden spoon aloft like a culinary sceptre.

"I trust Jax hasn't scared you off yet?" Knox grinned widely, his green eyes twinkling with mischief.

"Hardly," I replied, forcing a casual tone, though my thighs clenched involuntarily at the sight of him. How the hell was I going to survive this dinner with all these men without turning into a puddle? "I've been looking forward to seeing what you've whipped up in the kitchen."

"Good!" Knox's voice boomed again. "I made a simple carbonara, nothing fancy. I wanted to get more creative, but Tommy forbade it." A flicker of disappointment crossed his face.

Chapter 16

"Whatever it is, I'm sure it'll be fantastic," I said, offering a smile as I placed my hand gently on his arm. His grin widened, and for just a moment, I saw a flicker of vulnerability beneath the surface.

"Yerp, it's ready," Knox announced, his voice filled with pride. "Go ahead, take a seat."

Jax slid his arm around my waist, guiding me toward the dining area. The penthouse, with its cavernous open-plan layout, felt even more imposing as we moved further in. The table was set in the middle of the room, under the soft glow of recessed lighting, and as we approached, I could feel the tension in the air. It was subtle but palpable—like a predator lurking just beneath the surface, ready to strike.

"Hi," Declan greeted me with a warm smile as he slid into the chair across from mine. The sight of him reminded me just how similar he was to Jax, but there was a calmness to Declan, a groundedness that set him apart from his wild twin.

"Hello," I replied, my voice soft but steady. "Nice to see you again."

Declan's smile widened. "Likewise, Ember. Welcome."

Tommy entered the room last, his presence commanding without a word spoken. He moved with an air of authority, his eyes scanning the room like a king surveying his court. His gaze lingered on me for a moment, intense and unreadable, before he gave a curt nod and sat at the head of the table. There was something about Tommy that always made me feel like I was being weighed, measured, and found either wanting or worthy. But tonight, his coldness was even more pronounced.

I smiled at him, trying to bridge the distance, but he gave me nothing in return—just that icy stare. What had I done to warrant such an icy reception?

Knox busied himself serving the pasta, placing a plate in front of Tommy first before making his way around the table. His booming energy seemed to fill the room, making the tension between us all even more noticeable. Once he had dished out the food and settled into his seat next to Declan, he turned to me with a grin that sent a shiver down my spine.

"Can I fuck you?" Knox's voice cut through the air, blunt and without hesitation. My breath caught in my throat as the words hung in the silence, and I could feel every set of eyes in the room on me.

I blinked, caught off guard, my jaw dropping slightly. But Knox didn't back down. He leaned forward, his grin widening. "Jax told me he offered up our services to you. Said you like a rotation of dick."

I turned to Jax, my gaze sharp with accusation. "Did he now?" I said, my voice laced with irritation. "I think what I said was that I don't commit to just one man and that I don't do monogamy."

Knox shrugged, his tone casual. "Yeah, like I said, a rotation. Variety's the spice of life, right?"

The room went silent. I could feel the tension coiling tighter as the words sank in. Tommy scoffed from across the table, the sound low and dark, cutting through the thick air like a blade. I glanced at him, but his expression was unreadable, the storm brewing in his eyes impossible to decipher.

"Would you like some wine?" Declan's voice, warm and

Chapter 16

kind, broke the tension. He held up a bottle of red, the dark liquid shimmering in the dim light.

I shook my head, offering a strained smile. "No, thank you. Just water." I needed a clear head for this dinner—I had the distinct feeling that I was dancing on a razor's edge, and one wrong move could cut deep.

Tommy continued eating in silence, shoveling the last of his pasta onto his fork with a venomous intensity. As soon as he finished, he stood abruptly, the chair scraping against the floor with a sharp screech. Without a word, he turned and stalked out of the room, leaving a trail of unease in his wake.

"Is he all right?" I asked Jax, my voice soft as I leaned closer to him. "Did I offend him?"

Jax shrugged, his demeanor as careless as ever, though there was something darker lurking beneath his casual attitude. "No idea," he purred, his eyes gleaming with mischief. "But do you wanna stay the night?"

17

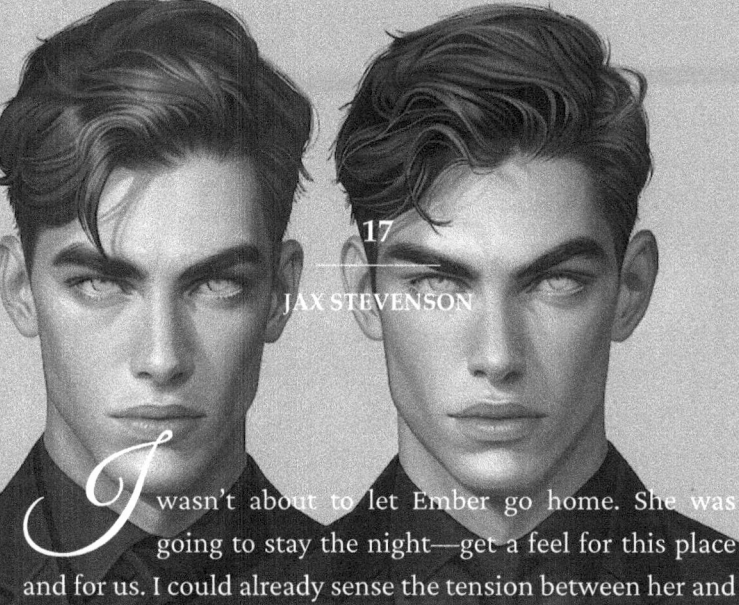

JAX STEVENSON

I wasn't about to let Ember go home. She was going to stay the night—get a feel for this place and for us. I could already sense the tension between her and Knox simmering beneath the surface. She acted tough, but I knew deep down she was intrigued, ready to dive deeper into what we had to offer. The question was whether she'd surrender to that curiosity.

"I'm not staying the night, Jax. But thanks for the offer," she said, her voice steady but her eyes giving her away as they scanned me. I could read her like an open book. That woman wanted to stay, whether she admitted it or not. She was practically dripping with desire, and I knew it wouldn't take much to persuade her.

"How about this," I said, leaning back with a casual grin. "Stay in the guest room. No pressure. Before that, you, me, and Knox can watch a movie in the theatre room." Her eyes flickered with interest, even if she tried to hide it. There it was—the crack in her armor. She wasn't as unaffected as she wanted to appear.

"What movie?" she asked, trying to sound indifferent, but I caught the subtle shift in her posture. She was hooked, and we both knew it.

"Dunno. Maybe a documentary. Knox loves those," I said, throwing a glance toward the kitchen where Knox was finishing up, wiping down the counters as if he hadn't been watching us this whole time. She raised an eyebrow, clearly not expecting that.

"Nature documentaries, to be exact," Knox chimed in as he strolled over, a smirk on his lips as he draped a muscled arm around her shoulders like it was the most natural thing in the world. "You in, sexy?"

Ember looked up at him with that same fierce attitude I loved, her lips curving into a seductive smile. "Just so we're clear," she said, her voice firm, "I'm not here to whore myself out, buddy." Then her eyes flicked back to mine, and she leveled me with that same look. "And neither are you, Jax. If I stay, if I engage with any of you, it's because it's my choice. I know what I want, and I'll take it when I'm ready."

I couldn't help but raise my eyebrows at her boldness. She caught me off guard, and I loved it. Knox chuckled softly, his grip around her shoulders tightening just slightly, enough to remind her that she wasn't in full control here.

"No one said anything about you acting like a whore, Ember," I said, my voice calm but firm. "I'd be happy to keep you all to myself, but you made it clear one man isn't enough for you. So, if that's what it takes to keep you here, I'm more than willing to share." My gaze held hers, making sure she

Chapter 17

understood I wasn't playing games. "But don't mistake this —you're not walking out of here tonight."

She stayed silent for a moment, her eyes searching mine, and I could practically see the wheels turning in her head. She was weighing her options, deciding just how far she wanted to take this. After a beat, she finally spoke.

"Fine," she said with a shrug, her composure slipping back into place. "But we're not watching some lame-ass nature documentary."

Knox grinned, clearly enjoying the back-and-forth. "What do you want to watch then, girly?" he asked, his voice light but challenging.

She leaned back in her seat, crossing her legs and flashing us both a playful smirk. "There's a snooker game on soon," she said. It was a surprising choice, but then again, nothing about Ember was predictable.

"Snooker it is," I replied, standing up and nodding toward the theatre room. Knox and I grabbed three glasses of wine as we followed her to the largest room in the penthouse. We'd converted it into a home theatre with four plush love seats facing an oversized screen. Heavy black curtains framed the massive windows, but with the London night stretching out beyond, we didn't need to pull them closed. The city lights added to the mood, casting a soft glow through the room.

Knox set up the channel for the game while I guided Ember to one of the love seats, handing her a glass of wine. She eyed it suspiciously before raising it to her lips.

"Anything in there that shouldn't be?" she asked, her tone accusatory, though her lips curved in a teasing smirk.

I felt a flicker of irritation but masked it quickly. "You think I'd need to spike your drink?" I asked, my voice lowering dangerously. "I thought we'd moved past that."

Her eyes remained locked on mine, sharp and unyielding. "I've known many men like you," she said, her voice steady, but there was something behind it—a hint of something darker. "Even a woman, in fact. She was my best friend growing up." Her lips quirked into a half-smile, though her eyes stayed cold. "So yes, I do believe you could. But I'm hoping you didn't."

Her words caught me off guard, a subtle jab that sank deeper than I cared to admit. My frown deepened as I studied her face, trying to decipher the meaning behind the statement. This wasn't just a casual comment; it was a challenge, and she was daring me to respond. I wasn't one to back down from a challenge, but there was something about the way she said it—something that made me pause.

Still, she was testing me, pushing my buttons, and it was working. I could feel the tension building, the air between us thick with unspoken promises, the edge of something dangerous. She took a slow sip of the wine, keeping her eyes on me the entire time as if daring me to cross that line.

I had to admit that she intrigued me more with every moment that passed.

Knox settled in beside her, grabbing the remote and leaning back. "All set, girly. The game starts in half an hour." He flashed her a grin before turning his attention to the pre-game chatter on the screen.

But I wasn't watching the TV. Neither was Knox. We were both watching her, studying every little move she made

Chapter 17

—the way her body shifted, the way she kept her legs crossed and uncrossed as if trying to ease the tension coursing through her. She could feel it, too.

After about ten minutes of watching the game, Ember sighed and turned to Knox, her gaze holding something darker, more dangerous. Whatever was coming next, she was ready for it. And so were we.

"Are you ever going to make the first move, or are we really going to have to watch this stupid game?" Ember's voice, playful and teasing, sliced through the tension in the room like a knife. Knox and I exchanged a look, both flabbergasted at her boldness, before turning back to her. She sat there, smiling, like she knew exactly what kind of fire she was stoking.

Knox moved first, leaning in to capture her lips in a searing kiss. His eyes met mine as their mouths connected, filled with heat, before he finally closed them, surrendering to the passion between them. I could feel the energy between them—raw, electric, pulsing through the air like a live wire.

My breath hitched when Ember's hand reached back, searching for mine. Her fingers brushed against my skin, a silent plea for me to join them. The touch sent a jolt of electricity straight to my dick, igniting a fire inside me that burned hotter with each passing second. I laced our fingers together, guiding her hand down to the hard bulge in my pants that had been torturing me all night.

"Feel what you do to me, Ember," I whispered, my voice rough and barely audible over the thunderous pounding of my heart. I needed her to understand just how much control she had over me, how easily she could unravel me with a single touch.

She broke the kiss with Knox, turning those smouldering, chocolate-brown eyes toward me. The mixture of lust, curiosity, and something deeper glimmered in her gaze, drawing me in like a moth to a flame. I could feel her need, her desire to push boundaries, to see how far she could bend us both.

"Strip," she commanded, her voice sultry and commanding, dripping with authority. "I want you naked."

A thrill ran down my spine at the sound of her words. There was no hesitation as I complied, unbuttoning my shirt slowly, savoring the heat in her gaze. Her eyes roamed over my body as I peeled away the layers, leaving me bare in front of her. My breath came in short, ragged pants as I kicked off my shoes and pants, finally standing before her completely naked, my cock standing at full attention.

Normally, I thrived on being in control—of women, of the situation—but with Ember, everything felt different. She had a power over me that no one else had. She didn't need restraints or submission to make me bend to her will. The way she held me in her gaze, the way she commanded the space—it left me vulnerable in a way I never imagined I'd enjoy. And fuck, did I enjoy it.

Her attention shifted back to Knox, who was already sliding his hands up her thighs, the black silk of her dress bunching around his fingers. The way his large hands gripped her hips, the way her body responded—it was intoxicating. She raised her arms, allowing Knox to lift the dress over her head in one smooth motion, revealing the matching

Chapter 17

black lace underwear that clung to her perfect body. My mouth went dry at the sight of her, sitting there like a dark goddess, bare and beautiful.

Knox wasted no time, tugging her panties down with a growl of appreciation as he exposed her to us. Her body glistened, every curve, every dip more beautiful than I had imagined. My desire for her only intensified, my need to touch, taste, and claim her growing unbearable.

"Jax, slip in behind me," she instructed, her voice softer now but no less commanding. I moved behind her, my body pressing against the warmth of her back as she leaned into me. The heat of her skin against mine sent waves of pleasure through me, and I wrapped my arms around her, my hands finding her breasts, kneading the soft flesh as I pushed the lace of her bra aside.

Knox was already buried between her legs, his mouth devouring her with an intensity that made Ember cry out, her voice rich with pleasure. I could feel every tremor, every moan vibrate through her body as she melted into me, her pleasure becoming mine.

Knox's tongue traced her slit, drawing a desperate moan from her lips that only drove me further into madness. I tugged on her nipples, rolling the hard peaks between my fingers as I pressed kisses to her neck, inhaling the intoxicating scent of her skin.

"Jax... harder," she panted, her voice breathless and full of need. I obliged, pinching her nipples harder, feeling her arch against me, her body trembling as Knox continued his relentless assault on her core.

"Fuck, Knox..." she gasped, her head falling back against

my chest. Her fingers tangled in his hair, pushing him closer as her hips bucked in time with the rhythm of his tongue and fingers. The room was filled with the sounds of her wetness, of Knox's mouth working her over, and the sinful moans that escaped her lips.

Knox looked up, his face glistening with her arousal, and smirked at me before returning to his feast. "Sweet like honey," he murmured, his voice a rumble of satisfaction before diving back in.

Her cries grew louder, her body taut with pleasure as she neared her release. I could feel her tightening, the tension building inside her until it was too much to contain.

"Knox... don't stop," she begged, her voice trembling with desperation. "I'm so close."

I watched, captivated by the way her body trembled, her muscles clenching as the pleasure overwhelmed her. Her orgasm hit like a tidal wave, crashing through her in waves that left her gasping for air, her body jerking with each pulse of pleasure.

"Fuck...!" she cried, her entire body quaking as she came, soaking Knox's mouth with her release.

Knox sat back, his lips glistening with her cum, and his eyes locked with mine. There was a wicked gleam in his gaze, one that promised more to come as he dove back in.

"God, Ember... you're so wet," Knox mumbled between fervent licks, his voice a mix of awe and lust. "I want to drink your cum, to have you soak my entire face."

"Fuck, Knox..." she managed to breathe out, her body trembling against mine. Her back was pressed against my chest.

Chapter 17

"Jax... pinch my nipples harder," she whispered, her voice barely audible over the cacophony of our shared desire. I couldn't deny her, not when she sounded so wanton and vulnerable. I tightened my grip on her breast, pinching her nipple just as she requested.

As I watched her stomach muscles contract, I knew she was close to reaching her peak again.

"Knox, don't stop... please," she begged, her eyes filled with wild desperation.

The tension coiled tightly within her, ready to snap at any moment. Feeling the impending release, I pinched her nipple once more, watching as she shattered into a million pieces around Knox's mouth.

"Fuck... !" she cried out as waves of pleasure crashed over her, drowning her in their exquisite depths.

Knox looked up at me, his face glistening with her cum, and the predatory gleam in his eyes spoke volumes.

Her eyes, glazed with lust, locked onto mine, and she commanded Knox to move to the other side of the loveseat, leaving me sitting there, utterly captivated by her.

"Jax," she purred, leaning her body over the backrest, offering herself up like a succulent feast for a ravenous beast. "I want you to fuck me."

My fingertips found the clasp of her bra, and I unhooked it with ease, watching the delicate fabric float onto the couch, leaving her exposed and vulnerable. The sight before me was intoxicating – her glistening pussy, swollen and slick from Knox's attention, beckoned me to indulge in its depths. Ember instructed Knox to stand in front of her.

"Are you ready for me?" I asked, my voice barely more than a whisper.

"Always," she replied, her eyes never leaving mine.

With deliberate slowness, I positioned myself at her entrance, feeling the heat radiating from her. As I began to sink into her, I was met with a tightness that bordered on painful yet was so undeniably exquisite that words could never truly capture its essence. She was a siren, luring me deeper into her embrace, threatening to consume me entirely with each passing moment.

"Jax... please..." Ember's voice reached out to me; I started to pound into her with a slow, steady rhythm, each thrust sending shivers down my spine as her body clenched around me, refusing to let go.

"Knox," she moaned, reaching out for him.

18

KNOX HOLLAND

My heart pounds as Ember's hot mouth wraps around the tip of my dick. Fuck, it feels like nothing I've ever experienced – hot, wet, and quite possibly the best feeling I've ever had.

"God, Ember," I groan, gripping the edges of the couch.

I've never had a mouth on my dick before. The women I usually fuck lie quiet and still, as if they're asleep. When I first started having fantasies about sexual encounters, they were always with unconscious women — something about the quiet, the control; it stirred something dark inside me. And now here I am, with Ember breaking all the rules I once held myself to.

"Like that, Knox?" she whispers, her breath warm against my cock.

"Fuck yes," I grunt, watching her lips slide along my shaft, the sensation sending shivers down my spine.

My mind wanders – back to med school when I realized my desires weren't like those of my classmates. Somnophilia, they called it. A sick fascination with having sex with sleeping people. But I couldn't help myself; the quiet, the stillness, it drew me in like a moth to a flame.

I once entertained the thought of engaging in necrophilia, hoping that the stillness and silence would be appealing. However, upon attempting it, I was unable to even achieve an erection. That experience swiftly put an end to that curiosity.

"Fuck," Jax grunts, snapping me back to the present. Sweat beads on his brow, his eyes locked on Ember's body bent over the loveseat, breasts swaying with each thrust. The sight makes my mouth water, and I can still taste her sweet arousal on my tongue – a flavour unlike any other I've ever known. The taste of her pussy was luscious and heavenly. It quickly became my new favorite flavor, leaving me wondering if I could somehow preserve its essence and spread it on my toast every morning.

Ember's moans echo in my ears, her body writhing in pleasure as Jax pounds into her relentlessly. The vibrations travel down my shaft, sending shivers up my spine.

"Fuck," she mumbles around my cock, her breath hot on my skin.

My heart races, a primal drumbeat in my chest. Jax's relentless thrusts echo through the room, and I find myself mirroring his pace. Ember's face reddens as she gags around me, but I don't want to hurt her – a first for me.

I pull my cock back from her throat, so she can take in lungfuls of air. "Can I do that again?" I ask, surprised by my own need for permission. My hand caresses her cheek softly, gentler than I've ever been.

Chapter 18

She nods, breathless. "Yes, but let me breathe every now and then."

I push back into her throat, our eyes locking. Jax pounds into her from behind, her moans audible throughout the house. I slide in and out, matching his rhythm.

"Fuck," I groan as my balls tighten, and I release down her throat suddenly. She pushes me away, a bead of cum on her chin. She reaches up, wipes it off, and licks her finger clean. The sight sends shivers down my spine, and dark fantasies cloud my mind.

If I were to cum into a cup, would she raise it to her lips and drink me down in one swallow? Or perhaps she would playfully spit me back into my eager mouth, allowing me the pleasure of savouring every drop of myself.

Jax finally empties himself inside her, just moments after me. I notice Ember's fingers working furiously between her legs, rubbing her clit in perfect rhythm with his final thrusts. Her face contorts, the sheer ecstasy flooding her features. Watching her come undone like this—fuck, it's something I didn't think I'd ever care to witness, but here I am, enthralled by every moan and shudder.

Shit. I want to be the one making her feel like that when she's wide awake, fully aware of every moment, every touch. This woman... she's gotten under our skin, woven herself into the fabric of our lives, and I don't think either of us can escape her grip now.

Obsession pulses in my veins, growing and spreading like wildfire, consuming every rational thought I had left. A storm's brewing inside me, making everything I thought I knew feel hazy and disjointed. I realize something chilling in the middle of all this—the idea of not keeping her close? Unbearable. But the thought of having to kill her? It makes my blood freeze in my veins, something I've never felt before. I've always been comfortable with death, even intrigued by it. But this? This is different. I don't want her gone—I want her with us, wrapped in our world, where she belongs.

"Jax," she purrs, dragging my attention back to her. She collapses onto the loveseat, spent, and drags her fingers through the mix of hers and Jax's cum, offering them to him. "Taste."

"Fuck," Jax rasps, eyes wide and dark with lust. He leans forward, taking her fingers into his mouth, licking them clean with deliberate slowness, his gaze never wavering from hers. It's a quiet act of submission, a side of him I've never witnessed before. She has him wrapped around her finger, and he knows it.

I'm still reeling from it all when Ember's sultry voice cuts through the thick tension hanging in the room. "Enjoy the show?"

Her gaze shifts past me, and I turn to see Tommy standing in the doorway, gripping his erection through his suit pants, a dangerous gleam in his eyes. I'd never pegged him as the voyeur type, but there's no denying the hunger in his expression.

Tommy locks eyes with me briefly before turning on his heel and walking away, leaving a trail of confusion behind him. What the hell is going on with him? I know he's been different lately, but this? I shake my head, trying to brush off the lingering unease.

Ember shifts beside me, standing up from the seat, her

Chapter 18

naked form glistening with sweat and satisfaction. "Where's the bathroom?" she asks, as if she hadn't just unraveled us both moments ago.

Jax reaches for her hand, pulling her toward the hallway. "I'll show you." They disappear down the corridor, leaving me sitting there, still trying to process the whirlwind that just tore through this room.

I pull on my sweats, sitting back down on the loveseat that's damp with the evidence of what just transpired. The fleeting thought of licking it off the cushions crosses my mind, but I push it aside. Instead, I grab the remote, flicking through Netflix, trying to find something—anything—to ground me. Will Jax bring her back? Will this night continue?

As if summoned by my thoughts, Ember walks back in, her body still radiating warmth and satisfaction, her confidence a palpable force in the room. She bends to pick up her clothes, slipping them back on without an ounce of hesitation. She's completely unbothered by my presence, by the fact that I've seen her in her most vulnerable moments, and I can't help but admire that.

"Put that one on," she points to the TV screen, indicating Harry Potter. "I love the last movie. Nothing better than watching Harry enact his revenge."

I click on the video, and the familiar sound fills the room. She settles in next to me, her warmth pressing into my side, a silent reminder of everything that's happened tonight. Jax returns, taking his place on her other side, completing this strange little triangle we've formed.

"Rub my feet," she commands Jax, and without hesitation, he complies. The way she so effortlessly gives orders, and the way we follow them—it's intoxicating. A soft moan escapes her lips as Jax's hands work on her feet, and I can't help but flick my gaze to her face, watching her enjoy his touch.

"Ember, don't start," I warn, trying to keep the growing tension at bay. She grins up at me, her eyes sparkling with mischief.

"No one told you not to," she replies, her voice dripping with playful defiance.

I laugh, taken aback by her boldness. She's fearless, and it's that same fearlessness that's pulling me deeper into this. "You like going more than once?" I ask, my curiosity getting the better of me.

"Baby," she purrs, resting her head on my lap, the heat of her breath brushing against my skin, "I can go all night." The sensation of her so close sends a jolt through me, my body reacting despite the exhaustion settling in.

The TV flickers in the background, casting a soft glow across the room, but my mind is miles away from the storyline on the screen. Jax's eyes, usually so calculating and cold, seem softer as he looks at her, his hands still gently massaging her feet. There's something shifting between the three of us, something unspoken but undeniable.

Jax breaks the silence with a grin. "Wanna play 20 questions again?"

Ember lifts her head, a wicked smile curving her lips. "Okay, but I go first." The energy in the room shifts, the playful tension returning.

Her eyes lock onto mine, and I know she's about to go

Chapter 18

straight for the jugular. "Is that the first time you've had your dick sucked?"

I can't help but laugh at her bluntness, caught off guard by the directness of her question. "Yeah, sweetness. How could you tell?" I answer, trying to regain some semblance of control in this conversation, but knowing full well that with Ember, control is an illusion.

She shrugs, her gaze never faltering. "The way you moved—almost shocked at the touch, so I assumed it was a first-time thing."

Jax's eyes widen in disbelief, his head snapping toward me. "What the fuck, really?"

I shrug, feeling oddly exposed. None of them know the full extent of my preferences when it comes to women—my history, my darkness. But with Ember, for some reason, I don't feel the need to hide it as much. There's something about her, something raw and real, that makes me think she might understand more than anyone else ever could.

"Ember, how'd you learn to use a gun so well?" Jax asks suddenly, his hands working skillfully over her feet as she lounges between us, her attention seemingly focused on the TV screen.

"Simple," she replies, her voice calm and collected, though the weight of her words lingers heavily in the room. "My dad was the president of an MC back in Australia. Grew up holding a gun."

The casual tone with which she says it sends a chill down my spine. It's clear she's no stranger to danger, and the darkness inside her mirrors something familiar within me. The power and violence she was raised around... it's intoxicating.

Jax pauses his movements for a moment, and Ember shifts her attention towards him. "Do you have a family, Jax?" she asks, her voice gentle, but there's something in her eyes—something probing like she's trying to unravel what makes us who we are.

Jax doesn't flinch. "Declan's my twin as im sure you have guessed," he answers easily, though I can tell there's a deeper truth he's weighing before saying more. "Tommy's like a father to me, and Knox here is like an older brother. As for blood relatives, I have no idea. My mum gave me up when I was five after I was diagnosed as a psychopath."

Ember's brow furrows, a flash of disbelief and disdain crossing her face. "Your mother gave you up because you're a psychopath?"

"Yup." Jax's voice is steady and cold, but there's an undercurrent of pain he hides well.

"Sounds like you were better off without her," she replies, her tone casual, shrugging off the weight of his past like it's nothing. She doesn't flinch, doesn't try to fix it. She accepts it as a fact, just as Jax does.

A twisted grin spreads across Jax's face, but there's something raw behind his eyes. "Yes, I was," he agrees quietly, his hands resuming their gentle massage on her feet.

Then Ember's gaze shifts to me, dark and unwavering, locking onto mine like she's peeling back the layers to see the real me. "What about you, Knox? Do you have a family?"

I feel the tension creep into my shoulders, my fingers digging into the armrest on my side. Meeting her eyes feels like exposing parts of myself I've long tried to hide. But for some reason, with her, I want to let it out.

Chapter 18

"I grew up in a loving family," I start, my voice lower than before. "My mother was a stay-at-home mom, and my dad was a gynaecologist. I went into medicine to follow in his footsteps."

"But?" Ember presses, sensing the weight of the untold story that follows.

Jax's gaze is now fixed on me, as he watches me expose parts of myself he knows I keep hidden.

"But... my parents were devout Christians," I continue, my grip tightening. "They found out about my... real desires when I was twelve. I killed our family dog just to see what was inside." I pause, the memory is dark and vivid, as if it's etched into my bones. "They tried to exorcise the 'devil' from me, brought in priests, sent me to therapy—anything to fix me."

Her eyes widen slightly, but there's no judgment, only fascination. "And?"

"And I learned to hide it," I say, a bitter laugh escaping me. "Until I became a surgeon. That's when it all came back. I couldn't control it anymore... lost my medical license after a patient died on my table."

"Shit," Ember breathes, her eyes locking onto mine. There's no pity in her gaze, just understanding. "What happened next?"

"Tommy had already been using me as an off-the-books doc for years," I explain, my voice steadying. "When I lost my license, he brought me into the fold fully. The Aces became my permanent family."

Ember nods, her expression softening. "Sounds like you found your true family here."

I glance over at Jax, who's been watching this whole exchange with a soft smile.

"Declan," Ember says, her voice shifting as she turns back to Jax. "I want to know about him."

Jax leans back, tapping his fingers on his knee, clearly considering how much to share. "He's... complicated," Jax replies slowly, his tone more guarded. "He doesn't touch women anymore. Don't expect much from him."

"Why?" Ember asks, her interest piqued.

"That's not my story to tell," Jax says, shaking his head. I can see the hear edge in his voice when it comes to his twin. He doesn't want to expose Declan's demons.

"Then tell me about Tommy," she says, switching gears effortlessly, her eyes flicking between Jax and me.

I lean back, the question hanging in the air between us. "Tommy... well, he's got his own demons to," I say, my tone darkening. "He doesn't care much for women outside of what they can offer. He'll fuck them if he wants to, but don't expect any affection after." Jax lets out a short laugh, emphasizing the truth in my words.

Ember's lips curve into a small smirk. She's intrigued, and I can tell she's still trying to figure us all out, trying to piece together the puzzle of who we really are.

As the conversation shifts, we start bouncing questions back and forth. She tells us about her work, the places she's flipped and sold, and how she built her empire from the ground up. I know Jax has already Googled every bit of information he could find about her, but we both listen anyway, captivated by the way she speaks, by her voice that weaves its way through our minds like a drug.

Chapter 18

Time slips away, and before we realize it, the night has worn on. Our eyelids grow heavy, the buzz of conversation slowly fading as exhaustion settles over us. We end up falling asleep on the couch, tangled together in a mess of limbs, the flickering light from the TV casting shadows on our faces.

It's strange, this closeness. But it feels right. It feels like home.

19

TOMMY PERCIVAL

Three months later

Three months. It had been three damn months since Ember sauntered into Jax's world, her presence altering everything like a storm reshaping the land in its wake. The changes she brought weren't just to him—they rippled through all of us, leaving indelible marks on our tightly knit brotherhood. I had seen transformations in Jax, sure, but it was the way she influenced Knox that made me truly uneasy. Knox, the unhinged butcher who had once reveled in his own proximity to madness, was now... soft.

It was surreal, watching him prepare pasta dishes for Ember like some lovesick schoolboy, his hands—hands that once knew only how to slice and carve—now tenderly kneading dough or rubbing her shoulders after a long day. He'd even started giving her vanilla sex. Knox? Vanilla sex? It was absurd. He ran her baths, for fuck's sake. And then there was Declan—the most grounded of us all—completely surrendering to her allure. That was the final betrayal.

Jealousy twisted inside me like a knife. It wasn't just that I wanted her—it was that I couldn't have her. She represented something forbidden, a temptation I couldn't afford to indulge. The worst part was she knew it. Every time she looked at me, her gaze filled with longing and desire, she dangled that forbidden fruit just beyond my reach.

Somehow, she had slipped into the fabric of our lives, weaving herself into our routines, our thoughts, our every damn moment. And before I knew it, resistance became futile. Ember wasn't just a guest; she had become a fixture, a constant presence in our home. But as much as I wanted to keep my distance, I found myself softening, little by little.

It wasn't long before I made the foolish mistake of offering her a project. One morning, I came across this charming old farmhouse—a sprawling property perched on a hill, an hour's drive from the city. It was exactly what we needed—a sanctuary, a fortress, a place that could be our version of Helm's Deep. Without hesitation, I bought it, imagining it as our refuge, a place to escape the world.

And like the fool I'd become, I invited Ember to help restore it. I didn't even get the offer out of my mouth before she shot me down with that withering glare of hers. "I work on my own projects," she snapped, her voice cutting through my enthusiasm like a blade. She had no interest in my vision, only her own.

For a moment, I stood there, feeling like an idiot, my confidence deflating as I watched her turn away. Anger

Chapter 19

flared, but before I could voice it, Declan stepped in—calm, collected, always knowing the right thing to say. He reminded Ember that the farmhouse would belong to all of us, including her. "It's yours as much as it is ours," he said, his voice gentle but firm. Declan knew how to get to her. He appealed to that sense of individuality, her need to leave her mark, to create on her own terms.

It was a masterstroke. She softened, her eyes flickering with interest as Declan urged her to envision the place through her lens, shaping it to fit her tastes rather than ours. It was subtle, but it worked. She began to see the farmhouse as her canvas, something she could mold into her own masterpiece, without even having the chance to see it yet.

And just like that, Declan became the latest to fall under her spell. It was only a matter of time before he succumbed, just like the rest of us. She took him on a date and showed him her properties, flaunting her skill with effortless charm. Watching her reel him in like a fish on a hook was mesmerizing. Declan, ever the romantic, was captivated. He basked in her attention, just like Knox, just like Jax.

I would hear them at night, the sounds echoing through the walls—the passion, the intensity of their connection. It drove me insane. Ember had this way of pulling men into her orbit, offering them something irresistible. And in return, they gave her everything—adoration, loyalty, devotion, and by the sound of it, some of the most intense sex any of us had ever experienced.

I... I found myself watching from the sidelines, torn between admiration and frustration, trapped in the knowledge that Ember had changed us all in ways we couldn't undo.

In a way, she had become our queen. Each of us played our roles—loyal subjects to her reign. But for me, it was a reign of frustration, watching her bend the men I called brothers to her will while knowing I could never let myself fall like they had. I couldn't afford to.

But that didn't stop me from wanting.

Ember's nocturnal habits had shifted. I'd catch her in the early morning hours, sometimes sharing a quiet breakfast with Declan or engrossed in a marathon chess match with Knox, the board likely being worked over from the night before. Sleep didn't seem to interest her much, but she craved intimacy. I'd see it in the fleeting moments—her hand brushing against one of the others, lingering glances, as though her desire for connection outweighed everything else.

I'd given up talking about her with the others. Jax, Knox, and Declan were firmly caught in her web, and there was no point trying to drag them out of it. But the most challenging part of it all? It wasn't just watching them fall. It was fighting the pull she had on me. Every passing day made it harder to resist. The temptation became almost unbearable, a dangerous dance on the edge of something I couldn't afford to give in to.

She wanted me, too. That much was obvious in the heated glances she'd throw my way, the way her fingers would linger on my arm for just a beat too long. I could feel the weight of her desire like a storm pressing against me, threatening to break down the walls I'd spent years

Chapter 19

building. But I couldn't—no, I wouldn't—fall for it. Not again.

Not after Natasha.

The mere thought of Natasha sent a wave of bitterness crashing through me. Her memory was like a knife twisting in my gut, a constant reminder of what happens when you give in to your desires and let yourself trust someone fully. Natasha had been my undoing once, and I wouldn't make the same mistake twice. I couldn't.

No one knew the full story of what happened to Natasha. They all thought it was just another casualty of a skirmish with a rival gang. But the truth? The truth was far worse. Natasha hadn't just died because of gang violence—she had been the reason for it. She was the mole. The one who had infiltrated Aces, using her charm, her doe-eyed innocence, her perfect body to lure me in, make me believe we had a future.

For two years, I thought I was building something real with her. Love. Trust. But all the while, she was working for someone else, undermining us from the inside. Five of my men paid the price when things finally went south. Five loyal soldiers. Five brothers.

When the truth came out, it broke me. It sent me spiraling. But in the end, it was my decision. I'm the one who had to put her down. To pull the trigger. No one else knew that. No one else would ever know that. Not Jax, not Knox, not Declan. And certainly not Ember.

Natasha's betrayal was mine to carry, and it was a heavy burden—one that weighed on me every time Ember looked at me with those sultry eyes as if she could pull me in and fix everything that had shattered inside me. But I couldn't let her. I wouldn't. Natasha had already broken me once, and I knew that if I gave in to Ember, it could destroy me all over again.

But still, the pull was there, gnawing at me.

She was different from Natasha—at least, I told myself that. Ember wasn't sneaking around with the intent to betray us. She was more like fire, burning everything in her path, consuming those around her. And despite my better judgment, I could feel drawn toward that flame.

But the memory of Natasha's final moments, the weight of the gun in my hand as I pulled the trigger, was enough to keep me grounded. She had fooled me once and led me down the path of love and trust, only to tear it all away.

That day... I could still see Natasha's face. She had stared at me with wide, pleading eyes, tears streaking her cheeks as she begged for her life. She'd said she loved me, that everything had been a mistake, that she was forced into it. But I knew better. The damage was done, and the consequences were too severe to ignore. In the end, love didn't save her. And it hadn't saved me either.

I couldn't go through that again. Ember, for all her allure, for all the ways she tempted me, was a risk I wasn't willing to take.

20

DECLAN STEVENSON

The first light of dawn had barely begun to seep into the room, casting soft, eerie shadows across the floor as I watched Ember emerge from Knox's room, rubbing her eyes, yawning as though she hadn't had a single moment of rest. She called herself a night owl, and she usually was, but lately, I'd noticed a change. Over the past month, she made it a point to get up at 8 a.m. to eat breakfast with me. A habit that, though subtle, hadn't gone unnoticed.

"Morning," she mumbled, her voice thick with sleep. She was wearing one of Knox's old t-shirts as a nightdress. The fabric hung loosely over her body but clung just enough to reveal the curves beneath. Her long black hair, wild from sleep, cascaded down her back in dark waves, framing her delicate face. She was striking, almost ethereal in the early morning light. It was hard not to feel drawn to her, not to admire the way she moved—effortless, yet grounded.

"Good morning," I replied, holding out my arms in an

unspoken invitation. Without hesitation, Ember walked straight into them, her body curling against mine like it had always belonged there. Her warmth seeped through my clothes, and she pressed herself into me as though seeking refuge and comfort. The feel of her heartbeat, the way her body molded to mine—it was enough to make my heart stumble over its own rhythm.

She slouched, her head resting against my chest, her breath soft and steady. For a moment, it felt like she had drifted back to sleep in my arms, her breathing slowing, her weight relaxed.

"Sleepy?" I asked softly, my hands instinctively moving to support her, to hold her closer.

"Mmm," she hummed in agreement, her voice barely above a whisper. She didn't move, didn't pull away. It felt natural to hold her like this, the weight of her head against my chest, her body a quiet reassurance that she was here.

"Are you sure you don't want to go back to bed?" I murmured, not wanting to push her, but offering her the chance to rest if needed.

"No," she replied, her voice still drowsy but firm. She tilted her head up to look at me, her eyes soft in the morning light, a vulnerability in them I wasn't used to seeing. "I want to be here with you."

Her usual fire, her sharp wit—it was gone, replaced by something quieter, more fragile. It was as though she had stripped away the armor she so carefully wore, letting me see the woman beneath. The raw, unguarded version of herself that she rarely showed anyone. Her eyes, typically fierce and

Chapter 20

full of defiance, now looked at me with a softness that made my heart swell.

"Thank you," I whispered, unsure what I was thanking her for. Maybe it was for trusting me, for letting me see this side of her. Or perhaps it was for something deeper, something I wasn't ready to name yet.

She smiled a small, genuine smile that crinkled the corners of her eyes. It was a smile that said she understood. It was one of those moments where words weren't necessary, and everything we needed to say had already been conveyed in her being here.

The smell of coffee filled the kitchen, its rich, earthy aroma grounding me in the present as I stood there holding her. I thought about how far we'd come, how much closer we had grown in such a short period. It felt surreal. Just a few weeks ago, Ember had stumbled into my arms, mistaking me for Jax. She had been so guarded then, all sass and fire, a whirlwind of chaos that had disrupted the fragile balance we'd all come to rely on. And yet, despite the chaos she brought, she had somehow found a way to settle into our lives, into my life.

The change had been gradual but undeniable. The walls she kept around her started to crack, and every time we had these quiet moments—just the two of us—I could feel them crumble a little more. It wasn't just lust or attraction that pulled me toward her anymore. There was something deeper, something far more dangerous.

As she stood in my arms, her head resting against my chest, I couldn't help but wonder if she felt it too—the weight of something bigger than either of us, something we couldn't easily define but couldn't ignore.

She pulled back just enough to look up at me again, her eyes searching mine for something. I wasn't sure what it was—reassurance, maybe? Or perhaps she just wanted to know if I felt the same pull she did. Whatever it was, I knew it was enough to keep her here, wrapped in my arms, instead of retreating into her usual defenses.

"I'm glad you're here," I admitted, the words slipping out before I could stop them. And I meant it.

Ember's lips curled into another soft smile, and for the first time in a long time, I felt like I was exactly where I was supposed to be.

I remembered the first time she hugged me, thinking I was Jax. I was bustling about in the kitchen, preparing breakfast for myself, the sizzle of bacon filling the air. Ember had emerged from Knox's room, her sleepy gaze scanning the space as she wandered in for a drink. She moved languidly, her bare feet barely making a sound on the cool tiles. From behind, she mistook me for Jax, and without hesitation, she slipped her arms around my waist, pressing herself into me as she needed me to hold her up.

The warmth of her touch sent a jolt through me, the unexpected intimacy catching me off guard. It had been a long time since anyone had touched me like that, and certainly not since Crystal. The feel of her body against mine was electrifying, even though I knew it wasn't meant for me. Her soft breath tickled the back of my neck, and for a moment, I froze, unsure how to respond.

But instinct took over, and I turned towards her, wrapping her in my arms without a second thought. I pulled her closer,

Chapter 20

holding her tightly, not wanting to let her go. The scent of vanilla shampoo mixed with the unmistakable musk of sex from the night before filled my senses, and I found myself nuzzling into her hair. My heart pounded in my chest, the stirrings of desire flickering to life for the first time since Crystal had betrayed me.

The soft morning light filtered through the curtains, casting a golden hue around her as she tilted her face to look at me. Her eyes, warm and rich like autumn leaves, searched mine with an intensity that made me feel exposed, as if she was peering into a part of me I'd kept hidden. Then, I saw realisation dawning on her face as she recognised her mistake. I wasn't Jax.

"Sorry, shit, I thought you were Jax," she stammered, her cheeks flushing as she tried to pull away, embarrassed by the mix-up.

But I couldn't let her go. Not now. Not when she was this close when her warmth was seeping into me, thawing the ice I'd buried myself in. I tightened my hold, wrapping my arms around her waist and pulling her closer.

"Please don't move," I said softly, my voice barely above a whisper. I searched her eyes, hoping she wouldn't pull back, would accept this. "I was enjoying it."

Her breath hitched, her surprise evident. I could see the curiosity in her eyes, warring with uncertainty. For a moment, it felt like she was seeing me. There was something more in her gaze—something I'd felt from Jax and Knox but had never understood until now.

She nestled closer into my chest, her voice soft and hesitant. "Jax told me you don't like women. I'm sorry I got confused between you two."

I gently kissed the top of her head, surprising even myself with the gesture. It felt natural, unguarded—something I hadn't done in years. "I don't usually get close to women," I admitted, the confession strange and foreign on my lips. "But I've found myself drawn to you... from the moment I met you."

Her eyes, vast and vulnerable, held mine. For a second, she looked fragile, like she was letting me in on something deeply personal. "What do you have planned today?" she asked, her voice barely more than a whisper. "I have a few things I need to do for a townhouse I just bought. Want to tag along?"

I couldn't deny her. I didn't even want to. "Of course," I said, the words coming quickly.

The townhouse she took me to was a classic London property, in desperate need of repair but full of potential. She wasted no time getting to work, talking to the builders on site, her commanding presence catching everyone's attention. They seemed surprised to see her there so early and even more shocked to see me by her side. I could see the unspoken questions in their eyes—what was I doing here with her? Why was she with me?

But they didn't ask. They wouldn't dare.

"Make sure everything is done properly," I instructed, my tone sharp and unyielding. They nodded in silent understanding, knowing well the consequences if they didn't meet expectations.

As Ember talked with the foreman, her sharp mind and passion for her work were on full display, and I couldn't help but admire her. She wasn't like any woman I'd ever known—strong, fiercely independent, and yet there was something so profoundly vulnerable about her, too. It was a contradiction that made her all the more captivating. She had a way of weaving herself into your life without you even realizing it, and by the time you did, it was too late. You were hooked.

Chapter 20

And I was. She'd found a way in despite everything I'd told myself and the walls I'd built.

"Hey, what's for breakfast?" Ember's voice jolted me back to reality, her playful tone cutting through the fog of my thoughts. I looked down at her, and there was that spark in her eyes, a mix of curiosity and mischief that always kept me on my toes.

"Bacon, eggs, and toast," I replied, trying to shake off the lingering feelings that had crept up on me.

"You were miles away, babe. You okay?" she asked, her brow furrowing slightly as she studied me.

I exhaled, feeling the warmth of something more than just the morning sun spreading through me. Something about being around her made me feel alive in a way I hadn't in years. "I'm great, honey," I said, a soft smile tugging at the corners of my mouth. "I was thinking... if you're not too tired, I could take you to see that farmhouse Tommy bought. He'd love to get started on it."

Her lips pursed like they always did when she was considering something, her gaze never leaving mine. I could practically see the gears turning behind those mesmerizing eyes, always calculating, always one step ahead. "Why can't he ask me himself?" she asked, her tone laced with just the right amount of defiance.

I couldn't help but smile at her challenge. That was Ember—she wasn't the type to back down easily, even with someone like Tommy. "That's something you'll have to take up with him when you see him," I said, keeping my tone light. The truth was, Tommy didn't like to ask anyone for anything, especially her. There was too much-unspoken tension between them, and I knew better than to get caught in the middle of it. But the thought of what might unfold when the two of them finally clashed sent a thrill of anticipation through me.

"Okay, well, I'm free," she said, her determination as sharp as ever. "But let's stop by Tommy's office on the way. I need to ask him a few things." There was a fire in her voice that told me this wasn't going to be just a friendly chat. She was gearing up for something bigger, and I had a feeling that whatever it was, it would be explosive.

The thought of Ember going head-to-head with Tommy wasn't something I'd ever thought I'd want to see, but now... I was eager to witness the sparks fly. Two forces like that colliding? It was bound to be unforgettable.

As I stood there, watching her, I couldn't help but wonder how much she knew about her effect on us all. She wasn't just some girl who'd accidentally walked into our lives. No, Ember had changed everything, and the question now was whether that change would bring us closer together—or tear us apart.

I watched as Ember walked out of Jax's room, now wearing a navy pantsuit; it was accentuating her curves and displaying a generous amount of cleavage. I couldn't help but feel a stirring of desire as I looked at her, wondering if she was trying to get a rise out of Tommy or if it was all for me. Either way, I found myself entirely on board with the situation.

"Ready?" she asked, her eyes flickering with mischief.

"Lead the way," I replied.

Chapter 20

As we walked up the stairs and then down the dimly lit hallway, the tension between us thickened. The silence was broken only by the subtle sound of her heels clicking against the floor. Each step she took seemed deliberate as if she knew precisely the effect she had on the people around her. I couldn't help but wonder how this meeting with Tommy would unfold.

Ember knocked softly on Tommy's office door, waiting for his response. "Ember?" he murmured from behind the door, his voice barely audible, though unmistakably curious. She turned the knob and walked in, leaving me standing at the threshold, observing the scene. None of us ever knocked on Tommy's door. We just walked right in. The fact that she did it now felt like another calculated move.

Inside, I caught a glimpse of Ember's reflection on the polished surface of Tommy's desk. The soft light from the light above cast a glow that accentuated the curve of her breasts, showcased perfectly by the plunging neckline of her pantsuit. Her eyes gleamed with a hint of mischief, and I smirked. She knew exactly what she was doing.

"Ember," Tommy's voice sounded strained, his gaze momentarily locking on her chest before he snapped it back up to meet her eyes. He swallowed hard, his attempt at maintaining composure betrayed by the tension in his posture. With a forced scowl, he straightened. "What can I do for you?"

"Declan is taking me to the farmhouse today," she purred, leaning forward just enough for her arms to push her breasts up further. "I wanted to get a feel for what you're after exactly."

Tommy's frown deepened as his sharp green eyes narrowed, scrutinising her. He wasn't sure what game she was playing, but he wasn't one to back down easily. "I just want to know how much work needs to be done," he replied, irritation already lacing his voice.

Ember smirked, the corners of her lips curling in a way that sent a shiver down my spine. "But you see, the work depends on what will be done."

Her words hung in the air between them, daring Tommy to engage. The tension was palpable, a power struggle between two formidable forces. I could feel my pulse quickening, caught between wanting to see Tommy put her in her place and knowing she wouldn't let him.

"Go on," Tommy urged his fingers drumming impatiently on the desk.

"Wouldn't you agree," she continued, her tone dangerously sweet, "that different plans require different resources? If I'm given complete free rein, the scope of the work—and the cost—will vary accordingly."

The room seemed to hold its breath. Their eyes locked, each refusing to give ground. It was like watching a predator and prey size each other up, except this time, it wasn't clear who the hunter was.

"Fine," Tommy said, at last, leaning back in his chair, though the tension in his jaw remained. "If I'm giving you free rein, how will that affect the work needed? And if you need specific guidelines, what will change?" His irritation was evident, but there was curiosity, too—he wanted to see what she could do.

Ember's lips curved into a smile, sly and victorious. She

Chapter 20

had him. "That depends on what you expect from me, Tommy. The amount of work will vary if I have full control over the design. If you have certain requirements, I can adjust."

Tommy studied her for a moment longer, weighing his options. "Fine," he finally agreed, his voice clipped. "You can have free rein. Just make sure there's space for an office and an armory. The rest? I don't care. Just remember, it needs to house all of us."

At that moment, I knew Ember had won. She managed to charm Tommy into giving her exactly what she wanted while simultaneously asserting her dominance in a way only she could.

"Okay," she said, her voice as sultry as commanding. "I'll pop back in when we return and review my plans with you."

She turned to leave, casting me a knowing glance before heading back down the hallway. I watched as Tommy sat there for a moment longer, silent, before returning to his paperwork, the tension still lingering in the air.

She'd managed to do what few could—bend Tommy to her will, if only for a moment.

As the tires crunched on the old dirt driveway, I couldn't help but admit that Tommy had outdone himself with this purchase. The old farmhouse loomed before us, its stone edifice a testament to the passage of time. It was clear he had Ember in mind when he bought the place.

"Wow," Ember breathed, her eyes wide as they swept over the dilapidated building. "This is... amazing."

"Tommy knew what he was doing," I replied, my gaze lingering on the worn stones and creeping ivy that clung to the walls like desperate fingers. The structure was magnificent despite its disrepair—a gothic masterpiece begging for resurrection, just like something Ember would fall in love with.

I turned off the engine and looked at Ember's face. Her eyes sparkled with shock and awe, reflecting the sunlight as she stared at the crumbling farmhouse. Tommy knew precisely what he was doing when he bought this place, clearly there was hope for those two yet.

"Declan..." she whispered, turning her wide eyes to me. "This is my dream home. This is what I've been working towards all this time." Without waiting for a response, her hand flew to the door handle, and she jumped out of the Mercedes, practically vibrating with excitement. The way her energy crackled around her was magnetic, making it impossible to look away.

The wind picked up, tossing her dark hair around her shoulders like a wild storm, and I could almost imagine her as some ethereal creature straight out of one of those gothic novels she loved so much.

"Can you believe it?" she called back, her voice full of excitement and wonder. "It's like something straight out of a story!"

She moved closer to the farmhouse, her eyes wide and captivated as she took in every detail—the weathered stone walls, the ivy creeping up like tendrils of forgotten memories, the once-grand entrance now hidden beneath layers of time and decay. Her gaze moved over the landscape, the

Chapter 20

rolling hills, and the distant line of trees. The old farmhouse had a presence, as if it was waiting for someone like her to breathe life back into it.

Ember's breath caught in her throat as she gazed out at the stunning view. Her hand reached out, tracing the outline of the ancient stone railing, worn smooth by centuries of weather and touch. "Declan, this... this is incredible," she whispered, her voice thick with reverence. It was as if the place had spoken to her, something I could feel too.

I couldn't resist capturing the moment. I pulled out my phone and snapped a few pictures of her, framed by the breathtaking view and the old farmhouse. The way she beamed, so alive in this place, I knew Tommy had to see it. He'd been fighting an internal battle ever since she entered our lives, but no matter how much he masked it, it was obvious to all of us that Ember had burrowed her way into his heart, whether he wanted to admit it or not.

I hit send on the photos and tucked my phone back into my pocket.

Jax had already declared her our queen, and I was completely on board with the title now. Ember was more than just a passing figure in our lives. Since her arrival, there had been no hookers at the penthouse, a far cry from the norm. Even Tommy, who still referred to her as our "occasional house guest," hadn't brought anyone else around. She had changed the dynamics of everything, and none of us could deny it.

I took slow, measured steps toward her, my pulse quickening as I closed the distance. Wrapping my arms around her waist, I pulled her back against me, savoring the warmth of her body as she leaned into my touch. Her soft gasp as she laid eyes on the view in front of us sent a thrill through me.

"Declan," Ember whispered, her voice barely audible over the rustling of the trees and the soft sigh of the wind. She pressed herself back against me, finding comfort and security in my arms. "This is like my dream home. I almost don't want to go through with it."

I frowned slightly, her words catching me off guard. "What are you talking about?" I asked, genuinely puzzled. My fingers traced slow, soothing patterns along her waist, making her shiver ever so slightly beneath my touch.

She tilted her head back to look at me, her deep brown eyes filled with uncertainty and something else—something that pulled at my heart. "What if all of this ends?" she murmured. "What if I never get to enjoy coming here? What if it all falls apart before I get the chance?"

Her vulnerability was rare, but it was raw and real in that moment. It wasn't like Ember to question herself or the future—she usually embraced everything head-on. The fact that she was sharing this fear with me made it feel even more significant, like she was letting me see a part of her she usually kept locked away.

I laughed then, a deep, throaty sound that echoed into the valley below. "Honey, Jax won't let you go," I reassured her, a teasing smile playing on my lips. "He's more likely to chain you to his bed for the rest of your life than let you slip away. And honestly, I'm inclined to help him."

She turned in my arms, her soft brown eyes locking onto mine with a sincerity that struck deep. "I know I'm not conventional," she said, her voice quiet, vulnerable in a way I

Chapter 20

hadn't heard before. "And this... this isn't what the world would call normal. But you three... you've crawled under my skin."

Hearing those words, something swelled inside my chest, a warmth spreading through me that had nothing to do with the crisp morning air. I leaned down, capturing her lips in a tender kiss, my hand gently cradling her cheek. When I pulled back, I whispered against her lips, "And you've crawled under ours too."

For a moment, we stayed like that, wrapped in each other's warmth, feeling more connected than ever. But then she surprised me with her next words, her gaze steady, her tone sincere.

"I understand if you want to see other people," she said, her voice clear but still hesitant, like she was laying bare a part of herself she wasn't used to showing. "But I would really like to keep this as just an 'us' thing."

I blinked at her, momentarily stunned by how open and understanding she was. I hadn't expected that, not from her. "Honey," I said softly, my heart swelling with affection for this woman who had turned our world upside down. "You might get to fuck all three of us, but you're technically in separate relationships with all of us exclusively. I mean, I can't speak for Knox, but I can for Jax and myself – we're one girl-at-a-time types. Plus, we're only okay with you fucking us... and Tommy."

At the mention of Tommy, her nose wrinkled, and she shook her head. "Maybe not Tommy. He has a stick too far up his ass."

I burst out laughing, appreciating her blunt honesty. "If

you think he bought this place for himself, you're wrong. This right here," I gestured to the farmhouse looming before us, "is his way of showing you that he's interested in you. He hasn't shown interest in anyone since his ex-wife, so trust me, you're in. Just keep doing what you're doing—it's working."

Her expression wavered between curiosity and a hint of uncertainty, the idea that Tommy might be slowly opening up to her clearly unsettling her in some way.

"Okay," she finally said, a quiet determination in her voice. "Let's go see what this beautiful building has in store for me."

I pulled out the heavy wrought iron key Tommy had given me, feeling the weight of it in my palm. "Hopefully this works," I muttered before sliding the key into the lock. The mechanism was stiff, but with a little force, it gave way, and the door creaked open, revealing the interior of the forgotten farmhouse.

"Wow," Ember whispered, her voice filled with awe as she stepped over the threshold. The space before us was bathed in the muted glow of filtered sunlight, casting long shadows on the stone floors. Woodfire stoves, stone hearths, and ancient beams overhead hinted at a time long gone. Dust clung to the air, mingling with the scent of damp earth and age, but underneath it all, there was something undeniably enchanting about the place.

"It's like stepping into another world," she breathed, her fingers tracing the worn edges of a stone mantle.

I nodded, mesmerized by the haunting beauty of it all. It was as if time had forgotten this place, yet it remained stand-

Chapter 20

ing, waiting for someone to come along and breathe life back into it. And that someone was Ember. This place was a reflection of her—wild, untouched, and full of untapped potential.

"Tommy definitely knew what he was doing when he bought this place," I murmured, more to myself than to her.

Ember turned to me, her eyes bright with excitement. "Let's explore," she said, her voice filled with anticipation. She handed me a notebook and a pen from her bag, her smile playful. "Take notes. Just write down everything I say, okay?"

I couldn't help but smile back at her. "Of course."

She walked through the space, her eyes sharp as she took in every detail. "Water damage," she muttered, running her hand over a damp spot on the ceiling. "Tiled roof, black mould..." She moved further into the house, her fingers lightly brushing over the walls as she mentally cataloged everything. "Sunroom, strangling vines," she noted, glancing out at the overgrown garden that lay beyond the cracked windows.

"New plumbing, new wiring," she added thoughtfully. "Maybe a 17th-century build? We'll need to get the original plans for that." She walked over to a crumbling section of the house, studying the stone with a critical eye. "What stone is this second add-on made of? Should it flow with the rest of the house or be kept separate?"

As I scribbled down her observations, I couldn't help but feel a growing sense of admiration for the woman before me. This wasn't just a job for Ember – it was her passion, something deeply ingrained in who she was. Watching her move through the decayed grandeur of the farmhouse, her fingers tracing the cracks in the worn stone, only heightened the pull she had on me. My body reacted to her presence, a tension coiling tightly in my gut and lower, my desire for her becoming almost unbearable.

"Declan," she whispered, her voice a soft echo in the large, empty room. The timbers above groaned under the weight of time, but her focus was elsewhere, her eyes roaming the space with a mixture of awe and excitement. "This place... it's like something out of a Gothic novel."

I nodded, my gaze tracing the contours of her body as she spoke, admiring how she fit so perfectly within the setting. This dilapidated, forgotten beauty of a house mirrored her in so many ways. Both wild, both captivating, both capable of resurrection into something extraordinary. The way she took control, how she saw the potential in the broken and the forgotten, it made my chest tighten—and made something else much harder.

As we reached the far end of the building, my restraint snapped. The pain in my dick was relentless, a dull throb that only intensified the closer I got to her. I moved behind her, wrapping my arm around her waist, my hand slipping possessively to her throat. She melted into me, her body softening at my touch, like she'd been waiting for me to take what I wanted.

I slid my other hand into the top of her suit, finding the soft, warm skin of her breast beneath the fabric. My fingers teased her nipple, rolling it gently between my thumb and forefinger as a soft moan escaped her lips, reverberating through the empty room.

Chapter 20

"Declan..." she breathed, her voice thick with lust, her eyes heavy as she leaned into my touch.

Emboldened by her reaction, I tugged the fabric of her suit off her shoulder, turning her around to face me. Her eyes were a storm of desire, her lips parted slightly, tempting me to kiss her. But first, I had to savor her, to take her in fully.

I bent down, taking her nipple into my mouth, suckling gently while my other hand roamed over her curves, exploring the soft skin now exposed to me. She gasped, arching into me, her fingers tangling in my hair as I worshiped her body.

"God, you're incredible," I whispered against her breast, the words slipping out before I could stop them. It was true. Ember had this way of commanding attention, a force of nature in every room she entered. But with me, here in this moment, she was soft, pliant, letting me take the lead, giving herself to me without reservation.

I continued to undress her, pushing the rest of her suit down until it pooled at her feet. "You know," I teased, my voice low and rough, "this is the most inconvenient outfit to get into, darling."

Ember laughed, the sound rich and sultry. "I know, but it looks hot as fuck, doesn't it?"

I grinned, unable to deny her that. "Hot as fuck," I agreed, my eyes roaming her now nearly naked form, her skin flushed with desire, her body practically glowing in the dim light of the old house. She was a vision, standing there, vulnerable yet powerful, every inch of her calling to me.

The reality of it hit me like a punch to the gut—how deeply

she had embedded herself in my life, under my skin. This wasn't just lust. It was something more, something dangerous. But for now, in this moment, all I wanted was to lose myself in her, to claim her, to make her mine in every way possible.

I felt my sanity unravel as the lustful hunger coursed through my veins. My hand slipped between her legs, pushing aside her panties and plunging a finger into her dripping wet cunt. Ember gasped, her eyes locking onto mine, filled with a desire that burned like wildfire.

"Declan," she whispered, trembling under my touch. I couldn't resist any longer.

Lifting her effortlessly into my arms, I carried her to the nearest wall, easily supporting her weight. The moment her back made contact with the wall, I set her feet back on the floor again; I hastily undid my pants, releasing my aching cock. I hoisted her back up, sliding myself into her hot, wet cunt – a place that had been calling out for me since we first laid eyes on each other.

"Fuck," she moaned, tightening around me like a vice. I struggled to hold back my pleasure as I drove into her. She was so incredibly responsive to me; it was intoxicating.

"Harder," Ember demanded in a breathless whisper. I obliged, thrusting into her with fervor and passion. She reached down, her fingers working her clit as I continued to fuck her against the old wall of the building. Its creaks harmonized with our desperate moans.

"Declan... I'm close." Her words were a siren's call, urging me to join her in the throes of ecstasy. I could feel her tighten around me even more, her body preparing for climax.

"Ember," I groaned, struggling to maintain control as I

Chapter 20

picked up the pace, driving into her with all the force I could muster. "Let go, darling."

Her body trembled in my arms, her climax still rippling through her as I spilled myself inside her. The sensation of her pulsing around me sent me over the edge, leaving us both breathless. My last thrust seemed to echo in the room, and just as we began to relax, I heard a groaning sound. Suddenly, the ancient wall behind her gave way, crumbling into a cloud of dust and debris.

I acted instinctually, grabbing her tightly to prevent her from falling backward through the now-exposed gap. The adrenaline surged through me, my heart pounding in my chest as I pulled her back into safety.

"Declan!" she gasped, her eyes wide in shock. But there was laughter there, too, mingling with the dust that now filled the air. "Guess we can add new wall materials to that list you made!"

Still holding her close, I chuckled, my body vibrating against hers from both the thrill of the moment and its absurdity. "Going on the list," I murmured, looking down at her face, smudged with dust and flushed with exertion. Something about her made even moments of chaos feel like they were spun with magic.

As I gently set her down, I noticed a small red streak running down her back. My grin faltered, and concern crept into my voice. "Hold on a second," I said, turning her carefully to inspect the blood's source. A scratch, probably from the rough wall behind us, marred her otherwise perfect skin. It wasn't deep, but it was enough to make me worry.

"Stand still," I commanded gently, pulling my phone

from my pocket and snapping a quick photo of the scratch. I sent it to Knox with a message asking him to check her out later, just in case she needed a tetanus shot or a stitch.

Ember glanced over her shoulder, frowning at me in an adorable and defiant way. "If I need a needle for that scratch," she declared with a mock glare, "you owe me a seafood dinner. I hate needles."

I couldn't help but smile at her, appreciating the strength and stubbornness she showed, even in the smallest moments. "Deal," I replied, brushing a stray lock of hair from her face. "But let's let Knox decide that. Better safe than sorry."

She sighed but nodded, letting the momentary seriousness pass. Her eyes, still shining with the remnants of desire and excitement, softened as she met my gaze. "You sure know how to make an inspection memorable," she said.

I laughed, pulling her into my arms again. The scent of dust and her skin filled my senses. "You make everything memorable, Ember."

21

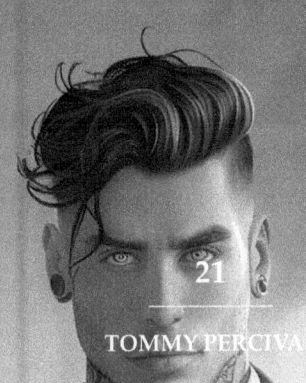

TOMMY PERCIVAL

The soft chime of the lift signaled their return. Declan and Ember, back from their little outing the farmhouse. I'd spent the last few hours brooding stewing over how seamlessly she had maneuvered me in giving her free rein over the place. She'd taken control; t much was clear. The farmhouse was in capable hands, an like it or not, it would be spectacular once she was finished. wasn't sure how I felt about her having that much swa over me.

The unmistakable rhythm of Ember's heels echoed down the hallway, and I braced myself for her usual knock at my door. But, instead of the polite rapping I expected, the door swung open without warning.

"I was told I wouldn't need to knock any more," she said, striding in like she owned the place. Her dark hair was a bit tousled, and there was a flush to her cheeks that hadn't been there when she left with Declan. The thought of them together—sex with her that I hadn't had—unsettled me more than I cared to admit. I pushed it away, locking down the emotion that threatened to crack through my stoic façade.

"So, Tommy, I've decided to take on the farmhouse. It's going to need much work, and I'm sure you'll have objections, but that's too bad. This is how it will be," she announced, settling into the chair opposite my desk as she had already won.

Her confidence, her commanding presence—it was infuriating and... intoxicating. I forced myself to look away from the low cut of her pantsuit and the way it clung to her curves. I needed to get control of this conversation, but before I could respond, Knox stormed into the room, a med kit in hand.

"Get undressed," Knox ordered, his voice more serious than I'd ever heard. Ember shot him a look of pure exasperation, clearly unimpressed with his dramatics. Still, she complied, lowering the shoulder of her pantsuit, revealing her perfect bare breast to me. I gripped the edge of my desk so hard my knuckles turned white, fighting the primal urge to look at her body.

Ember, of course, noticed. She always noticed. Our eyes locked, and she didn't break the stare even as Knox moved his hand over her back. He grabbed an alcohol wipe, and ran it over her back, I watched as her eyes crinkled at the sides in pain, as Knox said "its ok just a scratch, but you need a tetanus shot anyway."

"What the hell happened?" I asked, my voice steadier than I felt.

Her eyes flickered with something close to fear—an

Chapter 21

emotion I had never seen in her before. I tried to comprehend what had triggered her distress, and then I saw it—Knox holding a syringe.

"Don't freak out, baby," Knox said softly, his tone surprisingly contrasting to his usual bluntness. Ember's body tensed, her grip on the desk mirroring my own from earlier. Her breathing became shallow, and she was clearly trying not to panic.

"Ember," I called out, desperate to break her focus on the needle. The words came tumbling out before I could stop them. "How about dinner tonight? A date?"

Her head snapped toward me, surprise written all over her face. "What?"

I held her gaze, not backing down. "Yeah, why not? Let's get to know each other better."

Knox shot me a glance, his brow raised, but he stayed silent. I wasn't sure what had possessed me to say it. A date? I hadn't gone on a proper date in years, and certainly not with someone like Ember. But she needed a distraction, and... maybe I did too.

Ember blinked, clearly processing my offer. Then, as Knox stuck her with the needle, she winced but never looked away from me. After a moment, she tilted her head, a slow smirk spreading across her face. "Only if they serve seafood," she said, her voice laced with amusement.

"Done," I said, surprising myself with how easily the words left my lips.

The tension broke as Knox finished up, and Ember adjusted her clothes, pulling her top back into place with a casual elegance that made my pulse quicken. She pressed a quick kiss to Knox's cheek. "Thanks, big guy," she murmured, and I could've sworn I saw the man blush. It was like we'd all stepped into some alternate reality where Knox smiled at kisses and I asked women on dates.

Ember turned to leave, her hips swaying as she moved toward the door. She glanced over her shoulder, her eyes locking with mine once more. "9 pm sharp, Tommy. Don't be late."

"Yes, ma'am," I muttered under my breath, shaking my head as she disappeared from sight. A date. With Ember. What the hell had I just gotten myself into?

Knox leaned back against the wall, crossing his arms with a shit-eating grin. "A date, huh?"

"Shut up," I growled, though I couldn't help the small smile that tugged at my lips. "It's not like that."

"Sure it isn't," Knox replied, his grin widening.

I let out a soft chuckle, knowing full well I was in over my head. Ember had a way of turning the world upside down, and somehow, I'd let her pull me into her orbit. God help me.

At 8:55 pm, I knocked on the door of the room Ember had claimed in my apartment. I was dressed in navy blue pants and a crisp white shirt, casual yet sharp. After a few minutes, the door finally swung open. Ember stood there, her gaze locking onto mine, a smirk playing on her lips.

"I said 9 pm, handsome," she teased, her voice dripping with playful challenge. Without another word, she strutted past me towards the elevator, her scent lingering in the air as I stood there, momentarily dumbfounded.

Chapter 21

She looked absolutely stunning. Her hair was pulled back into a high ponytail, and the tight black trousers she wore accentuated every curve of her legs and ass. The forest green blouse she paired them with highlighted her skin tone, giving her a goddess-like appearance that was impossible to ignore. I could feel my heart skip a beat. "Jesus, Tommy, get it together," I scolded myself silently, shaking off the effect she had on me.

Half an hour later, we arrived at the restaurant. The drive had been relatively quiet, though I caught myself staring at her like a fool more than once. She noticed, of course, but only smirked in that infuriating way she had. We were quickly seated in a back corner, away from the bustling crowd. Ember's eyes lit up as the rich scent of food filled the air, and she let out a small, appreciative sound.

The waiter handed us a wine list, and Ember selected a Nero d'Avola without hesitation. We ordered oysters to start, and I couldn't help but notice the way her eyes darkened with desire as she ordered her shrimp and scampi linguini. She nearly salivated at the thought, and it was hard to ignore how her raw passion for food mirrored other... indulgences.

As we ate, our conversation flowed surprisingly smoothly. It was easy, natural. I found myself lowering my guard, laughing along with her as she recounted Knox's odd sense of humour and how easily Jax's darkness meshed with hers. She spoke about Declan's tender nature with genuine admiration, but when the topic shifted back to me, I couldn't resist asking.

"What do you like about me?" I asked, trying to keep my tone casual, even though my heart was pounding.

Ember raised an eyebrow, clearly amused. "Besides your good looks?" She grinned, leaning closer. "I admire your dedication to your brothers and the meticulous way you run things. You're methodical, in control, and it turns me on just how hard you're trying to resist me."

Her confidence hit me like a freight train, and I found myself grinning in return, despite the heat rising in my chest. I called for the waiter to clear the plates, and as I wiped my mouth with the napkin, I noticed how calm and serene she seemed after devouring her meal. She mentioned how there was nothing better than seafood and pasta, and we joked about how being English meant a mandatory love of seafood.

Just as she was about to say something, a loud commotion erupted at the front of the restaurant. My senses sharpened immediately, my body instinctively on alert. I turned just in time to see Garry, our security detail, rushing towards me, his face filled with urgency.

"Tommy!" he shouted, his voice cutting through the noise.

In an instant, I knew what was happening. Russians. My blood boiled as I saw the familiar faces of our enemies, weapons drawn. Without thinking, I grabbed the back of Ember's neck and shoved her under the table, not caring about anything else but keeping her safe. Shots rang out, and the restaurant descended into chaos. People screamed, ducking for cover as bullets flew.

Garry and I were outnumbered, six of them closing in fast. I barely had time to think as I pulled out my gun and started firing, trying to avoid innocent casualties while

Chapter 21

returning fire. These guys were good, too good. I could tell it was the Russian mob, coming after us—again. My patience had worn thin.

"Backup's thirty seconds out!" Garry shouted, managing to get close to me.

"Too fucking long!" I growled, ducking behind a planter. My mind raced, trying to figure out how we could hold them off until reinforcements arrived.

That's when I felt a hand at my back, reaching for the other gun I kept hidden there. I whipped my head around, fully prepared to shove them back, only to find Ember crouched next to me, her hand steady as she pulled the gun free.

"What the hell—"

Before I could finish, Ember stood, aimed, and fired in one smooth motion. The Russian I'd been tracking dropped instantly, a bullet between his eyes, just a split second before he would have shot me in the head.

I stared at her, utterly speechless. There was no time to ask questions. We needed to move. Ember, calm as ever, moved like she'd been born for this, seamlessly integrating herself into the chaos of the fight. I couldn't believe it.

She fired off another round, dropping another one of them, and for a moment, I just stood there, watching her. Admiring her.

We managed to take down the last of them just as our backup stormed in, the scene settling into a tense quiet. I holstered my gun, turning to find Ember standing there, breathing heavily but otherwise composed. Her eyes met mine, and she gave me a small, triumphant smile.

"Where the fuck did you learn to shoot like that?" I demanded, my voice rough with disbelief.

Ember shrugged casually, still holding the gun. "Told you before. My dad was in an MC back in Australia. Guns were part of my upbringing."

I shook my head, running a hand through my hair. "Jesus, this wasn't part of the plan."

She stepped closer, her eyes softening slightly. "Plans change, Tommy. If I wasn't here, you might not be standing right now."

I couldn't argue with that, even if my pride wanted to. Instead, I just stared at her, the woman who had just saved my life, feeling a mix of emotions I wasn't ready to unpack.

"I owe you," I muttered.

"Damn right you do," she said with a smirk, holstering the gun in the back of her own pants and walking past me, leaving me once again in her wake.

And just like that, I knew I was too deep.

22

EMBER DANG

The acrid stench of burning gunpowder filled the air, heavy and suffocating. My senses were overloaded, and the world around me blurred into chaos as bullets screamed past. Suddenly, Tommy's hand clamped down on the back of my neck, the pressure firm and urgent as he shoved me under the table. My body moved like it wasn't mine, responding to his command without resistance as I crumpled to the ground.

"Stay down," he hissed, his voice sharp, but I barely heard him over the deafening roar of gunfire.

My heart thundered in my chest, pounding so hard I thought it would burst through my ribs. Each shallow breath felt like a struggle, the air thick with smoke and fear. Panic clawed at the edges of my mind, threatening to take control, to drown me in helplessness. I felt trapped, suffocating, the fabric of my blouse suddenly too tight, too constricting. My vision narrowed as terror surged, locking my body in place.

Move, Ember, move, I screamed internally, but my limbs refused to obey.

A bullet tore through the back of a chair just inches from me, splinters exploding around me in a rain of jagged wood. The shock of it snapped me out of my paralysis. Adrenaline flooded my veins, white-hot and fierce, driving out the panic. I gasped for air, my heart racing, but my body was mine again.

Through the chaos, I saw Tommy crouched behind a large planter, his gun drawn. He was fighting for our lives, and here I was—frozen. No. I wouldn't stay frozen. I wouldn't be useless. Not now.

I caught sight of the gun tucked into the back of his pants, the cold metal gleaming like a lifeline. Before I could think, my hand darted out, grasping the grip with trembling fingers. My pulse roared in my ears as I pulled it free, the weight of it grounding me.

A man with a Colt 45 was moving towards Tommy, his face set with lethal intent. Time slowed as my instincts took over. My hands steadied, my breath slowed, and everything but the man before me faded away.

I stood, shaky but resolute, flicked off the safety, and aimed. My finger squeezed the trigger. The bullet flew, and in an instant, it was over. The man's body crumpled to the ground like a puppet whose strings had been cut, a single bullet hole between his eyes.

"Jesus, Ember," Tommy muttered, his voice low, almost disbelieving. His gaze was locked on the man I'd just killed. I thought I saw something like pride in his eyes for a moment, but there wasn't time to dwell on it.

Chapter 22

Before I could respond, two more men turned towards us, their guns raised, ready to end me. My heart hammered against my chest, but I didn't falter. Planting my feet, I squared my shoulders and aimed, my grip firm on the gun. I fired two shots, rapid and precise, each finding its mark. They dropped, lifeless before they could pull their triggers.

"Ember," Tommy's voice came again, but now there was an edge of concern beneath the awe. He rose from his cover and stood beside me; his gun raised as he scanned the room for any remaining threats.

But before either of us could move, a team of armed men flooded in from the kitchen, their weapons at the ready. I tensed, finger hovering over the trigger, but Tommy's hand was suddenly on mine, gently lowering the gun. His men. We were safe, for now.

Then, like a whirlwind, Jax, Declan, and Knox stormed into the room. Knox reached me first, barreling through the chaos like a freight train, his chest heaving with exertion. He was barely dressed, wearing only grey sweats, and in each hand, he clutched a gleaming meat cleaver. His wild eyes scanned me with desperation before he pulled me into a crushing embrace.

"Fuck, shit, Ember, you okay?" His voice was frantic as he dropped the knives, and then his hands roamed over my body, searching for any sign of injury. The intensity of his concern overwhelmed me, momentarily silencing the chaos around us.

"I'm okay, Knox," I managed, though my voice was shaky. My body still buzzed with adrenaline, my heart refusing to slow.

Jax arrived next, his blue eyes sharp and filled with worry and fury. He cupped my face, his thumbs brushing my cheeks, grounding me. "You're not hurt?" he asked urgently, his voice tight with barely contained emotion.

"I'm fine," I whispered, though the tremor in my voice betrayed me. The reality of what had just happened was sinking in, and my hands started shaking.

Meanwhile, Declan was already in Tommy's face, his voice low and dangerous. "What the fuck happened?" he demanded, his eyes burning with fury.

"The Russians ambushed us," Tommy growled, his green eyes flashing with anger. "They're not going to stop."

Knox's arms tightened protectively around me, his body trembling slightly with the force of his emotions. I could feel the frantic beat of his heart as it pulsed through his chest, the erratic rhythm matching the storm brewing behind his wild eyes. His concern was a tangible force, wrapping around me as fiercely as his embrace. I reached up, my hands gently cupping his face, pulling him back to the present, back to me.

"Hey, I'm okay, big guy," I murmured, my voice steady despite the whirlwind of emotions. "I'm okay, I promise."

His intense gaze softened as he looked down at me, the madness that so often gleamed in his eyes momentarily replaced with something rawer, deeper. In that moment, the world outside of us faded, and all that remained was the undeniable bond between us—a connection forged not just in lust but in something far more dangerous.

Knox's massive frame seemed to shelter me from everything. His warmth and the sheer size of him offered a strange comfort, a reassurance that, as long as I was in his arms,

Chapter 22

nothing could touch me. His breath ghosted across my skin as he leaned in, his lips brushing my ear.

"Ember," he whispered, his voice barely more than a growl. "I can't lose you. I won't survive it."

I exhaled softly, brushing my thumb over his cheek. "You're not going to lose me, Knox. I'm here, and I'm not going anywhere."

The tension in his body eased slightly at my words, but there was still an underlying edge, a darkness simmering beneath the surface that I knew was never far from exploding. Tommy's sharp voice cut through the moment, dragging us back to reality.

"Let's get out of here," Tommy commanded, his tone clipped as he strode towards us. "The clean-up crew is on their way, and our police contacts will act like nothing happened. This place will be spotless by morning."

I opened my mouth to object, but before I could get a word out, Knox scooped me up, cradling me against his chest as if I weighed nothing. My protest died in my throat as I wriggled in his grasp, but he held me tight, refusing to let go.

"Ember," he warned, his voice low and laced with a familiar edge of insanity. "If you don't let me carry you, I'll end up gassing this entire restaurant and posing the bodies like mannequins in Pompeii. Don't test me."

His words sent a cold shiver down my spine, reminding me of who Knox was beneath the tenderness—the same man who had no qualms about playing surgeon with living flesh, a psychopathic force of nature who kept his madness just barely restrained.

I sighed in resignation, my body still in his arms as I

looked up at him. "All right, all right," I whispered, my defiance ebbing away as I relented. I wasn't afraid of him, but I knew better than to push when his mind was teetering on the edge.

A low growl of satisfaction rumbled from Knox's chest as he held me tighter. "Good," he murmured, his grip firm but oddly comforting. There was something unspoken in how he carried me, primal and possessive, as if I was a precious thing he couldn't bear to lose.

Tommy shot Knox a knowing glance before leading out of the restaurant. I felt strangely safe—safe in the arms of a killer who would burn the world down just to keep me alive.

The cold London air kissed my cheeks as we finally pulled into the penthouse garage. Knox cradled me in his massive arms, his body tense as if he feared letting me go would invite disaster. Even though I felt ridiculous being squished into the car seat while he fussed over me, I let it slide. He was on edge, more protective than ever, and I wasn't about to fight him on it.

"Easy, big guy," I murmured, threading my fingers through his thick brown hair as he carried me inside. His green eyes met mine, softening for a moment at my touch before he refocused on our destination. With every step, the tension in his muscles coiled tighter, a silent promise that he wouldn't let anything happen to me. We entered the dining room where Tommy, Jax, and Declan were already seated, their eyes immediately tracking our entrance.

Jax's blue eyes sparkled with amusement as Knox carried

Chapter 22

me in like a delicate treasure, his lips quirking into a small smile. I shot him an exaggerated eye roll before Knox finally set me on his lap. His large, muscular arm wrapped securely around my waist, anchoring me to his solid frame while his free hand roamed over my body, checking for injuries. I knew he wasn't trying to be handsy, but the warmth and intensity of his touch had my heart racing, and I had to bite my lip to keep a moan from slipping out. His fingers trailed over my skin with the same precision and care as a doctor—well, a deranged one.

"All right, let's go over everything," Tommy said, his deep voice authoritative and commanding. After all, he was the head of the Aces Gang, and in moments like this, it showed. The room seemed to darken with the weight of his words as he recounted the chaos of earlier, the moment I'd taken out three Russians with deadly precision. My heart raced, adrenaline still pumping through my veins as I relived the scene in my head—the sharp crack of gunfire, the quick reflex, the cold focus.

Declan and Jax's eyes burned into me, their identical piercing blue gazes searing with disbelief and admiration. The intensity of their attention made my skin prickle.

"Ember," Jax's voice dripped with incredulity. "I knew you could shoot, but I didn't know you were that good."

I shrugged, forcing nonchalance, though the memories of my past stirred uneasily within me. "Well," I said, swallowing the tightness in my throat, "my dad taught me to shoot." The words tasted bittersweet as they left my lips, a reminder of the world I'd tried to leave behind.

Tommy, ever observant, leaned forward, curiosity sharp

in his green eyes. "Why did your dad teach you to shoot?" His voice was laced with genuine interest, his attention entirely on me now.

For a moment, I hesitated. The dark memories that had haunted me for years scratched at the edges of my mind. Part of me wanted to let it all out, to share the burden of those painful days, but another part feared what they might think—feared their judgment. Still, as I looked into their expectant faces, I realized that if anyone could handle the truth, it was them. They already lived in a world not far from where I came from.

Taking a deep breath, I began. "All right," I said, my voice steady despite the storm brewing inside me. "I was born into one of Australia's most notorious motorcycle clubs. My father was the president, and my mom, well, she was his old lady." I let out a soft, almost bitter laugh at the term, the weight of it pressing down on me. "They raised me in that world—teaching me to fight, to survive. MMA, guns, you name it, I learned it." A faint smile tugged at the corners of my mouth as I remembered my dad, his face beaming with pride whenever I hit a target dead center or pulled off a flawless takedown. "By the time I was seven, I could shoot like a pro, well that was until Mercy came along. My dad used to call me his natural."

The room fell into an almost eerie silence, their eyes never leaving me as I continued, drawing them into the darkest parts of my past. "When I was twelve," I started, my voice growing quieter, "a rival group attacked our compound. They wanted my father dead over some drug deal gone wrong. They didn't like his selling to the wrong

Chapter 22

people and wanted him to stop. The whole place turned into a war zone."

I paused, the sharp image of that day flashing through my mind. The sounds of gunfire, the screams, the chaos. "My father... he was shot right in front of me," I swallowed, my voice tightening as the memory washed over me. "He died right there, and they took me. For two weeks, I was tied up and..." My breath hitched, but I pushed forward. Knox's arms tightened around my waist, a silent promise of comfort and protection as I laid bare the darkest parts of my past. His touch, grounding yet tender, kept me anchored in the present while I delved into memories that still haunted me.

"For two weeks, I was trapped in their clubhouse," I said, my voice shaky but determined. "Until Michael, our vice president, came to rescue me. After my father's death, the club raised me and took care of my mother and me. A year later, she got cancer, and Michael took over as president. His son became the new vice president, and they ensured I was never left wanting."

I paused, swallowing the lump in my throat, trying to steady my breath. Knox's hand moved soothingly up my arm, his silent support giving me the strength to continue.

"My mother died when I was seventeen," I continued, voice soft but unwavering. "I stayed at the compound for another year before I left. I moved here, to London, two years ago."

The room was heavy with silence. Jax's mouth hung slightly open, shock and something like admiration flickering in his blue eyes. Declan's gaze softened, a new understanding settling into his usually guarded expression.

Tommy nodded, accepting my past as part of me without judgment.

"Okay," Tommy said after a long moment, his voice cutting through the tension. "Let's get some rest. Tomorrow, we'll figure out what to do about the Russians."

His words seemed to release the air from the room, a collective exhale of exhaustion. We all needed sleep, and our bodies and minds were worn from the day's events.

Tommy's eyes flicked to me, his expression unreadable. "You're staying in my bed tonight," he declared, his tone leaving no room for argument as he extended his hand to me. But before I could move, Knox's grip tightened around me, his protective instincts flaring up like wildfire.

I twisted in Knox's arms, gently touching his chest. "It's okay, big guy," I reassured him softly. I'll come to find you when I wake up, all right?"

Knox's jaw clenched, his reluctance palpable. His hands still gripped me like he was afraid to let go.

"Please," I whispered, gently touching his cheek. I felt the warmth of his skin under my fingers. "I'm fine."

He grumbled something under his breath, his dark eyes filled with hesitation. I sighed softly, pulling away from him. Standing, I stripped down to my bra and underwear, letting the cool air kiss my skin as I stood before him, vulnerable yet firm. Turning slowly, I gave him a full view of my body, letting him see that I was unharmed.

"See?" I said quietly, holding out my hand to him. "I'm okay, Knox. I promise. Let me go with Tommy, and I'll come to find you later, all right?"

Knox's Adam's apple bobbed as he swallowed hard, his

Chapter 22

eyes dark and conflicted. But eventually, he nodded, his grip on me loosening.

I turned toward Tommy, who stood with one hand outstretched, waiting for me. His expression softened, his green eyes watching me with a strange mix of admiration and control.

"This way, baby," Tommy said, his voice low, as he guided me out of the room.

As we walked down the dimly lit hallway, the weight of Knox's gaze lingered on my back. The air was thick with the unspoken emotions that clung to the night, and my heart raced in anticipation of what was to come.

"Your room's this way?" I asked, breaking the silence that had settled between us. My voice sounded too loud, too fragile in the stillness.

Tommy nodded, leading me down the hall until we reached a door. It looked like any other door in the penthouse, but as it creaked open, I knew this room held something different.

Darkness swallowed us as I stepped inside. The room was stark, almost devoid of life. Shadows clung to the walls, and the minimalist decor gave it a cold, distant feel. This wasn't a place meant for rest but a place for retreat.

"Your office is cozier than this," I remarked, my voice breaking the quiet as I glanced around the barren space. You really should have the fanciest room in the house. A bedroom should be where you recharge, decompress, and relax."

Tommy's deep chuckle rumbled through the room. "I sleep in here," he said, his voice gruff. "That's it. I don't need fancy."

He walked over to me, his hands finding my hips, pulling me close. His body pressed against mine, firm, and my heart skipped a beat at the sensation of his hardness against my belly. His green eyes bore into mine, filled with a mix of desire and something deeper, something darker.

"You're the first woman ever to step in here," he confessed, his voice low and rough. "I usually take my whores to my office."

A sharp laugh escaped me, though his words made my pulse quicken. "Am I just another one of your whores, then?"

His lips descended on mine before I could say anything more, kissing me with a hunger that left me breathless. His kiss was deep and possessive, claiming me in a way that left no room for doubt. When he finally pulled back, his eyes locked onto mine, and the intensity in his gaze sent a shiver down my spine.

"No," he growled, his voice thick with emotion. "You're not a whore. You're ours—Jax was right. You're our queen. And I intend to put you on that throne if you want it."

My breath hitched, my heart pounding as Tommy's words echoed in my mind. Queen. It was a title that weighed heavily with power, responsibility, and trust.

Smiling softly, I wrapped my arms around his neck and pulled him into another deep kiss. The heat between us grew as our lips melded together, a mix of passion and something more profound. This was the moment—the turning point. I had to either accept or reject what they offered me.

"Make me your queen," I whispered against his lips, my voice laced with a need mirrored his.

The dim lighting cast a soft glow over Tommy's face,

Chapter 22

accentuating the sharp lines of his jaw and the intensity of his gaze. He began walking us backward, our lips never parting as he guided me toward the bed. The scent of his cologne mingled with the lingering traces of gunpowder on his clothes, a delicious combination that only heightened the moment. It was as if the world outside ceased to exist, leaving nothing but us lost in each other's presence.

His legs hit the edge of the bed, and with a swift motion, he spun us around. My legs brushed the sheets as he gently lowered me onto the bed, his body hovering over mine. His eyes, dark with lust and emotion, locked onto mine. Deep like moss after rain.

"Ember," he murmured, his voice gravelly, filled with both desire and the weight of the promise he was about to make. "If we do this, you're ours. You'll belong to us four and only us. You can't touch another, and neither will we. You'll take on the role of queen, and once you do, there's no going back."

His vulnerability hung in the air, just beneath his commanding presence. It wasn't just about possession—it was about trust. It was about loyalty, commitment, and love. The way his voice softened and his hand gently caressed my cheek told me that this was more than a declaration—it was a plea.

I stared up at him, my heart racing, feeling the weight of his devotion. This wasn't a decision to be taken lightly. I could feel the gravity of the moment, the choice that would bind me to these men in a way deeper than anything I'd ever experienced. It was a choice that could either elevate me to a place of unshakable happiness or leave me vulnerable, shattered by the weight of the expectations.

But as I searched his face, I saw the unspoken promise in his eyes—the promise of unwavering loyalty, protection, and a love that would consume me in the best way possible. And in that moment, with my heart full and my mind clear, I knew what I wanted.

"Yes, Tommy," I whispered, my voice trembling but steady with conviction. "I'll belong to you all and only you."

A slow smile spread across his lips, his eyes darkening with a fierce possessiveness. His mouth found mine again, kissing me with a passion that seared into my soul as if sealing the pact we had just made. Every brush of his lips, every touch of his hand, carried a promise of devotion, desire, and a future bound by the most profound connection I'd ever known.

23

TOMMY PERCIVAL

The realization hit me like a freight train: Emily was the one. Not just my girl, but our girl—the inevitable Queen of the Aces. It wasn't the quiet moments we shared over dinner that sealed it, though those moments deepened my certainty. No, it was long before we ever stepped foot in that restaurant. The way she carried herself, the way she handled Jax's psychotic tendencies, soothed Declan's overprotectiveness, and even softened Knox's unrelenting bloodlust—it was all part of the larger truth I'd been avoiding for too long.

Sitting across from her, sharing more than just food, I realized I couldn't deny it any longer. The ease with which she navigated all of us, her grace and resilience, made me fall harder. She wasn't afraid of the darkness that surrounded us. Hell, she embraced it, just like we did. A strength in her, fierce and unyielding, demanded respect. And more than that, it demanded love. My love.

I'd spent weeks weighing the pros and cons, examining

every angle of a future with her. I tried to poke holes in it and find something that would make me hesitate. But every time I circled back, there was nothing. No reason to hold back, no downside, other than the constant knot of fear in my chest for our safety. Yet tonight, after seeing her take down those Russians without hesitation, I knew she could hold her own. She wasn't just capable—she was unstoppable.

And now, here she was, in my arms, dressed in nothing but her panties and bra. The air between us crackled with tension, thick with desire, and I could not resist the pull. Her kisses were intoxicating, leaving me aching for more, each touch making me lose myself in the heat. With one swift motion, I unclasped her bra, and the sight of her bare chest stole the breath from my lungs.

Her soft, perfect skin pressed against me, and I latched onto her nipple with my teeth, earning a sharp hiss from Ember's lips. The sound sent a surge of heat through me, my hunger for her growing by the second. Her back arched, bending in a way that made her body look like something sculpted out of a dream. I traced my teeth over her nipples, teasing her with just the right amount of pressure before following the trail with my tongue. Her moans were quiet but reverberated through me, low and gentle like music meant only for my ears.

I laid her down, her body splayed out like the most precious gift, and all I wanted at that moment was to worship her. My lips trailed a path down the smooth plane of her stomach, my fingers hooking the sides of her panties and sliding them down with efficiency. Every inch of her skin felt like heaven under my touch, but it was the intoxicating scent

Chapter 23

of her arousal that captivated me most, leaving me completely entranced.

I hovered over her, drinking in the sight of her—the rise and fall of her chest, the flush on her cheeks, the way her eyes darkened with desire. She was mine. Ours. The Queen of our dark kingdom, and I intended to show her how much that meant.

My tongue explored further, and Ember started to squirm beneath me, her body responding to every movement as if she had been waiting for this moment for an eternity. The taste of her arousal flooded my senses, sweet and intoxicating, sending a shiver of pleasure through me. She parted her legs wider, inviting me deeper into her warmth, her fingers tangling in the loose strands of my hair. With a gentle but insistent grip, she guided me to where she needed me most, and I was more than happy to oblige.

The moment my tongue found her swollen bundle of nerves, she was done for. Ember's body trembled as I lavished attention on her clit, circling and flicking it until I could feel her climbing toward the edge of release. Her breath hitched, and her thighs clenched around my head, her entire body arching off the bed. Then, with a guttural scream that echoed through the penthouse like a siren's call, she shattered.

Her orgasm crashed over her like a tidal wave, her legs quivering uncontrollably as she rode the waves of pleasure. The sound of her pleasure, the taste of her on my tongue, was enough to make me crave more—to show her just how thoroughly we, the four of us, could worship her in one night. And it was only the beginning.

I pulled myself up, my face hovering above hers, and looked into her dazed, half-lidded eyes. Her chest rose and fell rapidly, a faint smile tugging at her lips as she pulled me closer with a hand at the back of my neck. Her mouth found the side of my neck, leaving a trail of soft kisses that sent electricity coursing through me. The heat grew as her lips moved teasingly down, her breath hot against my skin.

I groaned softly, my desire for her spiraling out of control as her fingers traced delicate patterns across my chest. Each touch awakened something deeper inside me, something primal, something that craved to possess her completely.

I pulled back, quickly stripping off my clothes. My fingers fumbled in their haste—buttons were undone, the belt yanked free, pants and shirt discarded until I stood before her naked, my heart pounding in my chest.

"Tommy..." Her voice was a whisper, but it carried a weight that sent shivers down my spine. Her dark brown eyes roamed over me, taking in every inch of my body, her gaze lingering on the tattoos that marked my skin with stories of my past. She sat up slightly, propping herself on her elbows, and reached out to trace her fingers over the inked designs.

"Turn around," she commanded softly, twirling her finger in the air. There was no hesitation in her voice, no room for argument, and I obeyed without question.

As I turned, the tattoo on my back appeared—a giant skull wearing a crown, surrounded by four ace cards. It was a symbol of my leadership in the Ace Gang, a constant reminder of the power I held. But under Ember's gaze, all

Chapter 23

that power seemed to melt away, leaving me vulnerable in a way I had never felt before.

"You're beautiful," she murmured, her fingers trailing down my back, sending a shudder through me. Her words were sincere, but momentarily, I felt something unfamiliar—a sense of being indeed seen.

I turned back to face her, my desire for her burning hotter. "Ember..." My voice cracked as I spoke her name, the walls I had spent years constructing crumbling under the weight of her stare.

I leaned over her, my hand instinctively finding her breast, teasing the hardened peak of her nipple between my fingers. The sound of her soft moan spurred me on, my lips capturing hers in a deep, searing kiss. The taste of her mouth was intoxicating, and I lost myself in her, craving more with every second.

As if sensing my need, she parted her legs, allowing me access to her wet, waiting heat. My heart pounded as I positioned myself at her entrance, the warmth of her body drawing me in. Slowly, I slid into her, her wetness enveloping me in a way that felt almost sacred like we were two parts of a whole coming together perfectly.

"God, Ember," I groaned, my voice thick with emotion. "You have no idea what you do to me."

I began to move slowly at first, savoring the feel of her body around mine. Each thrust sent sparks of pleasure through me, her tight cunt gripping me as if she never wanted to let go. The room was cool, but her body was fire, every inch of her igniting something deep within me.

"Tommy," she moaned, her voice breathless with need as

she arched her back, urging me deeper. Her eyes locked onto mine, filled with a mixture of desire and something more—something more profound.

"Ember," I whispered her name like a prayer, my fingers reaching between us to find her clit. I rubbed it gently, in rhythm with my thrusts, and her body responded instantly. She moaned louder, her cunt tightening around me, pulling me deeper into her warmth.

"Harder, Tommy," she panted, her voice desperate. "Please."

I obliged, increasing the pace of my thrusts, my body crashing against hers with a force that made the bed shake. Her nails raked down my back, and the combination of pain and pleasure only drove me closer to the edge. Her pussy clenched around me, signaling she was close, and I moved my fingers faster, determined to send her over the edge once more.

"God, Tommy," she gasped, trembling beneath me. "I'm..."

Before she could finish, her orgasm hit, and I felt her clamp down around me, her body shuddering with the intensity of her release. Her moans filled the room, and the sight of her falling apart beneath me sent me spiraling into my climax.

As she milked me of every drop, I remained inside her, unable to bear the thought of separating from her. At that moment, I knew she was mine—ours. And there was no going back.

24

EMBER DANG

I was curled up naked in Tommy's bed, my head resting on his broad chest, the steady rise and fall of his breathing soothing me. My fingers traced the intricate patterns of his tattoos, the lines telling stories etched on his skin—stories I was only beginning to understand.

"Ember," Tommy's deep voice broke the silence, its timbre rich and velvety against my ear. His breath was warm, sending a shiver down my spine. There's something I need... well... want to tell you."

I looked up at him, meeting his emerald-green eyes, darker than usual, shadowed by something I couldn't yet name. The tension in his jaw and the way his fingers tightened slightly around my waist signaled that what he was about to say wasn't easy for him. I could feel its weight before he even spoke.

"Tommy, you can tell me anything," I whispered, brushing his disheveled hair from his forehead. His face, usually so composed, was different now—vulnerable in a way I'd never seen before. My heart tightened in my chest.

He hesitated, his eyes flickering as if searching for the right words. When he spoke again, his voice was thick with emotion. "My ex-wife... she was Russian. Part of the Russian mafia."

I stilled, my fingers pausing their gentle tracing along the snake tattoo coiled around his bicep. He had never mentioned her before, and now I understood why. The pain in his voice was palpable, cutting through the room's quiet.

"I married her knowing full well who she was, what she was involved in," he continued, his voice growing softer, more haunted. "But I loved her, Ember. I loved her so deeply that I thought it didn't matter. I could handle it."

He swallowed hard, and I could see the struggle in his eyes. The walls he'd built so carefully to protect himself crumbled, and he told me what lay beneath. I felt the weight of his words settle over me, and my heart ached for him.

"Her name was Natasha," he said, barely above a whisper now. "And she used me. She used me just like she used everyone else in her world."

The sorrow in his voice made my chest tighten, and I couldn't help but reach up to touch his face, my fingers gently brushing along his jaw. He flinched slightly as if not used to its softness. His life had been hard for someone who had once believed in love.

"Tommy..." I whispered, my voice breaking as I felt his pain ripple through me. "I'm so sorry."

His eyes, filled with sadness and resolve, met mine. "You don't need to apologize," he murmured, his voice steadier

Chapter 24

now, though the rawness still lingered. "It's in the past. But I wanted you to understand why I've been like I am. Why I've pushed people away."

The room, bathed in the dim glow of the moonlight, felt heavy with the secrets he had carried for so long. I saw the man beneath the façade—the one who had been scarred by betrayal, the one who had trusted the wrong person and had paid dearly for it.

"When I married Natasha," he began, his voice low and tentative. I thought it would bridge the gap between our gangs. I wanted to create an alliance, something substantial, something lasting." He let out a bitter chuckle, devoid of joy. "I thought love could conquer all—even hatred, even blood feuds."

His words hung in the air like smoke, thick and impossible to escape. It seemed almost impossible that someone like Tommy, a tough and guarded man, had once held onto such hope. But hearing him admit it made him feel more accurate, more human.

"Did it work?" I asked quietly, even though I already knew the answer.

He laughed again, this time more bitter than before. "No," he said, shaking his head. "For two years, I tried. But the Russians were biding their time. Playing games. Making promises they never intended to keep. All the while, they were working their angles."

I could hear the frustration, the anger still simmering beneath the surface. I watched as the memories of those years flashed in his eyes—the deals, the betrayals, the constant tension of being pulled in two directions. He had been torn between love and loyalty, and both had cost him.

"They wanted control," he continued, his voice tight. "They wanted to run part of the city, and I refused. I've worked hard to build what I have and wasn't about to let them tear it down."

I could see the fire in his eyes now, the fierce protectiveness that drove him to keep his empire intact, no matter the cost. It was the same protectiveness I had seen in him tonight, the same fire that made him who he was. And yet, beneath it all, a man had once believed in love. A man who had been burned by it.

Without thinking, I reached for his hand, squeezing it gently.

"Natasha..." Tommy's voice wavered, his grip tightening on my hand as if he were holding on to a lifeline. "She kept pushing, day after day, trying to convince me to give in. To let them—let the Russians—have a piece of our territory. She said it was the only way for us to move forward. She even talked about starting a family, settling down, trying to sell me this fantasy life where cutting ties with Jax and Deck was for the best."

I frowned, surprised by the mention of the twins. "Jax and Deck?" I echoed, unsure of their connection to all of this.

Tommy let out a heavy sigh, his emerald eyes clouding with emotion. "Years ago, I found them living on the streets, surviving by selling drugs. They were just kids, only 15. One of the foster homes they'd been placed in didn't give a damn about them, left them to rot." His voice softened with affec-

Chapter 24

tion, something rare for Tommy. "I took them in. I treated them like my own sons."

"Tommy," I whispered, my heart swelling at the realization. "You saved them."

He shook his head, releasing my hand to run his fingers through his disheveled hair. "Maybe," he said, his voice thick with doubt. "But Natasha... she wanted me to give them up. She saw them as nothing but dead weight, a liability." The haunted look in his eyes deepened. "She knew how much they meant to me and used that attachment against me."

Anger flared in my chest, hot and sharp, as Tommy's words sank in. Natasha hadn't just been cruel; she had been manipulative and calculating. "She wanted you to cut ties with your family," I said, disbelief and fury lacing my words.

"Yeah," Tommy admitted, a bitter edge in his voice. "She tried to convince me that they were holding me back, that if I let them go, we could build something better. She didn't understand—Jax and Deck weren't just part of the business. They were part of me. They were my family."

The weight of his love for the twins pressed on my heart. The man who ran this ruthless empire, the one who had the power to take down anyone who crossed him, was the same man who had opened his home and heart to two broken boys. It was beautiful, and it hurt to think that Natasha had tried to twist that love into something ugly.

"Natasha saw my attachment as weakness," Tommy continued, his voice cracking under the strain of reliving the betrayal. "She arranged for the compound to be ambushed, hoping to have the twins killed."

"Tommy..." I breathed, horror twisting my stomach. How

could anyone be that cold, that heartless? How could the woman he loved have betrayed him so profoundly?

He clenched his jaw, his eyes burning with the fire of old wounds. "Once I realized what she had done and knew she'd set it all up, there was no turning back." His voice dropped to a deadly whisper. "I shot her. Right between the eyes, Ember. I killed her to save Jax and Deck."

His confession, raw and brutal, hung heavy in the air. His words were laced with pain, but they were also final. His tone had no regret, only a chilling sense of resolve. And instead of recoiling from him, instead of feeling fear, all I felt was a fierce need to protect him. To show him he wasn't alone.

"Tommy," I whispered, my hand touching his cheek, forcing him to meet my gaze. His eyes were dark and tormented, and I wanted nothing more than to erase the pain that lingered there. You did what you had to do. You saved your family. You are human, and sometimes that means making impossible choices."

He leaned into my touch, closing his eyes for a brief moment before continuing. "Natasha never saw Knox coming. She thought she had everything under control."

I frowned, confused. "Knox? How does he fit into all of this?"

Tommy's expression grew darker, his gaze distant as he recounted the events of that fateful day. "Yeah, Knox," he murmured. "Natasha had no idea I'd called him in that day. He showed up at the compound for a completely different reason, but when he got there... he noticed something wasn't right."

Chapter 24

"What wasn't right?" I asked, leaning in closer.

"Too many unfamiliar faces. Too many Russians hanging around the compound. Knox, being Knox, sensed something was off immediately. He didn't wait for confirmation—he just started eliminating them."

My breath caught in my throat as I imagined Knox, cleaver in hand, slicing through enemies like a whirlwind. "He took them down?" I asked, awe creeping into my voice.

"Yeah," Tommy said, nodding. "He cut through a good number of them before they even had a chance to storm the place. Knox... he's ruthless when protecting what's his."

"Jesus," I muttered, picturing Knox's ferocity. I'd known he was capable of violence, but hearing about him taking down an entire group of Russians on his own—was terrifying, and yet, I admired him for it.

Tommy's voice softened, growing more reflective. "Knox warned me. He knew something was off, and that's when everything clicked. I realized Natasha had set me up and was trying to destroy everything I cared about. She would have killed Jax and Deck to get what she wanted."

My heart ached as I looked into Tommy's eyes. He was holding so much inside, so much pain and guilt. "And you told them she died in the ambush," I said, understanding the burden he had carried all these years.

He nodded, his jaw tightening. "I told them she was killed in the crossfire. I pretended to grieve, pretended I'd lost someone I cared about. But I wasn't grieving her death. I was grieving my stupidity for trusting her."

"You've carried that secret all this time," I whispered, captivated by the vulnerability in his gaze.

"I don't want them to know," Tommy said, his voice firm. "They don't need to carry that burden. It's mine to bear."

The weight of his confession settled between us, a dark secret shared in the room's stillness. But instead of feeling overwhelmed, I felt honored that he trusted me with this part of himself.

"Ever since I met you, Ember, I haven't been able to get you out of my mind." His voice softened, shifting from the past to the present. "You've consumed me. You're all I think about. The moment you walked into my life, I stopped calling the whores. I didn't need them anymore. I only want you."

His words hit me like a wave, washing over me with an intensity that left me breathless.

"Tommy..." I hesitated, unsure how to respond to the flood of emotion in his voice. But before I could say anything more, he continued.

"I don't know if I can trust again," he admitted, his eyes burning with sincerity. "But I want to try with you. You've already become my queen, Ember, and I don't want anyone else. It's you, now and forever."

The vulnerability in his confession and his love's rawness left me speechless. At that moment, I realized how deeply he had let me in. This man, who had been betrayed and scarred, was opening himself up to me in a way he hadn't done for anyone else.

"Jax was right about you," Tommy added, a faint smile tugging at the corners of his lips. "From the moment he met you, he knew. You were meant to be our queen."

25

JAX STEVENSON

A few hours later, I strolled past Tommy's room, and there it was—Ember's presence, unmistakable and thick in the air. Call me crazier than people think, but I could always tell when she was nearby like her essence pulled me in. Her scent was everywhere, delicate yet overwhelming, wrapping around me. For a moment, my chest tightened with an unfamiliar sensation. I knew then that Ember had done it—she had cracked Tommy open, breached the walls he'd built around himself for so long. And instead of jealousy, I felt something else... something warm, unexpected. Gratitude.

I couldn't pinpoint when the shift occurred, when my chaotic life, filled with cold survival and even colder killings, began to feel more stable. It wasn't just Tommy. It was all of us. Ember had stepped into our world like a storm—no, not a storm, more like a slow burn. She came in, dismantled our emotional armor, and made us realize that maybe we weren't destined to walk this earth alone. She was our

Queen, no doubt, the center of us all, holding the reins to a kingdom we didn't even know we needed.

The strangest part? I was never mad about it. It didn't feel like we were losing control or submitting. It felt like balance like she was the missing piece to the chaos we had become so accustomed to. Peace settled in my chest, and for someone like me, that's a miracle. If someone had told me a few months ago that I could feel this way—content, grounded, even... loved—I would've laughed in their face. Yet, I was standing outside Tommy's door, knowing Ember was inside with him, and all I felt was joy.

A small, crooked smile played on my lips as I imagined the walls Tommy had erected for so long crumbling beneath the weight of her love. If anyone could pull him out of the pit he'd buried himself in, it was Ember. She had the kind of strength that didn't come from muscle or brute force. No, her strength came from understanding, from the way she could see right through you, strip you bare, and still offer you her heart despite all the scars she might find.

But this wasn't just about Tommy's struggles. We had more significant problems looming—those fucking Russians. I couldn't get them out of my head since tonight's ambush. The sting of it still burned under my skin, the way they slithered into our territory, into our space. It wasn't just business; it was personal. And for Tommy, I knew it ran more profound than that. It wasn't just the Russians trying to encroach on us—it was the reminder of her. Natasha.

I'd done my digging, putting pieces together like a slow-building puzzle. There was always something off about how

Chapter 25

Tommy spoke of or didn't speak of her. I had known for a while now that Natasha had betrayed him, but what I hadn't known—what I suspected—was that Tommy had killed her. I didn't need him to tell me. Hell, I wouldn't dare bring it up. Some truths are better left unspoken, and this was one of them.

Tommy had been carrying that weight for years; I could see it in his eyes and his actions. The fleeting encounters with women, the emotionless sex, the constant distancing from anyone who tried to get too close. It was like watching a man swim more profoundly into the ocean, knowing he was drowning but refusing to return to shore.

That betrayal, the one Natasha left branded on his heart, shaped every facet of his existence. She had twisted the knife, and Tommy had been bleeding ever since. His reluctance to trust, to form any genuine connection, made sense now. His casual cruelty, the way he treated women as mere distractions—it was all because of her.

But here's the thing—Tommy wasn't beyond saving. As fucked up as he was, as deeply scarred, I knew he could be pulled back from the brink. And if anyone could do it, it was Ember. She had a power none of us fully understood yet. She could look into your soul, see all the darkness, and still hold out her hand, inviting you to walk through it with her. And for Tommy, that was everything.

I followed her scent, lingering like the promise of something better, something healing. It led me to Tommy's door, and I knew what was happening on the other side. Ember was there with him, offering him a chance to finally break free from the chains he'd wrapped around himself all these years. She was the key to unlocking that part of him that he'd buried along with Natasha.

Ember wasn't just our queen because she fit the role. She was our queen because she made us stronger and better. She made Tommy a leader again, not just a man running on autopilot. She gave Knox a reason to care beyond the bloodlust that drove him, and Declan... well, she made Deck remember that there was still kindness in the world, something worth protecting.

As for me? She gave me something I never thought I'd have. Peace.

As I stood outside Tommy's door, a strange sense of hope crept over me, blending with the anticipation of everything unfolding. Ember wasn't just some temporary relief in our chaotic world—she was the key to everything. Somehow, she'd become the one to unbind us all from the chains we'd shackled ourselves with. She had only started with Tommy, but I knew it wouldn't stop. With her at our side, we could face whatever came our way.

I lingered there momentarily, listening to the faint sounds coming from inside, imagining the walls Tommy had spent years building slowly crumbling down. It was both terrifying and exhilarating to think about. But this was Ember—she had a way of weaving herself into your soul, tearing you open, and piecing you back together without you even realizing it. She was doing that for him now, like she had for the rest of us.

Finally, I turned away from the door, leaving them to their moment. I had my own business to attend to. I headed down the hallway toward the theatre room, where I was sure

Chapter 25

to find Dec and Knox. The thought of them indulging in a cheesy rom-com at Ember's insistence made me smile. She dragged us into her world, making us do things we'd never usually consider.

Pushing the door open, I found them exactly as I expected—lounging on the love seats, eyes glued to the screen. The soft glow of the movie flickered across their faces; both were too engrossed in the on-screen romance to notice me at first. I chuckled, clearing my throat to get their attention.

"Got a minute?" My voice cut through the room, laced with a sense of urgency that I knew they'd pick up on.

Dec and Knox exchanged glances, and without a word, they straightened up. They knew something serious was coming. They'd felt it too—the tension mounting since the Russians had started closing in on us. We all knew it was only a matter of time before things came to a head, and tonight's ambush made it clear that time was running out.

I sat across from them, leaning forward as I laid out the rough outline of my plan. The pieces were slowly coming together in my head, but I needed their input. We discussed strategy, possible entry points, and contingencies, breaking it down piece by piece. With Dec's tactical mind and Knox's ruthless efficiency, I knew we could pull this off. Tommy would listen—he had to. The Russians needed to be dealt with before they tore everything apart.

As we discussed the threat posed by the Russians, I couldn't help but mention that Ember was still with Tommy. A flicker of surprise crossed Knox's face while Dec's expression softened into something like hope. The idea that Ember had succeeded where others had failed—breaking through Tommy's defenses—seemed to settle over the room like a quiet revelation. The disbelief I saw in their eyes slowly shifted into something else—optimism.

It wasn't just that Ember might have a chance at saving Tommy. It was the realization that maybe, just maybe, she could save all of us. Her influence had already reached further than any of us had expected. She had changed the way we moved, the way we thought, the way we felt. And if she could break through to Tommy, the one who'd shut himself off from the world the most, then maybe there was hope for us all.

As we talked, a newfound energy filled the room. Knox leaned in, his eyes gleaming with that dangerous focus he always got before a mission, and Dec's tactical mind kicked into high gear. But beneath the planning, logistics, and strategies, something else was driving us—hope. I hope that with Ember by our side, we can find a way to rid ourselves of the Russians and secure a future we hadn't even known we wanted.

With Ember, we weren't just fighting to protect what we had. We were fighting for something more—the chance at peace, redemption, and maybe even love.

26

KNOX HOLLAND

The door creaked open that morning, and there she was—Ember. Black lace panties hugged her hips, and Tommy's button-up shirt draped loosely over her frame, just barely concealing what lay beneath. Her long black hair fell in messy waves around her shoulders, and those eyes locked onto mine with a purpose.

"Kept my promise," she purred, stepping into the room. My heart hammered at the sight of her, the storm that constantly raged inside me, calming for the first time since she'd left.

"About time," I smirked, sitting up and leaning back against the headboard as I watched her move toward me. She had that sway about her, the kind that screamed confidence—the kind that made it clear she knew exactly what she wanted. And right now, that was me.

Last night's rom-com flickered through my mind, oddly peaceful amidst the usual chaos. Declan and I had watched it on her recommendation, but it wasn't enough to distract me from the gnawing thought: the Russians. Jax laid out his plan and clarified that we had to end the threat. I'd spent my life not caring about the danger, but everything was different with Ember now in the picture. I couldn't let anything happen to her.

"Hey," she whispered, her voice soft and inviting, pulling me back from my thoughts. "Missed you."

"I missed you too," I replied, my eyes drinking in the curves of her body and the way her skin seemed to glow in the soft morning light.

She had become the hurricane that tore through everything we once knew, and now, after the storm, I could see she was the best thing that had ever happened to us. Ember wasn't just changing us—she was completing us.

"Come here," I said, opening my arms to her. She slid into bed with me without hesitation, pressing her warm, soft body against mine. I couldn't help but smile as I felt her heartbeat, the steady rhythm syncing with my own.

"Knox," she purred, her voice low and seductive, "I want you to fuck me like you're used to."

Her words were like a punch to the gut, sending a surge of heat straight through me. My chest tightened, and I felt the hunger rise—raw and all-consuming.

"Are you sure?" I asked, my voice strained as I tried to keep control over the wild desire clawing at me.

"Absolutely," Ember whispered, her gaze never leaving mine. She leaned back on the bed, arms stretched above her head. "Tie me up with slip-able knots. I'll stay as still as possible."

I moved without hesitation, the command in her voice

Chapter 26

igniting something primal in me. Reaching under the bed, I grabbed the hidden silk ties, securing her wrists to the headboard. She was secured but also able to free herself; the knots would slip free if she pulled too tightly on them. I didn't want to trigger her, but I knew she wouldn't ask me for something she didn't like.

"Stay still," I instructed, my voice dark and cold.

"Ok," she whispered, her eyes fluttering closed as she sank deeper into submission.

"Keep your eyes closed. Slow your breathing," I ordered, my voice taking on a dangerous edge.

She obeyed without question, her chest rising and falling steadily, her lashes casting delicate shadows on her flushed cheeks. I watched her—studied how a predator might study its prey, savoring the anticipation of what would come.

My fingers curled around the top of her black lace panties, tugging them down her legs slowly and deliberately. Every movement was measured and precise as if savoring the moment before the hunt. Her body trembled under my touch, but she held still, playing her part perfectly as I had commanded.

"Keep your eyes closed," I growled, my voice barely more than a whisper. She nodded, breath hitching as I spread her legs wide, revealing the evidence of Tommy's attentions from the night before.

A deep, possessive growl rumbled in my chest. She was ours, and I couldn't wait to remind her how much we all intended to worship her in the coming nights.

The storm inside me quieted, and I focused on her. My hands roamed over her body, mapping every curve and inch of skin, knowing this moment was the start of something more profound. The room seemed to hum with the tension between us, every second dragging out like an eternity, every touch a silent promise of what would come.

Ember wasn't just part of our lives anymore—she was the center and knew it. The sight of her laid out before me, her pussy still swollen and used from the night before, sent a dark thrill coursing through my veins. A twisted satisfaction settled deep in my chest, knowing I wasn't the only one who craved control over her. But now, it was my turn.

"Did he fuck you hard?" I asked, my voice dripping with venom, watching her cheeks flush a deeper shade of red. She didn't answer, but she didn't need to. The evidence of last night's passions lay right before me, wet and inviting.

"My turn," I growled, my hunger roaring to life as her breath hitched. The delicate balance between anticipation and fear played out in her rapid exhales. My hand gripped her thigh, nails biting into her flesh as I leaned in, savoring the moment before I claimed what was mine.

Her body trembled ever so slightly beneath me, excitement and fear mixing in a cocktail of submission. The power I held over her was intoxicating, a high I didn't ever want to come down from.

I pushed my fingers into her folds, slow and deliberate, grazing her clit as I passed. Ember's moan slipped through her lips, soft but filled with need. I leaned in closer, whispering darkly, "Shhh."

She bit her lip, fighting to contain herself. My fingers plunged deeper into her cunt, watching her swallow them up to my knuckles. A wicked thought flashed across my

Chapter 26

mind: could I get her wet enough to take my entire fist? The depravity of the idea spurred me on, my need for her growing unbearable.

I crawled up between her legs, the sight of her exposed and ready driving me to the brink. Grasping my dick, I guided myself into her, her wet heat welcoming me with a sensation so overwhelming it stole my breath. She was still full of Tommy's cum, and the thought twisted something primal inside me, exciting me in ways I hadn't anticipated.

I imagined all four of us fucking her, filling her up until she was walking around with our cum dripping down her thighs. The image was so filthy, so perfect, it sent a pulse of pleasure through me.

I thrust in and out of her, watching as she struggled to maintain her composure. Her face contorted with the effort, but the pleasure was too much for her to keep still. I didn't care—I loved seeing her come undone, knowing I was the one to push her past her limits.

Needing more control, I sat up, kneeling between her legs. "You're mine," I growled, gripping her hips with a bruising force. I shoved her knees to her chest, angling myself deeper into her. My eyes locked onto the sight of my dick disappearing into her over and over, slick with her arousal.

The sound of her wetness echoed around the room, a twisted symphony of lust and dominance. My blood boiled as I pounded into her, my body drenched in sweat as I maintained the brutal pace.

"Take it," I snarled, watching her body beneath me, her breath coming in ragged gasps. Her eyes squeezed shut, wrinkles forming at the corners as she fought to keep still, to endure the pleasure building inside her.

I knew she was close. So was I. The thought of us unraveling together, two dark souls entwined in unbridled passion, pushed me closer to the edge.

"Come for me," I commanded, my voice rough with authority. "Now."

Her climax crashed through her like a tidal wave, her scream piercing the air as her body convulsed around me. "Knox!" she cried, her voice raw with release. Her pussy clenched hard around my cock, and the hot gush of her orgasm spilled over me, coating my balls as I continued to thrust into her.

"Fuck, Ember," I growled, my orgasm building like a storm inside me, ready to tear through everything in its path. "You're mine."

"Always," she panted, her chest rising and falling as she struggled to catch her breath. Our eyes met, and I saw the hunger, the need, the same dark desire that consumed me.

I thrust one last time, burying myself deep inside her as the storm inside me unleashed. My orgasm ripped through me, a roaring inferno of lust and possession. I emptied myself into her, claiming her.

"Knox," she whispered, her voice trembling as the aftershocks of her climax rippled through her body. She lay there, vulnerable and beautiful; her submission laid bare before me. She pulled hard on the silk bindings, pulled her hands free, and wrapped them around my neck, pulling me close. At that moment, she was mine, and I wasn't about to let that go.

27
DECLAN STEVENSON

I stood there, caught between sleep and wakefulness, when Ember emerged from Tommy's room. She was wearing nothing but black lace panties and Tommy's button-up shirt, which barely skimmed the tops of her thighs. Her long raven hair spilled down her back in soft waves, framing her body like a dark halo. She moved with a grace that felt almost feline, every step deliberate as if she knew the effect she had on me.

"Morning, handsome," she purred, her voice like silk. Before I could fully process her presence, she leaned in and pressed her lips to mine in a slow, lingering kiss. Her taste clung to my lips as she pulled away, leaving my thoughts scrambling to catch up.

"Good morning," I managed, though my voice betrayed the control I tried to maintain around her. Ember's brown eyes sparkled with mischief, her smile wicked as she strolled past me, her fingertips grazing my arm. The brief touch sent a jolt of electricity through me.

"No breakfast today, I made a promise to Knox. I'll see you later," she whispered, her words thick with promise. And just like that, she slipped into Knox's room, the door closing behind her with a soft click, the dark hallway swallowing her whole. I stood there, staring at the space where she'd been, her scent still hanging in the air like a ghost. My chest tightened with a mix of desire and something else—a dangerous longing that I hadn't felt in years.

I couldn't help but wonder what had happened between her and Tommy last night. Had they sorted things out? The thought of losing her now was unbearable. We had all fallen for her in ways none had expected, and I knew we wouldn't let her go without a fight. But Tommy had been distant, holding back in ways none of us fully understood. I only hoped that whatever barriers stood between them had crumbled overnight.

I moved to the kitchen, grabbed a mug, and poured myself a cup of coffee. The bitter warmth helped ground me, but my thoughts still circled Ember. The image of her, the feel of her lips against mine—like she had woven herself into my very bones.

A few moments later, Tommy strolled into the kitchen, looking as sharp as ever in his tailored suit. He grabbed a mug and poured himself a cup of coffee, his movements smooth and practiced.

"Morning," I greeted, overseeing him, trying to gauge his mood. The tension between him and Ember had been palpable lately, and I couldn't help but worry about where it might lead. Tommy was like a storm waiting to break—calm on the surface but with a fury brewing beneath.

Chapter 27

"Morning," he replied, his voice casual, but there was something different in how he carried himself today. He moved to the counter, sipped his coffee, and then glanced at me, a flicker of amusement dancing in his green eyes.

"Last night, go all right?" I asked cautiously, testing the waters.

Tommy smirked, his expression softening in a way I hadn't seen before. "I'll buy a crown for the queen today," he said, taking another sip. "Seems she's won my heart."

The relief I felt was almost overwhelming, as if a weight had been lifted from my chest. A grin tugged at my lips as I leaned back against the counter. "Good," I admitted, "Because I didn't want to give her up."

Tommy's grin widened, a touch of wickedness gleaming in his eyes, but beneath it was genuine warmth. "Oh, don't worry. We're not giving her up." His voice had an intensity, a possessiveness that matched my own.

I swirled the last of my coffee in my cup, watching the dark liquid spin into a tiny vortex.

"By the way," Tommy said, leaning against the counter more casually now, "we've got a shipment of drugs for the Irish to pick up today. You and Jax are going to oversee it."

I nodded, glancing at the clock on the wall. "What time?"

"1 pm, I think," he replied, pushing off the counter. "I'll go check." He disappeared down the hallway, leaving me alone with my thoughts.

The silence in the kitchen hung heavy, like a thick fog settling over the room, wrapping itself around my thoughts. Ember had changed everything. She wasn't just a part of our lives anymore—she was the center, the pulse, the heartbeat of this strange family we had formed. And the more time I spent with her, the more I realized how much that scared me. Not because I didn't want it—but because I did.

A FEW HOURS LATER, I WAS HUNCHED OVER THE PAPERWORK FOR today's shipment, trying to focus as my mind constantly drifted back to Ember. Her laugh, how she smelled, and how she felt when pressed against me. I tried to shake the thoughts away, but it was no use. She was a storm I couldn't escape.

I looked up just in time to see her emerge from Knox's room. Her wrists, marred by red marks, caught my eye instantly, and a flare of possessive anger rose in my chest. What the hell had they been doing?

She crossed the room toward me with that easy confidence, her hips swaying slightly. My gaze flicked back to her wrists, the marks screaming at me for attention.

"Hey," she said softly, settling into my lap like it was the most natural thing in the world. Her scent—heady, intoxicating—filled my lungs, a mixture of trouble and temptation I craved more than air.

"Hey," I replied, my voice rougher than intended. My eyes kept flicking back to her wrists.

"What are you working on?" she asked, resting her head against my chest like she belonged there.

"Shipment details," I muttered, still distracted by the red lines marring her delicate skin. She noticed my gaze and offered a smile that made my blood hot. She had this way of driving me crazy effortlessly.

Chapter 27

With a sigh, she shifted in my lap, her body fitting perfectly against mine. "I have to head home today," she said, almost regretfully. "I have a few calls to make and some builders to check in with about the compound, and the townhouse needs a visit this week to ensure it's all running smoothly. Think you could drive me?"

I swallowed hard, pressing a kiss to her forehead without thinking. Her skin was warm, flushed from whatever had gone down in Knox's room. "Of course," I murmured. My lips lingered a second longer, and I fought back the surge of protectiveness threatening to spill out. "But you might wanna put some clothes on."

She glanced down at the shirt she was wearing, laughing softly. "Good point," she said, flashing me that smile that always made my heart skip a beat.

"Wait here," I said, my voice a little rougher as I slid her off my lap. I needed a second to collect myself, so I headed to my room and grabbed a pair of black sweatpants from my drawer. "Got it," I called as I returned and handed them to her. She slipped them on without a second thought, the pants hanging loose on her hips.

"Thanks," she said, her voice softer now. She glanced at me, and the playful teasing faded momentarily, leaving something more profound in her eyes—something unspoken, lingering between us. But just as quickly, it was gone.

"Listen, Ember," I began, my heart thudding hard. "We have a shipment to oversee today. Jax and I can drop you off in about twenty minutes. Is that okay?"

"Sure," she said with a smile, though something about the look in her eyes told me she wasn't entirely present.

There was a shadow there, a heaviness she was trying to hide.

I gave her a playful tap on the rear. "Go grab your things. We're heading out soon."

Jax entered the room dressed and ready as she disappeared to gather her belongings. Ember came back just as quickly, giving him a once-over before grinning. "I think I have a thing for men in suits," she teased, making us laugh.

Within ten minutes, we descended the elevator to the parking garage, the tension between us lighter but still there. The drive to Ember's place was mainly quiet, the city traffic a dull hum around us. I watched her out of the corner of my eye as she stared out the window, lost in thought. I couldn't shake the feeling that something was pulling her away from us, and the thought sent a stab of unease through me.

Finally, we arrived. Ember unbuckled her seatbelt, leaning forward to kiss both Jax and me on the lips. "I'll see you later," she murmured, her voice soft but carrying a weight I couldn't quite place.

"Need us to pick you up?" I asked, the words coming out more protective than I intended.

She smiled, shaking her head. "No idea. I'll call you, okay?"

"Okay," I agreed, though I hated leaving her here alone.

I watched her walk into the building, the rain-slicked pavement glistening under her bare feet. She dangled her heels from her fingers, and with every step she took away from us, I felt the knot in my chest tighten.

Once she was gone, Jax finally spoke. "We need to move her in with us," he said, his voice low and steady but laced

Chapter 27

with urgency. "I'd feel much better knowing she's with one of us all the time."

I sighed, running a hand through my hair. As much as I wanted to brush off his suggestion, I knew he was right. Ember had become the center of our lives, and the thought of losing her to the chaos around us was unthinkable.

"Yeah," I said quietly, my mind racing with the possibilities. "We'll talk to her tonight."

28

EMBER DANG

The city's cold embrace greeted me as I stepped out of the car, the sharp bite of autumn air nipping at my bare feet. My heels dangled from my fingers like some forgotten accessory, giving me that *the walk of shame* look. Wearing Tommy's button-up shirt and Declan's black sweat pants, I couldn't have looked more out of place among the refined clientele of the upscale building.

Tim, the doorman, caught sight of me approaching, his face flushing as he quickly looked away. The judgment in his averted gaze didn't escape me, but I couldn't have cared less.

"Afternoon, Tim," I called, my voice laced with playful sarcasm.

"Afternoon, Miss Dang," he muttered, refusing to meet my eyes. I smirked, rolling my eyes as I strolled past him and into the building.

The soft chime of the lift signaled my ascent, the sterile walls of the elevator reflecting the image of a woman caught between two worlds. As I rode up to my floor, the quiet felt suffocating, the kind that presses in on you from all sides, leaving nothing but your thoughts to fill the space. It was a feeling I'd grown all too familiar with.

When I finally reached my door, I paused momentarily, inhaling deeply before stepping inside. The apartment was still, eerily so, the silence enveloping me like a thick shroud. Without hesitation, I made a beeline for the shower, needing to wash away the remnants of the last few hours.

The icy water hit my skin, each drop like a cold slap to the senses, but I welcomed it. As it cascaded down my back, it carried with it the weight of the night—of sweat, of cum, of sin. I leaned against the cool tiles, letting the steady stream of water drown out the noise in my head, giving me peace. In this place, I could hide from the chaos that constantly seemed to chase me.

Once the water cleared, I turned off the faucet and stepped out, shivering slightly as the cold air nipped at my damp skin. Wrapping myself in a towel, I went to the bedroom, swapping Tommy's shirt and Declan's sweats for my own—a fresh pair of gray sweatpants and an oversized t-shirt hanging loosely off my frame.

Settling at my desk, I opened my laptop, its soft glow casting shadows across the dim room. My fingers hovered over the keys before they began to move, sketching out the details of a new design. The creative process offered me a welcome escape, a way to disappear into a world of colour and texture, far removed from the complexities of my reality. Deep shades of red and green flooded the screen, each one a piece of a world I was crafting.

Just as I began to lose myself in the design's rhythm, the

Chapter 28

doorbell's sharp sound pulled me back to the present, the shrill noise slicing through the quiet like a blade.

"Who is it?" I asked through the intercom, my voice steady, though inside, I felt a knot of unease forming.

"It's me. Buzz me up." The gravelly voice on the other end made my blood run cold. Killer.

My heart stuttered, the familiar rush of adrenaline surging through me. What the hell was he doing here? The man had a way of showing up like a storm—unannounced and impossible to ignore. My hand hovered over the buzzer, shaking slightly before I pressed it, granting him access.

The clock's ticking seemed to slow as I waited by the door, each second stretching out longer than the last. My pulse quickened in my veins, my body on high alert. The knock on the door came sooner than I expected, and I hesitated before pulling it open.

There he stood—Killer, wearing faded jeans and a white shirt that barely concealed the swirling tattoos beneath. His dark, stormy gaze locked onto mine, and before I could react, he closed the distance between us, pressing his lips to mine in a bruising kiss.

"What the hell are you doing here?" I stammered, pulling back as my mind raced to catch up with what had just happened. The kiss lingered on my lips, a bittersweet reminder of a past I thought I had left behind.

"Ember," he said, his voice low and rough, "I want you to come home."

I stared at him in disbelief, struggling to reconcile the memories of the man I once knew with the imposing figure who now stood before me.

"Home?" I scoffed, folding my arms across my chest defensively. "You know damn well that place stopped being my home a long time ago."

"Things have changed, Ember," Killer insisted, his eyes pleading with me, trying to reach a part of me that had long since moved on. "You don't belong here. You belong with us, with your people."

The dim light from the hallway cast eerie shadows across Killer's face as he walked past me into my apartment, his tattoos looking even more striking against the stark white of his shirt, as I stepped in after him and closed the door behind me.

Before I could fully register what was happening, the sound of the door opening again drew our attention. Declan appeared in the doorway, his presence a sudden and welcome lifeline amidst the turmoil. His arrival brought a wave of relief, grounding me in the present and pulling me away from the shadow of my past.

"Baby, what are you doing here?" I asked, surprise and hope clashing in my voice. He held up my phone, his blue eyes flicking between me and Killer, assessing the room.

"You left this in the car," he said, his tone even though his eyes flashed with the unmistakable intensity that only Declan could wield. His gaze swept over Killer, sizing him up without saying a word.

I reached for my phone, our fingers brushing briefly, sending a spark of warmth through me. "Thank you," I breathed, grateful for the small connection amid the growing tension.

"Want to come in?" I called out, my words almost plead-

Chapter 28

ing, desperate for him to stay, to shield me from whatever this confrontation with Killer was about to become. But Declan shook his head, his jaw tight as his eyes locked with mine.

"No thanks, you look busy," he replied, clipped and distant. Then turned on his heels and walked out and down the hall to the lift. With a press of the lift button, the doors slid open then shut, and just like that, he was gone—leaving me alone with Killer once more.

The sting of Declan's retreat lingered as I closed the door, trying to shake off the rejection. My mind raced with thoughts of why Declan had left so abruptly. Did he feel threatened? Angry? Or maybe he was just irritated that I'd left my phone behind, making him come back when he had more pressing things to deal with.

With a deep breath, I turned back to Killer, who stood watching me, his presence heavy in the small room. I smiled, keeping my emotions in check as best as possible.

"Please, make yourself comfortable," I said with forced politeness as I moved toward the kitchen, hoping that making coffee would give me time to collect my thoughts. I quickly prepared two cups, my hands trembling as I stirred in the milk and sugar for Killer's—just as he used to like it.

I handed him the cup as he settled into a chair.

"Thanks, Ember," he muttered, his eyes searching mine as I sat across from him, maintaining as much distance as the space would allow. I perched on the edge of a chair, the vast distance between us reflecting the years that had passed and the canyon that had formed between who we once were and who we had become.

"Killer," I began, my voice soft but firm, "what are you doing here?"

His gaze bore into mine, his expression revealing the cracks in his tough exterior. There was a vulnerability in his eyes I hadn't seen since we were kids, running wild through the streets of our old neighborhood.

"I came to take you home, Ember," he said quietly, his words carrying the weight of a man trying to right the wrongs of his past. "Back to the compound."

My heart stuttered in my chest, the memories of that place—the club, the chaos, the violence—flooding my mind. "Why now?" I asked, my voice barely above a whisper.

"Because," he replied, leaning forward and setting his cup on the table. "I want you to be my old lady. I've loved you since we were kids, and I never stopped, not even after all this time. I thought giving you space and letting you live your life might change things, but it didn't. I can't let you go."

His words hit me like a punch to the gut. Love. The weight of his confession pressed down on me, heavy and suffocating. For so long, I'd fought to carve out a new life away from the shadows of that world, and now Killer was here, dragging me right back into it.

"Killer," I began, my throat tight with emotion. "I can't love you like that. Not anymore."

His face twisted with pain, the storm in his eyes darkening. "Ember..."

"I've moved on," I interrupted gently but firmly, "and I've found a new family now." The words sounded strange coming out of my mouth, but they were true. The love I had

Chapter 28

for Tommy, Declan, Knox, and Jax was something I never thought I'd experience, something that filled every part of me.

Killer's hand clenched into a fist, the anger and hurt swirling in his eyes as he processed my words. Before he could speak, I reached out and placed my hand on his arm, a gesture meant to calm him, to offer some semblance of comfort.

"I'm sorry," I whispered, "but my life is here now." I watched as Killers shoulders slumped.

"Let's not do this here," I quickly suggested, feeling the weight of Killer's presence pressing against the familiar walls of my apartment. Let's grab some food and talk. We've got a lot to catch up on."

Killer nodded, his rough exterior softening just slightly as he agreed. "Sounds good."

I quickly gathered my things, threw on a jacket, and slipped my phone into my pocket. Opening the door, I led the way out, eager to escape the claustrophobic air that seemed to thicken every second we stayed inside.

The steam from the coffee curled upward, bringing some warmth to my chilled hands. I had missed Killer, I missed how we laughed together. Our voices carrying through the quiet room as we lost ourselves in the memories of our shared past, as we sat at the Cafe just outside my building.

"Remember when you were ten, and we went on that school bushwalk?" Killer grinned, a wicked gleam in his eyes. "You were terrified of that spider and ran so fast you slipped down the hill, covered in mud. The teachers thought you'd shit yourself. You had to walk around with that massive stain on your pants the rest of the day!"

I groaned, burying my face in my hands at the memory. "Oh god, I'd almost blocked that out. Do you have to bring it up?"

"Absolutely," he said with a chuckle, sipping his coffee. "It's not every day I see you squirm like that."

I shook my head, laughing despite myself. No matter how much time had passed or how different our lives had become, moments like this reminded me that some things never changed. The weight of our shared history, both the good and the bad, kept us tethered. The cafe soft chatter faded into the background as we lost ourselves in the moment, but I could feel the darkness of my past trying to creep in around the edges.

Determined to keep things light, I leaned forward with a mischievous grin. "Speaking of embarrassing memories," I began, "do you remember ninth grade? You had that massive crush on Emily, and when the bus arrived, you tried to kiss her so fast you smashed your head into her nose. Gave her two black eyes!"

Killer burst into laughter, running a hand through his messy hair. "God, I'd forgotten about that! Poor Emily, she probably hated me after that. I was such a dumb kid."

"We both were," I agreed, smiling as the warmth of our laughter settled between us. We'd been through so much, yet somehow, our friendship had remained intact. It was a lifeline in the chaos that had been our lives.

As the moment softened, Killer's hand reached mine, our

Chapter 28

fingers naturally interlacing. The gesture was not romantic; it was more like comfort, the touch shared between two people who had seen the darkest parts of each other's souls and still stood by each other's side.

"Killer," I said quietly, barely above a whisper, "you know I love you, right?"

He nodded, his expression turning serious, his smile fading. "Yeah, Em, I know. But you're not in love with me?"

His words cut deep, hitting a truth I hadn't wanted to face. Once, years ago, maybe there had been the faint possibility of something more between us. But the tides of our lives had changed, and we'd been swept along in different directions. The past held memories of what could have been, but that was all they were now—memories.

"Maybe I used to think about it," I admitted softly, my voice thick with the weight of those old thoughts. "But we've both changed, Killer. Things are different now."

The café seemed to fall quieter around us, as if the city was listening to our conversation. The cold wind blew through the narrow streets outside, carrying the scents of wet stone and the Thames. The buildings outside, with their weathered Gothic facades, loomed over us like sentinels from another time, reminding me that the past never indeed left—it was always there, lingering, even as we tried to move forward.

Killer's eyes softened, and I could see the glimmer of unshed tears. He squeezed my hand, his voice low and thick with emotion. "No matter what happens, Ember, I will always be here for you. You're my best friend. That's never going to change."

My chest tightened at his words, a mixture of gratitude and sadness washing over me. I squeezed his hand in return, feeling the truth of his words settle into my heart. Killer and I had a bond that went beyond the physical; it was forged in the fires of survival, facing the darkness together and coming out the other side. We might not be meant for each other in the way some people were, but we were each other's constants, and that was enough.

"Killer," I began softly, my voice trembling as the weight of the past pressed down on me. "Before... I was taken; I might've thought about being your old lady. Maybe I could've seen us together back then." I paused, shaking my head slowly as if I could physically push away the memories that had shaped my life since. "But now... things have changed."

His eyes softened, understanding flickering in their depths, though sadness lingered just beneath. "Things have changed?" he asked, his voice gentle but laced with the sorrow that comes from years of unspoken truths.

"More than you could ever know," I whispered, glancing down at our fingers still entwined. Our bond was unspoken but strong, forged through years of pain and survival. But one thing hasn't changed... you were my first friend, Killer."

The words settled in the space between us like an anchor, weighing me down, grounding me in the here and now, while the past swirled around me like a storm. When I met his gaze, I saw the reflection of the girl I once was—a girl who had been broken, shattered by the darkness that had overtaken her life, yet somehow pieced back together. And

Chapter 28

Killer? He was the boy who had stood by me through it all, his presence the only constant in the chaos.

A tear slid down my cheek, unbidden, and I wiped it away quickly. "Thank you," I whispered, my voice breaking under the weight of emotion. Our friendship, the bond that had survived the cruel hands of time and distance, had transcended all of it—pain, loss, laughter. No matter how far we'd gone from each other, this tether had never frayed.

Killer's grip tightened ever so slightly, his thumb rubbing gentle circles against the back of my hand. The warmth of his touch was a balm, soothing the ache that had built in my chest, but I could feel the shift coming, the truth I had yet to tell him looming just on the horizon.

"Killer," I said, hesitating for a moment, the words tangled in my throat. My heart raced with trepidation. I wasn't sure how he'd take what I was about to say, but I needed to get it out. "There's something you need to know about my life here in London."

He leaned back in his chair, his brows knitting together in concern as he studied me. "What is it, Em? You know you can tell me anything."

I drew in a deep breath, trying to steady myself. "I've become involved with a group here," I admitted, my voice barely above a whisper. "They're called the Aces. It's complicated... they're complicated. But they have a lot of power, more than I realized when I first got tangled up with them." I could see the shift in his expression, the concern deepening in his eyes, and I pressed on before he could interrupt. "I'm in a relationship with all four of them. At the same time."

The admission hung heavy in the air, and my cheeks

burned with its weight. I had no idea what Killer would think. Would he judge me? Would he walk away? I braced myself for the inevitable shock, maybe even anger.

But instead, Killer's lips twitched upward, and before I knew it, he broke into a wide grin. "Four of 'em, huh?" he chuckled, shaking his head in disbelief. "You think if I head back home, I could get some of the club whores to share the old lady title too?"

The tension cracked, and I couldn't help but laugh. Of course, he'd find a way to lighten the moment, even now. That was Killer for you—able to make me laugh even when I felt like the world was crumbling around me.

"Honestly," I said, wiping a tear from my eye, "if you want more than one, go for it. Life's short, and you never know, it might just be what you need." My laughter faded into a small smile, and the weight on my chest lightened, just a little.

The conversation ebbed, and the café around us seemed to fade into the background. Outside, the cold wind swept through the streets of London, carrying with it the sound of the city's heartbeat. But inside, there was only the quiet hum of the ghosts of the children we used to be, running wild through the sun-drenched streets of Australia.

"Killer," I whispered, my voice barely audible above the soft murmur of the café. "Promise me something." He looked at me, waiting. "No matter what happens—no matter how much changes, or how far apart we get... promise me you'll never forget the bond we share."

His eyes locked onto mine, a gaze so intense it felt as if it could pierce through my very soul. There was a deep

Chapter 28

sincerity in his voice, a rare vulnerability that Killer rarely let show. "I promise, Ember. No matter what happens, you'll always have a piece of my heart. We should stay in touch more, you know? Call each other, text... I don't want to lose what we have, even if our lives have taken us in such different directions."

A bittersweet warmth filled my chest, making it hard to breathe. Looking at him now, I was reminded of everything we had survived—together, yet apart. "I'd like that, Killer," I replied, my voice soft but steady. "We've come too far to let time or distance tear us apart now. We've been through too much."

He nodded, a small smile tugging at the corner of his lips. There was an unspoken understanding between us, something that didn't need to be said out loud because we already knew it too well. Killer glanced down at his watch, the golden hands ticking away with precision, each second pulling us closer to the inevitable goodbye.

"I've got a flight out tomorrow morning," he said, his tone shifting slightly as reality began to settle in. "But I want to make the most of my time here in London."

I returned his smile, though it didn't quite reach my eyes. "You should explore the city while you're here. London's a place full of hidden treasures—if you're willing to look hard enough, she'll reveal them to you."

For a brief moment, neither of us spoke, the weight of what had been said hanging between us. Killer stood up from the table, his eyes lingering on me with a mix of affection and sadness. "I guess this is goodbye, then," he said, his voice quiet but resolute. "For now, at least."

"Goodbye, Killer," I murmured, my throat tightening with the emotion I wasn't ready to show. As we embraced one last time, I held on just a little longer than usual, as if trying to absorb all the love and comfort I could before he was gone.

With one final look, Killer turned and walked out of the café. I watched as his silhouette disappeared into the crowd, swallowed by the sea of faceless people moving in every direction.

For a moment, I stood frozen in place, caught between the memories of who we once were and the uncertainty of what we had become. Then, slowly, I gathered my things and headed back toward my apartment.

29

DECLAN STEVENSON

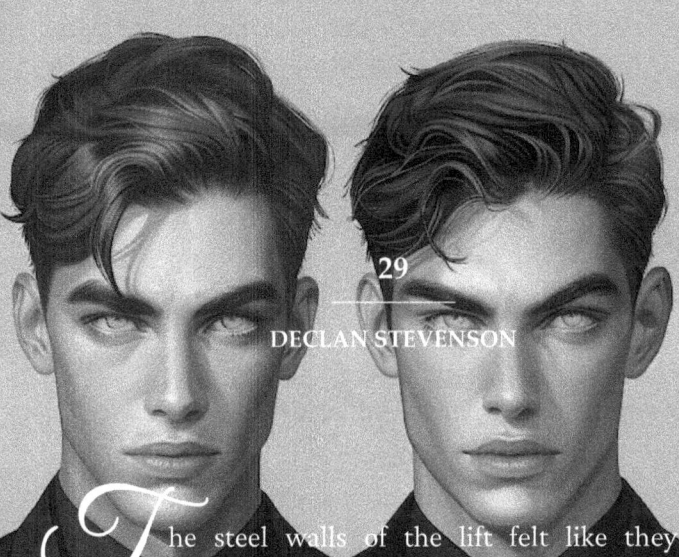

The steel walls of the lift felt like they were suffocating me, closing in as I descended to the ground floor. My pulse thrummed wildly in my throat, choking me with every beat. I could still see him—that tattooed guy standing there with Ember, too familiar and comfortable in her space like he belonged. And I didn't. The image clawed at me, tearing at something raw and unhealed deep inside.

"Fuck," I muttered, the word coming out like a growl as I squeezed my fists until my knuckles turned white. The pressure in my chest was unbearable, but it was nothing compared to the feeling of betrayal gnawing at my insides.

When the lift doors slid open with a whisper, the cold air of the lobby hit me, sharp against my skin. But even that icy bite couldn't cool the fire burning in my chest or douse the fury swirling in my gut. My feet carried me toward the car on autopilot, each step heavy, weighed down by the storm brewing inside me.

Jax was already waiting, leaning against the car with a scowl. His voice cut through the haze, tight and laced with impatience. "Declan! What the hell, man? We're late."

"I know," I grunted, yanking open the passenger door and sliding into the seat. Each breath felt too fast, too shallow, like I couldn't get enough air. My mind was still trapped in the hallway outside Ember's door, replaying how she'd let that guy in, like I didn't exist, like everything between us was nothing.

Jax started the car, his eyes flicking to me as the engine rumbled to life, breaking the silence. "You good?" he asked, his tone casual, but I could hear the edge of concern buried beneath it.

"Yeah," I lied, my throat tight. The word felt caught in my chest, scraping its way out. I wasn't good. I was far from it.

Jax's eyes narrowed, his gaze flicking between me and the road. "Doesn't look like it," he muttered, more to himself than to me, but he didn't press. He knew me too well and knew when I wasn't in the mood to talk. Still, I could feel him watching me out of the corner of his eye, waiting for me to crack, to spill whatever was eating me alive.

I stared out the window, the city blurring past in streaks of light and shadows. The buildings and the streets bled together, just a backdrop to the chaos in my head. My thoughts circled back, spiraling into a memory I tried so hard to bury.

A betrayal. Not the first time. That same damn sting. Walking into my old apartment—our apartment—and finding her tangled up with someone else, limbs twisted in the sheets that had once been ours.

Chapter 29

"Declan?" Her voice, barely a whisper, echoed in my head. I'd stood in that doorway, my heart in my throat, as I saw her tangled in someone else's arms. My blood had run cold.

"Get out," I had managed, my voice hollow, the room spinning around me.

"Please, just let me explain—"

"Get. Out." My world had crashed that night; everything I thought I knew turned to ash. I hadn't let anyone in after that, not until Ember.

And now, here I was again, standing in the rubble of my trust, that old wound tearing itself wide open, raw and unhealed despite the years. The scene replayed in my mind—the way Ember had let that guy into her apartment, the casual ease between them, the way her body language spoke of familiarity. My stomach twisted into knots, each second feeding into the anger simmering beneath the surface.

"Dec, man, you gotta tell me what's going on. You're all over the place," Jax's voice pulled me back, his usual light tone laced with concern.

"It's nothing," I bit out, the words like poison on my tongue. I wasn't ready to tell him about the man I'd seen, the tattooed guy who seemed so comfortable around Ember. I wasn't even sure what it meant, but it gnawed at me.

Jax shot me a look, his eyes scanning my face as we weaved through the busy streets of London. His hands gripped the wheel tighter, knuckles turning white. "You're a terrible liar, bro."

I clenched my jaw, biting back the urge to spill everything. We had a job to do. Drugs to move. Business first. That's how it had always been—focus on the task, shove the personal shit down deep. I couldn't afford to let my emotions derail me. Not again.

The warehouse loomed ahead, a hulking structure of rusted metal and cracked concrete. The air outside was thick with the smell of damp asphalt, gasoline, and the faintest hint of decay. As we stepped out of the car, the chill of the night settled in, wrapping around me like a vice.

Inside, the Irish were waiting, their faces sharp and hard. Eyes watched us from every corner, like predators waiting for the perfect moment to strike. Jax was in his element, his voice smooth and calculated as he led the deal, his every word precise and cold. But my mind kept drifting. I couldn't shake the image of Ember, the softness in her eyes towards that man. That look wasn't something you gave a stranger. It wasn't a look you gave someone who didn't matter.

"Declan!" Jax's voice snapped through the fog of my thoughts, sharp and impatient. "Grab the crates."

I moved mechanically, loading the heavy boxes into the truck, but their weight was nothing compared to the heaviness in my chest. It sat there, a gnawing ache I couldn't shake, twisting more profoundly every time I thought about her. I hadn't asked for much—just honesty. And now, I didn't even know if I had that.

One of the Irishmen, a skinny guy with too many tattoos and a nose crooked from being broken too many times, watched me. His gaze lingered too long, his eyes narrowing as if he could see straight through me. "Somethin' eatin' at ya, boy?" he asked, his accent thick and mocking like he knew something I didn't.

"None of your business," I snapped the edge in my voice

Chapter 29

sharper than I'd intended. His grin widened, but he raised his hands in mock surrender, backing off. The look in his eyes, that knowing glint, grated on me. Everyone could see through the cracks I desperately tried to hold together.

With the truck loaded, Jax nodded, signaling it was time to go. We climbed back into the car, and as the engine roared to life, I couldn't stop myself from reaching for my phone. I thumbed the screen, hoping—half-hoping—that maybe there'd be a message from Ember. Some explanation. Some sign. But the screen remained dark and empty, as hollow as the pit forming in my gut.

Jax didn't say anything for a while, the silence between us heavy, broken only by the engine's hum and the occasional bump of the road. But I could feel his eyes on me, studying, waiting. Finally, he spoke, his voice low but firm. "Listen, whatever this is—whatever's fucking with your head—you need to talk to her. Don't let it sit, man. Don't let it fester. I've seen what happens when you bottle it all up. You're not the same when you do that, Dec."

I nodded, but the weight of his words only made the ache in my chest grow tighter. Jax was right, of course. I'd learned the hard way what happens when you bury shit too deep. It eats at you and festers like a wound until it's too infected to heal. But even knowing that, I wasn't ready. Not yet.

The thought of talking to Ember, of confronting whatever she might tell me, twisted my insides into knots. What if she admitted it? What if she told me the worst thing I could imagine? Could I handle that? Could I handle the truth if it was another betrayal, another knife in the back? I wasn't sure.

And the uncertainty, the doubt... it was slowly killing me.

I couldn't stop replaying the scene in my head—Ember so casually letting that guy into her apartment. Who the hell was he? The way she stood with him was so comfortable; it was like a slap.

"Declan, seriously, what's going on?" Jax's voice cut through the chaos in my mind, barely audible over the low hum of the engine. His gaze flicked toward me, but I couldn't find the words to explain the storm raging inside.

"Nothing," I muttered, forcing a tight-lipped smile. It felt like lying through my teeth, but I couldn't handle it. Not now. Not yet.

I shifted my focus back to the streets outside the window, watching as the dark shapes of buildings blurred into one another. Each corner we passed only seemed to tighten the knot in my chest, like the city was closing in on me.

As soon as we pulled up to the penthouse, I barely waited for the car to come to a complete stop in the underground car park. When the tires stopped moving, I shoved the door open and stalked toward the lift, not even waiting for Jax to catch up. The rage bubbling inside me needed an outlet, and I knew exactly where I was heading—Tommy. He would understand.

My heart hammered in my chest as I stormed into the elevator and rode up in tense silence. The moment the doors opened, I stormed straight into Tommy's office, the sound of the door slamming shut behind me, startling him from whatever paperwork he'd been focused on.

"Declan?" Tommy's voice was sharp, concern etched

Chapter 29

across his face as he took in my expression, his green eyes narrowing slightly. "What's wrong?"

"Ember," I choked out, barely able to get the words past the knot in my throat. "I saw her with another man. She let him into her apartment. She said she needed to go home to work, but this guy? Big, tattooed, looked like a fucking biker." The words poured out of me in a rush, my voice raw with anger and something else, something darker, like betrayal, creeping into my veins.

Tommy raised an eyebrow, leaning back in his chair with maddening calm. He crossed his arms over his chest, watching me closely. "Are you sure he's not someone from one of her building projects? A contractor or something?"

I clenched my fists, frustration prickling under my skin. "I'm sure," I snapped, my voice harder than intended. "He wasn't just some contractor. They looked... familiar, like they had history. The way she was with him..." I trailed off, unable to finish the thought, the image of them together burning behind my eyes.

Tommy didn't flinch; his gaze was steady, and his calmness only made the storm inside me rage harder. "Ember used to belong to a motorcycle club," he reminded me, his voice as level as ever. "Maybe he's someone from her old life, still part of that world."

The logic of it should've been reassuring, but it only fanned the flames of my doubt. "I don't know," I muttered, running a hand through my hair, tugging at the roots in frustration. "It felt different. More than just some old acquaintance."

Tommy stood slowly, clearly sensing the weight of the

situation. He grabbed his jacket from the back of his chair, his movements deliberate. "Let's go find out," he said, his tone leaving no room for argument. "No use sitting here guessing. Best to get the truth straight from the source."

The suggestion sent a jolt of adrenaline through me. Finally, action. Answers. My pulse thudded hard in my throat, the sound of my blood rushing in my ears as we headed toward the elevator. The ride down was tense, the silence between us heavy with unspoken thoughts. When we reached the parking garage, I was wound so tight it felt like I would snap.

Tommy slid into the driver's seat of his car, the engine roaring to life as he floored it out of the garage. The city streaked past us in a blur, but my mind was elsewhere, fixed on Ember—on the man she'd let into her life so quickly. The image of their easy familiarity gnawed at me like a wound that wouldn't heal.

Each mile we covered felt like a lifetime, the anticipation building in my gut like a ticking bomb. The knot in my chest tightened with every minute, my stomach twisting into knots as we sped toward her street. Tommy didn't say a word, his hands gripping the wheel, his focus razor-sharp as we neared our destination.

When we finally pulled onto Ember's street, my heart leaped into my throat. I wasn't ready for this confrontation, but there was no turning back now. Tommy slowed the car as we rounded the corner and the Cafe near her building came into focus.

There he was. The guy is big, tattooed, and they sat at the window seat in the Cafe. Tommy pulled his car into a park as

Chapter 29

we sat and watched. I saw them talking, and I watched as she laughed, and smiled at him. They looked... comfortable. Familiar. The way their bodies leaned into each other and his hand reached out to brush against hers felt like a betrayal, even if I couldn't fully explain why.

"Lets go in." Tommy said as he reached for the door handle of the car.

"Wait," I whispered, my breath catching in my throat.

Tommy's gaze followed mine, his eyes narrowing as he watched. "Declan," he said softly, his voice low, "we don't know the whole story here. Just... be cautious."

But as we watched, the man reached out and covered Ember's hand. She didn't pull away. Instead, their fingers intertwined in a way that felt too intimate and close, like they shared something I didn't understand. Something I wasn't a part of.

My stomach dropped. The cold, sickening sensation swept through me like a wave, washing over everything.

"I can't... I can't fucking believe this," I muttered, my voice barely more than a whisper. The pain was sharp, immediate, like a knife twisting in my gut.

Tommy exhaled quietly beside me. After a moment, he said, "Let's head back," his voice steady but sympathetic. He knew I needed space.

A single tear slipped down my cheek, cold against my heated skin. I swiped it away angrily, trying to hold myself together. Tommy glanced at me briefly, but said nothing more, his hand tightening on the wheel as he turned the car around and drove away from the scene. Away from Ember and the man she was so comfortable with, away from the betrayal that twisted inside me like a slow-burning fire.

The streets of London passed by in a blur, the towering buildings and ancient architecture casting long shadows over us. It felt like the city was mocking me, reminding me that love was fragile in this cold, unforgiving world—too fragile for someone like me.

Tommy's voice finally broke the silence, rough and filled with regret. "Shit, Declan... I'm sorry."

"Don't," I muttered, staring out the window, my heart still in pieces. The weight of what I had seen settled deep into my bones, making breathing hard.

Tommy didn't waste any time when we pulled up to the penthouse. He fished his phone from his pocket and dialed a number. "Candy, I need you at the house," he said, his tone clipped before he hung up. He glanced at me briefly, his face unreadable, before retreating to his office.

30

TOMMY PERCIVAL

My heart dropped like a lead weight in my chest as I stared through the café window, watching Ember laugh with the man across from her. He was everything I imagined from her past—the rugged biker type, inked up and rough around the edges. The kind of guy I never envisioned her associating with. Yet, they were locked in a shared intimacy that hit me like a punch to the gut.

Beside me, Declan's expression mirrored the ache that clawed at my insides. His pain was so raw, so palpable, that it twisted the knife even deeper. Ember's betrayal wasn't just a dagger to his heart—it pierced mine too, a sharp reminder of how fragile trust could be.

I couldn't tear my eyes away. Each laugh they shared, every casual touch, felt like another layer of deception unraveling before me. Memories of her crept up, uninvited—the whispered promises, the fleeting moments when I let myself believe we were building something real. Was it all a façade?

Had she just been playing us, hiding the truth behind that damn perfect smile?

It hit me hard, harder than I cared to admit. I'd been a fool. I thought we had something solid, something real. But Ember had secrets, ones she never let us in on. My chest tightened, the realization settling like a weight I couldn't shake off. I was pissed, sure, but there was something worse beneath the anger—an overwhelming sadness. The trust, the dreams I'd begun to build, the future I thought was possible shattered like glass.

As we pulled away from the café, the betrayal sat heavy in the car, a thick silence that neither Declan nor I could break. My grip tightened on the steering wheel, the anger burning hotter with each passing second. But as that fury roiled inside me, another feeling rose to meet it—determination. I wasn't going to let this destroy me. Ember's actions wouldn't define us and wouldn't break me.

"Fuck," I muttered under my breath, reaching for my phone. Without a second thought, I dialed Candy's number. She'd always been there for quick jobs that helped me forget, even if only for a while.

"Tommy," Candy answered after the first ring, her voice carrying that familiar tone of curiosity and flirtation.

"Candy, I need you at the house," I said, my voice cold and clipped, not in the mood for pleasantries. The words felt heavy, loaded with everything I wasn't saying.

Without waiting for her response, I disconnected the call. The anger simmered just below the surface as I stepped into my office, pulling the gun from my waistband and tossing it onto the desk with a loud thud. It didn't matter how often I

Chapter 30

tried to steady myself; the betrayal kept gnawing at me, each unanswered question slicing deeper.

I sat alone in the shadows of my office, the dim light casting long, dark shadows across the room. Ember's face haunted me, her laugh, her touch—it all felt like a twisted mockery now. Why? Why had she done it? What more could she possibly need beyond what we offered her? The four of us had given her everything, hadn't we?

I couldn't stop the questions from coming, each one more suffocating than the last. Did Ember genuinely need more than what we could offer? Had we fallen short somehow, leaving her to seek comfort elsewhere? Or was this just a pattern, the same vicious cycle I'd seen before, a cruel echo of Natasha's betrayal?

The parallels between Natasha and Ember gnawed at me, dredging up memories I'd fought to bury. I thought I'd moved past it, but now it felt like history was repeating itself. Natasha had used me and twisted the knife in ways I didn't see coming. Was Ember doing the same? Was this who she was? The idea felt like poison in my veins.

I stared at the gun on the desk, feeling the weight of the past pressing down on me, and I couldn't shake the bitterness rising in my chest. How could I have let this happen again? How could someone I trusted and opened my heart to betray me like this? And what did it say about us—that we were so easily deceived that we couldn't see the truth staring us right in the face?

The silence in the room grew heavier, the weight of Ember's betrayal settling over me like a suffocating blanket. No matter how hard I tried to rationalize it, to find some explanation that made sense, I came up empty. All I knew was that my trust in her had been broken, and with it, we had started to build the fragile bonds.

But I wouldn't let it end here. I wouldn't let her actions define me or the life I had built. I had survived betrayal before, and I would survive it again. Ember might have broken my heart, but she wouldn't hurt me. Yet, amidst the turmoil of my thoughts, one chilling possibility lingered in the shadows—could Ember's betrayal be more than personal? Could it be calculated or premeditated? Was she a part of something darker, biding her time until she could dismantle everything I'd worked to build?

The thought curdled in my stomach like poison.

A soft knock at the door shattered the storm swirling inside me. "Come in," I barked, not bothering to mask my voice's frustration.

Candy entered, her long black trench coat clinging to her body, framing her in a way that would've excited me once. Her blonde hair cascaded over her shoulders, and her lips painted the deep crimson shade she knew I liked.

"Tommy," she purred, her voice sultry and teasing, as though my name was a sin she was savoring. She closed the door behind her, locking us in with the tension that simmered beneath my skin.

"Suck me off," I commanded flatly, sliding my chair back to give her access, barely sparing her a glance.

Her wicked grin spread and her hips swayed as she approached. Usually, the sight of her naked under that coat, knowing she'd come prepared precisely as I'd ordered,

Chapter 30

would've sparked a fire in me. But today, that fire was cold ash. My mind was elsewhere. It was with her.

Candy didn't seem to notice my detachment as she poured me a glass of whiskey, the amber liquid swirling like temptation in the dim light of my office. "Here you go," she whispered, pressing the glass into my hand with a practiced, seductive smile.

I took a sip, letting the warmth spread through my chest, dulling the sharp ache of betrayal, but only for a moment. It wasn't enough. Nothing was enough right now.

With slow, deliberate motions, Candy undid her belt, allowing the trench coat to fall in a pool at her feet. She stood there, fully naked, save for the pair of red heels I always liked. She sank to her knees, reaching for my belt and unbuckling it without hesitation. Her fingers slid inside, finding my dick soft and uninterested.

She started to stroke me, her touch firm and practiced, but nothing. I felt numb, dead inside—because I wasn't thinking about Candy. I was thinking about Ember. Ember, with her untamed fire, was the one who had gotten under my skin and now roamed free in my mind.

Candy's mouth enveloped me, hot and wet, her head bobbing as her moans filled the room. She was good at this, always had been, but I couldn't escape the shadow of Ember. Candy's efforts were mechanical, lacking the wild passion Ember's touch always seemed to spark in me.

I leaned back in my chair, drowning in the whiskey and the bitterness of my mind. Ember had betrayed us. Me. And still, I couldn't get her out of my fucking head.

Candy's movements grew more intense, her lips working

harder, but all I could see was Ember—the memory of her standing in front of me, raw and untamed, driving me to the brink with nothing more than her presence. I could almost hear her laughter echoing in the corners of my mind, mocking me for letting her in.

And then, the door creaked.

31

EMBER DANG

I couldn't wait to see the boys again. My boys. The ones who had brought me back to life in ways I never thought possible. Tommy, Declan, Jax, and Knox—they had become my everything. It was strange to think that I could love again after all I'd been through. But here I was, deeply, irrevocably in love.

God, they each brought out something different in me, something unique. It was like I had four different sides, four different versions of myself that had always been waiting for someone to unlock them. Tommy made me feel powerful, like I could conquer the world with him by my side. Declan showed me a softness I hadn't thought existed in me anymore—he peeled back the layers of my heart, one tender moment at a time. Jax awakened a wildness inside of me, a reckless freedom I craved, and Knox… Knox gave me the kind of safety that was almost terrifying in its intensity. It was as if I needed all four of them, each one completing a different piece of the puzzle that made up my fractured soul.

I grabbed my phone, dialing Declan's number, hoping he would pick up and come get me. As the phone rang on and on without an answer, I sighed. No matter. I was determined to see them, with or without a ride. They would be home now. And I needed to be home.

I gathered my laptop and work materials, realizing that I hadn't gotten much done today anyway. The penthouse was a better place to focus, especially with Tommy there to help me pick between two different shades of green for the compound. The thought of his steady presence by my side, guiding me through even the smallest decisions, brought a smile to my lips.

As I descended in the lift, the cold air clung to my skin, the metallic walls reflecting the glimmer of anticipation I felt. I couldn't wait to see them. The ding of the lift snapped me out of my thoughts, and I stepped out into the lobby, my bag slung over my shoulder.

"Hey!" I waved down a black cab from the curb, sliding into the back seat and giving the driver the address to the penthouse. As we sped through the city streets, I watched the world outside rush by in a blur, a strange detachment settling over me. It was as if the rest of the world had become background noise—my real life was waiting for me at the penthouse. With them.

"Here we are, miss," the driver announced, pulling up outside the building. I paid the fare and climbed out, taking a deep breath of the crisp air before heading toward the front door.

"Evening, Miss Dang," the doorman greeted, scrambling to open the door for me. Another pressed the button for the

Chapter 31

lift without me even asking. I raised an eyebrow at the treatment but nodded my thanks as I stepped into the lift.

I had always been driven straight into the underground car park, avoiding the main entrance and keeping my head down. But now, I walked through the front doors like I belonged here. Because I did. I was theirs, and they were mine.

The penthouse was quiet when I stepped out of the lift, the silence wrapping around me like a shroud. The air felt heavy, almost too still, and something strange crept at the edges of my mind. But I pushed it down, chalking it up to nerves. After all, I was eager to see Tommy and the others. I could already feel my pulse quicken as I walked up the stairs then down the hallway, each step echoing in the vastness of the space.

When I reached Tommy's office, my heart was racing, excitement buzzing through me. Grabbing the doorknob, I turned it with a sense of anticipation. But the moment the door swung open, everything inside me froze.

My heart stopped.

Tommy sat there in his chair, a glass of whiskey lazily cradled in one hand. And there, kneeling between his legs, was a woman, her lips wrapped around his cock, moving with a slow, deliberate rhythm. My world tilted on its axis.

My words died in my throat.

I stood there, frozen in place, the door ajar, the weight of betrayal sinking deep into my chest like a stone. My breath hitched, my heart a wild, erratic beat as my eyes locked onto the scene before me. Tommy—my Tommy— sat in his office chair, whiskey glass in hand, while a woman knelt between his legs, her lips wrapped around him in a way that made my stomach turn. The shock of it sent a jolt through me, my body frozen in place as I tried to make sense of the betrayal I was witnessing.

The moment our eyes locked, time itself seemed to stand still. Tommy's green eyes widened in horror, his face paling as he realised I was standing there, watching everything. The whiskey slipped from his grasp, shattering against the cold, unforgiving floor, much like the fragile trust I had in him.

"Ember," he croaked, his voice barely a whisper, as if my name held the weight of a thousand apologies. But it was too late. The damage was done. My heart felt like it had stopped beating, suspended in the agony of the moment, the world crumbling around me.

I couldn't breathe. Couldn't think.

"Tommy," I whispered, my voice thick with the betrayal that wrapped around me like a vice. We had made a promise last night—just us, no one else. Yet here he was, breaking that vow as easily as the glass that now lay in shards at his feet. My pulse hammered in my ears, drowning out everything but the sound of my world collapsing.

The scream tore from my throat, a raw and desperate sound that I didn't recognize as my own. I lunged forward, my hand closing around the cold metal of the gun he'd carelessly left on the desk's edge. My fingers trembled as I raised it, aiming it at the man I had started to fall for, the man I thought I knew.

"Ember, wait!" Tommy's voice broke through, thick with panic, but I couldn't hear him. The rush of blood in my ears drowned everything out. My heart pounded like a wild

Chapter 31

drum, the betrayal slicing through me like a jagged blade, Tommy stood from the chair, hand outstretched for me.

I pulled the trigger.

The gunshot cracked through the air, its violent sound reverberating off the walls, mixing with the scent of gunpowder and whiskey. Tommy staggered back, clutching his shoulder as crimson bloomed beneath his fingers, staining his suit a deep, unforgiving red.

Before I could fully grasp what I had done, a strong arm wrapped around me from behind, pulling the gun from my grip with swift precision. Declan. I could feel his steady presence, but I couldn't focus on anything other than the betrayal that still gnawed at my insides.

"YOU LIAR!" I screamed, tears blurring my vision as they streamed down my face, hot and unrelenting. My voice cracked with the weight of my pain. "I trusted you! I let you in, and you lied to me!"

Tommy grimaced, his hand pressed firmly against the bleeding wound, but his eyes—those eyes that I had loved—burned with anger. "Ember, you cheated first!" he snarled through the pain, his voice hoarse. "I saw you! You were holding hands with a man in a Cafe!"

"What?" I spat, the disbelief and confusion twisting in my chest. "You mean Killer? Do you think that was cheating? Declan saw him, too! He's the VP of my father's club, you idiot!" My voice cracked under the weight of it all, the truth tumbling out in a rush. "He came to check on me. There's nothing between us, and you know it!"

Declan's arms tightened around me, holding me in place as I struggled to free myself, my emotions spiraling out of control. I had trained for years in MMA, but at this moment, I felt powerless. The betrayal had sapped every ounce of strength from my body.

"Your jealousy is pathetic," I spat at Tommy, my voice icy and trembling with rage. "You accused me of cheating when it was you who destroyed us. You who broke our trust."

Tommy faltered, his gaze softening, filled with regret. "Ember, I—"

But before he could finish, Declan began pulling me from the room, his grip firm but gentle. I didn't resist anymore. I didn't have the strength. My heart felt like it was being ripped apart, piece by piece, and I didn't know if I could ever put it back together.

The hallway outside was dark, and the tension in the air was suffocating. My breaths came in ragged gasps as the reality of what had just happened began to settle in.

"Ember!" Jax's voice rang out as he and Knox appeared, skidding to a halt when they saw my state. "What the fuck happened?"

I shook my head, unable to form words. Jax's gaze flickered toward the office, his eyes narrowing as he took in the scene—Tommy bleeding, the woman cowering under the desk. The expression on Jax's face was a mirror of my devastation.

"Tommy, what the hell is going on?" Jax demanded, his voice sharp, while Knox stood behind him, his usually calm demeanor replaced by a mixture of disbelief and anger.

Tommy didn't answer. He just stood there, blood soaking through his shirt, his pants undone, looking like the broken

Chapter 31

man he had become. He tried to speak, but the words failed him. No explanation could fix what had been shattered.

"You need to get out of here," Declan said quietly, his arm still wrapped around me, guiding me away from the carnage. I barely registered the movement, my mind still replaying the betrayal repeatedly.

I was so happy. I had let myself believe that I could love again and trust again. I had fallen for Tommy, Declan, Jax, and Knox, each bringing a different part of me back to life. It was like I needed all four of them to feel whole.

But now, with each step I took away from Tommy, I felt that wholeness was crumbling, and I didn't know if I'd ever get it back.

32

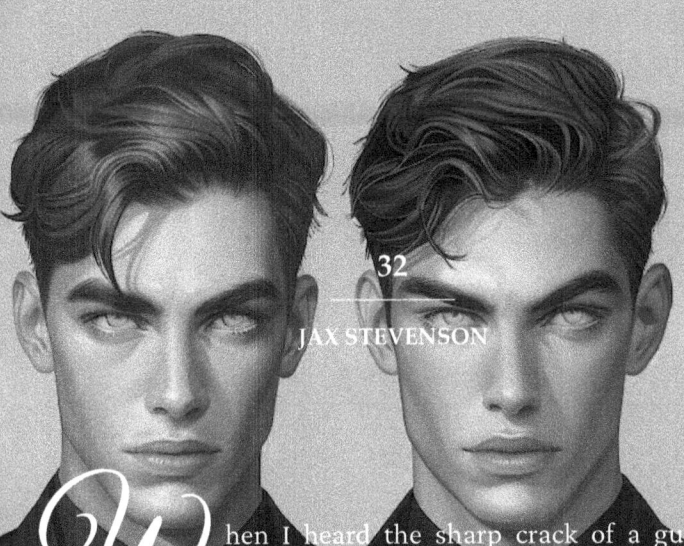

JAX STEVENSON

When I heard the sharp crack of a gunshot echo through the penthouse, my blood froze for a split second. Gunshots in our home? That could only mean one thing—something had gone wrong, and we might've been infiltrated.

I was pouring over some paperwork when the chaos erupted, and I shot out of my chair, adrenaline surging through me. As I rushed down the hallway, I heard the unmistakable sound of Ember's screams.

Fuck.

My heart pounded as I bolted toward Tommy's office, my mind racing with a thousand scenarios, none of them good. When I skidded into the room, the scene before me was nothing short of a nightmare. Tommy was standing there, bleeding from a gunshot wound—nothing too serious, but still, the sight of him shot was enough to throw me off. Declan was dragging Ember toward the lift, her body writhing in his grip as she fought to break free, her voice thick with anguish.

"Ember," was all I had managed to get out as Knox stormed in behind me, his massive form nearly knocking me over in his rush. The guy was like a bull, ready to charge through whatever stood in his way.

But amidst all the chaos, there she was. Candy. The little whore was cowering under Tommy's desk like a scared animal. It hit me like a freight train. Holy shit.

Tommy, you absolute fuckwit.

I stood there, momentarily stunned, as Ember's screams filled the air, echoing down the hallway as Declan shoved her into the elevator. Her words cut through me, raw and searing—accusations of betrayal and heartbreak that twisted something deep in my chest. Watching her like that, seeing her so broken, it hurt in a way I wasn't sure I could explain. She'd become everything to us, and now it felt like she was slipping away.

I wanted to stop her. I tried to grab, hold, and tell her it was all a misunderstanding. But if she stayed, Tommy might end up worse than shot.

As soon as the elevator doors slid shut, the room became eerie. All eyes turned to Tommy. His shirt was splattered with blood, his shoulder wound dripping onto the floor. And then there was the raw guilt and rage written all over his face. He was mumbling something incoherent about a guy he saw Ember with. I loved Tommy like a brother—hell, more than that, like a father figure at times—but if he hurt the woman I loved, we loved, I knew where my loyalty would lie... with her. No questions asked.

Chapter 32

"Tommy," I growled, my voice barely restrained. "You best explain yourself. Now."

He looked at me, his usually slicked-back hair in disarray, his eyes wide with a mixture of pain and frustration. He wasn't the unflappable leader I was used to seeing—he looked vulnerable. The last time I'd seen him like this was after Natasha.

"Mate," Tommy started, his voice cracking. "I saw her. With my own eyes. In that fucking café, holding hands with some guy. She's been fucking around behind our backs, probably working with the enemy."

I felt my blood run cold. It all clicked into place. Tommy's weakest point, his Achilles heel—jealousy and paranoia. It had always been there, festering since Natasha. I knew then that my suspicions about her betrayal were likely right.

Before I could respond, Declan reappeared, looking almost as wrecked as Ember. "Let Knox look at your shoulder," he muttered, nodding toward Tommy.

Tommy nodded silently, and we made our way to the kitchen. As we left the office, Candy, the opportunist, scurried out from under the desk, making a beeline for the exit.

"Fuck off outta here!" I barked at her, watching her sprint stark naked to the lift, her perfume trailing behind like a bad memory. Damn, she could run when she needed to... heels or no heels.

Once we were in the kitchen, the tension was suffocating. Declan started in, his voice tight and fury. "I saw her too, Jax. And Tommy's right."

I shot Declan a look—the kind that only the two of us understood. If he were wrong about this, I'd beat his ass myself. But he stood firm, determined in his conviction. He explained everything—how he saw Ember with a man and how it led up to her shooting Tommy. The more I listened, the more I felt like I was drowning in the insanity of it all.

The kitchen grew quiet, and I noticed Knox, standing by the sink, gripping a kitchen knife way too close to his arm. His face was tight with pain, not from the situation but from the emotional shitstorm swirling inside him. Knox needed to feel pain to release it, and I knew he'd go through with it if we didn't stop him.

Declan moved fast, yanking the knife away from Knox before he could do any real damage. Knox looked at him, his voice low and desperate. "Dec, you know I can't deal with this shit. I need to bleed it out."

But Declan wasn't having it. He shoved the knife aside, leaving Knox to start pounding his head with the palm of his hand instead. I didn't understand how Knox could only find solace in pain, but that's how he worked. And I loved the big guy too much to change him, even if it meant stopping him from hurting himself.

Tommy let out a heavy sigh, and I felt my patience wearing thin. Ember was gone. Tommy had fucked up, Knox was about to knock himself out, and Declan was caught up in the madness.

"Let me get one thing fucking clear here," I snapped, my voice cutting through the tension like a blade. All heads turned toward me. "You idiots. I'm not sure how much Ember has told you about her past, but Killer is Ember's childhood friend. She told me about him ages ago. You all

Chapter 32

would've known if you bothered to ask her instead of letting your egos drive her away!"

I pointed at both Tommy and Declan, rage burning in my chest. "But no, apparently, we don't ask questions in this house. We just fuck things up and deal with the fallout later."

Declan glared at me. "You know I've got issues."

"We all have issues, brother," I shot back, gesturing to my head and then to Knox, who was still punching his skull like a madman. "But that doesn't mean we get to drive the woman we love away."

Then I turned to Tommy, slumped in a chair, holding his shoulder like it was some badge of honor. "You fucked up big time, Tommy. Let that sink in."

I stormed out of the kitchen, done with all of them. If Ember didn't forgive them—and frankly, I wouldn't blame her—I'd claim her for myself. Maybe Knox could pull it together, too. But Tommy and Declan? They were on their own.

Back in my room, I started to hatch a plan. I needed to get Ember to listen to me and trust me, without killing me first. It would be tough, but I couldn't let her stay gone. Not when she meant everything.

I just hoped I wasn't too late.

33

EMBER DANG

I lay on my bed, staring blankly at the ceiling above me, a once-familiar landscape that now felt foreign, as though I were looking up at a distant sky I no longer recognized. The shadows across the plaster mocked me, like spectres of a life that had slipped from my grasp. My apartment, which had once been my haven from the chaos of London, now felt suffocating—a gilded cage where the air grew thicker with every breath.

Sleep had long since abandoned me, replaced by a restless ache that gnawed at the edges of my sanity. Each tick of the clock reminded me of time slipping through my fingers, a cruel tally of the hours since I had left the Aces' penthouse. The sanctuary I had found in their arms—Declan, Tommy, Jax, Knox—felt so distant now, a beautiful dream unraveling into a nightmare.

I let my eyes drift over the room, taking in the books on the shelves, their spines turned toward me like rows of tombstones. I used to find solace in the pages of Lovecraft and Stoker, in the dark worlds they created, where horror was tangible, something you could fight or flee from. But now, the absolute horror was inside me, twisting and churning, making the darkness feel less like an escape and more like an accomplice to my pain.

Tommy's betrayal hung over me like a storm cloud, heavy and ominous, seeping into every corner of my mind. How had it come to this? I had been truly happy for the first time in what felt like forever. I had given myself to each of them, and they had filled parts of me I hadn't even realized were hollow.

But now, that wholeness felt shattered, scattered across the floor like the broken pieces of the whiskey glass Tommy had dropped when he saw me standing there. How could he do this? After everything we had shared, after the promises we made? It wasn't just the act itself—the woman on her knees, her lips wrapped around him—but the violation of trust, the crack that splintered the foundation of what we had built.

I closed my eyes, trying to block out the image, but it replayed relentlessly. The feel of Tommy's skin against mine, the way his green eyes had locked onto mine with that dangerous mix of possessiveness and passion—how could that same man betray me so quickly? My chest ached with the weight of it, a hollow echo of the love I had given him.

A bitter laugh escaped me, harsh and empty in the silence of my apartment. I had never thought I could love again—not after everything that had happened, after the years of fighting, surviving, and protecting myself from the world. And yet, against all odds, I had fallen for them, let

Chapter 33

them in. Tommy, Declan, Jax, and Knox had each unlocked a part of me I thought was long dead. But now, it felt like Tommy had ripped those pieces from me and left me bleeding.

The soft light of morning filtered through the window, a weak and unwelcome reminder that life would go on regardless of my heartache. I turned my back to it, curling up on the bed as if shutting out the world could somehow numb the pain.

But then, as I lay there in the quiet, I heard the faint creak of the kitchen door. I pushed myself up, my body heavy with the weight of exhaustion, and made my way into the room. There, sitting at the kitchen island, was Jax. He was hunched over, a bottle of whiskey dangling from his hand, his usual sharp suit now rumpled and hanging off his frame like an afterthought.

"Jax," I murmured, my voice barely louder than a whisper. He didn't look up, didn't react. The silence between us was thick with unspoken words, with the rawness of everything that had happened.

I stepped closer, the sight of him sending a new wave of emotion crashing through me. Jax was the wild one, the one who laughed in the face of danger, who took whatever the world threw at him and threw it right back. But now, sitting there, he looked...broken.

"Ember," he finally said, his voice rough with something I couldn't quite place—regret, maybe, or sorrow. He took a long drink from the bottle, his blue eyes meeting mine over the rim, and I could see it then—the vulnerability he tried so hard to hide.

Without thinking, I crossed the room and sat beside him. He didn't speak, nor did I. We didn't need to. The silence between us spoke volumes—about the love we had shared, the trust that had been broken, and the pain that now bound us together.

He took another swig, then set the bottle on the counter with a dull thud. "I'm sorry," he said, slurred but sincere. "I'm sorry for all of it."

I reached out, placing my hand over his, the warmth of his skin grounding me in a way I hadn't expected. "Me too," I whispered, my voice barely holding together under the weight of it all.

The sight of him—so broken, so desperate—should have filled me with disgust. A man like Jax, who could take a life without flinching, now sat before me, crumbling under the weight of emotions he rarely allowed himself to feel. But instead of revulsion, I felt a pang of compassion deep in the hollow space where my heart once thrived. With his lethal hands and surprising tenderness, Jax was a victim of love's cruel design, just like me.

I sat there, watching him silently. My instinct was to reach out, to offer him something—anything—but the wounds were still too fresh, too raw. The memory of Tommy's betrayal clung to me like a suffocating fog, clouding my thoughts and keeping me frozen in place.

"Jax," I finally whispered, my voice sounding foreign in the quiet of the room. The name felt heavy on my tongue. "What are you doing here?"

He looked up slowly, his disheveled hair falling over his eyes, eyes that held the intensity of a storm but were

Chapter 33

tempered by a vulnerability that startled me. His usual sharp blue gaze was soft now, pleading. "You can't leave me," he rasped, each word thick with emotion. "I won't survive."

The room seemed still around us, the weight of his words sinking deep into the silence. In that moment, I saw something in Jax I had never fully understood before—his fragility, hidden beneath layers of bravado and chaos.

A bitter laugh escaped my lips before I could stop it, shattering the fragile calm. "You've got to be kidding me," I said, my voice edged with disbelief as I leaned back against the cold countertop, needing something solid to hold me up. "This whole reverse harem thing? It's done, Jax. Tommy made sure of that." The name tasted vile in my mouth, reminding me how quickly trust can be shattered.

Jax's eyes flickered with something more profound—something raw and painful. "Do you want me to leave the Aces?" His voice was low, but the question hit like a punch to the gut.

"What?" I blinked, thrown off by the vulnerability in his words. "Why would you even ask that?"

His expression didn't change. "Because if that's what it takes to keep you, I'll do it. I'm yours, Ember," he said, his voice breaking through the fog of my thoughts with brutal clarity. "I can't live without you."

The sincerity in his voice shook me, but I couldn't let myself fall for it, not after everything. I sighed, trying to keep my emotions in check, fighting against the tears that threatened to spill over. "Jax, you're drunk. You need to go." I tried to make my voice firm and steady, but even I could hear its cracks.

Without warning, he dropped to his knees before me, the impact reverberating through the quiet room. His eyes, usually cold and calculating, were filled with a desperation that left me breathless. "I can't... I can't live without you," he repeated, his voice trembling. "I know you didn't do anything wrong. I know the truth. Don't throw Knox and me in with those idiots. We need you. I need you."

I felt something inside me splinter at the sight of him—this strong, violent man, reduced to a pleading wreck on my kitchen floor. The tears I had fought so hard to keep at bay slipped down my cheeks, scalding my skin with their betrayal. "Jax, you have to leave," I said, my voice breaking under my heartache. "Please. If you don't go, I will."

He rose slowly, the intensity of his gaze never faltering as he stepped back. His presence filled the room, even as he prepared to leave it. "I'm yours, Ember," he said, his voice resolute as if making a vow to the universe. "No one else's. I'm not going anywhere. I'll do whatever it takes to have you back."

And then he was gone, the door closing behind him with a quiet finality that left the air heavy and suffocating. I stayed seated, my back pressed against the cold counter, tears still falling as the emptiness settled in. The ache in my chest grew with each passing second, the loss wrapping itself around me like a cold, unrelenting weight.

The clock on the wall ticked forward, indifferent to the storm that had just passed through my life. I was left alone, my world again fractured, the pieces scattered around me in ways I wasn't sure I could ever put back together.

34

TOMMY PERCIVAL

The apartment was too quiet. The kind of silence that gnawed at your insides, amplifying every thought, every regret. I sat in the dark, nursing a glass of bourbon that tasted like ash in my mouth. The liquid burned as it slid down my throat, but it couldn't numb the ache inside me. Nothing could. Not now.

I glanced at my phone for the hundredth time, the screen lighting up with the same damning silence as before. No calls. No texts. Just that glaring void where Ember's name should have been. My fingers hovered over the screen, tempted to send another message, but I stopped myself. She hadn't answered the last dozen. What difference would one more make?

"Fucking hell," I muttered, tossing the phone onto the couch beside me. It hit the cushion with a dull thud, mocking me with its stillness. I'd reached out in every way I could—texts, calls, even sending gifts to her apartment. But nothing. Ember had shut me out, and I couldn't blame her.

I'd fucked up. There was no way around it. The wound in my shoulder, though healing, was a constant reminder of that fact. Every time it twinged and the ache flared up, it returned that moment. The gunshot. The look in her eyes. The betrayal. She had pulled the trigger, but I had been the one who loaded the gun.

The pain in my shoulder? I welcomed it. Liked it, even. It kept me grounded in reality and reminded me of my failures. Of the trust I'd broken, not just with Ember but with Jax, Declan, and Knox. It was a sharp, physical echo of the emotional wreckage I'd left in my wake.

Jax had mentioned a few days ago that he'd gone to see her. He hadn't said much, just that she had sent him away. Every time he showed up, she sent him packing. And if she was shutting out Jax, the one she had always had the softest spot for, what hope did I have?

I leaned back in the chair, letting the room's darkness close in around me. The weight of it pressed down on my chest, making it hard to breathe. Ember's absence was suffocating. She had become the glue that held us together, bringing light into the darkness we all carried. And now that she was gone, everything felt... hollow.

I rubbed a hand over my face, feeling the stubble that had grown in the last few days. I hadn't been sleeping much, barely eating. Just going through the motions, trying to keep the gang running while my mind spiraled. But focusing and caring about anything was getting harder when she wasn't here. When I knew I had driven her away.

"Jesus, Tommy," I muttered, staring at the glass in my hand. "You fucked it this time."

Chapter 34

I replayed that moment in my head for the thousandth time. Watching her in that café, seeing her with Killer. The way they had laughed and their hands had touched across the table. I had jumped to conclusions and let my jealousy get the better of me. And then, instead of talking to her, I had let my anger fester, let it drive me to make the worst decision of my life.

Then... Candy in my office, the gunshot that followed... it all played out in slow motion now, like a bad dream I couldn't wake up from. I could still hear Ember's scream and see the devastation in her eyes as she pulled the trigger. And the look on her face when she realized what I had done had broken something inside me.

I took another sip of bourbon, the alcohol doing little to dull the edges of my thoughts. I had to fix this. I had to make things right. But I couldn't do it alone. We had to come together—me, Jax, Declan, Knox. We needed a plan. Something solid, something that would show her we were serious. We were willing to fight for her to prove we deserved her.

But how were we supposed to do that when she wouldn't let us through the door?

My shoulder throbbed, a sharp reminder that time was running out. The longer we waited, the harder it would be to bring her back. I couldn't let this end like this. I wouldn't.

I stood up, the weight of the bourbon settling in my stomach as I walked over to the window. The city stretched out beneath me, lights twinkling in the darkness, indifferent to the turmoil inside me.

"We need a plan," I muttered, staring into the night. "Something that will show her we're not giving up."

She deserved more than words. She deserved actions—actual, tangible proof that we were willing to do whatever it took to win her back and show her that we could be better.

My phone buzzed, pulling me from my thoughts. Hope flared in my chest for a split second, but it wasn't her when I glanced at the screen. Just a business notification. Another deal is going through, another task I had yet to be interested in handling.

With a frustrated growl, I tossed the phone on my desk and grabbed my jacket. I needed to clear my head and figure out how to correct this.

35

KNOX HOLLAND

The morning light sliced through the blinds, unforgiving in its brightness. I blinked, groggy, still clutching the remnants of a restless night in my head. My body groaned in protest as I hauled myself out of bed, muscles stiff and aching, but I pushed through it. Today was different. Today, there was no room for hiding. No more avoiding the truth that had gnawed at me for five long days.

"Five days, eleven hours, thirty-three minutes," I muttered, the time since I last saw Ember etched into my mind like a scar. It was a countdown I couldn't escape.

I grabbed my clothes, pulling them on with the same mechanical motions I'd repeated a thousand times before, but everything felt off. Nothing fit right. Not anymore. The roar of my Harley as I climbed on was the only thing that gave me any sense of normalcy. The engine's rumble beneath me, the hum of the city, the rush of wind—all of it blurred together as I tore through the streets toward her apartment.

I barely remembered the ride. The roads, the turns—none of it mattered. Only the destination did. Only her.

When I reached her building, my heart pounded harder than the motorcycle engine ever could. By the time I stepped into the lift, that rhythmic thud echoed in my ears, filling the sterile silence. I watched the numbers tick up to her floor, each dragging my stomach lower, twisting it tighter.

Her door was in front of me now, solid, imposing, yet flimsy. My hand trembled as I knocked, the sound reverberating through the empty hallway like a gunshot.

"Ember?" I called out, but my voice cracked under the weight of everything I couldn't say.

Minutes dragged on, each one suffocating me a little more. And then, finally, the door opened.

She stood there, disheveled, wearing a black tracksuit and no makeup. Her wild and messy hair fell around her face, yet she was still the most beautiful thing I'd ever seen. But I could see the toll everything had taken on her: the fatigue in her eyes, the hollowness beneath the surface.

I clenched my fists at the thought of Tommy being the cause. That asshole.

Her eyes flicked to my hands, her gaze softening with concern. She reached out, slowly unfolding my fingers, peeling them open like she was releasing me from the tension that had built inside me since the moment she left.

"Come in," she said softly, stepping aside to let me in.

I walked into her apartment, and what I saw surprised me. It was a mess—takeout containers scattered across the table, blankets strewn everywhere, and a scene from The Proposal where Sandra is dancing around the bonfire frozen

Chapter 35

on the TV. It wasn't the meticulous, put-together Ember I remembered. But then again, nothing was the same anymore.

She slumped back onto the couch, wrapping herself in the cocoon of blankets like a wounded animal. She lifted the corner and gestured for me to join her, her vulnerability bare.

"Come here," she whispered, her voice rough.

I didn't hesitate. I couldn't. I sank into the blankets beside her, my body pressing against hers as I pulled her close. She felt small, frail, almost, in a way that sent a ripple of fear through me. The takeout containers showed she was eating, but something about her seemed... diminished.

Her body heat seeped into mine, grounding me and calming the storm raging inside my head for days. When Ember was close, the beast within—the part of me that craved violence and chaos—quieted. She had that power over me.

Her hand reached up, gently brushing against my cheek, wiping away a tear I hadn't realized had fallen.

"Knox," she murmured, her dark eyes searching mine with an intensity that made my heart clench. "I'm still here. I love you, big guy. I couldn't erase my love for you if I tried." Her voice cracked slightly, and she paused, taking a shaky breath. "But Declan and Tommy? They broke my trust. They hurt me in ways I can't forgive. But you... you and Jax... I can't let go of you two. I just can't."

Her words hit me like a sledgehammer, knocking the air from my lungs. I gripped her tighter, my lips finding hers in a desperate kiss, full of everything I couldn't say out loud. The hunger, the fear of losing her, the raw need surged to the surface.

Ember's hands roamed over my body, tugging at my shirt and lifting it to show off my stomach. Her fingers danced across my skin, tracing the hard lines of muscle and tattoos, sending shivers through me. Each touch, each breath shared, made me feel more alive than I had in days.

But it was more than just the physical. Her touch seemed to pull me back from the brink, as she reminded me that I wasn't just the monster I sometimes feared I'd become. With Ember, I was more. I was someone worth loving.

Her fingers trailed lower, but I stopped her, pressing my forehead against hers, breathing her in.

"I need you, Knox," she whispered against my lips, laced with the same desperation I felt. But I pulled back slightly, cupping her face and staring into her eyes.

"I'm not going anywhere, Ember," I said softly, my voice rough with emotion. "But I need you to promise me something."

"What?" she asked, her brow furrowing in confusion.

"I need you to let us fix this," I whispered, my thumb brushing her cheek. "Me and Jax... we'll figure this out. We'll make it right. Just... don't shut us out."

She nodded, her eyes shining with unshed tears.

We were all broken, but we might just have a chance to heal together.

My hands traced the curve of her back, skimming over the smooth fabric before slipping lower, lifting her into my lap.

She gasped into the kiss, and that sound cut through the

Chapter 35

chaos in my mind. The sudden hardness between my legs reminded me of my humanity, of the pull she had over me. I focused on Ember—her warmth, heartbeat, and body pressed against mine like we were meant to fit this way.

"Knox," she whispered, grinding herself against me. The friction sent shivers down my spine, and I tightened my grip on her, desperate not to let go. Terrified that if I did, she'd slip through my fingers for good.

"Ember," I muttered, pulling back from our kiss. My hands trembled as I gripped the hem of her shirt. I lifted it, my fingers brushing the bare skin underneath, feeling her softness against my calloused hands. The sight of her, the vulnerability in the moment, made me feel alive in a way that terrified me as much as it thrilled me.

I dived in to suck on her nipples hard, not caring about the bruises that might bloom beneath my lips. Her moans fill the room like sunlight breaking through a storm, and I can't help but chuckle at the symphony of pleasure we create together.

"God, I've missed you," I admit, dragging my teeth across her sensitive flesh. The taste of her, the way she writhes in my lap – it's a drug I crave more than anything else.

The world tilts as I grab her hips, lifting her off my lap and standing. Her feet dangle above the ground, and I can feel her heart racing against mine as I lower her back down slowly. My hands find the waistband of her pants, peeling them down over her hips until they pool at her ankles. The fabric whispers like a sigh as it slides away, exposing her to me.

Her pussy is beautiful – a small patch of hair, dark and

wild, just enough to make my mouth water. Fucking hell, I love it. I lean in, hooking one of her legs over my shoulder as I dive into her, tasting her like heaven itself. She's musky and sweet, intoxicating like honey on the tip of my tongue.

"Knox," she moans, her fingers tangling in my hair. I devour her with an intensity born from days of denial and hunger, wanting nothing more than to hear her cries of pleasure fill the room.

"God, don't stop," she gasps, her voice trembling with need. I quickly stand up and undo my jeans, pushing them down my legs to free myself. Ember looks at me with those piercing eyes, her gaze full of desire and trust.

I sit back on the couch, gripping myself. I hold steady as Ember stands and straddles my lap. The raw vulnerability in her eyes strikes something deep within me. I watch intently, remembering how her lips curve into a smile and her brow crinkle when she's focused. I've spent years pushing away the thought of love, but now, with Ember, it consumes me like wildfire.

"Knox," she breathes, wrapping her arms around my neck and lowering herself on to my hard dick, "you feel so good." She moans as she settles on my lap, her pussy lips wrapped around my dick, drawing me in as deep as she can.

With every movement, our bodies meld together, my dick sliding in and out of her wet pussy. I can't imagine living without this connection. She's not just any woman—she's my soul mate. And I'll be damned if I don't make her mine for life.

"Ember," I choke out between gasps; I want to marry her.

Chapter 35

I don't need her permission. I'll fill out the paperwork, and make her mine forever.

I suck on her nipple again, the taste of her skin a sweet torment. My eyes flick open, and I spot the steak knife on the coffee table—a remnant from some meal she'd had.

"Knox, what are you doing?" she asks, a mix of curiosity and concern in her voice.

"Trust me," I say, wiping the blade on the blanket before pressing it against her throat. I watch as her pulse races under the cold steel.

"Fuck, Knox," she moans before closing her eyes and continuing to ride me. I run the knife down her chest, circling her nipple, feeling her pussy clench around my cock with every movement. The thin line of blood that follows the blade excites me further.

"Mine," I growl, carving a 'K' into her flesh, the top of one breast to the middle of the line, then from the bottom back to the centre. The perfect letter K in her blood. It has to scar—she'll be marked as mine forever.

"Yours," she whispers, her voice filled with a mix of pain and pleasure.

I place the knife back on the couch, watching her eyes flutter open. Her gaze locks onto the bloody 'K' carved into her chest, a wicked smile blooming on her lips. She reaches for the knife, pausing when she notices my shirt still on.

"Off," she commands, pointing at my shirt with the blade. I obey, hastily pulling it over my head and tossing it aside. The cold steel of the knife presses against my heated skin, and she carves an 'E' into my flesh. The sharp pain mingles with pleasure as I gasp.

"Sweetness, I'm gonna cum if you keep cutting me like that," I warn her, desperate for release.

Her laughter sends shivers down my spine as she drops the knife, lifting herself before slamming back down onto my cock. My grip tightens around her hips, guiding her to ride me hard and fast. She clenches around me, her moans growing louder as she shatters around me.

"Knox," she breathes, pressing her fingertips into the fresh cut on my chest. The pain intensifies, pushing me over the edge. I spill myself inside her, her spasms milking me dry.

"Ember," I panted, pulling her against me as she collapsed onto my chest. "Marry me, Mrs. Holland."

"Mr. Dang sounds better," she giggles, her breath hot against my skin.

"Mr. Dang, it is," I reply, taking her face in my hands. Our eyes lock, and I kiss her roughly, sealing our bond.

Tomorrow, I'll make sure the paperwork's delivered to her door. This woman is mine, now and forever, even if she was just joking.

36

EMBER DANG

I stood in the soft glow of the morning light, adjusting the hem of my fitted pencil skirt. The black blouse clung to my frame like shadows at dusk, an armour of elegance against the day's inevitable chaos. My fingers lightly trailed the blueprints spread across the marble countertop, my mind already racing ahead to the meeting with William Henry, the architect who shared my love for the macabre. His designs always spoke to me, blending the beautiful with the eerie, much like the life I found myself leading.

A steaming cup of coffee sat nearby, offering a fleeting promise of comfort for the hour pf day I very rarely allowed myself to be up at, though my body had gotten used to being up with the sun, mainly to have breakfast with Declan. The thought of him made my heart clench. God I missed him. I wrapped my fingers around my coffee mug, inhaling the rich aroma, relishing the brief pause before the day would truly begin. Then, the sharp knock on the door broke through the stillness, pulling me from my thoughts.

"Probably Knox," I murmured, the slightest curve of a smile playing on my lips. His persistence was predictable, endearing even, like the haunting pull of a familiar nightmare. Knox had always been a man of habit, returning time and again with the same dark energy that matched my own.

I breathed and moved to the door, my heels clicking softly against the floor. With a resigned sigh, I swung it open, bracing for whatever storm Knox would bring today. But a stranger stood in his place instead of his familiar, tattooed frame.

The man before me wore a suit so crisp it seemed almost out of place at this hour. His expression was neutral, his presence bland—forgettable, even. Yet the yellow envelope he held in his hand carried an air of foreboding. My instincts prickled.

"Ember Dang?" he asked, his voice as unremarkable as the rest of him.

I narrowed my eyes slightly, assessing him. "Yes," I replied, the edge in my voice unmistakable.

Without a word beyond the necessary, he handed me the envelope, his movements precise and efficient. I took it, feeling the slight crinkle of the paper beneath my fingers, a sudden and unwelcome shift in my otherwise controlled morning. He disappeared as swiftly as he'd come, leaving only the quiet hum of the apartment as I stared at the envelope in my hand.

I shut the door softly, the click reverberating through the empty hall like a distant echo. Back in the kitchen, the envelope felt heavier than it should. I set down my coffee and tore

Chapter 36

it open, half-expecting nothing of consequence yet bracing for anything.

The contents, however, were absurd. A marriage license. Knox's name was scrawled in bold letters alongside mine as though some legal document could bind me to the man whose heart was more scalpel than muscle. A sharp and incredulous laugh burst from my lips, bouncing off the cold steel appliances surrounding me. The whole thing was absurd, but somehow, it was exactly what I should have expected from Knox.

"Wild ideas indeed," I muttered, tossing the document onto the countertop, watching it slide amongst the meticulously arranged blueprints. The world Knox lived in, the world I found myself tangled in, was nothing if not unpredictable. He was chaos, wrapped in precision, and somehow, that had become an anchor for me—a dangerous one, but an anchor nonetheless.

I sipped my coffee, letting its warmth calm me as the surreal reality of the morning settled in. My thoughts drifted back to Knox, to how he moved through the world, dissecting everything with that clinical gaze of his. He could be unnerving, yet it was that same intensity that had drawn me to him in the first place. The man was a puzzle—beautiful, terrifying, and utterly captivating.

As I stood there, caught between amusement and frustration, another knock echoed through the apartment, shattering the brief calm I had reclaimed.

"Knox," I muttered, shaking my head with a smirk. Of course, it was him. He was probably here to explain—or maybe not. With him, explanations weren't always necessary. Chaos had a way of speaking for itself.

The rhythm of the day shattered the moment I opened the door. Tommy was standing there, swaying slightly, his suit wrinkled and disheveled. The smell of alcohol clung to him like a desperate ghost, haunting every breath he took. Once sharp and calculating, his eyes were now bloodshot and dull, swimming with a mixture of regret and something darker.

For a moment, everything stilled. My heart didn't skip; it thudded, slow and steady, as if bracing for what would come next. The lightness that had filled my morning with absurdity evaporated, replaced by the oppressive weight of his presence. Tommy had always been able to change the atmosphere, his mood controlling the room like a conductor with his orchestra. But today, there was no music—only tension, heavy and suffocating.

"Tommy," I breathed, the name dropping from my lips like a stone sinking into a still pond. It sent ripples of unease through me, touching every nerve and muscle. My sanctuary —the one place untouched by his chaos—now felt invaded, his presence turning it into a battleground.

"Ember..." His voice cracked, raw with emotion, barely audible. That single word was a plea, a confession, and a weighty apology.

"Inside," I ordered, the command clipped and cold. We didn't need an audience for this theatre of our lives. I stepped aside, allowing him in, and the scent of whiskey and regret wafted past me as he stumbled forward. I couldn't shake the

Chapter 36

feeling that the shadows in the apartment had grown darker, more menacing, in his wake.

I led him to the kitchen, the one place that still felt somewhat grounded. "What the hell are you doing here, Tommy?" My voice cut through the silence, sharp as a knife. I spun around to face him, my pencil skirt hugging my form like armor against whatever storm he'd brought with him today. His disheveled appearance, once so put together, mirrored the chaos he always brought into my life.

Without warning, the glint of cold metal caught my eye. A gun. He had a gun. My heart lurched, but outwardly, I remained steady. "What the fuck, Tommy?" I hissed, my voice low, venomous.

His suit, always pristine, now hung on him like a forgotten memory of the man I once knew. The tattoos hidden beneath those expensive fabrics were like the scars he never let anyone see—dark, intricate patterns that told a story he only shared in the dead of night when the world was asleep, and his mask could fall. But now, standing in my kitchen, vulnerable and dangerous, he looked like a man on the edge.

In a reckless move, Tommy grabbed my arm, and placed the gun in my hand then pressing the cold barrel of the gun against his own temple. "I can't do it," he rasped, his voice broken, a melody of despair and need. "I can't live without you, Ember."

His green eyes—those once mesmerizing pools of chaos and calm—now pleaded with me, begging for something I wasn't sure I could give. Salvation or damnation, I couldn't tell which. The weight of the gun in my hand was nothing compared to the gravity of his confession. Here stood a man, who once seemed invincible, stripped bare before me. His demons were now mine to face.

The morning light fought its way through the blinds, casting pale shadows across the room, illuminating the deep cracks in Tommy's façade. Outside, the city roared on, oblivious to the drama unfolding within these walls. The disconnect between the two worlds—the bustling, indifferent city and the raw emotion in my kitchen—was almost too much to bear.

I tried to wrestle the gun from him, but he held firm, his resolve unshaken. "You should have figured that out before you put another woman's lips on your dick," I spat, my words laced with fury. The memory of his betrayal, sharp and fresh, gnawed at me like a festering wound. But Tommy remained steady, the gun still pressed against his temple.

"I'd rather be dead than live without you," he whispered, his voice so low it was barely audible. "I know I fucked up. I let my own issues—my past—destroy what we had. And I'm so sorry, Ember. I'm sorry." His words, heavy and fragile, a desperate attempt to salvage something from the wreckage.

The seconds ticked by, each one marked by the blinking of the microwave clock, the soft hum of the city outside. I could feel the weight of his regret pressing down on me, mingling with my own pain. This man, once so strong, so untouchable, was crumbling before me, undone by his own actions.

With trembling fingers, I finally managed to half pry the gun from our joined hands, the cold metal now heavy only in my grip. "What are you doing, Tommy?" I whispered, my

Chapter 36

voice barely more than a breath. "I'm not coming back. We're done. I can't trust you anymore."

He sighed, a long, heavy sound that seemed to drain the very life from him, and his gaze dropped to the floor. "I know," he said, his voice hollow. "But what about Declan? Jax? Knox? They need you, Ember. I'll stay away. You won't have to see me. But they—" his voice broke, "they need you."

His words hung in the air, a plea not for himself but for the men who had also fallen for me, who had somehow become entangled in this web of betrayal and longing. Tommy's desperation was palpable, his love for me tangled in his guilt, his fear, and the unrelenting pull of the past.

The gun in my hand felt like an anchor, a grotesque reminder of how far things had spiraled out of control. I placed it gently on the countertop, as if it were a fragile thing that could shatter with the slightest touch. But it wasn't the gun that was broken—it was us. All of us.

I exhaled, the sound heavy and resigned, a quiet surrender to the chaos that had consumed my life. Jax and Knox—no matter how hard I tried to distance myself from them, they pulled me back. Their presence was as inescapable as shadows cast by flickering flames. Jax, with his disarming innocence that masked the darkness beneath, and Knox, with his raw strength and the scars that ran deeper than skin—they were part of me now, stitched into the fabric of my being. And now, Tommy had invoked Declan, dragging him into this tangled mess I could never seem to escape.

"Declan, too?" The words slipped out, carrying the weight of a battle I hadn't even realized I was still fighting.

Declan wasn't Tommy—he didn't wield the same sharp edges that could cut you in a thousand ways before you even felt the pain—but he was no less dangerous in his way. The distrust that simmered beneath his surface had always been a barrier between us, one I wasn't sure could ever indeed be dismantled.

I turned back to face Tommy, his gaze locking onto mine, those emerald eyes filled with deep sorrow I rarely saw. It was like looking at a ghost of the man he could have been—if life and his choices hadn't torn us apart. For a moment, I saw through the façade of the criminal mastermind, catching a glimpse of the man buried underneath the layers of power and violence. But that man was long gone, buried beneath the weight of London's underworld.

"Okay," I murmured, the decision heavy on my tongue like a stone dropping into the abyss. The word was final, carrying the end of something I had held onto for too long. "But you better keep your promise." My voice was cold and resolute, leaving no room for debate. "You and me? We're done."

Tommy nodded, a hollow movement as if agreeing had drained the last bit of life out of him. "Okay, baby, I promise." The term of endearment, once warm and intimate, now felt like a bitter echo of a love that had long since died. It chilled me, like the touch of something cold and lifeless, and I knew there was no going back.

37

TOMMY PERCIVAL

The weight of my promise felt like a noose tightening around my neck, growing tighter with each passing day. When I left Ember's that day, I swore I would stay away—to retreat into the shadows and leave her to my brothers. It wasn't a promise I made lightly, but one born out of a twisted kind of love, a desperate attempt to protect her from the chaos I brought, even if that meant protecting her from myself.

It was both a blessing and curse; as the days blurred into weeks, and the weeks stretched into months, the gnawing ache of her absence in my life grew like a hunger I couldn't satisfy. It was relentless, like a thirst for something I couldn't drink. Not having her in my life was a torment, an everyday kind of hell that gnawed at me from the inside out; seeing her every day wrapped around one of the others but I having to slink in the shadows and not be seen tore at me.

Every single day. Just out of reach. A haunting presence, a specter who lingered in my mind no matter how hard I tried to stay away. I saw her with my brothers, their laughter, their closeness—a constant reminder of everything I had lost, of the love that could never be mine again. Watching them with her was like twisting a knife more deeply into a wound that refused to heal.

The irony was cruel. The four of them together, unaware of the storm that raged inside me. With her frosty demeanor, Ember would only speak to me when absolutely necessary, her words clipped and professional. It was a mask, but even so, I could feel the sharp edges of her disdain cutting into me with every exchange.

The more she immersed herself in the farmhouse project, the more I found myself pulled toward her despite the agony it caused. My involvement in the project was unavoidable; it was practical and rooted in business. But I knew the real reason I stayed close was that invisible tether between us, which wouldn't let me go no matter how hard I tried to sever it.

Every day felt like a battle to keep my promise, resist the pull of my desires, and stop myself from reaching out. I watched her love Jax, Declan, and Knox in ways I could only imagine. I saw how they adored her and held her, and the jealousy burned so hot I thought it might consume me. But I knew I couldn't give in. I had to stay strong to honor my promise no matter how much it hurt.

So, I stayed in the shadows. I watched them all from the sidelines, a silent witness to their happiness, my heart torn apart by a love I could never fully claim. I made a choice, and I knew I'd have to live with it—a sacrifice for the woman I

Chapter 37

loved, even if it meant sacrificing my happiness in the process.

In the dim light of my office, surrounded by stacks of paperwork that I couldn't bring myself to care about, Jax was the only one who could pull me out of my head. He'd always been my closest confidant when it came to matters of the heart, always steady when I couldn't find my footing.

"She'll come around, brother," Jax said, breaking through the thick silence. His words were like a rope pulling me out of the dark. "Give her time. She'll come back when she sees that you only have eyes for her, that it's her love you want."

I wanted to believe him. God, I wanted to. I tried to think that Ember's heart would soften, that she'd see past the hurt and the anger and find the love still there—burning inside me, waiting for her. But with every passing day, her distance felt like a wall growing higher between us. The chasm between us seemed unbridgeable, and I feared the gap would swallow us whole before I could make things right.

The paperwork before me blurred, and I cursed under my breath. Forging documents had never been my favourite task, but it was a necessary evil in our world. The deal with the Irish was just another piece of business, another transaction to keep things running. Despite my distaste for it, the Irish had proven to be valuable allies, and their connections were crucial to maintaining our operations flowing.

But today, even that didn't matter. Not the paperwork, not the business, not the deals. Nothing mattered except for the overwhelming need to win her back. I couldn't live in this limbo forever. Watching her with my brothers was tearing me apart, and if I didn't come up with a plan, I was afraid I'd lose her for good.

Jax was right. I needed to give her time to show her the truth. But time was running out, and I wasn't sure how long I could keep my promise.

I just needed a way to reach her and make her see that I was still waiting.

I offered only a brief nod to Jax in response to his words of encouragement, unable to articulate the storm of doubts and fears that had become my constant companions. Winning Ember back felt more like an unattainable dream than any real possibility. It was a fantasy I couldn't afford to entertain for fear of shattering the fragile hope I clung to like a lifeline.

In my darkest moments, the idea of ending it all had crossed my mind more than once. There was an old myth whispered among the Irish—a belief that if a gangster took his own life, he'd be condemned to purgatory, a fate worse than death. I never put much stock in myths or superstition, but such tales held weight on this world of woes where reality often blurred with legend. They crept into the darkest corners of my mind, warning me against the temptation of a final escape.

And so, I played my part—the disgraced lover, cursed to watch from the sidelines as the woman I loved found solace in the arms of my brothers. It was as if the universe had handed me a sentence of endless punishment. I was drowning in a sea of regret, watching Ember give her heart to the very men I had raised like family. The cruel irony left me hollow.

Chapter 37

. . .

THE HEAT OF THE SUMMER AIR HUNG THICK AS WE FINISHED THE final touches on the compound. It was a testament to Ember's brilliance, her vision brought to life in every corner of the place. Yet, with the changing season, her summer dresses reminded me of everything I could no longer claim as mine. The flowing fabrics clung to her body, a siren call I had to ignore.

On one particularly humid evening, the guys decided to host a barbecue—a chance to unwind after long work days. They hired a catering service to spare Knox from kitchen duties, giving him a rare break. We gathered outside on the patio, a space Ember had transformed with her eye for detail. But beneath the jovial atmosphere, a sense of dread gnawed at me, the oppressive heat only amplifying the tension that had settled in my chest.

The oak decking beneath my feet was solid, offering a sturdy platform that kept me physically distanced from her. But I couldn't escape the turmoil no matter how far I stayed. I could've made an excuse to skip the dinner and retreated to my office, but that wouldn't have solved anything. This was my life now—sharing the same space with Ember while pretending everything was fine.

As I took my seat at the head of the table, the weight of my regret pressed down on me. Ember moved around the patio, setting the table with her usual grace and precision, the sun casting a warm glow on her skin. She wore a black dress that hugged her curves just enough to stir the desire I had tried to suppress. Her hair was pulled back into a loose bun, with strands framing her face in a way that made her look effortlessly beautiful. The tattoos on her arms shimmered in the fading light, like the intricate secrets she kept hidden beneath her tough exterior.

I watched her, unable to look away; every movement she made reminded me of what I had lost. She moved with such ease and purpose, yet there was a coldness in her disregard for me. Her silence was deafening—a punishment more brutal than any words she could have spoken.

I couldn't help but wonder how she could still be so blind to the love that burned within me. Did she not know that every mistake I made was from fear, desperation, and trying to protect what little was left of my heart? Or maybe she did, and the truth was that I wasn't worth forgiving.

Only Ember knew the answer to that question. And so far, the answer had been no. Still, I couldn't ignore the subtle glances she threw my way when she thought no one was looking. But I was always looking. Always watching her. My heart and mind were wholly consumed by her, even when I knew I should've let go.

I noticed her gaze softened ever so slightly when her eyes met mine. Was she breaking? Was she feeling the loss of me, too? Known for acting impulsively, I felt the urge to get up, talk to her, and close the distance between us. I gathered every ounce of courage, ready to make my move. But before I could act, the others spilled out onto the patio, filling the air with their voices and laughter. I silently cursed them for their impeccable timing, watching as the moment slipped away from me once again.

Maybe tomorrow, I told myself. Perhaps tomorrow, I'll

Chapter 37

have the courage to fix this. But tonight, I was stuck in the shadows, watching the woman I loved from a distance, unsure if I'd ever get the chance to make things right.

My fists flexed under the table, the muscles straining with the need to hit anything. The frustration bubbling inside me was unbearable, a volatile mix of anger and desire that grew stronger with every passing second. The chance to finally speak with her, to fix things, had slipped through my fingers once again. But now wasn't the time for recklessness. I had to bide my time, wait for the perfect moment to confront her, to show her how much I still cared.

Ember moved effortlessly among the group, her laughter carrying the warm summer breeze. It was a sound that once had the power to light up my world, but now it felt distant, unreachable. She was right there, yet miles away, and the space between us felt insurmountable. I watched her, the ache in my chest growing more assertive as she smiled at Knox, Jax, and Declan, her interactions with them full of warmth. But me? I was just an outsider in my own life, trapped on the fringes of her affection.

Everyone took their seats at the table, the tension palpable as Ember deliberately sat as far from me as possible. The distance wasn't just physical—it was emotional and spoke volumes about the widening chasm between us. The chef reappeared with the entrees, but I could barely taste the food. My mind was far away, consumed by thoughts of the conversation I knew would happen soon. I couldn't keep doing this—watching her from a distance, pretending that everything was fine while my heart ached for her.

The patio buzzed with conversation, an air of forced

normalcy hanging over the gathering. In their well-meaning but misguided attempts to help, my brothers kept trying to pull Ember and me into the same conversations. She brushed them off every time they tried, though, with that same cold, distant tone she reserved just for me. Her dismissals were like knives to my chest, each cutting deeper than the last.

I caught Jax's apologetic glance from across the table, the silent "sorry, man" in his eyes as he realized his efforts were in vain. Declan and Knox threw me similar looks, their faces full of regret for the tension hanging over what was supposed to be a relaxed evening. I gave them a slight nod, a signal that I understood, but the frustration gnawed at me inside. They were trying; I knew that. But it wasn't enough.

Underneath the surface, a storm was brewing, and I knew it wouldn't be long before it erupted. I couldn't stand the distance between us any longer, couldn't keep pretending like everything was okay when it wasn't.

38

EMBER DANG

I sat on the plush sofa in the movie room, a space shaped by my design, cocooned within the Gothic grandeur of the fortress the Aces now called home. It was a refuge, yet it wasn't quite my home. That word still belonged to my apartment, my sanctuary away from all this—a reminder that I could escape if I needed to.

"Isn't it eerie how the shadows play on the walls?" I murmured, more to myself than anyone else, as the flickering light from the screencast grotesque shapes across the room, dancing along the darkened corners. The film, a horror classic, played on, but my mind wandered, drifting through thoughts that had nothing to do with the story on screen.

I practically lived here now, moving through these grand halls and Gothic rooms as if I'd always belonged. Yet, my apartment remained my safe harbor, untouched by the chaos that had woven itself into my life. The scars—both seen and unseen—reminded me why I needed that backup plan. No matter how deeply I was pulled into this world, I wasn't ready to give up my independence.

"Ember, you've gone quiet," a voice pulled me from my thoughts, someone's gentle reminder that I was still in the room.

"Just appreciating the screen's glow amidst all this darkness," I quipped, my smirk faint but ever-present, as if the shadows around me were more of a muse than a threat. Snark was my shield, and I wielded it as naturally as breathing.

On-screen, the protagonist fought against some looming terror, and I felt a bitter sense of kinship. We were all fighting something, weren't we? Whether it was the demons from our past or the monsters we faced in the mirror each morning. The movie played on, its gothic horror matching the mood in the room, the house, the life we'd all built here.

"Love this part," I added, pointing to a scene where the shadows twisted into grotesque figures. "Art imitating life, or maybe it's the other way around." A few nods from the others acknowledged my words, but I could feel their focus drifting. Everyone was locked in their battles tonight, the weight of our lives pressing in like the walls of this fortress.

But I had responsibilities, too, and Tommy's approval was needed for the latest construction plans. The garage, a hulking concrete addition meant to house their collection of cars and bikes, still required his sign-off before the builders arrived in the morning.

"I need to run something by Tommy," I muttered to no one in particular, standing up and leaving the cozy darkness of the movie room behind. My footsteps were quiet against

Chapter 38

the polished floors as I made my way to his office, the weight of the conversation looming ahead.

The door to Tommy's office was heavy, almost foreboding, as always. I pushed it open gently, the creak barely a whisper against the silence. There he was, sitting behind his desk, though tonight he looked more like a man unraveled than the stoic leader I was used to seeing.

"Tommy?" I called softly, hesitant, unsure if I was intruding on something private. His hands were buried in his hair, his usual control over his emotions slipping away. His green eyes, ordinarily sharp and commanding, were clouded with sorrow, the weight of something deep and personal etched into the lines of his face.

He didn't look up at first, his broad shoulders hunched over like a fortress crumbling under the pressure of too many battles. Seeing Tommy like this—this powerful man who carried so much authority—reduced to someone who could barely hold himself together was a strange, heartbreaking sight.

"Are you alright?" I asked, knowing the question was futile. He wasn't. Anyone could see that. But sometimes, you had to ask anyway, if only to open a door, to give them permission to let you in.

His only response was a shuddering breath, a silent plea for understanding that transcended words. As I closed the door behind me, shutting out the world, I knew that here—in the presence of his vulnerability—I would find a connection deeper than anything words could convey.

His voice broke the silence, raw and jagged, clawing its way out of the depths. "I miss you, Ember," he confessed, the weight of his admission hanging in the air like a fog between us.

Seeing him like this—so fractured yet still holding onto some semblance of control—struck a chord deep within me. The shadows seemed to deepen in the room, holding their breath as I reached out. My hand trembled ever so slightly as it met the cool skin of his cheek. His flesh was cold to the touch, a stark contrast to the warmth and fire that always simmered just beneath his surface. He leaned into my palm, a gesture so simple yet heavy with meaning.

"Tommy..." I whispered, my touch soft, as though it could ease the torment flickering behind his green eyes—those eyes that had seen too much, carried too many burdens. He pressed closer into my hand, seeking something he couldn't put into words.

We were kindred spirits, bonded by the same harsh life that had forged us into the people we were. There was no innocence left between us, no room for the naivety of youth. We were shaped by betrayals, loss, and pain—a story carved into our souls, and that's what brought us back to each other time and again.

"I'm broken Ember, I don't know how to be a normal person. I didn't have a normal childhood, I never learnt how to do things the normal way.' Tommy confessed.

"None of us grew up right," I murmured, the truth heavy and undeniable. It wasn't just him, wasn't just me—it was all of us. This makeshift family we'd cobbled together was built from the ruins of the lives we'd left behind.

Compelled by something far older than words, I leaned in, my lips finding his in a kiss that was more than just an

Chapter 38

apology or forgiveness. It was a promise. In that kiss, I told him everything I couldn't say aloud—that I missed him, too, despite everything.

The kiss deepened, and the room fell away. Every second was stretched, every movement a testament to the longing we had both kept buried for too long. There was an urgency between us now, a need to reclaim what had been lost.

Tommy's grip on me tightened as the kiss intensified, but there was no rush for more. He wasn't demanding; he wasn't pushing. It was as if he was asking for permission with every movement, waiting for me to decide how far we would go. But I wasn't content with just tenderness. There was something wild in me, something that needed to be let out.

My hands, driven by desire, began to undo the buttons of his shirt. The fabric parted beneath my fingers, revealing the inked canvas of his body—a proof of his life, his scars, his survival. Each tattoo was a story, a piece of him laid bare.

He hesitated, stepping back slightly, as though he was afraid to let me get too close. "You don't have to," he murmured, a crack in his usual confidence.

A smirk tugged at my lips, amusement lacing my voice as I whispered, "Oh, Tommy, I want to."

At my words, his restraint snapped, and he closed the distance between us with a single, purposeful step. The air between us thickened with tension, charged with the scent of leather and desire. His arms wrapped around me, pulling me close. His voice, rough with emotion, slipped out before he could stop it. "I love you, Ember... I love you so much it feels like my heart breaks every time I see you."

His confession hit me like a wave, and the intensity in his

green eyes—wild, desperate, and full of emotion—was almost too much to bear. But I didn't shy away. Instead, I leaned into him, kissing him with the same fire he gave me. My fingers moved to his belt, unbuckling it with a practiced ease, and then slid down to his pants, pushing them to the floor.

We stood there, two broken souls in the middle of his office, surrounded by the symbols of his power. But none of that mattered right now. It was just us, isolated in our own world, the night wrapping around us like a protective shield.

His hands moved with a precision that belied the urgency of the moment, my shirt slipping away under his touch. The warm air hit my skin, but it was nothing compared to the warmth of his hands as they traced the curves of my body. With a slow, deliberate movement, he eased my pants down over my hips, his fingers lingering on the path they left behind.

We were together in the way we always had been—two souls intertwined by fate, by pain, by a love that was as fierce as it was flawed.

"Up you go," Tommy murmured, his voice a low rumble that echoed through the marrow of my bones. He lifted me with an ease that belied his raw strength, setting me on his desk.

The wood beneath me was polished to a sheen, reflecting the ambient light that played across the surface, turning everything into a kaleidoscope of desire. My heart galloped, a wild thing within the cage of my ribs, as I reached for him. My fingers wrapped around his hardened length with a possessiveness that bordered on reverence.

Chapter 38

"Shit, you're so wet," he rasped as I guided him to my core, his eyes alight with a hunger that mirrored my own. "Have you missed this?"

"Yes," I breathed, the word dissolving into a moan as he slowly claimed me, filling the void that had been left aching and empty. We were locked in a timeless dance, our bodies finding the rhythm that had always been ours alone.

He leaned in, his mouth capturing the sounds I couldn't contain, kissing me with a fervor that swallowed the night itself. As he withdrew only to surge forward once more, our connection became the axis upon which the world spun—a pivot point of flesh and need.

His deliberate pace was a delicious torture, each slow thrust a testament to the longing that had built between us. "Faster," I whispered against his lips, my voice laced with desperation.

"No," Tommy breathed out, almost reverently. His green eyes bore into mine, fierce and unyielding. "I've missed the feel of you so much, Ember. I need to savor it, need to feel every damn inch of you around me."

Tommy's thumb found its way between the entangled map of our bodies, teasing the bundle of nerves at my core. A gasp escaped me as he began to rub in rhythmic circles, coaxing the building tension tighter. My back arched off the hard surface of the desk, creating an altar of my body beneath the cathedral of his touch.

"Are you going to cum for me?" he murmured, his voice a dark promise that vibrated through the hazy room. "Squeeze me tightly, milk me of my cum."

The echo of his chuckle reverberated through the

cavernous office, a sound darkly melodic against the patter of rain on the windowpanes. "If you keep talking like that, I'll do anything you ask me," I breathed, the words tumbling from my lips in a mixture of desire and surrender.

Tommy's response was a subtle increase in rhythm, a gentle escalation that coaxed a deeper hunger from within me.

"Your cunt was made for me," he declared with the reverence of someone who had discovered a sacred text hidden among the detritus of the mundane. "We fit together like a puzzle, perfect." His voice broke slightly, imbued with raw emotion. "I should have known from day one you were the missing piece we needed."

A sharp pinch to my clit sent ripples of ecstasy cascading through me, and I exploded around him, my body clenching tight as if to never let go.

Tommy's movements became fervent, with each thrust, he chased his own release, a storm that brewed in the depths of green eyes turned dark with passion.

And then, with a finality that seemed to shake the very foundation of the room, he found it. Stilling as he unloaded inside me, coating my core with his cum, marking me as his again.

As he pulled away, there was a moment of stark vulnerability—a fleeting glimpse of the man behind the leader of the Ace gang. He looked down at me, at the evidence of our union slowly dripping out of me, and his fingers moved with purpose, scooping it up and pushing it back in.

"Keep that inside you," Tommy commanded, his tone edged with a possessiveness that sent shivers down my

Chapter 38

spine despite the warmth that enveloped us. "Where I belong."

I collapsed back against the cool, hard surface of Tommy's desk, my chest heaving, trying to catch my breath after the storm. I was adrift in the aftermath, floating in that liminal space where pleasure and reality blur into a single, indistinct haze.

"I love you," I whispered into the silence that had settled over us. My voice sounded alien, as if the words were carved from the darkness itself, heavy with emotion yet light enough to rise through the air and wrap around him.

Tommy's eyes met mine, green orbs that shimmered with unspoken depth—a verdant forest after the rain, alive and vibrant. "I love you too," he murmured back, his voice a low thrum that resonated within my very marrow.

Then, in the quiet that followed, I reached for something more profound, a truth that had crystallized in the crucible of our passion. "I love all of you," I added.

A smile tugged at the corners of his lips, the curve softening the harsh lines etched by a life of ruthless decisions. "I knew if I had a queen, she would belong to all of us," he said, his tone touched with reverence.

39

EMBER DANG

"You ready?" Declan's voice was a low rumble, still thick with the last remnants of sleep.

I turned to see him leaning against the doorframe, his eyes scanning me with an intensity that always set my nerves alight. His tousled hair fell over his forehead, giving him a casual, yet undeniably rugged look.

"Yeah, I'm ready," I said, snapping my laptop shut and slipping it into my leather bag. "I just need to go over a few details for the garage with the builders before we head out. The concrete foundation should be dry by now, but there's some finishing work I need to sign off on."

He gave me a nod, his expression unreadable, but I caught the faintest trace of amusement in the twitch of his lips. Declan always enjoyed watching me in action—whether I was bossing around builders or sketching out plans for the next phase of construction, it was as if he found some quiet pride in seeing me work.

We stepped outside into the crisp air, the farmhouse

fading behind us as we made our way toward the open lot where the garage was taking shape. The hum of machinery filled the air, and I spotted the foreman, a burly man named Mark, waving us over.

"Morning, Ember. We've got the foundation set, and we're starting on the walls today. You still want the brick finish on the exterior?" he asked, his clipboard in hand.

"Yes," I replied, my mind already racing through the logistics of the design. "Make sure the exterior matches the tone of the house—dark brick, black trim. I don't want any mismatched materials."

Mark nodded, jotting down notes as I continued. "And the soundproofing needs to be done before anything else. The insulation should be delivered today, right?"

"Should be here by noon," he confirmed.

"Good," I said, satisfied. "Keep me updated if anything changes. I'll be at the townhouse, but you can call me."

We walked back to the car, the weight of responsibility lifting slightly now that the garage construction was progressing smoothly. Declan slid into the driver's seat as I settled in beside him. He reached a hand over the middle and laid it on my leg, as he looked at me and smiled and said, "You can boss me around like that any day." Making me laugh, maybe Declan would allow me to treat him the same way I treated his twin... I wasn't apposed to giving it a try.

As the road blurred beneath us, I thought about one thing that still needed attention—soundproofing. The garage definitely needed it. With the lives they led, it wasn't just a matter of privacy; it was a necessity. The farmhouse was a sanctuary, but with everything that happened within

Chapter 39

our walls, we needed to make sure that what went on inside stayed inside.

Particularly that small room in the back of the garage I had built just for Knox. Knox had been adamant about its inclusion in the plans. A room designed for him to retreat into, away from the rest of us. A place where he could be free to indulge in his darker urges, where Tommy could send whoever he pleased for Knox to "play" with. That room wasn't just a space—it was Knox's haven, his own twisted little corner of the world, and the last thing we needed was anyone outside those walls hearing what went on inside.

As Declan drove, the thought lingered. The farm had become more than just a home; it was an extension of the Aces, a reflection of thoer lives. And I needed to protect it at all costs. Soundproofing was a small price to pay for the secrets it would keep.

I hadn't shown Declan the townhouse for months now, and I could feel his curiosity growing as we neared the city. My townhouse was freaking amazing, William knew me well, and had helped me design the whole thing. It already had a buyer, one who was on a wait list with many others.

When we pulled up to the building, Declan's eyebrows rose slightly. "Holy shit!" he said, his voice tinged with surprise.

I smirked as I stepped out of the car, feeling a surge of pride. "Yeah. It's finally done, but there are a few small details I need to sign off on before I officially hand over the keys."

The townhouse was everything I had wanted it to be. The exterior was sleek, modern, with a Gothic edge that nodded to my darker tastes. The black iron gates swung open as we approached, and I led Declan inside, my boots echoing off the polished floors.

"Come on, I'll give you the tour," I said, turning to see him standing just inside the doorway, his eyes scanning the space with a silent appreciation.

The main living area was open, the dark wood floors contrasting with the black and steel furnishings. Floor-to-ceiling windows flooded the space with natural light, but the heavy velvet drapes could easily plunge the room into shadow.

I led him upstairs to the master bedroom, where the bed —a custom-made four-poster with black wrought iron details—stood as the focal point of the room. The walls were painted a deep, rich grey, and the furnishings followed suit—dark, minimal, with a touch of elegance.

Declan wandered to the window, looking out over the cityscape below. "You've outdone yourself, Ember," he said, his voice low. "This place is… beautiful."

I smiled at his words, feeling a warmth in my chest. "I wanted something that felt like home without it being my home."

We made our way back downstairs, where I walked over to the kitchen counter and grabbed a stack of papers I needed to go through. I signed off on a few minor adjustments—the lighting in the downstairs hallway, a small issue with the plumbing in the guest bathroom—before finally setting the pen down.

"That's it," I said, exhaling a breath I didn't realize I'd been holding. "It's done."

Chapter 39

Declan watched me in that way he always did, with quiet intensity, his hands resting casually in his pockets. "So, when does the sale go through?"

"Not sure yet. Maybe in a few days once everything is finalized," I said. "I think the photographer arrives tomorrow to catalogue the place, then I think *House to Home* is going to feature it before the keys are handed to the owner."

His gaze lingered on me for a moment longer before he walked over and wrapped an arm around my waist, pulling me close. "You deserve this," Declan murmured, his breath warm against my ear.

I felt his lips brush against my skin, sending a shiver down my spine as he held me tight. His voice was filled with sincerity, a quiet reverence that made my heart ache in the best way possible.

"You're possibly the most talented interior designer on the planet," he said softly, kissing the side of my neck.

I couldn't help but giggle, leaning into him. "I'm the only one you know," I teased.

He pulled back just enough to look at me, a crooked smile playing on his lips. "So what? I mean, look at Tommy's penthouse," he said. "It was done beautifully. Then I saw what you could create in your own apartment, then the farmhouse, and now this."

His gaze softened, his fingers tracing a gentle line down my arm. "I know, deep in my soul, your talent is one of a kind. People are on a waitlist just to buy anything you design. They don't even need to see it before you hand over the keys—they have that much faith in what you create."

His words stirred something inside me, something that

made my chest tighten with emotion. I'd always had faith in my skills, but hearing him say it like this, with such admiration and pride, hit differently. There was no pretense, no need to impress me—just pure, unfiltered honesty.

"There's so much feeling in every room, every single corner of these places," he continued, his voice deep and sincere. "I'm so proud of you and even happier that you returned to us. I couldn't live without this in my life—without you."

I smiled at him, my heart swelling at how his words wrapped around me, grounding me in a way only he could. He leaned in and kissed me deeply, a kiss that spoke of all the unspoken words between us—of longing, belonging, and love that had been tested.

When he finally pulled back, his eyes sparkled with mischief. "So," he said, with a teasing lilt, "can we christen that bed before you sell it?"

I burst out laughing just as he wrapped his arms around my waist. He walked us back up the stairs and threw me onto the bed, the soft mattress enveloping me as I landed. Before I could catch my breath, Declan was on top of me, his grin wide and boyish as he leaned down to kiss me again, deeper this time.

His lips trailed down my neck, leaving a trail of warmth and fire in their wake. My body arched instinctively toward him, my fingers tangling in his hair as I pulled him closer, needing more. His hands moved over my body with a tenderness that belied the passion behind his touch, and soon, we were a tangled mess of limbs and desire, the rest of the world fading away as we lost ourselves in each other.

Chapter 39

His kisses became more urgent, more demanding as he slid his hands beneath my blouse, peeling it off with careful precision. His fingertips grazed over my skin, sending waves of heat through me as I gasped against his mouth. Declan's shirt was discarded quickly, and I felt the solid warmth of his chest press against mine, the sensation of his skin on mine igniting something primal inside me.

"You drive me crazy," he murmured, his lips finding my collarbone as his hands worked on the waistband of my pants.

"Likewise," I breathed, my fingers tracing the lines of muscle along his back as I helped him slide the last of our clothes away, leaving nothing between us.

He entered me slowly, every inch of him stretching and filling me as we both gasped at the sensation. His eyes locked onto mine, and for a moment, everything stilled—time, space, the air around us. All that existed was this: the rhythm of our bodies moving together in perfect sync, the intimacy of our breaths mingling as we shared this moment.

Declan's hands gripped my hips as he set a slow, steady pace, his gaze never leaving mine. Each thrust was a promise, each kiss a reminder of how deeply we belonged to one another. I wrapped my legs around his waist, pulling him closer, wanting to feel every part of him as he pushed deeper inside me.

Our moans and gasps filled the room, a symphony of pleasure that drowned out everything else. Declan's hand slid down to where we were joined, his fingers circling my most sensitive spot as his thrusts grew more urgent, pushing me closer to the edge with every stroke.

"I love you," he whispered, his voice rough with need as he watched the way I trembled beneath him, the pleasure building in my core until I could no longer hold back.

"I love you too," I gasped, my body shattering beneath his touch as waves of ecstasy crashed over me. Declan followed moments later, his release hitting him with a force that left us both breathless.

He collapsed beside me, pulling me close as we lay tangled in the sheets, our bodies still humming with the aftershocks of what we'd shared.

"I could get used to christening every bedroom you design," Declan whispered with a grin, pressing a kiss to my temple as we lay there, basking in the warmth of our connection.

I chuckled softly, feeling a sense of peace I hadn't felt in a long time. "You're impossible," I murmured, resting my head against Declan's chest as the steady beat of his heart lulled me into a contented silence. The warmth of his body beneath mine, the soft rise and fall of his chest, made everything feel so right like all the jagged pieces of my life had somehow started to fit together.

For a few moments, there was nothing but the quiet hum of our breathing and the comfort of being wrapped up in each other. Then, Declan broke the silence, his voice tinged with playful curiosity.

"So... you and Tommy..." he trailed off, a smirk tugging at the corner of his lips as he shifted slightly to look at me.

I laughed, unable to resist the grin spreading across my face. "Yes, me and Tommy," I teased, rolling my eyes at the obvious question. I knew where this was going.

Chapter 39

Declan's smile grew wider, and he wiggled his eyebrows suggestively. "Oh, come on, spill! I need the goss. Are you two back on? Did you work it out, or were you just scratching an itch? Because, trust me, we all heard the noises coming from his office last night."

My laugh bubbled up, full and unguarded. "Yes, we're back on," I admitted, shaking my head at his teasing tone. I could see the relief wash over Declan as he let out a dramatic sigh and pulled me closer, his arms tightening around me.

"Thank God," he said, his voice sincere now, his teasing giving way to something deeper. "We're a team, Ember. Even though Tommy was willing to sacrifice himself so the rest of us could be happy, I knew we needed to all be together. You just needed the room to sort out the feeling side of it all."

I looked up at him, his face illuminated by the soft light filtering in from the windows. There was something so genuine in his expression, a deep understanding that made my heart swell. He wasn't just saying this for Tommy's sake —he meant it. We were all connected, inextricably tied to each other, our broken pieces fitting together in a way that made sense, even if the world around us didn't.

"We're all broken, Ember," Declan continued, his voice a low rumble that vibrated through his chest. "All of us. We've got issues that run so damn deep, we don't know what's up or down half the time. It's what makes us so good at the jobs we do, but it's also what makes this... us... a little more complicated."

I smiled at him, feeling a rush of affection for this man who could so easily read me, who understood the complicated layers of our lives. "Oh, I know," I said, my fingers absentmindedly tracing the lines of his tattoos. "It's why I was drawn to you all so quickly, why I threw out my 'no relationships' rule without even thinking twice. You're all... irresistible, in your own twisted way."

He chuckled softly, the sound rumbling through him like a distant storm. His hand brushed a strand of hair from my face, tucking it behind my ear as his eyes softened.

"I know Tommy and I still have some way to go," I admitted, my voice quiet but certain. "But I forgive him. I know he won't make the same mistake again."

Declan nodded, his gaze steady and filled with understanding. "He won't," he agreed, his tone firm. "Tommy's been through hell and made some stupid choices. But he loves you, Ember. And he'll do whatever it takes to ensure he doesn't lose you again."

I leaned in, pressing a soft kiss to his lips, feeling the truth of his words settle deep within me. "And I love him," I whispered, my breath mingling with his. "I love all of you."

Declan's smile was complete, a look of pride and contentment etched across his features. "We're lucky to have you, you know," he said, his fingers tracing gentle patterns along my arm. "None of this would work without you."

He kissed the top of my head, his hand stroking my back in slow, soothing motions.

And in that moment, wrapped in Declan's arms, I knew that no matter how messy or complicated things got, we would always find our way back to each other. Together.

40

KNOX DANG

The hum of my Harley echoed through the quiet streets as I weaved my way across London, the city's lights reflecting off the damp asphalt. Tommy had called me into his office, looking more serious than I'd seen him in a while. He had a big lead from Adrian Romano—something that could shift the balance of power. But there was a catch. Tommy had made a promise to Ember, which had shocked us all. He was going to cook her dinner tonight, something none of us had ever witnessed, and he wouldn't break that promise. So, the responsibility of meeting Adrian fell to me.

The engine purred beneath me as I pushed the Harley faster, my mind focused on the task ahead. Adrian's mansion sat on the far side of London, a sprawling estate that screamed wealth and power. As I neared the gates, the iron bars slowly swung open, welcoming me into the lion's den.

I rolled up the driveway, the mansion looming in front of me like something out of a dark fairy tale—grand, imposing, and more than a little unnerving. I killed the engine, the silence that followed thickening the air around me. Adrian's men were always lurking, unseen but ever-present. This was their territory, and they liked ensuring everyone knew it.

The front door opened just as I stepped off the bike, and there he was—Adrian Romano himself. He was the picture of controlled chaos, sharp features, and cold eyes that could charm or intimidate depending on the situation. But today, there was a strange calmness about him.

"Knox," he greeted, his voice as smooth as the whiskey I knew he probably had waiting for him inside. "Tommy send you in his place?"

"Had other plans," I replied, my voice low and steady as I followed him into the mansion. "He has a Queen that needs attending to."

Adrian raised an eyebrow, a smirk tugging at the corner of his lips. "Ah, I had heard the rumors that you had all succumbed to the same woman. Seems unbelievable."

I shrugged, meeting his gaze with a steady calm. "Yeah, I guess it sounds that way from the outside. But with Ember, it's different. She's... everything." I paused for a moment, searching for the right words. "We all have our demons, our dark sides. Declan, Jax, Tommy, and I're all cut from the same messed-up cloth. But somehow, she balances us. Keeps us from going over the edge. There's something about her that works. It's not about possession or control. It's about trust, respect... and love."

Adrian's smirk faded slightly as he considered my words. "Love, huh? I still don't get it. How do you stand it, however? Sharing her, knowing you're not the only one? I'm not built

Chapter 40

that way. I would slit the throats of anyone who touched what was mine." His tone was cool and matter-of-fact, like describing something as simple as taking out the trash.

I chuckled, the memory of my own possessiveness rising to the surface. "I thought the same thing once. I was sure I'd lose my mind at the idea of sharing. I'm a killer, Adrian. My first instinct is to protect what's mine, and anyone who threatens that is as good as dead." I took a breath, thinking of Ember. "But then I met her, and... well, she changed everything. I don't feel like I'm losing anything. She gives each of us what we need; in return, we give her everything. And that keeps me sane. Keeps all of us sane."

Adrian's gaze softened, but his eyes still had that calculating edge. "Interesting," he murmured, watching me closely, his curiosity piqued. "I can see it in you... she does ground you, doesn't she? Curious... very curious." His words were laced with intrigue, but I could tell his mind was already turning over the possibilities, as though trying to reconcile the idea of love and loyalty with his own need for control.

"Yeah," I said, smirking back at him. "She does. And that's why she's ours. All of ours."

As we stepped into the foyer, I was drawn to the opulence around us—marble floors, intricate chandeliers, and artwork that probably cost more than my Harley. Adrian led me through a series of corridors until we reached a grand sitting room, where another figure waited.

"Knox, meet London Deluca," Adrian introduced, motioning to the woman sitting comfortably on the leather sofa. London, daughter of Frank Deluca—another name that carried weight in our world.

She stood up, her piercing eyes meeting mine. There was an undeniable fire behind them, a spark of something dangerous yet captivating. "Nice to finally meet one of the infamous Aces," she said, her voice soft but laced with power.

I nodded, taking her in—a striking woman with dark hair and a look that said she was used to getting what she wanted. "London," I acknowledged, keeping my tone neutral but respectful. There was something about her that demanded it, even without words.

Adrian poured himself a drink, the amber liquid swirling in his glass. "I have some information for Tommy," he began, his gaze flickering toward me. "Something that could change the game."

I crossed my arms, my gaze steady on him. "Let's hear it."

Adrian sipped his drink, letting the tension in the room grow. "Frank's dead," he finally said, his voice cold, emotionless.

I nodded, unphased. "We know." Word traveled fast in our world, especially when someone as high-profile as Frank DeLuca was taken out of the picture.

Adrian glanced at London, who stood beside him with a quiet but commanding presence. "She's the head of the DeLuca family now," he said, nodding toward her. "Frank played all of us, but London's in charge now."

I shifted my gaze to London, sizing her up. She was composed and tough—definitely had the look of someone who wouldn't be a pushover. "That's usually how it works," I

Chapter 40

said, my voice flat. Power doesn't wait; when one player falls, another takes their place. And now it was London's turn to carry the weight of the DeLuca family.

Adrian's jaw tightened, frustration evident in his expression. "You don't know that Frank wasn't just dealing with us. He was playing everyone—using us all as pawns in his little game. We're not just talking about running shipments; he was lining his pockets and cutting deals behind our backs. And now, all the shit he left behind? It's on her shoulders." He nodded toward London again, and her eyes flicked down, unreadable but hard.

I crossed my arms, absorbing the gravity of Adrian's words. This wasn't just about taking over Frank's business; it was about cleaning up the mess he left behind and surviving the fallout. "So what's the move?" I asked, cutting straight to the point.

Adrian leaned back in his chair, swirling his drink before taking a slow sip. "There's some blood ahead in the future," he said, eyes gleaming with the prospect of what was to come. "The question is—will you and Tommy help?"

I raised an eyebrow. "I'll ask Tommy, but he'll want the same for the Russians in return. You know how it works."

Adrian smirked, clearly already expecting the answer. "Oh, I've wanted to jump in on that one for a while now. There are too many of them in this city. I want more space."

I couldn't help but chuckle, the tension breaking slightly as I glanced toward London. "Marry that one," I said, nodding toward her. "You'll get more space instantly."

London blushed, a light pink dusting her cheeks, while Adrian let out a low laugh, his eyes sparkling with mischief.

"Are you on board or not?" he asked, his gaze shifting back to me, all business again.

"Tommy will likely say yes," I said, knowing Tommy's stance on the Russians and how much he hated their encroachment on our turf.

Adrian's smirk widened. "So, here it is—Frank was screwing us all bad. He was selling information from every family to the others. Selling secrets to other groups. The Salvo's, the Moretti's... he had no loyalty."

London folded her arms across her chest, her expression hardening. "Some serious things are coming out on the Moretti's side," Adrian continued. "Frank was knee-deep in something with them. We're still working through it, but by the looks, Moretti's mum might be involved."

That made me swear under my breath. "The mum that went missing, like, what, twenty years ago or some shit?" I asked, my mind racing.

"That's the one," London said, her voice tight with frustration. She had more information than she was letting on, but this was neither the time nor place to press her.

I rubbed the back of my neck, trying to wrap my head around the mess that Frank had left behind. "Okay... well, do we know what information about us he sold?"

Adrian handed me a thick folder, his expression grim. "This is what we have so far."

I flipped through the documents, each page making my blood run colder and colder. It was a disaster. Everything from our shipment routes to some internal family dynamics had been compromised. Frank had sold us out to anyone

Chapter 40

willing to pay, and it was clear that the fallout was far from over.

"Fuck," I muttered, slamming the folder shut. My mind raced, my heart pounding as I tried to process the extent of Frank's betrayal. This wasn't just about business deals or alliances gone sour—this was personal. Frank had sold us out in ways that cut far more profound than I ever could have imagined.

My fingers gripped the folder's edge tightly, knuckles white as I forced myself to breathe, but the tension escalated as my eyes flicked down to the last page. The address of our new farmhouse—the one we had just spent months building, the one Ember was currently eating dinner in—was listed at the bottom. Frank had given away the location of our sanctuary. The place that was supposed to be safe, hidden.

Panic began to creep in, a slow, suffocating pressure that squeezed my chest. I could feel the blood rushing to my ears, drowning out everything else in the room. This wasn't good. This was worse than bad—this was catastrophic.

"Adrian," I rasped, barely recognizing the fear that coated my voice. "I need that help. Now."

Adrian's eyes narrowed, his easy smirk fading as he caught on to the gravity of the situation. "What is it?"

I tossed the folder onto the table between us, pointing to the address. "The farmhouse. That's where we're based. Ember's there." My breath came faster, the words tumbling out in a rush. "If Frank sold us out if he gave that address to the Russians... we gotta go. Now. We can't waste any time."

Adrian's gaze flicked from the folder to me, then to

London, who had grown eerily quiet. The weight of the situation settled between us, thick and oppressive.

"Shit," Adrian muttered, standing up abruptly. "You're right. This is a fucking mess." He barked orders to someone in the hallway called Matteo and Domino before returning to me. "We're moving. I'll get my men on it, but we must go now."

I barely registered his words, the adrenaline pumping through my veins as I yanked my phone from my pocket. My fingers shook as I dialled Tommy, the ringing in my ears mixing with the dial tone on the other end. Come on, come on, pick up.

41

TOMMY PERCIVAL

I stood over the stove, stirring the simmering sauce, the rhythmic sound of the wooden spoon against the pot calming my frayed nerves. Tonight wasn't just about dinner—it was a chance to reconnect with Ember, to close the distance that had stretched between us for too long.

"Smells amazing in here," Ember said, her voice soft and melodic as she stepped into the kitchen.

I turned to look at her, and for a moment, my thoughts scattered. She looked radiant, her dark hair spilling over her shoulders in soft waves, her eyes bright with a hint of playful mischief.

"Just wait until you taste it," I replied, a smile tugging at my lips. "I've been perfecting my pasta recipe. If it turns out well, you might have to give up your fancy apartment."

Ember chuckled, the sound warming something profound inside me. "Is that your way of suggesting I move in permanently?"

"Something like that," I said, a note of seriousness creeping into my voice as I turned back to the stove, trying to hide the mix of excitement and nerves building inside me. The idea of her moving in filled me with anticipation and apprehension. I wanted her here to share this life with us, but I knew it was a huge step.

"Tommy, this is delicious," Ember said, leaning against the counter, her eyes gleaming with delight as she sneakily took a quick scoop of the sauce. "You've outdone yourself."

"Glad you approve," I replied, feeling warmth in my chest at her words. I finished plating the pasta and set the table, the soft clinking of dishes breaking the comfortable silence in the kitchen.

Jax and Declan grabbed their plates and headed to the movie room, shooting me a grin as they left. It was their not-so-subtle way of giving us space, and I appreciated it. I turned back to Ember, who was already sitting at the table. This felt like a quiet little date, just the two of us, something simple yet meaningful.

As we sat down and started eating, I couldn't help but take a moment just to watch her. She looked content, and the sight of her here—back with me—made my heart feel lighter than it had in months. The past few months had been hard, and I didn't realize how much I missed this, missed her, until now.

"I'm really happy you're back," I said, my voice soft but filled with meaning. "I know it took some time, but seeing you with the others... watching you from a distance... it was tough. I struggled a lot. But I had to keep my word, to give you the space you needed."

Chapter 41

Ember's fork paused midway to her mouth. She lowered it slowly, her eyes meeting mine with a tenderness that made my chest tighten. "I missed you too, Tommy," she said softly. "I'm glad you gave me the time. I needed it to sort through everything, but it wasn't easy. I never stopped thinking about you. I never stopped missing you."

Her words hit me like a wave, a sense of relief flooding through me. I reached across the table, gently taking her hand in mine, the warmth of her skin grounding me.

"I'll never hurt you again, Ember. I promise," I said, my voice steady but full of emotion. "No matter what, I'm here for you. Always. I'm not going anywhere."

She squeezed my hand in return, her eyes shining. "I know," she whispered, her voice filled with quiet assurance. "And that's why I'm here now. Because I believe you."

For the first time in a long while, it felt like everything was falling into place. Sitting there with her, sharing dinner like it was just the two of us in the world—it felt right. And I wasn't going to take that for granted again.

After we finished dinner, Ember and I worked together to stack the dishwasher, our movements in sync as we cleared the plates. It was a small, mundane task, but there was something intimate in the simplicity of it. Once everything was set, we headed to the movie room to see what Jax and Declan were watching, laughing quietly as we joined them on the couch.

The cozy glow from the screen cast flickering shadows across the room, wrapping us in a comfortable intimacy that felt safe. The soft hum of the movie in the background blended with the quiet moments we shared. I wanted to hold on to this feeling—the warmth, the connection—while I still could.

Ember tucked her legs beneath her, her arm brushing against mine as she settled in.

"Ember," I began, my voice low as I turned to face her.

She glanced over, curiosity flickering in her eyes.

"I was serious before when I said... about you moving in here, officially. Giving up your apartment."

Her brows knit together slightly, and I could feel the shift in the air, the tension coiling tighter.

"Tommy, I—"

"Just hear me out," I cut in, the edge of desperation creeping into my tone. "We've built something real, something incredible. I don't want you to feel like you're living in two worlds anymore. You belong here—with us. I want you here."

She shifted slightly, her eyes still focused on the screen as she let out a soft chuckle. "You know, even if I wanted to, I wouldn't be allowed to officially go back to my place."

Jax, who had been half paying attention, scrolling through his phone, looked up, furrowing his brow. "What do you mean?"

Declan turned his head too, curiosity piqued. "Yeah, what are you talking about?"

Ember smirked, her eyes twinkling mischievously. "Knox would never allow his *wife* to live anywhere else but with him."

The silence that followed was almost comical, like the air had been sucked out of the room for a second. I felt my own

Chapter 41

head tilt slightly, trying to figure out if I'd heard her correctly. "Wife?" I echoed, the word hanging in the air.

Declan's confusion turned into a burst of laughter, breaking the tension. "Wait—w*ife?* You're saying what I think you're saying?"

Ember shrugged, laughing softly. "A few months ago, Knox sent me a marriage license. At first, I thought it was a joke. Something he'd done to make me laugh. But now... I'm not so sure."

Declan slapped his knee, still laughing. "That makes so much sense! He's been wearing a wedding band for months now! I thought nothing of it, just Knox being Knox, but now it all clicks."

Jax, sitting on the far side of the room, was frozen in place, his mouth slightly ajar. "Wait, wait, hold on a second. Are you saying you're married to Knox? For real?"

I couldn't help but smile, shaking my head in disbelief. "That sneaky fuck," I muttered, rubbing my hand over my jaw. "He slid right in without any of us even knowing."

Jax finally blinked, coming back to life, looking from Ember to me, then to Declan, trying to process it. "So... how can we marry you now too, if Knox beat us to it?" His voice held a mix of shock and something close to panic, which made Ember burst into laughter.

She looked over at him, grinning. "Relax, Jax. I didn't even agree to it."

Declan wiped a tear from his eye, still chuckling. "Knowing Knox, he probably just had his judge friend push it through."

Ember laughed harder at that, the sound brightening the room. "Well then, Mrs. Holland," I teased, winking at her.

She leaned into me, still laughing. "Oh no, I'm not Mrs. Holland. He took my name."

That was it—Declan howled with laughter again, and even Jax cracked a smile, shaking his head in disbelief. "Wait, wait, what? Knox took your name?"

Ember nodded proudly. "Yep. He's Mr. Dang now, or so the paperwork says."

The room erupted with laughter, and I couldn't help but join in. "How in the world did you get him to give up his name?" Declan managed between fits of laughter.

Ember's grin widened. "I just told him I wouldn't be Mrs. Holland. I guess he didn't like that very much."

I leaned back against the couch, pulling Ember closer into my side, feeling the weight of everything settle into a strange, but comforting, normalcy. Knox always was the possessive type, and of course, he would've done something like that. But the fact that Ember was sitting here, with all of us, laughing about it—that was something else.

"Mr. Dang, huh?" Jax finally said, shaking his head in disbelief. "Never thought I'd see the day."

"Neither did I," I muttered, chuckling. "But that's Knox for you."

As the laughter died down, Ember looked at each of us, her smile softer now. "It's crazy, right? I didn't see it coming either. But... I don't mind. Knox is Knox. He does things his way. And I guess... I'm okay with that."

We all sat there for a moment, the weight of her words settling in. This was our life now—a life full of chaos,

Chapter 41

surprises, and unconventional love. And I wouldn't trade it for anything.

"Well," I said, raising an imaginary glass in a toast. "To Mr. Dang."

Everyone joined in, their laughter filling the room once more.

42
JAX STEVENSON

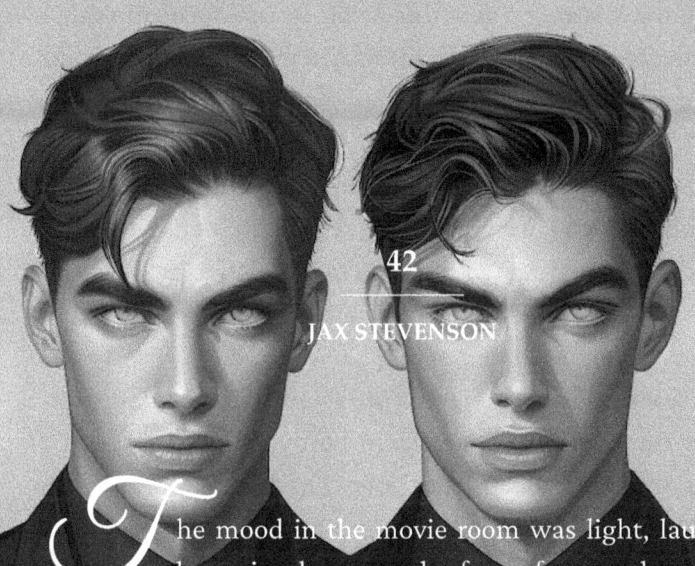

The mood in the movie room was light, laughter bouncing between the four of us as the credits rolled on some action flick none of us had really been paying attention to. I glanced over at Ember, the soft glow of the TV playing across her face as she leaned back against the couch, her legs tucked beneath her. She had that look of contentment, the one that always made my chest tighten just a little.

But I couldn't stop thinking about the whole marriage license thing. Knox, sneaky bastard, already got his name in the game, and now it felt like we were all playing catch-up. I shifted, looking at Ember, and said, "Okay, so how do I get to marry you if Knox beat me to it? There's gotta be a way, right?"

Ember laughed, her voice warm and teasing, but it didn't hide the surprise in her eyes. "How about I wear a dress, and we throw a party? Would that work for you?"

Before I could respond, Declan chimed in, smirking. "What if we *all* want to marry you, hmm?"

Tommy, sitting a few feet away, leaned forward with a mischievous grin on his face. "Yeah, Ember, what about us? You're not leaving the rest of us out of this equation, are you?"

I watched as Ember's expression shifted, her eyes widening as the weight of our words hit her. She paled slightly, her laughter fading into a nervous chuckle. "Hold on a minute, guys. One thing at a time. I never even agreed to Knox's... let alone all four of you."

Her voice trailed off just as the sharp sound of glass shattering ripped through the air. Instantly, all of us froze, our heads snapping toward the door. The movie room, which had been filled with easy laughter just moments ago, now felt like a pressure cooker about to explode.

Tommy was the first to react, his body moving with the kind of speed that came from years of living on the edge. He was already halfway to the door, his muscles tense and ready for whatever was coming.

My own pulse kicked into high gear, and I instinctively reached for the guns we kept stashed in the couch cushions. My fingers closed around the cold metal of the Glock, and I cocked it, the sound echoing in the sudden stillness.

Declan was already in motion too, his hand on Ember's arm as he gently but firmly pulled her down, laying her flat on the floor and crouching over her like a human shield. "Stay down," he ordered, his voice low and controlled.

I stood, gun in hand, moving behind Tommy as we both faced the door, waiting for whatever threat was about to come crashing through. My mind was racing, adrenaline surging through my veins, but I forced myself to stay

Chapter 42

focused. If there is one wrong move, everything could go sideways.

Tommy gave me a glance, his green eyes hard with a determination I'd seen countless times before. He raised a hand, signaling for silence, as we both strained to hear the source of the noise. Another crash echoed from the hallway, followed by the unmistakable sound of footsteps—heavy, deliberate.

"Get ready," Tommy muttered under his breath, his grip tightening on the gun in his hand that he had pulled from god knew where.

My heart pounded, the anticipation building with every second that ticked by. I could feel the familiar rush of the hunt, the thrill of danger, but there was also a gnawing fear at the back of my mind. Not for me. Not for Ember.

Declan still had her pinned beneath him, his large frame covering hers entirely as he whispered something to her that I couldn't hear. She looked pale, but her eyes were alert, scanning the room like she was trying to find a way out if things went south.

The footsteps grew louder and closer until they stopped just outside the door.

For a moment, everything was eerily still.

Then, without warning, the door burst open, slamming against the wall with enough force to shake the frame. A group of men dressed in SWAT uniforms surged into the room like they'd known exactly where we were the whole time. They moved with precision, too fast, like this wasn't just a lucky break—they'd been planning for this. How the hell did they know?

My mind raced as I took in the scene. Whoever sold us out knew more than they should've. The house, sure. But the exact room we were in? That was something else entirely. Betrayal laced every thought as I glanced at Tommy, who had already started firing.

The sharp crack of gunfire split the air, Tommy's shots precise and controlled, but all they did was ping off helmets and vests. A couple of them staggered, but none went down. I watched in disbelief as the men dove on us with military precision, closing the distance in seconds.

"Fuck!" I shouted, grabbing for another weapon stashed under the couch cushion. My fingers wrapped around the cold steel of the pistol just as one of the SWAT guys lunged at me. I fired off a shot, but he was too fast, knocking the gun out of my hand before I could get a clean hit.

They were on us, pushing us down, their grips iron-tight. One of them grabbed me, twisting my arm behind my back with a strength that had me gritting my teeth in pain. I thrashed, trying to shake him off, but these guys weren't regular thugs—they were trained for this. I could hear Tommy cursing as they tackled him to the ground, Declan's furious grunts as he fought back, and Ember's muffled scream as she struggled beneath the weight of one of the attackers.

Adrenaline surged through me as I twisted in the guy's grip, slamming my elbow into his ribs. He grunted, loosening his hold for just a second—enough for me to turn and slam my fist into his face. His helmet absorbed most of the impact but threw him off balance.

In the chaos, I spotted one of the men pinning Ember to

Chapter 42

the floor. My blood ran cold. They had her on her stomach, her face pressed against the hardwood, her arms wrenched behind her back. I saw red.

"Get the fuck off her!" I roared, charging at him. I tackled the guy, knocking him off Ember, but before I could land another punch, another one of the SWAT guys was on me, dragging me back.

"Who the fuck are you?" I snarled, trying to break free as the guy yanked my arms back.

They didn't answer. They didn't say shit. That silence only made everything worse. I knew what we were dealing with—this was calculated and precise, and they knew exactly what they were doing.

Declan was still fighting off two of them when one of the guys pulled out a taser. I saw the flash of electricity before Declan's body seized, his muscles locking up as he collapsed to the floor. I winced as the same fate awaited me. I needed to get to Ember to ensure she was all right, but they were too fast and well-prepared.

Tommy was the last one to go down, his face twisted in rage as they overwhelmed him, forcing him to the ground next to Declan. They got him in a chokehold, his voice cut off mid-shout, and all I could hear was the deafening sound of my heartbeat in my ears.

How the hell had it come to this?

The SWAT team moved like a well-oiled machine, efficient and merciless. They were tying us up now, making sure none of us could even twitch without their say-so. My wrists burned as the zip ties bit into my skin, the plastic digging in harder with every flex of my arms. I growled under my breath, glaring at the guy who had tied me up. His mask covered his face, but I could see the cold detachment in his eyes—this was nothing to him, just another job.

Across the room, Tommy's eyes locked on mine. He wasn't speaking, but his lips moved just enough for me to catch the word: *Russians.* My blood boiled. One of the guys securing Declan's hands spoke rapidly, clipped Russian to another, confirming Tommy's suspicion. It made sense. The Russians had been circling us for a while now, sniffing around the edges of our operations, looking for weaknesses. I should've known they'd make their move like this, a full-on ambush.

The thought of being outplayed by those bastards only fueled the rage simmering inside me. But I couldn't do shit. My arms were pinned, the ties biting in deeper, and all I could do was watch as these assholes made sure we were fully restrained. Declan was fighting them, as usual, his body jerking as they secured his wrists behind his back. He swore under his breath, but the fury in his eyes told me he wasn't done yet.

But then my gaze shifted to Ember. She hadn't been tied up, not yet, at least. One of the Russians was standing near her, probably waiting for an order. But what unnerved me more than the fact that she wasn't resisting was the look on her face—blank. Hollow. Like she wasn't even there anymore. Her eyes weren't wide with fear or narrowed in anger like I'd expected. They were just... empty. She wasn't moving, wasn't fighting, wasn't Ember.

"Ember?" I called out, my voice rough, but there was no response. She didn't even flinch. It was like she didn't hear

Chapter 42

me or recognize me—or anyone else in the room, for that matter. She wasn't the same person I knew. The fire, the fight in her—it was gone and terrified me more than anything else.

One of the Russians looked down at her, confused, and I felt a rush of panic rise in my chest. What the hell was happening to her?

"Hey!" I shouted, struggling against my restraints. "Get the fuck away from her!"

The Russian ignored me, his attention still on Ember, but he didn't touch her. I thought maybe they'd leave her alone for a moment, but then another man—one who looked like he was in charge—stepped forward, speaking to his men in Russian again. Whatever he said made the others pause, their eyes flicking to Ember.

Tommy's gaze was locked on the scene unfolding before us. His jaw clenched, veins popping at his temple as he glared at the man in charge. He couldn't do anything either, but I could see the wheels turning in his head, the rage bubbling beneath the surface.

I glanced at Declan, who was watching the same scene with wide eyes. His body was still tense, like a coiled spring, but I could tell he was just as helpless as I was.

We all were.

And Ember? She was still there, physically at least, but mentally? She was somewhere else. The fire in her eyes—the one that had always burned so brightly—was completely gone.

It was like she'd disappeared right in front of us.

And I had no idea how to bring her back.

43

KNOX DANG

I had never been more grateful than I was right now for Adrian Romano standing at my side. We pulled up at the farmhouse just as the gunfire erupted, the staccato bursts echoing across the darkened landscape. My heart was racing, the adrenaline coursing through my veins, but the sight of Adrian and his crew rolling up alongside me brought relief.

Adrian had left London behind despite her insistence on coming. I knew she had that fire in her, which reminded me of Ember, but this wasn't the place for anyone unprepared for bloodshed. Even thinking about Ember being caught in this mess made my chest tighten, blood boil. This wasn't a place for her—*not my Ember*. She was stronger than anyone I knew, but this... this was war.

The anger crept over me, that familiar, suffocating veil of rage that sometimes swallowed me whole. My hands tightened around the grips of the twin guns in my hands, their weight a comfort, but I had to keep my head clear. I had to focus. The only thing that mattered was getting inside and ensuring Ember was safe.

The gunfire had stopped now, and an eerie silence settled over the farmhouse. I motioned for Adrian and his team to follow as we approached the side door. I led the way, my heart pounding louder than the blood rushing in my ears.

Two guns, one in each hand, safeties off. Every muscle in my body coiled, ready to strike, to tear apart anyone who stood between me and the people I loved. I reached for the door, my fingers barely brushing the handle before I pushed it open with a quiet precision. The door gave way without a sound, and we filed inside like shadows slipping through the cracks.

Adrian's men moved like ghosts, disciplined and deadly. I could feel Adrian at my back, his presence a solid weight, like a pillar of ice keeping my rising fury in check. He was as calm as ever, a man who'd seen more blood and betrayal than most. But every breath was a struggle not to let the rage consume me. I had to keep it together. I had to think about her—Ember. Every step brought me closer to finding her, to pulling her out of this nightmare.

The dimly lit hallways of the farmhouse stretched before us, and the scent of gunpowder still lingered in the air. My mind was already racing, playing out every scenario, every possible way this could've gone down. I tried to ignore the gut-wrenching thought that something might have already happened to her.

Adrian's voice was low, barely a whisper, but it cut

Chapter 43

through the silence like a knife. "We need to be quick. This place reeks of an ambush."

I nodded without looking back. I didn't need the reminder, but it helped to have someone like Adrian with me—calm, calculating. I could hear his men moving ahead, checking corners and ensuring we wouldn't fall into a trap.

We passed through the hallway, edging closer to the kitchen. The air grew heavier, and every step felt like walking toward the edge of a cliff. My grip tightened on my guns, and the cold metal ground me.

And then, we heard a faint rustling sound, the scrape of boots on wood, from the left, the movie room.

I cracked my neck, the tension building up in my shoulders loosening momentarily before I locked eyes with Adrian. His eyes widened, a silent warning flashing as he shook his head slightly, but I just smiled—cold and hard. He didn't get it.

"They have my wife," I growled, the words a snarl of pure fury, and without waiting for any more protests, I walked straight into the movie room.

Time slowed the second I stepped through the door. My mind went razor-sharp, hyper-focused on what was in front of me. The room was filled with men dressed in full SWAT gear, their faces hidden behind helmets, their bodies covered in bulletproof vests. My eyes swept over them, taking in the layout, the angles, the openings—and I immediately knew where to aim. These bastards thought they were untouchable, but they forgot one thing: I wasn't aiming for the vests.

I squeezed the trigger, round after round, my shots

aimed at their exposed necks. One by one, the men fell, crumpling like paper as I landed shot after shot. The hot sting of a bullet hit my arm, but I didn't flinch. Pain was nothing. Not compared to the rage burning inside me. It's not compared to the need to get to Ember.

The gunfire around me was deafening, but my focus was absolute. My world had shrunk to a single point, and that point was Ember.

And then, I saw her.

Kneeling on the floor, her arms behind her back, her face pale but calm in that eerie way she got when things were really bad. Our eyes locked across the chaos, and I saw the slightest flicker of relief in her expression. She was alive. She was still there.

But something dark had settled over her, a blankness I hadn't seen in her before. She wasn't resisting, wasn't fighting back, and that worried me more than anything. It was like she had switched off, disconnected from the violence surrounding her.

"Ember," I whispered under my breath, just as I took down another man who had aimed his gun toward me. My blood was roaring in my ears, my vision narrowing as I pressed forward. Every fiber of my being screamed at me to reach her, to rip apart anyone who stood in my way.

Adrian and his team surged in behind me, gunfire erupting as they took out the stragglers, but my focus never left her. I took a step forward, another shot ringing out as I dropped the last man standing between me and Ember.

Blood splattered across the room, and across my face. I wiped the warm droplets from my cheek, my heart still

Chapter 43

racing with the fading adrenaline. My gaze locked on Ember, her wide eyes meeting mine. In that instant, something snapped in her eyes—a ferocity, a fire that I had only glimpsed before, now fully unleashed.

I smiled at her, a silent reassurance, but I barely had time to process what was happening before Ember pivoted. She moved so fast, so fluidly, that the man holding her barely had time to react. He released her arms, stunned by the sudden motion, but it was too late. In one swift, graceful movement, Ember swept her leg under his feet, sending him crashing to the floor with a heavy thud.

Before anyone could move, she was on him. Her legs wrapped around his neck, and with a strength and precision I had never seen before, she began to choke him. The man struggled, his hands clawing at her legs, but it was no use. Ember's face was a mask of cold, focused fury, her movements quick and calculated.

The room went deathly silent as we all watched, frozen in place, as she finished him off. The man's gasps for air became weaker, his body jerking beneath her before finally going limp. The crack of his final breath echoed through the room, a haunting reminder of just how deadly she could be when pushed.

Ember held her position for a moment longer, her body tense, her eyes still locked on the man beneath her. Then, slowly, she released him, her legs uncoiling with the same lethal grace she had used to strike. She stood, her chest heaving, the room eerily quiet as everyone processed what had just happened.

I took a step forward, my heart hammering in my chest

as I moved toward her. "Ember," I whispered, my voice low, almost reverent.

She turned to face me, the fire in her eyes still burning, it was like she didn't see me, didn't know who I was.

44

EMBER DANG

The room felt like it was closing in, the walls shifting and twisting as the men in SWAT gear swarmed into the space. But they weren't just men in uniform anymore. They morphed, twisted into something more sinister, something my mind recognized but refused to acknowledge. My heart hammered in my chest, each beat a deafening drum in my ears. The world around me blurred, faded, until I was no longer in the movie room.

I was back there.

The cold, damp room where they kept me when I was a child. The sweat, blood, and fear stench clung to the air like a suffocating fog. My hands were tied behind my back, the rough ropes cutting into my skin, my body naked and vulnerable. I could feel the scratchy fabric of the old rug beneath my knees, the bruises on my flesh from the countless times they had taken from me. Over and over again, they had come. I couldn't stop them. I was just a child.

My breaths came in ragged gasps, each one more difficult

than the last. I couldn't get enough air. I couldn't move. My body was frozen in that horrific memory, locked in the cage of my mind. The present, the farmhouse— all vanished, replaced by the nightmare I'd tried to forget.

I could hear them—dark and menacing voices circling me, closing in. I tried to scream, but no sound came out. My throat felt raw, tight, like something was choking me from the inside out. I couldn't speak. I couldn't fight.

Then, through the fog of terror, I saw him.

A figure stood before me, his face shrouded in shadows, but his eyes... I recognized those eyes. There was something in them that whispered of safety, of protection, something that promised this nightmare wasn't real. His gaze was piercing, grounding, and for a fleeting moment, I clung to it.

He's safety.

That thought echoed through my mind, the only thread of reality I had left. I focused on him, trying to pull myself from the abyss. But the pressure on my wrists grew tighter, the ropes binding me digging into my skin, and my panic surged again. I couldn't breathe, I couldn't—

Snap.

Something inside me broke. The fear, the helplessness— it all shifted into something else. Rage. Raw, unfiltered rage. My body moved on instinct, years of survival training kicking in as my muscles tensed, ready to strike.

I wasn't that child anymore.

I wasn't weak.

I wasn't powerless.

A primal scream ripped from my throat as I twisted, using the momentum of my body to throw off the hands that

Chapter 44

had held me. The men around me were no longer those from my past. But my mind was still locked in survival mode, and all I could think was to fight, to destroy anyone who tried to take from me again.

The man holding me stumbled, his grip faltering as I broke free. My legs moved before I could think, sweeping beneath him and sending him crashing to the floor. Without hesitation, I was on him. My legs found his neck, squeezing with a strength I didn't know I possessed. His eyes bulged as he struggled beneath me, his hands clawing at my legs, but I didn't let go. I couldn't.

I had to survive.

I had to fight.

The room went silent, but I didn't stop. I squeezed harder, my body trembling with the force of my fury. His gasps became weaker, fainter, until finally, they ceased altogether.

And then, the silence hit me.

The man beneath me was still, lifeless. My body shook as I released my grip on him with my legs, my heart pounding in my chest. My gaze darted around the room, confused.

The man beneath me was still, lifeless. My body shook as I released the grip I had on him with my legs, my heart slamming against my ribs in a chaotic rhythm. My breath came in shallow gasps as I glanced around the room, my vision blurred, confusion clouding my thoughts. The faces around me were familiar, yet distant. I knew those eyes—those deep, piercing gazes—but the faces, they didn't make sense.

Everything felt out of place, twisted and wrong. My mind was still trying to crawl out of the dark, out of that memory that had swallowed me whole. The room seemed to tilt, and I swayed on my feet, the adrenaline in my veins faltering.

Just then, one of the men lunged toward me, and instinct kicked in before I could process the movement. In a flash, I grabbed the gun from his hand, my fingers steady, as though they were made to wrap around the cold metal. There was no struggle, no hesitation from him. I aimed the barrel right between his eyes, my hands shaking slightly, but my grip unwavering.

His expression shifted, and to my confusion, a look of understanding crossed his features. His eyes softened, the tension draining from his body as he relaxed, resting his forehead gently against the gun's muzzle.

And then he spoke, his voice low and tender. "Ember, it's ok, baby. It's just us. We're all ok. If you need to pull the trigger, it's alright. I love you. I'd die for you anyway."

His words cut through the fog, the weight of them grounding me, pulling me back from the edge. I stared into those eyes—soft, warm, filled with a love I didn't deserve. The haze in my mind started to clear, and I gasped as recognition hit me like a sledgehammer.

"Tommy?" I whispered, my voice trembling as I stared at him, at the man who had just offered himself up to me, without hesitation, without fear.

He smiled gently, that crooked, boyish smile I knew so well. "Yes, baby. It's me."

The gun slipped from my fingers, clattering to the ground as my legs gave out beneath me. But before I could crumble completely, Tommy caught me and held me close. His arms were warm, strong, and safe. I buried my face in his chest,

Chapter 44

my entire body trembling, the weight of what had just happened crashing down on me like a tidal wave.

But then, another presence wrapped around me, pressing against my back, solid and familiar. His scent hit me before his voice did, a deep growl vibrating in my ear, the sound both possessive and protective. "It's ok, sweetness. We got you now."

Knox.

I knew him by feel alone. The hard planes of his chest against me, his body seemed to fit perfectly against mine, as though he was made to be my shield. His arms encircled me, a barrier between me and the world, as if he could block out the darkness that threatened to consume me.

I sagged into them both, the fight draining from my body, my mind too exhausted to cling to the terror that had held me captive. Tommy's hand gently stroked my hair, his lips brushing my forehead in soft reassurance, while Knox's grip tightened, his presence steadying me in a way only he could.

They were here. Safe. I was safe.

Tears slipped down my cheeks, silent and unchecked, as I finally let go, letting them carry the weight for me, just for a little while.

45

DECLAN STEVENSON

I stood there, frozen for a second, watching Tommy scooping Ember into his arms like she was the only thing that mattered. She pressed her face against his chest, clinging to him, and Knox—always her silent protector—followed right behind. I couldn't tear my eyes away as the three of them disappeared from the room, leaving the chaos and blood behind.

The silence that followed was suffocating. My mind raced, trying to process everything, but I could only focus on that image of Ember, shaken but alive. Relief coursed through me, but it didn't loosen the tight knot in my chest.

I exhaled, my gaze slowly shifting toward Adrian Romano, who stood casually by the door, surveying the mess with that calm, amused look he always wore. He didn't even blink at the carnage around us. His eyes flicked over the scene like it was just another day at the office. Then, he met my gaze, and the smirk on his face widened.

"What the fuck are you doing here?" I asked, my voice

low but heavy with genuine surprise. Not that I wasn't grateful—I was. But Adrian Romano didn't do things for free.

He chuckled, that rich, smooth laugh that always made it sound like he knew something no one else did. "Collecting future IOUs from the Aces," he said casually.

I couldn't help it—a laugh escaped me, though it was more bitter than anything else. "Well, this one was well deserved," I admitted, my tone softening with gratitude. "Thank you. I don't know what I would've done if they'd hurt her."

Adrian's smirk shifted, the amusement dimming just enough for something more real to surface in his eyes. He nodded once, slowly, like he understood exactly what I meant.

"I get it," he said, his voice quieter, almost sincere in a way that caught me off guard.

I arched a brow at that, his words hitting me differently than I expected. "You get it?" I repeated, not sure if I believed him.

His smirk returned, but it wasn't as sharp as before. It was softer, like he was letting me in on something. "Men like us... we always get it when it comes to women like that."

I didn't know what to say, so I just nodded, letting the silence hang between us for a moment. For all his swagger and bullshit, I could tell Adrian knew exactly what Ember meant to me—almost like he had an Ember of his own. That connection and fear of losing someone like that didn't need explaining.

Adrian pushed off the doorframe and clapped a hand on my shoulder as he passed by. "Alright, let's clean up this

Chapter 45

mess, yeah?" he said, his voice casual but with a steel edge that told me he was already planning his next move.

I let out a long breath, feeling the weight of the night press down on me again. "Yeah. Let's clean this up."

As I turned, my eyes landed on Jax, who was still almost frozen in the same spot. His usual carefree expression was gone, replaced with something I rarely saw in him—fear. Real, bone-deep fear. He hadn't moved, his eyes wide and haunted as they stared at the spot where Ember had been. I stepped toward him, concern tugging at my gut.

"You okay, mate?" I asked, my voice low, trying not to startle him.

Jax blinked, his eyes slowly lifting to meet mine, and for a second, I wasn't sure he was there. Then, in a voice so unlike him—quiet, almost broken—he whispered, "I... I don't know what would have happened if they had hurt her, Dec. If they had hurt her..."

I felt my chest tighten at his words and looked at my brother. Jax, the one who always played it cool and laughed in the face of danger, was crumbling right in front of me. This wasn't the time for him to spiral, not now. I stepped closer, grabbing his shoulder and grounding him in the moment.

"Hey, it's okay," I said firmly, meeting his eyes. "She's okay. I'm fairly certain Tommy's in his office right now, probably refusing to let her out of his arms. She's safe, Jax. She's okay."

Jax looked away, his jaw working as if he was trying to hold back something. He swallowed hard, his Adam's apple bobbing. "Maybe we should let her go," he muttered, his voice cracking slightly. "Keep her away from all of this... from us. It's selfish. The four of us forced her to stay in this life. To love us."

My stomach sank at his words. I could see where this was headed, and it wasn't good. Jax had never voiced doubts like this before, but I could hear the guilt lacing every word. He was spiraling, and if I didn't pull him back now, he might try to push Ember away—for her sake, sure, but it would destroy him in the process.

I gripped his shoulder tighter, giving him a shake. "Snap the fuck out of it, Jax," I growled, my voice low but sharp. "She chose us. She's strong. Stronger than any of us sometimes. She's okay. She's here. And we're here."

He looked at me, his eyes searching mine like he was looking for reassurance that he wasn't the only one drowning in these thoughts.

"Listen," I said, softening my tone but keeping it firm. "Why don't you go find her? Head to Tommy's office. You need to touch her, hold her, remind yourself of a few things."

Jax hesitated for a beat, then gave a slow nod. "Yeah... yeah, maybe you're right." His voice was steadier now like he was coming back to himself. He gave me a weak smile, the weight in his eyes still there but less overwhelming. "Thanks, mate."

I watched him walk out, his shoulders still tense but with a bit more purpose in his steps. He'd be fine once he had Ember in his arms again. She was the anchor we all needed.

As soon as Jax was out of sight, I turned back to Adrian and his men, who were still standing there, watching the

Chapter 45

scene unfold. "All right, enough staring," I snapped at them, my voice harsher than before. "Get this shit cleaned up."

Adrian's men jumped into action, quickly clearing the bodies and the mess left behind. I noticed Matteo, Frank Deluca's right-hand man, standing off to the side, whispering with Adrian. My blood ran cold at the sight of him.

"What the fuck are you doing here?" I barked as I marched over to them, my anger simmering beneath the surface.

Matteo turned to face me, his expression unreadable, but something flickered in his eyes. "Relax, Declan," Adrian said, stepping between us before things could escalate. "He's here on business."

"Business?" I shot back, my eyes narrowing. "What kind of business brings Frank's right hand to our doorstep after Russians have just attacked us?"

Matteo smirked, but it didn't reach his eyes. "The kind of business that's about to change everything."

46

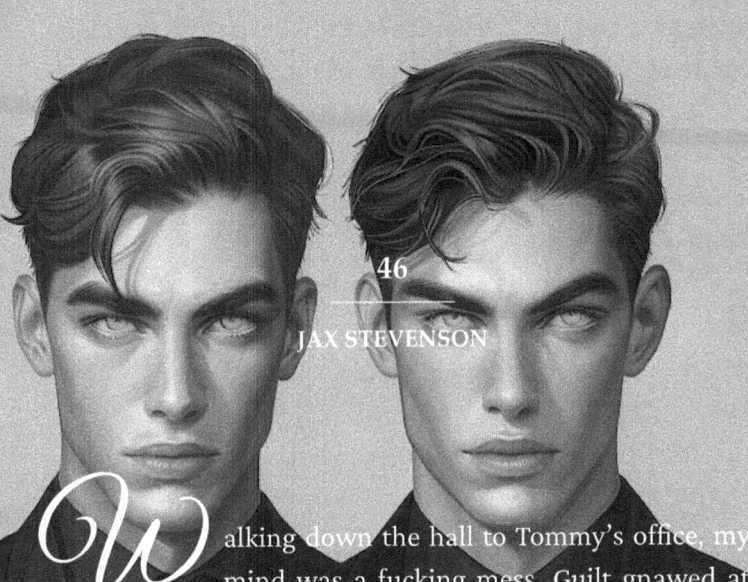

JAX STEVENSON

Walking down the hall to Tommy's office, my mind was a fucking mess. Guilt gnawed at me, twisting my insides into knots that I couldn't untangle. My footsteps echoed in the quiet, too loud, too sharp, like they were mocking me with every step.

This was my fault.

I was the one who pushed for Ember to be part of us, to be mine, to crown her our queen without thinking twice. I didn't consider the danger, the enemies, the shitstorm that was always circling us. I was selfish. She'd become my obsession, my everything, and I wanted her with us, no matter the cost. And now? Now I wasn't sure if she was okay.

Fuck.

That look in her eyes before she choked that guy out—Jesus, it's haunting me. That blank, faraway stare like she wasn't even there, like someone had switched off the light inside her. I knew that look. I'd seen it in my own reflection after I did things I shouldn't have, things that stayed with me long after the blood was cleaned up. But seeing it in her—someone so fierce and alive—shook me to my core.

I couldn't shake the image of her legs wrapped around that guy's neck, the way she moved with such brutal efficiency. She snapped, and part of me felt like I had pushed her to that edge. I dragged her into this world, made her a part of us, and she was nearly... hurt? Broken? I didn't know. Fuck, I didn't even know if she'd been hurt because I hadn't checked. I had just stood there like a fucking idiot, watching her, too caught up in my head.

My heart was pounding now, loud enough to drown out everything else, the guilt weighing me down like chains around my ankles. The thought of her getting hurt—or worse—because of me was unbearable. I swallowed hard, my throat dry, finally reaching Tommy's office.

The door was slightly ajar, and I could hear the low murmur of voices inside. Tommy, probably holding her, whispering reassurances. My chest tightened. Tommy's got her. He's with her. But that didn't make it any easier. It didn't stop the guilt from ripping through me.

I paused at the door, my hand resting on the doorknob. Part of me wanted to turn around and leave, to avoid facing her right now, to avoid seeing the damage I might have caused. But I had to know if she was okay. I had to see her, touch her, make sure she was real and breathing, and not lost to whatever darkness had flickered in her eyes when she snapped.

Taking a deep breath, I pushed the door open.

The sight inside hit me harder than I expected. Tommy was sitting on the new occasional couch, which was massive,

Chapter 46

fluffy, and comfortable, which Knox had demanded when she designed Tommy's office.

He cradled Ember in his arms, her head resting against his chest. She looked so small, so f and fragile at that moment, but her eyes were closed, and her breathing was She wasn't crying or trembling—she was just... there. Tommy's arms were wrapped around her like a shield, and his expression was unreadable, but I could see the tension in his shoulders, the fear just beneath the surface.

I stepped inside, the guilt tightening its grip around my throat. "Is she...?" I couldn't finish the question, my voice barely above a whisper.

Tommy looked up at me, his green eyes hard but understanding. "She's okay, Jax," he said quietly. "Just needs some time."

I nodded, my hands flexing at my sides, restless. I didn't know what to say or how to explain the storm brewing inside me. So I just stood there, staring at her, trying to make sense of everything.

"I shouldn't have made her our queen... I didn't think...," I started, my voice breaking under my guilt.

Tommy's gaze never left me. "We all wanted her here, Jax," he said, his voice firm but not accusing. "But you're not wrong to feel the way you do. This life—it's not easy. And maybe we didn't think about all the ways it could fuck with her. But she's strong. She's with us because she chose to be."

I shook my head, the knot in my chest tightening. "But look what happened. She—she wasn't even there, Tommy. She snapped, and it was like... like I didn't even recognize her."

Tommy's arms tightened around Ember as he glanced down at her, his face softening. "She's been through hell, Jax. We've all got our demons. That was hers."

I let out a shaky breath, taking a hesitant step closer, my eyes never leaving Ember's face. "I didn't think she'd be in danger like this. I didn't think… fuck, I was so selfish."

Tommy's eyes narrowed slightly, his tone shifting. "You're not selfish for wanting her with us. We all wanted her here."

I nodded again, feeling the sting of tears I refused to let fall. I couldn't lose her. Not like this. Not after everything.

"Go ahead," Tommy said softly, nodding toward Ember. "She needs to know you're here."

I stepped closer, my heart hammering as I crouched beside the couch. Gently, I reached out and touched her hand, my fingers brushing against hers. Her skin was warm and alive, and that simple contact grounded me, like I could finally breathe again.

"Hey, poison," I whispered, my voice breaking. "I'm here."

Ember's eyes fluttered open, her gaze meeting mine. And in that moment, everything else faded—guilt, fear, and doubt. She was here, and she was mine. Ours.

"I'm sorry," I murmured again, my voice barely audible as I crouched beside the couch. "I should've done more."

Ember's brow furrowed in confusion as she looked down at me, her hand still resting in mine. "More what, Jax?" she asked, her voice soft but laced with concern. Without hesitation, she climbed out of Tommy's arms and into mine, wrap-

Chapter 46

ping her legs around my waist and arms around my neck, holding me tightly.

The sudden warmth of her body against mine, her weight in my lap, broke whatever fragile control I had left. The tears I'd been holding back started falling, and I couldn't stop them. I didn't even try. They fell freely, silently at first, and then with a force that made my chest ache.

"Shhh," Ember whispered, her lips brushing against my ear as she cradled my head against her shoulder. "It's okay, Jax. It's okay. Pick me up."

I didn't hesitate. I wrapped my arms around her tighter, standing with her held against me like my only lifeline, and sat back down on the couch where Tommy had just vacated. Her body was so small, so fragile in my arms, but she felt like the strongest person I'd ever known.

Ember didn't loosen her grip as I sat, and I didn't want her to. I needed this, needed her. My tears kept falling, my body shaking with the weight of my guilt, and all I could do was hold her close.

Tommy, who had moved to give us space, walked across the room toward his desk. Knox was already there, sitting in the chair, his eyes fixed on Ember like they hadn't left her since the moment they'd come into the room. His gaze was intense, almost too much, like he was afraid if he looked away, even for a second, she might vanish.

"Knox," Tommy said softly, but Knox didn't respond. His focus stayed on Ember, unmoving, unwavering.

Ember shifted in my lap slightly, pulling back just enough to look at me, her hands cupping my face as she wiped away my tears with her thumbs. Her touch was soft, gentle, but her eyes were filled with determination, with understanding.

"It's okay," she whispered, leaning her forehead against mine. "I'm here, Jax. We're all here. You didn't do anything wrong."

I swallowed hard, trying to find the words, but all that came out was, "I was scared." My voice cracked, and I hated it—I hated how vulnerable I felt. "I was so scared."

Her arms tightened around me, pulling me back into her warmth. "I know," she said, her voice soft but sure. "But I'm okay. We're okay. You did everything you could."

I nodded, even though the guilt still gnawed at me. I didn't know if I'd ever shake it. But right now, I could breathe again with her in my arms. The tightness in my chest eased just a little.

Across the room, Knox's eyes never wavered. He hadn't said anything since I'd entered, but I knew his feelings. The fear, the need to hold her, to make sure she was okay. We all felt it.

I closed my eyes, my forehead resting against hers, and whispered, "I love you, Ember. I'll never stop loving you."

"I know, Jax," she whispered back, her lips brushing against mine in the softest, most reassuring kiss. "I love you too. Always."

47

TOMMY PERCIVAL

I paced my office, my heart still pounding from the night's events. The scene replayed in my mind—the breach, the violence, and the sickening reality that they had gotten too close. Way too close.

"We need better security," I growled, my voice tight with frustration. "They just fucking walked right in. How the hell did they get in?"

Knox sat at my desk, his eyes never leaving Ember, still curled up in Jax's arms on the couch. His hands rested on the arms of my chair, gripping it tightly, knuckles white. He was in control, at least on the surface, but I knew him well enough to see the rage simmering beneath.

"Frank Deluca," Knox muttered, the words laced with disgust. "He was selling information about every single group in London. Playing all of us against each other."

I stopped pacing and stared at him, trying to process what I'd just heard. "Selling information? About us?"

Knox nodded, his jaw clenched, still not tearing his gaze

away from Ember, like she was the only thing grounding him. "Yeah. This house, for starters. The plans, the entire blueprint, and every inch of security we had in place."

I cursed under my breath, feeling a fire ignite in my chest. "This house?" I spat, anger making my hands shake. "What the fuck else, Knox? What else did Frank sell?"

Knox finally looked at me, his expression dark, his voice steady despite the fury bubbling beneath. "The penthouse, too. Every detail of how it's laid out and what we've got in place there. And... Ember's apartment."

My heart stopped for a moment. "Ember's apartment?" I whispered, my voice low and dangerous.

Knox nodded. "There's more. There was an entire file on her, Tommy. Frank had it compiled. Every detail about her life, her habits, her movements. And worst of all..." He hesitated, his eyes flicking back to Ember, who was still in Jax's arms, her small frame wrapped around him for comfort.

I stepped toward him, needing to hear it, even though I already knew. "What, Knox? What was it?"

Knox's gaze turned hard, his voice lowering to a growl. "She was labeled as our weak point. Frank convinced them that if they took Ember... we'd break."

The rage inside me erupted. I slammed my fist against the wall, needing something to hit, to destroy. "Motherfucker!" The sound echoed through the room but wasn't enough to ease the fire burning through my veins. "That slimy piece of shit sold her out. Sold us out."

I turned back to Knox, my mind racing with a hundred questions. "How long have they known? How much do they know about us?"

Chapter 47

Knox's eyes hardened. "Enough to know exactly where to hit. They knew every entrance, every blind spot. And they knew she was the key."

I clenched my fists, trying to keep myself in check. The idea of someone using Ember as a pawn in their game and thinking they could get to us through her made me sick.

Knox's face was just as grim, but he remained calm; the only sign of his anger was the way his fingers tightened on the edge of my desk. "We were exposed, Tommy. And not just us. They've been selling everyone out—Russians, the Moretti's, Romano's, even the Salvio's."

I took a deep breath, forcing myself to focus. This wasn't just about revenge. It was about protecting what was ours. Ember. The Aces. Our future.

"So what's the plan?" I asked, my voice cold and calculating, the fury still simmering beneath the surface.

Before Knox could respond, the door creaked open. I turned just in time to see a tall, broad-shouldered man stride into the room, flanked by six armed men dressed in full SWAT gear. His presence immediately shifted the atmosphere, like a dark cloud descending over us.

"No plan needed," the man said, his deep Russian accent cutting through the tension in the room. His lips curled into a chilling smile as he stepped forward, his eyes cold and calculating. It was unmistakable who he was. I would know that voice with my eyes closed and in my sleep. Sergei Ivanov.

Knox barked in fury, his body tensing as he stood, guns ready. Jax, still on the couch with Ember, twisted, his reflexes lightning quick as he threw Ember behind him, shielding her with his own body. His eyes blazed with protective rage, while wide-eyed but silent Ember kept low behind him.

I stood, my fists clenching. Every instinct in me screamed to rip this bastard apart. "What the fuck do you want, Sergei?" I growled, stepping forward.

Sergei's smile widened. "You really should hire better security, da? Or perhaps get better men. I just walked right in the front door... and straight in here."

A low snarl escaped from Knox. He was ready to blow; I could see it in his eyes. But now wasn't the time. Not yet.

I met Sergei's gaze, my heart thudding in my chest as I resisted the urge to lunge at him. "What do you want?" I demanded, my voice seething with barely controlled rage.

Sergei's eyes flickered with amusement before he took a step closer, his armed men fanning out behind him, their weapons trained on all of us. "You killed Natasha," he said smoothly, his voice cold as ice.

My brow furrowed, confusion twisting my thoughts. "Natasha?" I spat, though I knew precisely who Sergei was talking about. The name wasn't just familiar—it was burned into my past. Natasha, my ex-wife. Sergei's daughter. But I wasn't about to show him the cracks in my armor.

Sergei's smile vanished, replaced by a stern, cold glare, the kind that spoke of years of hatred and resentment. "Don't play stupid with me, Tommy. Natasha. My daughter, your wife. You killed her," he growled, his voice thick with venom.

The room went deadly silent. My heart pounded, the weight of his words settling in like a lead ball in my stomach.

Chapter 47

This wasn't a power move or some calculated mafia play. This was personal. Blood.

I clenched my jaw, trying to keep my voice steady. "I didn't kill Natasha," I said through gritted teeth. "She made her choices, Sergei. You know that. She chose her path."

Sergei's eyes flared with fury, and for a moment, I thought he might order his men to open fire right there. But instead, he chuckled—a low, dark sound that sent a shiver down my spine.

"Maybe you didn't pull the trigger yourself, or maybe you did and blamed it on my men...Either way, I know what happened," Sergei said, his voice a sinister promise.

Knox stepped forward, his jaw tight and knuckles white as he gripped his gun, ready for whatever came next. "You're a fool if you think you can walk in here and make threats," he growled, his voice laced with rage.

Sergei didn't flinch, his cold gaze shifting between me and Knox. "Threats? No, this isn't a threat, Tommy. It's a fact. You've taken from me; now, I'll take everything from you. Every. Last. Thing."

I could feel the anger rising inside me like a tide of molten lava, ready to explode. Every word from Sergei's mouth was like gasoline on a fire I was barely holding in check. My fists clenched tight at my sides, muscles straining as I fought the urge to tear him apart right then and there. But I couldn't. Killing him here, with so many witnesses, would ignite a war that would engulf all of London. No one would be safe, least of all Ember.

"Get the fuck out of my house," I growled, voice low and dangerous.

Sergei's lips curled into that same sick smile, his eyes gleaming with a sinister glee. He wasn't done yet.

"Oh, I am going," he sneered, "but I'll take her with me." His finger pointed directly at Ember, his gaze gleaming with malicious intent.

Knox growled like a caged animal, stepping forward. "Like fuck you are," he snarled, his voice dripping with menace.

Jax was in front of Ember, shielding her with his body, his eyes locked on Sergei's men. The room tensed like a drawn bowstring, all of us ready to explode into violence.

But before we could react further, a figure moved from behind Sergei. It happened so fast that I almost didn't catch it. A small woman, lithe and quick, stepped up behind him, and in one smooth, silent motion, she slid a blade across his neck.

Blood was sprayed in a red arc, painting the room in a gruesome mist. Sergei's eyes went wide with shock as his hand flew to his throat, gurgling in disbelief as his life drained out of him. He dropped to his knees, crumbling like a puppet whose strings had been cut.

Who the fuck was she? Where the hell did she come from?

The room erupted in chaos. Knox reacted first, his gun already drawn. He aimed straight at the necks of the six men in SWAT gear who had been standing like statues just moments before. His bullets flew with deadly accuracy, taking down the first two in seconds, each hit clean through the exposed flesh of their necks.

Jax wasn't far behind. He pulled a gun from behind the

Chapter 47

pot plant next to the couch, following Knox's lead and aiming for the vulnerable spots. His shots were just as precise, taking down another two men before they knew what hit them.

I was slower off the mark, momentarily caught off guard by the sudden shift in the room. The sight of Sergei bleeding out in front of me had rattled my focus. But that didn't last long. I snapped into action, drawing my gun and firing off rounds like Knox had done, aiming right at the necks. The sound of bullets tearing through flesh and the sickening thud of bodies hitting the floor filled the room.

In a matter of seconds, all six of Sergei's men were down, lifeless on the floor, their SWAT uniforms now stained with their blood.

The silence that followed was deafening.

I turned, eyes landing on the woman who had slit Sergei's throat. She was standing there, calm as a breeze, wiping the blood from her blade with a small cloth she pulled from her jacket.

"Who the fuck are you?" I demanded, voice rough, the adrenaline still coursing through my veins.

48

DECLAN STEVENSON

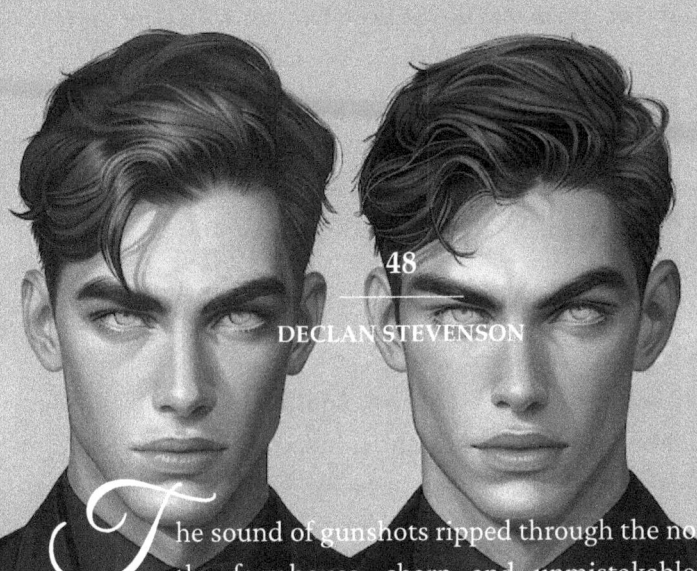

The sound of gunshots ripped through the noise of the farmhouse, sharp and unmistakable. My heart lurched in my chest, and I bolted from the room without a second thought. Adrian was behind me, his heavy footsteps pounding the floor as we sprinted toward Tommy's office. Fear gnawed at me with every step, the dread of what might be waiting in that room tightening my throat.

I didn't hesitate when I reached the room and skidded inside, my feet sliding in the blood on the floor.

What I saw made me stop dead in my tracks.

The room was a goddamn bloodbath. Sergei Ivanov, the head of the Russian mafia, was lying in a growing pool of blood, his throat sliced open, gurgling as his life slipped away. His cold, dead eyes stared at the ceiling, lifeless, while six men in full SWAT gear lay crumpled on the floor, each one shot cleanly in the neck. The air was thick with the coppery scent of blood and gunpowder.

And then there was a tiny little woman with long brown hair.

She stood casually next to Sergei's body, wiping a long, gleaming blade on a cloth with the same calm you'd expect from someone wiping down a dinner knife after a meal. The scene felt surreal, like something out of a twisted nightmare.

"What the fuck, London?" Adrian's voice rang out beside me, filled with shock and fury.

My eyes snapped to Adrian, confusion swirling in my mind. London? I knew Adrian had connections, deep ones, but this woman? There was something about her I couldn't place. But Adrian's reaction—he knew her.

Tommy, standing just feet away, his face a mask of fury and disbelief, turned toward Adrian. "London?" His voice was low and dangerous. "As in London DeLuca?"

Adrian sighed, running a hand through his hair, the weight of the situation heavy in the air. "Tommy, meet London DeLuca," Adrian said, his voice dripping with pride and exasperation. "She's the head of the DeLuca Family now."

I stared at her, dumbfounded. The head of the DeLuca group? That name carried weight—dangerous weight. The DeLuca family wasn't a family you fucked with lightly. And now she was standing here, cool as ice, after just taking out the head of the Russian mafia.

London DeLuca. Jesus.

Her eyes flickered to me briefly, almost dismissively, before she returned to cleaning her blade as if this whole thing was just a minor inconvenience.

Chapter 48

"What the hell happened here?" I finally managed to ask, my voice rough with the adrenaline still surging.

Adrian crossed his arms, staring at the bodies on the floor with regret and amusement.

"Sergei came to collect on something that didn't belong to him. London here ensured he wouldn't be collecting from anyone again." Knox growled as he stalked to where Ember was peeking from behind Jax's body.

Tommy took a step forward, still processing everything. His eyes were glued to London. "So, you just waltzed in here and slit his throat?"

London smirked, "He made it easy. Too busy running his mouth to notice who was standing behind him."

I shook my head, trying to catch up with the situation. The Russians. Sergei. This wasn't just a usual fight for territory—this was personal, family-level shit, the kind that sparked wars that could burn cities to the ground. And London, this small, lethal woman, had just lit the fuse.

"Why?" I asked, my voice low, still trying to piece together the chaos. "Why take him out now?"

London turned her gaze toward me, and for a moment, her eyes softened with something resembling sadness and determination. "He killed my father," she said bluntly. "So this was a blood debt that is now settled."

My mind reeled. I hadn't known her father, but for her to carry that weight—to carry a vendetta of that size—made everything feel even heavier. As she turned to Adrian, something shifted in her expression, her posture relaxing slightly. "Sorry, big guy," she said, a slight smirk tugging at the corner of her lips. "Didn't mean to steal your thunder."

Adrian, always one for theatrics, smirked right back at her, a glint of amusement in his eyes. "It's ok," he said smoothly, his voice lowering as he leaned toward her. "I'll punish you later."

London blushed, her cheeks turning a soft shade of pink that only seemed to confuse me more. What the actual fuck was happening here? One second, this woman was slicing Sergei's throat with terrifying precision, and the next, she was blushing at Adrian's words like some smitten woman. I was more confused now than I had been before.

She turned back to face us, the coldness returning to her eyes. "Sergei killed my father," she repeated as if grounding herself in that truth. "It was in a file I read."

She glanced at Adrian briefly before locking eyes with Tommy. "My father sold information to all the other groups," she continued, her voice steady and unflinching. "I intend to not follow in his footsteps. I've been informed that I am now the boss—a role I didn't want but will fulfill. However," she paused, her gaze growing firmer, "I won't be running what was known as the DeLuca family."

I blinked, trying to process her words as she pointed toward Adrian with a casual gesture. "I'm marrying this brute," she said, the corners of her mouth twitching upward again. "So I'll be known as London Romano. My business will be absorbed into his."

Tommy's face was unreadable, though I could see his jaw tightening slightly as he tried to absorb the bombshell she had just dropped.

"For future business," London continued her voice busi-

Chapter 48

nesslike and to the point, "you will need to contact Adrian. I'll be destroying all the files I find on the family's and returning all the information I uncover to those it concerns."

She gave us one last look—a mixture of finality and a strange, quiet resolution—and then she turned on her heel, striding toward the door. She moved with the confidence of someone who knew exactly where she stood, no hesitation in her step. Adrian followed close behind her but paused before leaving, casting a glance back at us.

"You heard the boss," Adrian said with a smirk, then casually gestured to his men. "Clean this place up and dispose of the body before you leave."

With that, they walked out, leaving the rest of us in stunned silence as the weight of the night—and everything it had become—settled around us.

I glanced at Tommy, who hadn't moved from where he stood. His eyes were locked on the door where London and Adrian had just left, a mix of fury and understanding battling behind them.

Still standing protectively in front of Ember, Jax exhaled deeply, finally loosening his grip on her. Knox stood nearby, his jaw clenched as he wiped the blood from his face, still processing everything. But it was Tommy who broke the silence first.

"We need better security," he muttered, his voice low but steady. "No one walks into our home like that again."

I nodded in agreement, but my mind couldn't shake the image of London, standing over Sergei's body, blood on her hands and no regret in her eyes.

The night had been chaotic. Lines had been crossed. But one thing was clear: our world had just shifted, and things would never be the same again.

49

EMBER DANG

3 Months Later

I sat at the dining room table, staring at the four slices of cake placed neatly in front of me, my brows furrowing in confusion. The room was bathed in the soft, warm glow of the chandelier overhead, casting a golden hue over everything. Knox stood across from me, arms crossed, his face unreadable.

"What is all this?" I asked, my eyes darting between him and the cakes. I couldn't help but feel a little amused. This was Knox, after all.

"I need to know which one you like," he said, his voice steady, though there was an edge of something behind his words. Something... important.

I raised an eyebrow, my amusement growing. "Why?"

"Just take a bite of each and tell me," he replied, sidestepping my question entirely.

I narrowed my eyes at him playfully, but his expression remained serious. He wasn't giving anything away, and now my curiosity was piqued.

"All right," I muttered, picking up the small fork beside the plate. I glanced at him once more before slicing off a bite of the first cake—chocolate. I let out a slight hum as soon as it touched my tongue. It was rich, decadent, and unforgettable. The kind of cake that melts in your mouth and makes you forget the world for a moment.

"Good," I said, nodding my approval as I swallowed. Knox remained silent, watching me closely, but I could see the intensity in his gaze.

I moved on to the second slice—vanilla. It was... okay. Not bad, but not life-changing either. Just simple and sweet. I gave a half-hearted shrug as I tasted it and looked up at Knox.

He didn't react, so I moved on to the third cake—red velvet. The vibrant color caught my eye as I took a bite, and immediately, I was hit with a mix of sweetness and cream cheese frosting that danced across my taste buds. Another winner. I gave Knox an approving smile, but he remained tight-lipped.

Finally, I picked up the last slice—sponge cake. It looked unassuming compared to the others, but my eyes widened as soon as the first forkful touched my lips. The flavor was light yet rich, with a buttery softness that melted into my senses. It was divine—like biting into a cloud, but somehow better.

Chapter 49

I set my fork down and pointed to the sponge cake. "That one," I said firmly, a satisfied grin spreading across my face. "Now, tell me why."

Knox's lips curled into a slight smile as he uncrossed his arms and walked closer to me. "The sponge cake, huh?"

I nodded, leaning back in my chair, still watching him. "Yep. Now spill. What's going on?"

Knox grinned, his expression softening just a bit, and said, "Okay, sponge cake it is," as he stood up and started walking away.

"Wait, can you take the other cakes and leave the sponge?" I called after him, half-joking but still wanting to finish the sponge cake.

He stopped, turned back, and, with a quick stride, came over, grabbed the three remaining plates, and slid the sponge cake closer to me. He leaned down, kissing me, then paused to lick his lips, smirking as he said, "Yep, the sponge is the winner."

Before I could respond, Knox gave me his smirk and sauntered off, leaving me even more confused.

What the hell was going on? I reached out, grabbed the rest of the sponge cake, and dug in. Each bite was just as incredible as the last, the buttery sweetness melting on my tongue. I couldn't help but hum in delight as I devoured the rest of it.

Then, a voice cut through the moment from behind me, low and teasing. "Keep moaning like that, and I'll have to fill that mouth with something better."

I couldn't help but smile at the familiar voice. "Sorry,

Knox gave me cake," I replied, my tone playful, not even turning around.

Tommy's laugh echoed softly through the room as he stepped closer. "Which one did you pick?" he asked, though I could tell from his smirk that he already knew the answer.

I narrowed my eyes at him, finally catching on to the game. "You know why I got cake, don't you?"

Tommy just smiled, leaning down to kiss me, the warmth of his lips brushing against mine. When he pulled back, his voice was soft and full of affection. "Yes, I do. But I'm not telling you either."

I groaned, mockingly annoyed, as he chuckled and walked off, leaving me even more curious than ever. What were they all planning? Something told me this was going to be more than just cake.

***

That night, we all sat at the table, a comfortable rhythm to our movements, as Knox handed out dinner plates. He'd made my favorite—seafood pasta, the rich smell of garlic, butter, and fresh shellfish filling the air. The plate in front of me was piled high, and I couldn't help but smile at the sight. Knox always knew how to get me to relax, even if I still wondered what the hell the cake situation was about earlier.

He sat beside me, his shoulder brushing mine as we all dug in. The conversation flowed naturally, as usual, when we sat down to eat together. Declan and Jax started replaying the day's visit with the Irish about the latest gun shipment.

"They want a bigger amount next time," Declan said between bites, shaking his head slightly. "The deal's been the

Chapter 49

same every three months, but now, out of nowhere, they're saying they need more."

Tommy frowned, his fork paused mid-air. "They get plenty every damn quarter. What the fuck do they need more for?"

Jax shrugged, barely looking up from his plate as he spoke. "I don't know. They weren't exactly forthcoming about it. But I can find out if you want."

"Yes, I think we should look into that," Tommy said, his voice firm but measured. His eyes drifted towards me momentarily before turning back to Jax, his brow still furrowed. "I don't like surprises."

As the conversation moved forward, Knox, ever the one to keep things light yet informative, grinned and added his little tidbit. "That little guy I got to play with this morning before I went cake shopping was... invaluable."

I glanced at him, raising an eyebrow, as did Tommy. Knox leaned back in his chair that dangerous glint in his eye telling me this wasn't just an innocent chat.

"Adrian and London have been feeding us some solid intel on the Morettis," Knox continued, twirling some pasta onto his fork. "There's been some shit brewing on that side, and Tommy, you figured it was a good idea to get involved, remember? So you gave me the go-ahead to, you know, do my thing." He took a bite, looking far too pleased with himself.

Tommy gave a slow nod, piecing it together, his gaze sharpening. "That's right. I didn't think they'd be this sloppy, though."

"Sloppy doesn't even begin to describe it," Knox added,

his eyes flashing with amusement. "The guy practically sang everything the moment I walked into the room. Let's say the information is massive, like world-shattering massive."

"Well, I hope you passed it along," Tommy muttered, a hint of sarcasm in his voice. But there was also approval.

I watched them all as they spoke, the ebb and flow of this life we lived pulling me in like it always did. As much as the day's intensity still weighed on my mind, sitting here with them—sharing food, conversation, and maybe just a little chaos—was grounding in a way. Knox's hand found its way to mine under the table, reassuring me that I wasn't just a spectator. I was part of it, thoroughly entangled in their world.

"So, Adrian and London," I said, breaking my silence, curious about this new power couple. "They are getting married?"

Knox grinned again, his eyes twinkling. "Already married if the rumor is to be believed. London's running her father's old operation now, and Adrian's more than happy to absorb it into his. They will make quite the team, and it benefits us too. We're all in this together."

Tommy nodded, a satisfied smirk crossing his face. "Good. I'm glad it's only the Salvio's we must look out for now."

There was a pause, a weight settling in the air as we all thought about what that meant. The Salvos had been a growing problem, and we all knew it. If London's intel could help tip the scales in our favor, it was a move we needed to capitalize on.

Knox stood up suddenly, stretching a bit before grinning

Chapter 49

at all of us. "All right, no more work talk for tonight," he announced, walking towards the kitchen. I watched him curiously as he returned with a massive sponge cake, placing it on the table before me with a satisfied smirk. "We have some celebrations to get to," he said.

I frowned, utterly confused. "What for?" I asked, my brow furrowed as I glanced from the cake back to Knox.

He reached into his pocket and pulled out a neatly folded piece of paper, handing it to me with a knowing grin. I took it from him, unfolding it carefully, and my eyes widened when I saw what it was. It was an official letter declaring that I had been named this year's Best Interior Designer in London. The memory of the email I'd received months ago hit me. I knew I was in the running, but I had been up against some huge names, so I didn't think much of it.

"Oh my God," I whispered, my heart racing as I stared at the letter. I blinked up at Knox, feeling a little dazed.

"We have a celebrity in our mix," Knox teased, his grin widening as the rest of the table looked at me with proud smiles.

I blushed, shaking my head. "No, no, it's nothing like that..."

Knox leaned closer, his eyes gleaming with mischief. "Oh yes, Ember. You're officially number one."

Before I could protest further, everyone at the table except for Knox stood up at once, each holding out small boxes in their hands. My heart leaped into my throat as they all spoke in unison, "Will you marry *all* of us?"

My hands flew to my mouth, a squeal escaping my lips before I could stop it. The emotions hit me all at once—

surprise, joy, love—and I felt the tears welling up in my eyes. "Yes," I managed to gasp, my voice barely holding together. "Yes, yes, I will!"

Laughter erupted from the table, but it was warm and full of love. Knox, Declan, Jax, and Tommy were all beaming at me, each holding out their box as if it were the most precious thing in the world. And to me, it was.

Knox was the first to step forward, pulling a small ring from his pocket, a minimalist band that was exactly my style. I smiled at him, and he leaned down to kiss me softly, whispering against my lips, "Sponge cake and all; you're stuck with us."

One by one, they each handed me a ring—each different, each perfect in its way. Declan's had an intricate Celtic design, Jax's was a sleek, modern band of diamonds, and Tommy's was classic but bold with a massive diamond in the center, just like him. The room felt lighter, the weight of the world outside disappearing momentarily as I looked at the men who had become my everything.

"I can't believe this is happening," I whispered, blinking back tears of happiness as I looked down at the rings, one on each finger. They all smiled at me, their eyes full of love and promise.

Knox says to me, "Sweetness, we have been married for 6 months, 2 weeks, and 3 days; it's been happening for a while now." This makes me burst out laughing.

"This is just the beginning," Tommy said, his voice soft but steady. "We're in this together, all of us."

I nodded, unable to find the right words to express my feelings. Instead, I pulled them all in, wrapping my arms

Chapter 49

around their necks, feeling the warmth of their love surround me.

My lips collided with Knox's first, his mouth parting to take mine instantly. His growl vibrated against my lips as he spoke, "I'm going to lay you out on this table like the feast you are."

My eyes darted between them all, their hungry gazes locked on me. "Okay," I whispered, my voice trembling with anticipation. This had been a secret dream of mine, getting all of them at the same time.

Knox picked me up, and my legs wrapped around him, holding him close. He placed my ass on the top of the dining table and pushed me back. All four of them looked down at me, smirking, and said in unison, "We're going to eat you now."

One by one, they each took hold of a piece of my clothing and removed it. My mouth watered as I watched them discard their garments. Then, four large, hard cocks came into my sight, and I moaned. "Fuck me, please."

Knox lowered himself between my legs and licked me so slowly that I squirmed on the dining table. Tommy reached out and grabbed some of the cream from the cake, placing it on my nipples before slowly licking it off. My nipples turned into hard peaks, and I moaned even louder. "Fuck me," I gasped, feeling the pull in my core. "I need you."

But Knox continued to lick me slowly, and Tommy focused on my nipples. I felt four hands roaming my body, caressing the inner parts of my thighs and the crook of my neck. The sensation was insane and addictive. I would need more of this, if this is what four at once felt like.

As my core tightened and I started to climb towards my orgasm, I could tell Knox sensed it. He licked me harder while the other hands roamed further, and Tommy pinched my nipples. I couldn't hold back any longer, crashing over the edge and coming all over Knox's face. I was a panting, writhing mess by the time I came down.

Knox didn't waste any time, lining up with my entrance and pushing right to the hilt. "Fuck me hard," I screamed, and he obliged, setting a brutal rhythm.

I felt a dick slap against my mouth and turned to see Tommy standing there. "Open wide," he commanded, and I did as he asked. Spit slid down the side of my face as I took him into my mouth. Those hands, oh god, continued to explore and roam. The sensations were wild as Tommy face-fucked me and Knox pounded into me.

My mind swam in the chaos of pleasure, each touch igniting a fire within me.

Knox hit that sweet spot inside me making me moan around Tommy's dick. The sensation of him in my mouth was overwhelming, and I felt a primal need to please him, to draw out his pleasure. His balls tightened, and I sensed he was close to the edge, so I reached out with one hand and slowly sank a finger into his ass.

The effect was immediate – Tommy fucked me harder and faster, his dick ramming into the back of my throat over and over again. I explored deeper into him, finding that spot that made his knees buckle. "Ember!" he screamed as he came, ropes of hot seed spurting down the back of my throat. The taste of him, the raw intensity of his climax, triggered my orgasm. I clamped down on Knox, feeling my

Chapter 49

pussy walls sucking him in, and he growled low in his throat as he found his own climax and filled me full of his cum.

Just as I started to come down from the high, two sets of hands grabbed me, lifting me and placing me onto Jax's waiting dick. He was sprawled out on the floor next to the table, a wicked grin on his face. I slid down onto him, gasping at the feel of him inside me. A set of hands pushed me forward until my chest was flush with Jax's muscular form.

"Stay still, okay?" Jax whispered, planting a tender kiss on my forehead. I nodded, trying to catch my breath, my body still trembling from the intensity of what had just happened.

As I lay there, I felt another dick start to push into my pussy alongside Jax's. The stretch was intense, a little painful, but also pleasurable. Declan seated his dick inside me next to Jax, and I moaned loudly at the sensation of being so full. They began to move in unison, pulling in and out of me, and Declan's hands reached around to palm my breasts softly.

"Fuck, Ember, you take us so well," he murmured. "Your pussy is so greedy, stretching to take us both." "Look at you." Jax joined in with his brother, their voices mingling in a symphony of dark desire as they pushed in and out of me. "Your pussy is so tight like this."

Then, they slammed into me, their movements synchronized as they took what they wanted from me. I was powerless to stop the orgasm that washed over me, wave after wave, leaving me breathless and weak. My arms turned to jelly, and I collapsed onto Jax, feeling them continue to fuck me hard and fast together.

"Ember..." Jax growled, his voice strained as he neared his climax. His brother followed suit, and soon, they both released inside me, filling me full, marking me as theirs before slowly pulling out.

Fuck this is what home felt like. Pure bliss.

BONUS CHAPTER

The morning sun streamed through the window, casting soft golden light across the room as I stood in front of the mirror, adjusting the delicate lace of my wedding dress. It wasn't like any traditional gown; it was uniquely mine—simple, elegant, and completely black. It represented me and the life I was about to share with them.

I smoothed my hands over the fabric, feeling calm and anticipation in my chest. Today wasn't a legal wedding, not in the eyes of the law. I was technically only married to Knox, but today was about something more profound. It was about committing myself to them, standing before our closest friends and family, and symbolizing what we already knew in our hearts: that I belonged to them, and they belonged to me.

Laws be damned.

Each of them—Tommy, Jax, and Declan—would take my last name today. Dang. Something about it made my heart swell with pride and love. They were choosing to carry my name, to wear it as a mark of our bond. It was beautiful in a way that words couldn't fully capture.

A soft knock at the door pulled me from my thoughts, and I turned to see Mercy peeking her head in, her sharp eyes sparkling with excitement.

"You ready, babe?" she asked, stepping inside. Her presence was a comfort, a piece of home brought from Australia. Beside her, Ruhn and Frost waited, watching with their signature silent intensity. Killian, too, stood nearby, his massive frame filling the doorway. My family—those I grew up with and fought beside. They were all here for me today.

I smiled at her, feeling a rush of warmth in my chest. "I think so. Just... taking it all in."

Mercy grinned, stepping closer to adjust my veil. "You're going to knock them all dead. They're never going to know what hit them."

I laughed softly, but the moment was interrupted by a sudden wave of nausea that rolled through me. My stomach lurched violently, and before I could stop it, I bolted to the bathroom, barely making it to the toilet in time to empty my stomach.

Mercy was right behind me, her voice laced with concern. "Whoa, hey. You all right?"

I sat back on my heels, wiping the corner of my mouth with a shaking hand. "Yeah... yeah, I think it's just nerves."

But even as I said the words, a nagging thought crept into the back of my mind. My hand rested on my stomach, and I couldn't ignore the sudden realization that hit me like a freight train.

My period was late. Like, late.

Bonus Chapter

Fuck.

I blinked, my thoughts racing as I tried to process it. Could it be? My heart pounded louder than before as if it had added a new layer of anticipation to this day.

Mercy crouched down beside me, her hand on my shoulder. "You sure it's just nerves?"

I nodded quickly, forcing a smile, but I knew she could see the doubt in my eyes. "Yeah, yeah. I'm fine."

She raised an eyebrow, clearly unconvinced but not pushing me on it. "All right, but if you're about to puke during your vows, maybe let me know so I can move a bucket under your face, right?"

I laughed at that, though my mind was still spinning. Standing up slowly, I leaned against the sink, staring at my reflection. Today was already monumental, but now this? A new possibility, a new life... my hand drifted to my stomach again.

I wasn't going to tell them yet. Not today. Today was about us. But I knew, deep down, that this moment—this wedding—was about to take on an even deeper meaning than I'd imagined.

I took one last deep breath, steadying myself as I nodded at Mercy. "Let's do this."

As I stepped out of the room, the warm air of the farmhouse wrapped around me like a reassuring hug. My heart pounded as I walked through the back door, onto the deck, and down toward where they waited for me.

Knox, Tommy, Jax, and Declan look like something straight out of a dream.

Knox stood tall, his broad shoulders straining against the

perfectly tailored suit that hugged his body in all the right places. His hair was slicked back, but a few rebellious strands fell over his forehead, giving him that rough, dangerous edge that always sent shivers down my spine. And even though his face was hard, his expression challenging, I could see it. The emotion. The tears. He was crying. Knox was crying, tears streaming down his face as he blinked rapidly, trying to hold himself together. It broke me and healed me all at once.

Beside him, Tommy was the epitome of control and power, but even he had a broad, boyish grin across his face. He wore a dark, perfectly fitted suit that clung to every muscle, his dark hair slightly tousled, and those green eyes locked on me, filled with a depth of emotion that only Tommy could carry. He had the air of someone who knew what was his and wasn't afraid to protect it. How he looked at me—like I was everything he needed—made my chest tighten with love and anticipation.

My wild one, Jax, had his black hair styled perfectly, and his suit was tailored but undone enough to show off that devil-may-care attitude. His blue eyes sparkled mischievously as they met mine, but there was something else too—something tender, a hint of vulnerability I rarely saw in him. He stood with his hands in his pockets, his grin stretching wide as if he could barely contain his excitement. And at that moment, I could see how much he wanted this and us.

Then there was Declan, my sweet, nurturing soul. He was all clean lines and elegant, his suit deep charcoal accentuating his quiet strength. His black hair was slicked back, and his blue eyes gleamed with pride as he watched me approach. Declan had always been the calm in the storm, but even now, I could see the raw emotion brewing beneath the surface, his gaze never leaving mine. His smile—wide and full of love—radiated warmth and made me feel like I was walking toward my forever.

They were all there, waiting for me and us, and I couldn't stop the wave of joy that surged through me.

As I took my first step toward them, my heart swelling with love, I saw Knox break entirely. He was bawling like a baby, tears streaming down his cheeks, his hands wiping at his face as he tried—and failed—to stop the flood. His body shook with emotion, and I couldn't help but smile, my heart soaring as I continued toward them.

Tommy, Jax, and Declan were grinning ear to ear, their eyes never leaving mine. They were filled with a joy and anticipation that matched my own. They were my future, and I was theirs. This was our beginning, a bond no one could break.

Our future started now, and I had never been more excited.

Three days later, I found myself pacing around the farmhouse, the nervous energy coiling in my chest like a tight spring. I had made up my mind—there was no more avoiding it. I needed to know for sure, not just from some faint test strip I had taken in the bathroom but from a professional. An ultrasound, something solid. And I needed to do it alone, well... almost alone.

I glanced at Mercy, leaning against the kitchen counter,

her eyes watching me with that knowing look she always had.

"You sure you don't want to tell them first?" she asked, raising an eyebrow as she sipped her coffee.

"No. Not yet," I said, shaking my head. "I need to know for sure before I even say anything."

She nodded, understanding exactly what I meant without needing me to elaborate. This wasn't just about being pregnant; it was about how much my life and our lives would change. And if I was going to tell the guys this news, I needed to know every detail.

The excuse I gave was simple—lunch with Mercy. They wouldn't question it; they trusted me, and in a way, I felt a pang of guilt for keeping them in the dark, but I had to do this my way. I needed to process it on my terms before the whirlwind hit.

Mercy and I hopped into the car, the hum of the engine filling the space between us as we made our way to the clinic. Ruhn drove us in, thankfully with Frost in the passenger seat. I was sure that Mercy had filled those two in on what was happening; there was no way Frost would ever let her out of his sight; his possessive nature towards her made Knox look soft. I stared out the window, my heart pounding in my chest, nerves fluttering like wild birds trapped inside me.

"You ready for this?" Mercy asked, her voice gentle as she pulled into the clinic's parking lot.

"As ready as I'll ever be," I murmured, unbuckling my seatbelt and stepping out of the car.

The clinic was small, tucked away in a quiet part of town

Bonus Chapter

—exactly what I needed. I didn't want to risk running into anyone or answering too many questions. It was just me, Mercy, and whatever awaited me behind those sterile white doors as Ruhn and Frost waited in the car.

Inside, the waiting room was cool and calm, and I tried to match that energy as we waited for my name to be called. My hands were clasped tightly together, my knuckles white with tension. I kept glancing at the clock on the wall, watching the second hand tick by as if the answers to my future were locked in every passing moment.

Eventually, the nurse called my name, and Mercy squeezed my hand before letting me go. I followed the nurse down the hall, my heart pounding harder with each step. The exam room was clinical and sterile, with the faint scent of disinfectant. It all felt surreal, like I was walking through a fog, unsure of what I would hear.

The technician was kind and professional, and she got straight to it. I lay back on the table, my breath catching in my throat as she spread the cold gel across my stomach. The machine whirred to life, the sound filling the small room as the ultrasound began.

My eyes were glued to the screen, my heart pounding so loud I could barely hear anything else. And then I saw it—two tiny flickering lights, two heartbeats.

"Twins," the technician said softly, pointing to the screen. "You're having twins."

For a second, everything stopped. My world narrowed to that screen, those two little lives growing inside me. Twins.

My breath hitched, and I blinked rapidly, trying to process it. I wasn't just pregnant—I was carrying twins.

Bonus Chapter

Mercy's gasp echoed from the corner of the room, and I turned my head to see her standing there with her hands over her mouth, her eyes wide with shock and awe.

"Twins," I whispered, my voice trembling.

"Yep," the technician confirmed, her tone warm. "Both are measuring right where they should be. Congratulations."

Tears pricked my eyes, and I didn't know if I wanted to laugh, cry, or scream. Maybe all three. My heart swelled with so many emotions that I could barely contain it. Twins. I wasn't prepared for this, but somehow, it felt right. It felt like the universe had given me something I didn't even know I needed.

I wiped my face with the back of my hand as the technician finished, handing me a printout of the ultrasound before leaving the room to give me a moment.

Mercy crossed the room, wrapping her arms around me tightly. "Twins, Em. You're going to be a mom of two."

I let out a shaky laugh, nodding as I clutched the ultrasound photo to my chest. "Yeah... I guess I am."

We stood there for a while, holding onto each other, the weight of what I had just learned settling in. This wasn't just my secret anymore. Soon, I would have to tell them, but for now, I needed a little more time to process, to hold onto this moment with just Mercy by my side.

As we returned to the car, the ultrasound photo tucked safely in my bag, I knew everything was about to change.

But for now, I kept the secret tucked away, a small smile playing on my lips as Mercy and I headed home.

Bonus Chapter

The warm sun beat down on us as we lay sprawled across loungers on a pristine white sand beach. The waves gently lapped at the shore, a soothing melody that lulled me into a state of pure relaxation. Our honeymoon had been nothing short of perfect so far—a mix of adventure and lazy days like this, soaking in the peace that had been so elusive back home.

Tommy, Knox, Declan, and Jax were all lounging around me, each looking more at ease than I had seen them in months. Knox had his signature smirk as he sipped from a tall glass of something alcoholic while Jax was flipping through a magazine, now and then sneaking glances at me over the top of it. Declan was grinning, looking out at the horizon like he had finally found the calm he'd been searching for, and Tommy... Tommy was already three-quarters of his drink, looking relaxed as he propped his feet up.

I glanced down at my drink—a mocktail, bright and fruity but missing the unmistakable punch of alcohol. I had been waiting for the right moment, and now, with the sun kissing my skin and the joy of being surrounded by the men I loved, I knew it was time.

I cleared my throat, sitting up a little in my lounger. "Hey guys, there's something I need to tell you."

All four heads turned toward me, curious and attentive. I wasn't often calling the shots like this, but they knew me well enough by now to recognize that tone in my voice. I wasn't nervous but could feel my heart racing excitedly as I prepared to drop the news.

"What is it?" Tommy asked, sitting up straighter, his glass dangling loosely from his hand.

Bonus Chapter

I raised my glass, swirling the liquid around, the bright red color catching the sunlight. "I'm drinking a mocktail."

Jax quirked an eyebrow. "You don't like the fancy cocktails they make here? That's not like you."

Knox gave me a teasing smirk, clearly not catching on. "Come on, baby. Live a little. It's our honeymoon."

I smiled, shaking my head. "Trust me, I'd love to. But alcohol isn't exactly good for a baby... let alone two."

For a split second, there was silence—just the sound of the waves and the faint chatter of other vacationers enjoying their day. Then, as if all at once, the realization dawned on them.

"Wait—what?" Declan's eyes widened, and he nearly dropped his drink, his gaze snapping to my belly.

Jax, his jaw-dropping open, stared at me. "Are you serious?"

I nodded, my smile growing wider. "Yep. I'm pregnant. And not just with one baby—twins."

Knox's smirk vanished, replaced with an expression of pure shock. His glass was frozen halfway to his lips as if he couldn't quite process what I said. "Twins? You're... you're pregnant with twins?"

"That's right," I said softly, feeling the warmth of their stunned gazes on me. "You're all going to be dads."

Tommy blinked, his expression shifting from confusion to something deeper, something raw and filled with emotion. He set his drink down and ran a hand over his face before letting out a soft, disbelieving laugh. "Holy shit, Ember."

Bonus Chapter

His voice's happiness was unmistakable, making my heart swell.

Jax was already out of his lounger, rushing over to me and wrapping his arms around my waist, his face pressing against my belly as if he could hear the tiny heartbeats already. "Twins?" he repeated, his voice muffled. "I can't believe it. Twins."

Knox, who had been frozen for a moment, finally set his drink down and came over, a grin spreading across his face as he looked at me. "Damn, you don't do anything by halves, do you, sweetness?"

I shook my head, laughing. "Nope. I guess not."

Declan was the last to move, but when he did, it was with purpose. He walked over and knelt beside me, his eyes searching mine. "We're having a family. A real family."

I nodded, feeling the weight of the moment settle in. "Yeah. A real family."

He reached out, resting a hand on my stomach as if he could feel the life growing inside me, and I saw the emotion flicker across his face—hope, joy, love. The same feelings were mirrored in all of their eyes as they crowded around me, touching my belly and wrapping their arms around me in a protective circle.

"I can't believe it," Tommy murmured, his voice low and filled with awe. "You've given us everything, Ember. Everything."

Tears pricked at my eyes, but I blinked them away, overwhelmed by the love surrounding me. "We did this together," I whispered, my voice thick with emotion. "All of us."

Knox leaned down, pressing a kiss to my forehead.

Bonus Chapter

"Twins," he said again, shaking his head in disbelief. "Two little Dang babies."

"Two little Dang babies," I repeated, smiling at him. "I'm going to need much help."

Jax, still holding onto me tightly, grinned. "You've got four of us. I think we've got this covered."

Declan's hand tightened on mine as he whispered, "We'll take care of you, Ember. All of us. Always."

As the sun continued to set over the horizon, bathing us in its golden light, I felt a deep sense of peace wash over me. This was the start of something new, something beautiful and profound—our family, our future, together.

And as I looked at the four men surrounding me, I knew that no matter what came our way, we were ready for it—together.

ABOUT CASSANDRA DOON

Cassandra Doon hails from New South Wales, Australia, where she was nurtured between the bustling streets of Sydney and the serene snowy mountains of Tumut. Today, she finds inspiration in the breathtaking Scenic Rim of Queensland's Gold Coast. A versatile author with a lifelong passion for storytelling, Cassandra has penned over 16 novels and 5 children's books, exploring a variety of genres. Known for her daydreaming and a head often lost in the clouds, she admits to being more at home in her fictional worlds than on social media. Outside of her literary pursuits, Cassandra is a devoted mother to two boys, dedicating her days to their endless energy as both a soccer mom and Pokémon master.

ALSO BY CASSANDRA DOON

The 4 Seats Series:

Matteo 🎧

Felix 🎧

Gabriel 🎧

Catcher 🎧

Ruhn & Frost (Coming Soon)

Standalone:

The Boys Of Hastings House 🎧

The Kings of Willows Peak 🎧

Damaged Goods 🎧

Tuesday May 🎧

The Devils Cut 🎧

The Detectives Mate (🎧 Coming Soon)

Bittersweet Snapdragon (🎧 Coming Soon)

Dark Dahlia Rite

Aces

Phantom Navis (🎧 Coming Soon)

Obsessed Shadows (🎧 Coming Soon)

Second Chances at The Riverbend Café (🎧 Coming Soon)

Still Waters (Coming Soon)

Lavender (Coming Soon)

The Dead Zone (Coming Soon)

Shadow Prince (Coming Soon)

Ravenwood Manor (Coming Soon)

Summer (Coming Soon)

Oakland Harbour Series:

Missing

Found

Home

Second Chances Series:

The Waterfall

Wicked Bonds (Coming Soon)

The Restaurant (Coming Soon)

Haunted Tales and Withered Old Flowers Series:

A Field of Tulips and Bones (Coming Soon)

Muddy White Lillies (Coming Soon)

The Queens of Ombres Series:

Follow Poppy (🎧 Coming Soon)

Protect Poppy (Coming Soon)

Crown Poppy (Coming Soon)

ABOUT J.N. KING

From a young age, J. N. King has been captivated by the art of storytelling, writing countless books in both German and English purely for the love of writing and her wildly vivid imagination. But everything changed when someone told her, "Your words are frickin' amazing," inspiring her to pursue a journey as a published author. Now residing in the English countryside, J. N. King spends her days crafting tales and dreaming up book boyfriends.

ALSO BY J.N. KING

Out Now:

The Boys Of Hastings House

His Majesty

The Waterfall

Bittersweet Snapdragon

Aces

Veada

Coming soon:

Wicked Bonds

The Restaurant

The Crimson Crown

Nailah